SHADOW OF THE HORDE KING

ALSO BY ZOEY DRAVEN

Warriors of Luxiria
The Alien's Prize
The Alien's Mate
The Alien's Lover
The Alien's Touch
The Alien's Dream
The Alien's Obsession
The Alien's Seduction
The Alien's Claim

Horde Kings of Dakkar
Captive of the Horde King
Claimed by the Horde King
Madness of the Horde King
Broken by the Horde King
Taken by the Horde King
Throne of the Horde King

Warrior of Rozun
Wicked Captor
Wicked Mate

The Krave of Everton
Kraving Khiva
Prince of Firestones
Kraving Dravka
Kraving Tavak

Brides of the Kylorr
Desire in His Blood
Craving in His Blood
Hunger in His Blood

Hordes of the Elthika
The Horde King of Shadow

Standalones
Rescued by the Luxirian
The Midnight Arrow

THE HORDE KING

SHADOW OF

USA TODAY BESTSELLING AUTHOR

ZOEY DRAVEN

THE HORDE KING OF SHADOW

The fearsome creature came from across Drukkar's Sea…and there was a rider on its back.

As a scholar in Dothik's library, Klara has spent her life trying to understand the strange dreams that have plagued her since she was a child—visions of dragons and a world with no written record. Rejected by her royal bloodline after her mother's death, Klara hides her chilling secret, knowing her rare magic could get her killed.

But when a dragon suddenly appears in Dothik, those dreams become a monstrous reality.

Sarkin Dirak'zar, king of the Sarrothian horde, cares only about finding heartstones—the dwindling power source for their revered dragons. Ice-cold and merciless, the last thing Sarkin wants is a wife, especially a weak and unwanted princess who likely won't last one night on dragonback. Yet the key to acquiring heartstones lies in Klara's visions, and so he gives her a cruel choice: marry him to save her people…or let Dothik burn.

Her first duty as queen? Claim a dragon of her own. What's even more alarming is that unexpected desire begins to simmer with her beguiling but guarded husband…even though his barbed cage of a heart is only meant to keep her away.

CONTENT CONSIDERATIONS

The Horde King of Shadow contains some themes and depictions that might be sensitive to certain readers. Please go to my website for a full list of content considerations.

Scan this QR code for easy access:

KARAG GLOSSARY

Akymor: holiday after Elthikan mating season

Aralye: darling or 'sweet'

Arasykin: heartstones

Elthika: dragon race; 'death wind' in Karag

Endrassa: thank you

Ethrall: death mist

Faryn: stop

Illa'rosh: choosing ritual at the Tharken cliffs

Sy'asha: dragon song

Karath: territory leader

Kya'rassa: rider horde

Lyiss: rest

Mysar: divine, mandatory atonement commands

Naro: apple-like fruit

Osh'ila: a novice rider

Sen endrassa: thank you *(sen is a respectful term when used to address an Elthika)*

Sethra: diving command

Shy'rissa: sleep

Sorrina: queen

Syn'ra: pleasure bump

Tarosh: work

Thalara: heartstone tree

Thryn'ar: flying command

Thryn'rosh: the final commitment ceremony

Trilikki: pepper spice on Dakkar

PROLOGUE
KLARA

The fearsome creature came from across Drukkar's Sea.

At the time of the first sighting, I had yet to be born, but I'd heard the stories all my life. Over the years, the account of that fateful day—the day the entirety of Dakkar realized it knew nothing at all—had become so tangled and twisted that it was difficult to ascertain what was true and what was merely grotesque, frightened fantasy.

Had the creature landed on the rocky shores of the West Lands and viciously gobbled up a traveling horde? Or had the creature stalked the horde on its travels, disappearing from view with a lift of its mighty wings whenever threatened, vanishing into the cloud cover like a ghost? Or had the horde stabbed it through the heart with a volley of spears and arrows, one striking true, and it had fallen to Kakkari's earth with a great tremble, its body sinking into the soil upon its death?

No one knew the truth anymore.

But what held true was that after that first sighting, nearly a year later, another creature had been discovered. Again in the West Lands. Again it was thought to have landed among the rocky shores of Drukkar's Sea. The *saruk*—a small village—of

Rath Hidri was near. The *Sorakkar* himself, a trusted and great leader descended from that ancient bloodline, had told the king what he'd seen.

The creature had circled the *saruk, flying* in the sky, its great wings flapping hard enough to send gusts of wind swirling below. It circled the *saruk* for three days, using the dense, coastal fog in the mornings to remain unseen, though the beat of its wings had been like the throbbing of a mighty heart. No one had slept. Many had retreated into the forests, hiding their children and sheltering beneath the thick boughs, until the creature had left, until it had become quiet again.

It was the *Sorakkar's* account that had sparked fear and hysteria and awe among Dakkar's people. The news had traveled quickly until it spread from village to village, from horde to horde.

What great creature, larger than any witnessed and catalogued in our lands, could *fly?*

And where had it come from? What lay beyond the shores of our land?

Ships had been built on the foundation of that question, explorers and warriors sent across the tumultuous waves at regular intervals for the next several years. Some had been gone for months, though eventually most of them returned with no news of discovery. One ship had been lost forever, never to return.

Memory faded. Many stopped looking up at the sky in trepidation every morning. Another horde king was selected, the ensuing grand celebration in Dothik helping to dampen and distract from our fear. Another *saruk* was built in the South Lands. Life continued, though there were those who believed it was foolish to ever pretend to forget.

The creature wasn't seen again for nearly two decades.

Long enough for it to become a distant memory, the edges softened with time.

When I turned twelve, the creature came to Dothik. It perched itself on the mountain range, called Bekkar's Shield, that protected the capital city from the western coast. From our little tower room in the market district, I could see it with my naked eye, though small in the great distance.

I wouldn't get a good view of it until the next day when it flew over the city.

Like the old tales of our human ancestors, the creatures resembled *dragons*. Fearsome to behold, their size was intimidatingly awe inspiring. The flash of its black scales in the early-morning light was something I could never forget. Like the scales on a *pyroki*, the loyal creatures our hordes rode across the wildlands, they shined and gleamed, tapering down to pointed ends like teeth, overlapping one another, crafting a natural and thick armor over the beautiful beast.

Its eyes were red, glowing from its dark, scaled face. The jaw was wide, four sharp horns curling close to its skull. Its limbs were thicker than turrets, each ending in wicked claws it kept curled as it flew. The tail behind it ended with a sharp spike that could easily impale a dozen Dakkari at once, swaying purposefully in the wind as its wings suddenly tilted, veering toward the south of the grand city.

I'd been in the market when the dragon flew overhead. I'd heard the panicked screams, the chaos and rush. But I'd been stuck, rooted in place, fractions of dreams becoming my reality, all pieces of a disjointed puzzle that *finally* began fitting into place, all at once.

That morning I saw something even more terrifying. Because when the dragon veered south, its whole body slid sideways, exposing what I hadn't been able to see from beneath it.

The fearsome creature came from across Drukkar's Sea...

And there was a rider on its back.

CHAPTER 1
KLARA

Red fog swirled in the glass flask stoppered with a black wax seal.

Stepping up to the vendor stall, I nearly got elbowed out of the way by a clamoring Dakkari female, who snatched up a vial shaped like a moon fruit, rounded at the bottom and tapered at the top.

Next to me, Sora called out, "Watch yourself."

The female's narrowed red eyes swung to Sora, but my brave friend only tilted back her chin. Then the stranger huffed, cradling her vial close as if it were gold, and pressed real gold into the vendor's hand before shuffling away.

"*Grimalkin*," Sora murmured under her breath.

There was a churning in my belly, reflected in the swirl of red beneath the crystal-clear glass before me. My eyes tracked the wispy sway, wondering what had created it.

"*Grimalkin*?" I repeated, half-distracted. "That's a new word from you."

"Heard it from a human at that tavern off the Twelfth Limb. He told me it means *old shrew* in their ancient language."

"Ah," I commented, tearing my eyes away from the red mist in the vial to peer at the vendor, an elderly Dakkari male with

5

golden eyes, tending patiently over his wares. I smiled. "And you liked the word and committed it to your beloved vocabulary of insults."

"Eighteen words and counting. Isn't it a delight to say?" Sora asked, laughing musically, a beautiful laugh that belied her crass tongue. Even the vendor turned abruptly to observe her. "*Grimalkin.*"

"It is," I agreed, tightening my arm around the book pressed to my chest.

Sora finally stepped up the vendor cart to look at what had caught my attention. She whistled, low and soft. To the vendor, she said, "A little morbid, isn't it? Considering how many it killed?"

He sniffed, then glared. "Don't like it? Then go."

"Come on," I said, pulling on my friend's arm before she started something. Again. When we were a distance from the vendor stall, I said, "You know it's fake anyway. Like he *actually* has the red fog bottled? Where has he kept it hidden away for the last two hundred years?"

"Actually, I need one," Sora announced before flitting back. Shaking my head, I watched her beam innocently at the vendor, who looked like he wouldn't sell to her before finally caving when he saw her glittering gold, pulled from her tunic pocket.

Turning, I absorbed the bustling marketplace, eyes darting, a small smile on my lips as I observed the chaos.

I needed a brief reprieve from the quiet of the archives, given the stiffness in my neck and the lethargy in my legs. I needed to *feel* the pulse of excitement of the market as I absorbed the plethora of colors and scents and sounds. The vibrant clothing for the special occasion, the waving flags, the mark of my family's line decorating them, the musical beat of distant drums, the scent of smoked and spiced *wrissan* meat from a nearby vendor cart.

A seller passed me holding a thick vertical pole that was three times his height. Pinned to it were dozens of colorful silks and cloaks, swaying from his wobbly grip.

"Anything catch your interest?" he asked, his gaze already sliding to seek out other customers. "The gold scarf would bring out your…"

His words trailed when he finally looked back at me, his eyes zeroing in on my scar. His brow ticked up, the pole swaying forward in his surprise.

I shook my head hurriedly, letting my hair fall over my cheekbone, and he left—thankfully without comment.

Overhead, I spied the crooked banner hung between two buildings. It heralded the two hundredth anniversary of the red fog's defeat in the Dead Lands. On another banner, across the market, were the beautiful faces, drawn in perfect likeness with an expert hand, faces copied from the golden statue at the front of the city of the *rivalla lo'kilan*.

The Five.

The five females who'd each played a part in eradicating the scourge of the red fog that would've certainly killed us all, wiping out the entirety of the races on our planet. Only because of them had we survived.

A spark of pride—and despair—burst in my chest.

"Look," Sora ordered, shoving the largest vial the vendor had had stocked toward my face. She shook it, and I watched the red smoke inside gently sway. "Likely *kreki* ink dyed red and suspended in a water solution. Quite genius, actually, though he has questionable morals."

"*You* just purchased those questionable morals," I pointed out, my gaze lingering on the red fog—ink—continuing to swirl. My lungs felt tight.

"What is it?" she asked, concern touching her tone.

"Nothing," I said, shaking my head, tearing my eyes away from the vial to hers. I offered her a small smile before it died. "Just…today of all days, I've been wondering what it was like.

The fog. I don't think I've ever truly tried to imagine it, have you?"

Trapped in it. Suffocated by it. The sinking realization that every breath wound its way down one's throat like a parasite—feeding, draining.

I nearly shuddered.

"Maybe you should ask them," Sora pointed out, nodding her head at the banner. My gaze snapped back to the Five, to their beautiful faces. "Maybe like Vienne, the great white-haired sorceress, you can ask her in your dreams," she teased. "You more than anyone."

I heard the slight mockery in her tone, and it made my shoulders tighten. "You don't believe she had visions in her dreams?"

Sora scoffed. "The evidence is subjective at best. There is no denying she possessed a great power. But I think it was the lore surrounding her husband that sparked *those* rumors."

I knew what was true. Sora didn't.

I forced a small smile, my gaze landing on a cart that sold *kuveri* bread, the small, dark berries spilling their juices into the spongy baked good. I shuffled forward, purchasing a slice quickly, offering half to Sora, who shoved it eagerly into her mouth.

Across from the fountain in the center of the market, a vendor was shouting. Calling out bets for the shadow moon tonight. A crowd grew around him, gold being shoved and waved into the air to catch his attention.

Sora dropped the bottle of red fog into her bag, and it clinked against a quill tip. "Maybe we should place a wager. Seems like a sure thing. What do you think?"

"They always come," I replied, picking at my bread. "It's not a question of *if*."

Now people placed bets on *when*. Exact times. On how *many* would come. On which dragon would be in the lead. If it would rain. If a cloud passed over the moon when they landed at the East Gate.

That was where the gold was.

"Will you try to speak with them again?" Sora asked. Her lip curled, and I felt a flash of shame in my chest. I knew she didn't mean for her teasing to feel malicious…but sometimes it felt like she was poking fun at my expense. "Or get caught by the guards? Don't make me tail you all night."

Just like my family, Sora was infinitely skeptical of my theories on the dragons and the world I believed lay beyond Drukkar's Sea. She was Dothik's leading scholar. Her mind and its limits were infinite. She could recount a book she'd read as a child, word for word, could tell you which pages had been ripped, which ones had held stains. She could tell you what she'd eaten while she'd been reading that book and what lecture her mother had given that evening.

Still, she didn't believe me. When it was her that I wanted to believe in me the most. Sometimes I thought she pitied me. That she only humored me because of our unlikely friendship. Or perhaps because of my bloodlines, which was even worse.

"I told you before—that was a misunderstanding," I said. "I was out on the wildlands. I'd forgotten it was the shadow moon."

I knew Sora didn't believe my lie. But she was wrong about me trying to *speak* with them. I wasn't insane. I'd just wanted to see them. Up close.

The tavern bells began to ring, filling the marketplace with a rush. Soon, the temple bell would sound.

"I need to get back," I told her, eager to leave. I didn't want to fight about this again.

"Klara," Sora said, catching my arm. "I'm only teasing…"

"I know," I said, giving her a smile I hoped looked genuine. "It's not that. The feast—I didn't realize how late it was."

Sora didn't believe me. I knew it was one thing she didn't respect about me. That I retreated and fled instead of standing my ground. *She* always held her ground. She was better suited to be a high-ranking guard of the *Dothikkar* rather than tucked away in the quiet archives, spouting off her evening lectures to whomever would listen.

Sora huffed out a sharp breath through her nostrils, her tail flicking. "Don't lose that," she commanded, her eyes sweeping to the book clutched against my chest.

I felt a twist of discomfort when she turned her back, stalking to the bets maker in the center, shouting something I couldn't hear over the crowd while fishing out gold from her pocket, waving it over her head.

For a moment, I stood perfectly still, observing the growing crowd. Listening to the cacophony of hundreds of voices enclosed in the marketplace, bouncing off buildings and funneling down the road.

In that moment, in a moment that nearly stole my breath, I felt incredibly lonely.

Someone jostled my shoulder, a drunk staggering into me, a slurred curse on his lips. The movement shoved me into a tall, imposing figure, and I felt my chest seize in panic when the book tumbled out of my grasp.

The drunk's boots kicked the book—one of the archives' most cherished tomes—when he stumbled off, and I gasped out my alarm as it skidded across the filthy road.

Before I had a chance to react, it was retrieved by the male I'd run into, his large figure bending low to snag it off the worn cobblestones.

When he turned toward me, my eyes latched onto the book. Quickly taking stock of its condition, I was relieved to see it had no significant damage on the leather-bound cover, at least from what I could see.

Then I watched the stranger flip open the pages. Curiosity, perhaps, but I nearly cried out in protest, my feet carrying me closer without a second thought. My love of books was perhaps the only thing I had in common with Queen Kara. This was *her* book. The one she'd painstakingly hand copied from the original text, of Bekkar's history. It was priceless.

And his hands are filthy, I thought in alarm, my gaze catching on a black chalky dust coating the male's palms. He turned a page, and I saw a black smudge linger on the delicate parchment.

Sora would *kill* me.

"Don't," I said quickly. "Please don't—"

For the first time, our eyes met. Whatever words I'd been about to utter died pathetically in my throat.

The male in front of me reminded me of the horde kings of old, of their imposing statues that had been erected in every outpost, in every village throughout Dakkar, even in the priestesses' temple in the North Lands and here in the districts of Dothik.

Only he wasn't a horde king. Whether living or dead, I knew every last *Vorakkar* of our history.

This mysterious stranger seemed to make the western market slow on the periphery of my vision. My heartbeat became both a lazy, languid thing, while also fluttering like a caged *thissie* in my breast.

His silken black hair was cut short, curling slightly at the nape of his neck. His eyes were multicolored, like golden jewels in their very center before expanding outward to a light brown, ending with a circle of deep green. I'd never seen their likeness before.

Though he had sharply pointed ears, I didn't spy a tail swaying behind him and thought it likely, given his eyes, that he had human blood running in his veins.

The golden richness of his skin only made his eyes glow brighter. I could envision him hundreds of years ago, on the back of a battle-bred *pyroki*, sword unsheathed, as he rode across the wildlands, like the ancient Dakkari.

His jaw was wide. His dark lips were full, large enough to make a little shadowed divot just beneath them. Nearly three heads taller than me, he had broad shoulders and his thighs were straining against the tight black trews that encased them. He was wearing a black, fitted, long-sleeved tunic. Over it was a black vest that molded to the stretch of his wide chest, resembling flexible armor. It shimmered with triangular scales that caught the afternoon sunlight.

I frowned. *Pyroki* scales? No. *Pyroki* scales were more flattened along the top edge.

"Are you done staring, *aralye?*" came his voice, deep and rich, though I thought I caught a stray edge of irritation too.

As heat flooded my cheeks, my gaze dipped to the book. Initially curious about the commotion, the onlookers started to disperse around us, but I let my dark hair fall even further into my face, wanting to hide from the nosy gossips. I only hoped they didn't recognize me.

"*Hanniva,*" I croaked, not meeting his eyes. *Please.* "I'll take that back now."

"So eager to reclaim it," he murmured. His words struck me as…careful yet deliberate. "Did you steal it?"

"What?" I breathed, frowning. "No, of course not."

Those eyes skimmed over the open book in his possession, but I felt my patience snap when he ran the pad of his thumb down the parchment, leaving that black dust in its wake.

"Your hands are filthy," I informed him, only imagining Sora's horror in my mind as I stepped forward, firmly snagging it from his grip. "And this book is very old."

The stranger's eyes narrowed. "My apologies, *aralye.* I forget how much of a brute I am around such delicate things."

I stiffened. Was it my imagination, or were his words dipped in warning?

"I know every dialect spoken on Dakkar," I informed him carefully, wary now. "I've never heard that word before. *Aralye.*"

The male's lips curled. The small, mocking grin made my knees nearly buckle.

"Perhaps it's one I made up" was all he replied.

Something in my gut told me he was dangerous. Despite his beauty, I knew I needed to get away from him and fast.

"Thank you for your help," I rushed out quickly, tucking the book close to my chest. A gust of wind funneled down from the Spine—the main road that cleaved the city of Dothik into two separate halves. The wind spread its fingers across the marketplace and briefly blew back the shadowed curtain of my hair. "But I must be going."

The skinned flesh on my knees gave an aching protest when I pivoted away, but then I felt a warm, strong, sudden hand clamp down on my forearm. The stranger turned me back to him, his eyes utterly trained on me. *Focused.* The hairs on the back of my neck rose, a sensation I knew all too well.

Frozen, I watched as his hand flashed forward, sweeping back the hair from my left cheek to expose the scar there.

I watched as his lips pressed together. Shock? Disgust? I knew what he saw—a flesh-colored scar resembling the wild roots of a tree, beginning at my left temple and curling down my cheek, slashing through one eyebrow.

"Who are you really?" he rasped, the edge of his words sharp and dangerous like a blade.

Wrenching myself away with strength that surprised even me, I blew out a sharp breath, unable to shield my glare. He'd left a black smudge on me in the wake of his palm.

Not answering, I took a step back. Then another, clutching the book I'd spend my evening painstakingly cleaning after the feast. The male never moved, and I felt like prey.

When there was enough distance between us, I turned on my heel and fled.

I felt his eyes on me until I reached the Spine. When I made it to the *Dothikkar's* palace, only then could I breathe again.

CHAPTER 2
KLARA

"Stop fussing, Klara," Dannik ordered, though amusement curled in his tone. He slid into the empty space beside me, tucking his shoulder against the column of the open window. "You don't have a hair out of place."

I huffed out a sharp breath, and my hand dropped away from my head, from where I'd been nervously smoothing down my hair. "That's not—"

"The guards said you were down in the western market today," he said, cutting me off, bumping my shoulder with his arm. "Why'd you go there?"

I shot my brother a sharp look. "You had me followed?"

"It's the shadow moon" was all he replied, shrugging one shoulder, as if that would answer my question. And well…it did.

"Then you'll know I was with Sora. I'd been in the archives all morning, I wanted to get some air before *this* tonight," I explained, waving a hand before us.

We were tucked against the far window of our father's grand throne room. I could hardly hear my own thoughts with all the chatter, music, and laughter, a headache starting to bloom behind my right eye.

There was an edge to my brother tonight. More guards were in the throne room for this celebration than for any other throughout the year. Even the laughter of the guests seemed louder, more forced.

Perhaps we were all trying to pretend that dragons wouldn't land at the East Gate any moment, if they hadn't already.

Across the room, I spotted the *Laseta Kalliri*—the high priestess of Dothik. She was watching me across the crush of bodies, and I pressed my lips together, inclining my head in respect. Then I looked away swiftly, telling myself to relax my shoulders and to smile softly at no one at all, like I was enjoying the merriment of the gathering, like I was at ease with her piercing eyes on me. Like I had nothing to hide.

Out of the corner of my eye, I waited until she turned her back, speaking with a male I recognized as a powerful merchant, and I blew out a steady, slow breath through my lips.

"What is it?" Dannik asked.

"Nothing," I said, turning to him with a small grin.

My brother frowned, his golden eyes cutting to the *Laseta Kalliri* before fastening back on me. His lips parted, but before he could say anything, a guard approached.

"*Rukkar*, your father is requesting your presence on the dais," he said. *Prince*, he'd called Dannik. His proper title.

A jolt went through my belly, a spear of disappointment cutting through me.

"Come," Dannik ordered me, grabbing my hand.

The guard said, with evident hesitation, "Only you. The *Dothikkar* made it clear."

He stared down the guard, who was a head shorter than him, until the other male dropped his gaze to the floor.

"It's all right," I told him, pressing my fingers to the back of his scarred hand. "Go."

Dannik's gaze cut to mine. I hadn't expected to see the burn of anger there.

"There is always defeat in your eyes, sister," he told me, cupping my cheeks in his warm palms. "I wish you would fight more for what is yours by blood."

Then he released me. He turned away while I struggled to swallow the sudden shame in my throat. I was alone again, watching my brother spear through the crowd, which parted for him like curtains in the morning, welcoming the dawn.

That was what he was for Dothik. It was common knowledge he was my father's favored heir, though my half sister, Alanis, was his firstborn. My father was expected to step down from the throne in the coming years. A new rule would come. Dannik would likely be at the helm.

From my corner in the throne room, I watched my family rise together on the dais. My father, with his graying hair and unyielding green eyes; a pink, thin-lipped mouth; and ruddy, wrinkled cheeks. My stepmother was next to him, though she hated when I made any mention of that title. Instead, I called her *Lakkari* just like everyone else. Queen of Dothik. And my half siblings.

Alanis, with her waist-length blonde hair and black *pyroki* scales sewn to her clothes in a way that resembled armor—not unlike the male from the market, I noted. She had never warmed to me, thinking me nothing more than a bug beneath her boot, another competitor for the throne she coveted.

Lakkis, in all her ethereal beauty that left the guards' tongues tied in her wake. My sister—while she'd always been kind to me —was still practically a stranger, an impenetrable wall I'd never been able to break through.

And Dannik, the unspoken heir to it all.

Together they made a pretty picture. The longing to join them on the dais burned so hot in my stomach it made nausea rise.

Across the room, my siblings' mother caught my eyes. Her chin lifted, brow raising. The gold crown seated on her brow sparkled under the lights as the throne room quieted, eager to hear the *Dothikkar's* welcoming speech.

This blatant rejection was growing more humiliating every year. I'd thought it would get better. It only ever got worse.

Leave, came the thought that had been surfacing more and more in recent months. *Rent the little room we had above the tavern, and live as you please. Or return to the wildlands, where you remember Mother best, where we were happy.*

But then I would truly be alone…and that scared me more than anything in this life. At least here, in this cold palace, I had Dannik.

The *Lakkari's* serene smirk followed me out of the throne room when I fled, keeping to the outskirts of the room like a rodent, hoping that I drew no one's eyes but hers.

Unfortunately, I felt the burn of *dozens'* as I slipped through the door, the snickering whispers erupting in my wake.

⁂

"I knew I'd find you here," came my brother's voice, cutting through the hushed, dark chamber.

I raised my head, confused. Then I jolted and wiped my right cheek with the back of my hand, my spine straightening as I smoothed my dress.

"It's only me," Dannik said. "You don't have to do that, Klara."

I was sitting on a bench across from an unyielding pedestal, one that held a gleaming sword. Dannik was regarding me carefully, and I couldn't help but frown.

"Have they come?" I asked immediately. "How many are there this time?"

My brother and I looked nothing alike. I looked like my mother—all dark, wavy hair and small features. And Dannik? Well, he looked like *his* mother. With golden hair and light eyes,

17

his skin warmed and blessed by the sun, with a wide, bold smile that had broken the heart of at least ten different females.

"You spend more time in here than you do in your precious archives," he grumbled, his booted feet crossing to me, ignoring my questions. "You'd think Arik's sword would've lost its appeal by now."

"It was Bekkar's sword first," I told him. The first great king of Dothik, passed down to my own ancestor. There was a white glowing stone still embedded in its hilt, its energy palpable. *The heartstone.* The last one in existence.

"And then Kara gifted it to Arik after the red fog's defeat, *lysi*," Dannik said, impatience threading in his tone, making me bite back a smile. He wasn't interested in history, in our ancient line, in all the little roots and paths and stories that had brought us here to our present. It didn't matter. I cared for more than the both of us. "We all know the story. I could recount Bekkar's campaign trail and the history of the Five in my sleep."

I turned my gaze back to the sword. The power of the heartstone was warm. It felt like a heartbeat to me. Comforting. Tangible. I could feel the tendrils of power floating over my skin, and if my mother was still alive, maybe I could ask her *why.*

Dannik took a seat on the stone bench next to me. There was an edge to him that I couldn't quite pinpoint. We were in the bowels of the palace. Once a dungeon, this place had been made new. It housed a vast collection of our history, of our family's history, Bekkar's sword included.

No one had wielded it since King Arik. It burned any who touched it. And yet it remained gleaming throughout the years, not a speck of dust or sign of mottled age marring the metal. The blade was as sharp as it had been in Bekkar's own hand.

"What does it feel like to you?" Dannik asked suddenly, taking my palm. I frowned, but then he waved his other hand to the sword. "The heartstone."

I swallowed, my spine snapping. "What?"

"I heard you and your mother speaking once, shortly before she was sent away," he started, his voice hushed, as if we weren't alone in this crypt of a place. "Shortly after you came to live here. Right here."

I swallowed, dropping his hand quickly. "Dannik, that was a long time ago."

"You told her you had seen them in your dreams. For *years*," he said quietly. "What did you mean? Because I *know* a sword injury when I see it. And that scar? It didn't come from a sword."

"Dannik," I whispered, averting my gaze from his to drop to the ground. "I—I don't... You know I cannot..."

"You think I'll let them take you to the *orala sa'kilan*? You think I'll let them take you away to the priestesses in the North Lands, to live out the rest of your days in training and servitude, *used* as a conduit to try to create more heartstones?" Dannik asked me, his tone bitter and aghast. "Your mother lied to them. What makes you think I wouldn't lie to protect you too? You *know* me, Klara. I would do anything to protect you. You're my *sister*."

Blood is blood, Klara. You are of me. He is of another. You cannot trust him fully.

My mother's words. Permanently embedded in my mind. I'd wanted to tell Dannik. My mother had forbidden it. Now she was dead. So why couldn't I shake her words?

"Even go against your own mother?" I asked. "Because we all know what she did."

Dannik reared back.

"She's wanted me gone since I first came to the palace," I told him. "Any hint of weakness... I'm surprised she hasn't married me off to a *darukkar* in one of the hordes. If only so she never has to look at me again."

"You are of royal blood," Dannik argued. "Even more so than any of us. She...resents that. Alanis too. They fear you."

I laughed, but it sounded hollow. My eyes were stinging from the tears that had already dried in my lap. "Because I'm so frightening. With all my books and half-mad theories."

"You didn't answer my question."

"Which one?" I returned.

His eyes cut back to the sword, a muscle in his jaw ticking. He was on edge, his tail skittering across the stone.

"What is it?" I asked, turning on the bench to face him more fully. Something was wrong. Had the celebration feast already ended? "Dannik?"

"The riders landed at the East Gate."

His words weren't unexpected, however. Yet there was something I couldn't place in his tone that made nerves curl in my chest, skittering my heartbeat.

"How many?" I asked, repeating my earlier question.

"Too many this time."

I straightened. "What does that mean?"

Dannik said quietly, his voice hushed, "If you know anything of them that might be of use, it's your duty as a descendant of the royal line and to your *people* to speak it. You must trust me, Klara."

"They're just dreams! They aren't real," I told him, unable to withstand him feeling betrayed. Like I *didn't* trust him. Because I did. I trusted him with my life. And if the priestesses caught wind of *this*, my life would be given to them. *That* was what at stake. "They are unclear. No words are spoken. I've never seen another person in them. Only…"

Only the dragons.

Two in particular.

A terrifying black creature with eyes as gold as the sun and teeth as sharp as swords.

The other…

I blew out a sharp breath, standing to pace to Bekkar's sword. I stared down at the white heartstone shimmering in its hilt. The last heartstone in existence on Dakkar…as far as we knew. It had been the heartstones that helped the Five banish the red fog in the Dead Lands. It had nearly cost them their lives.

"*If*," I started quietly, my words barely a whisper, "I possess fragments of our ancestors' magic, it is a useless thing."

Dannik's hand came to my arm, right over where the male in the market had gripped me, where he'd left that strange black residue on my skin.

"You might believe that," he whispered, as if we could be overheard. "But I don't."

My lips parted—

"Through our father, you are a descendent of Queen Kara, the Banisher and the Wielder of the Heartstones, and King Arik of Rath Serok. And your mother's line of Rath Drokka? You descend from the Mad Horde King and of Vienne the White Sorceress. There is power, electric in your blood, and it chose *you*. Not Alanis. Not Lakkis. Not even your mother. *You*, Klara."

My throat went tight.

"Can you feel it?" he asked, voice suddenly guttural. My lips parted when I heard the trepidation in his voice. "The power leeching from the land? Our home? This heartstone is growing dimmer with every passing day. Have you noticed?"

The hairs on the back of my neck stood up. My gaze cut to the heartstone. It hummed in answer. I could feel it. For the first time, I wondered if Dannik could too.

"These dragon riders?" my brother continued, shaking his head, and I heard the gold beads in his hair clicking together. "I think they want what we cannot give them. And I fear what they will demand in its stead. They are much too at ease. They have no fear. The only reason they would have none is if they knew there was no need for it. Because they know they could snap this city in two within the jaws of their beasts. I only wonder why they haven't yet."

"Dannik, what—"

"It was foolish of us to believe that there was nothing beyond

Drukkar's Sea," he continued, his lip curling in a mocking, sad smile. "I have a feeling that we know nothing at all and that we will pay for it in due time."

My brother took my hand again. "You need to have strength, Klara," he said, trepidation in his eyes. "More so now than ever before."

"Why?" I asked, hearing a thread of warning in his tone. "Dannik, what's happening? You're scaring me."

"They've asked for you."

"What?" I asked, thinking I heard him incorrectly. "*Who?*"

"The dragon riders."

All my breath left me. Dannik's grip tightened around my palm.

"Their leader. He asks for you at the East Gate."

CHAPTER 3
KLARA

They came every year.

On the tenth month just after the shadow moon.

Sometimes with many dragons, sometimes with just a mere few. But they always came. Every year they left almost as quickly as they'd arrived.

Only this year, they lingered.

I felt the palpable tension in the air, thick like heavy, black smoke, when I stepped beyond the East Gate. My legs froze, my feet not catching up quick enough, and Dannik caught my arm before I tumbled to the tightly packed dark brown earth.

The East Gate, unlike the well-manicured and paved northern entrance, looked out across the wildlands of Dakkar in all of its raw, unforgiving beauty. It was an entrance used primarily by *Vorakkar*—the horde kings—or the *Sorakkar*—the kings of the outposts—when they entered or exited our capital city.

I'd snuck through it often, a secret not even Dannik knew. And sometimes I sat out on the wildlands long into the night, uncaring that sand and dirt streaked my hair from the winds, as I listened to the quiet and felt a peace I'd never known within the confines of Dothik. I missed the wildlands. I missed my mother.

For a moment, my eyes fastened on the blackness of the night, only lit by bright starlight. Tonight, however, the shadows of the mountains seemed ominous and the vastness to them seemed insurmountable.

The clearing had been made with lines that no one dared to cross. Bright torchlight illuminated the wide circle, my father and his legion of guards on one side, protecting the council, the *Lakkari*, and my half sisters, and a line of strangers on the other.

Behind them, a great dragon seemed to materialize out of the darkness. I felt my chest go tight, shock piercing through my lungs like a dagger.

"Strength," Dannik whispered into my ear. A reminder. A softly spoken word, and yet it seemed amplified as I stared in the golden eyes of the dragon that I *recognized*. My scar gave a mighty throb, and I squeezed my eyes closed, feeling that panic and confusion rise in me, hearing my mother's hushed horror as she'd tried to quiet me in her arms.

"Dannik…" I said, my tone a strange mixture of a plea and a realization. *It can't be true…because then that would mean it's* all *real,* I thought.

I felt my brother's grip on my arm tighten before I felt him step in front of me.

The dragon roared, so sudden and violent that it trembled the earth beneath our feet, and I heard the startled cries from my father's council. Dannik froze. I heard a breath loosen from between his lips.

On the wildlands, I heard the other dragons respond. Now we knew they were there, hidden in the darkness, the weight of them shaking the earth as they stamped their limbs like a warning rumble. It sounded like thunder.

Then all at once it went quiet. Not just quiet…*silent.*

"Zaridan recognizes you, *aralye*," came the voice.

My eyes snapped open, fastening on the male who had stepped forward into the circle, breaking away from the line of the dragon riders that had come this night. Familiar eyes met mine, and all at once, I remembered the strength and warmth of his hand on my arm, leaving behind a glittering black dust.

It was *him.*

The danger I'd sensed in the marketplace with him only seemed amplified with the dragon looming over his shoulder.

"My wonder is if you recognize her," he continued, never taking his eyes off me on his approach.

"Zaridan," I whispered, blinking, the name stretched out on my tongue.

Out of the corner of my eye, I saw the guards trying to right my father, who'd fallen over at the dragons' chorus of roars. Alanis stood away from my stepmother and Lakkis, who were safely hidden behind a circle of guards. My eldest sister was standing next to the *Laseta Kalliri*, the priestess's lips pressed together as she regarded the stranger, her beautiful gown stained by dark earth at the hem.

"No," I said, swallowing the lump in my throat. "I don't."

"She denies you, Zaridan," the male announced, his eyes never leaving mine. A maelstrom of colors were swirling in his eyes, all reflected in warm torchlight.

Behind him, the dragon stomped and her hot breath blew into the circle, blasting my hair away from my face and snuffing out all the torchlight until I blinked into the darkness, my hand scrambling to find Dannik's.

"Get them lit!" came Alanis's hiss to the guards.

"She is one of the ancients, you must understand," came the stranger's voice, amplified in the dark, and I saw those glowing golden orbs behind him, fastened on me, stealing my heaving breaths. "Proud in her bloodline. All of the Elthika are. But Zaridan has lived much longer, and she deserves your respect."

"I…" I trailed off, and the torches began to light, one by one again, until I saw the male, standing closer than he'd been.

There were nine others behind him in a line. They hadn't moved an inch, but all of their hands rested on the hilt of a blade at their hip. All were dressed in varying colors—dark greens and blues, silvers and blacks—but all of them wore the same scaled clothing that this male wore. *Armor,* I realized now. And they weren't *pyroki* scales. They were dragon scales.

"I believe she does," I replied, lifting my chin. I pressed my fingertips to my brother's hand and gently stepped away from his grip, approaching the male. "Yet you give her name so easily for one to be respected."

"Names should not be hidden, Dakkari," the male rasped, his eyes narrowing as he studied me. Surprised that I stepped beyond my brother's protection? "Names should be feared."

"Then what is yours, dragon rider?"

The edge of his lip lifted. He moved. I heard the creak of leather on my brother's hilt as his hand tightened on his sword.

The stranger circled me, and I stiffened when he ran his hand over my waist, sliding it down until it cupped my hip. That palm dragged over my backside, and when my brother made a sound in the back of his throat, I shook my head, my hand gesturing for him to stay away.

This male was sizing me up. Studying me and inspecting me, like I was something for purchase at the market.

His palm was searing through my thin dress. Strong and sure. When I looked down at my waist, I saw the same black dust glittering in the torchlight, smearing across the white material. A mark. A warning.

He came to stand in front of me, and it took everything in me to hold my tongue, to not swallow too loudly, to not tremble beneath his gaze. His hand cupped my cheek, tilting back my face so he could inspect my scar. Internally, I cringed though I held still. I couldn't stand anyone to look at it. The curtain of my hair hid it, and I always made sure it was partially covered except when I was alone in the confines of my room.

But this male could do whatever he wanted to me with a dragon at his back. I knew that. Dannik knew it. Even my father knew it—the *Dothikkar*, the king. I imagined he was watching the exchange closely and carefully…but he would not interfere. Not like I feared Dannik would.

"I am Sarkin Dirak'zar," he told me, his voice gentle like how I imagined a lover's might be. But there was no mistaking the edge of malice in his gaze. "Rider of Zaridan. And king of the Karag horde of the Sarrothian."

My lips parted as I stared, as my heart pumped mightily in my chest. I could feel the ripple of that name as it made its way across the clearing. I thought maybe even the stretch of mountains heard them and felt the quake of their power.

No, it wasn't a name. It was a warning of what would come if we didn't submit to him.

My dreams told me what he wanted. They'd been woven through my veins like a tapestry, and now the image they made was suddenly clear.

"And what is your name, *aralye?*" he asked, his tone slightly mocking, the dangerous glint in his gaze making my tongue feel like a heavy stone in my mouth.

"Don't you already know it?" I asked, realization slotting into place.

In the market, he'd asked, *Who are you really?*

Those words had struck me as odd. Now I understood why.

He'd known who I was the moment I'd bumped into him. He'd known my bloodlines…but my scar had surprised him, taken him off guard. Why?

Sarkin's eyes narrowed. Behind him, his dragon stomped, shaking the earth.

Strength, I thought.

"Klara of Rath Serok and Rath Drokka," I told him. "I have

no great name like yours, Sarkin Dirak'zar, rider of Zaridan, king of the Karag horde of the Sarrothian."

Sarkin's chin lifted, and behind him, the line of dragon riders made a simultaneous chanting sound, a rumble of deep, short thunder. Like a war cry that the hordes would make upon a *Vorakkar's* return.

My gaze flashed to them. Six males and three females, I noticed.

Sarkin curled his finger under my chin, reclaiming my eyes.

I continued with, "I have no great name, but I am descended from greatness. From great Dakkari and humans alike who made this kingdom what it is now. I know what you want, Sarkin Dirak'zar. And I know you will only bring destruction in your wake if you take it."

"It is not so difficult to guess what I want, Klara," he told me, his lips pinched down, a glare in his gaze. He released my chin, and my head bobbed back from the force, my legs swaying underneath me, the pull of his eyes like a dizzying magic.

"I have seen your forests of heartstones," I whispered to him. "Perhaps you're greedy for just one more."

Dannik cut me a sharp look, but the *burn* of Sarkin's eyes held my full attention.

My loose tongue would get me into trouble, but I had spent the majority of my life tucked away in quiet places, out of sight and safe. For once, with the glowing golden eyes of a dragon upon me, I wanted to be fearless. With the *Laseta Kalliri's* piercing gaze on me—her eyes hungry like a thief's hand—I knew my fate had already been sealed. After tonight, I would likely be sent to the priestesses in the North Lands, just like my mother had always feared.

"*Dothikkar,*" Sarkin called out suddenly, making me jump. When my father said nothing, he continued, "You have a choice to make for your people."

"Dakkari do not accept threats, rider, even if you proclaim

yourself to be a king. You are no king here," my father spat. "*I* am. You are in Kakkari's realm now, and our goddess will—"

Zaridan's roar drowned out my father's words, and her mighty tail struck the ground behind her. After long moments the echo of it trailed away, though the mountains in the distance sung with it, and my father was silent. She was still snorting out sharp huffs, a low growl in her throat.

"We answer to the Elthika, *Dothikkar*," Sarkin said with cold patience as his eyes ran over my face. I had the impression he was looking for a weakness or trying to memorize every fault. "They are our gods and our goddesses. We are not Dakkari."

I saw his eyes change, and he turned to meet my father's gaze, stepping toward him though the guards unsheathed their swords at Sarkin's approach. He didn't even flinch.

"We are the Karag—riders of the mighty Elthika," he growled, a low rumble that mirrored his dragon's. "The gods of the sky. The death from above. You would do well to remember that before you speak to me. You might be king but only because of your bloodline. Where is the honor in that? Where is the sacrifice in that? The kings of Karag…we *earn* our thrones."

The Karag.

"You have a choice to make, *king*," Sarkin said, mocking distaste dripping from his tongue. "Give me the heartstone…"

A murmuring went through the clearing, the members of my father's council loosening their tongues in their shock.

"Or give me your daughter."

The world spun, the starlight brightening above as my vision blurred.

Dannik was the first to react.

"No," came the word, growled from my brother's lips. "Absolutely not."

And yet…my father's eyes had widened when he'd heard the Karag's offer. As if he couldn't believe his good fortune. Here was his opportunity to offload the daughter who had only ever brought shame and embarrassment, whose birth had nearly torn apart his legacy. *And* he could keep the heartstone?

His shock might've been mistaken for the shock of a loving father. Maybe that was what Sarkin would see. Maybe he would even revel in it.

My father knew that.

"No," he said quickly, mirroring Dannik's rejection. I saw my sister, Alanis, cut him a sharp look, her lips pressed together.

"Then perhaps I will take both," came Sarkin's simple reply.

A chorus of muted gasps and murmurings went through the clearing, and I stood there, unable to feel my feet planted firmly to the earth. Strangely, I thought of Queen Kara's book in my room, the one that Sora had let me borrow from the archives, and I wondered how she could reclaim it if I was gone.

"Do you know why the Elthika are feared?" Sarkin asked. "Because of their strength? Because of their might? No. It's because of their *ethrall.*"

My brow furrowed. *Ethrall?*

"It has toppled kingdoms and created civilizations. Would you like to see it, *Dothikkar?* Would you like to be reminded of what it can do?"

"Reminded?" my father rasped.

"Your people have seen it before. The last was two centuries ago. It wiped out an entire race on your planet…I wonder what it would do to your glittering city?"

"Impossible," Dannik breathed. But except for him, no one moved.

Horror rooted me into place.

I saw Sarkin's lips curl into a devastating grin. "You will learn to fear us. And only then can we come to understand one another, Dakkari."

It happened quickly.

Sarkin's eyes cut to mine, studying me again.

"Zari, *ethrall,*" he commanded.

Behind Sarkin's line of riders, Zaridan reared back, the scales on her chest glittering as she inhaled deeply, the gust of wind she sucked in whipping my hair around my face. I didn't understand...until I watched a silent roar, her jaws wide, razor black fangs exposed.

The red mist that streamed out of her crashed into the clearing like violent waves against a sea cliff.

"Klara!" I heard Dannik's call, but I couldn't see him. I was frozen into place as red fog trapped us, streaming around us like a river, one with no end. I heard Lakkis's scream, her cry of horror. I heard a cacophony of voices rise up into the air, the panic and confusion and then the despair of *realization*. Of swords unsheathing, metal ringing, like they had a chance against *this*.

We hadn't known what power these Karag possessed...and now we did.

The Elthika could create the red fog that had nearly destroyed our entire race two hundred years ago. The red fog my own ancestors had fought to defeat...and it had nearly killed them in the process.

All I saw was bloodred around me. I'd often wondered what it felt like, what it had been like. It was just as horrifying as I'd imagined.

Dannik was calling for me...but it was like another realm. I was lost. I could wander for centuries and never be found here. But the fog was weaving into my lungs. A *poison*.

Then behind me, his voice came.

"Are you afraid, *aralye?*"

"Yes," I whispered.

"Good," he said, stepping in front of me. I could make out his face in the mist, the only face I could see, and suddenly he felt like an unyielding pillar as chaos erupted around us. "Since your father will not answer, I will give you the same choice I gave him."

"Please stop this," I pleaded, thinking about Dannik. My

sisters. No one knew how long the red fog took to poison the body. Some succumbed to it in moments, others days. I didn't want to take the risk. "*Please!*"

"The heartstone or you. Make your choice."

"Me," I cried out immediately. "I will go with you! Stop this!"

Sarkin called out, "*Faryn.*"

Another gust came. I blinked and before my eyes, the red fog disappeared in an instant. As my eyes adjusted to the darkness, I saw the loose swords hanging from the guards' grip, I saw my father slowly rising from the ground and Dannik with rage in his eyes, pinned on Sarkin. Lakkis's sobs filled the quiet as her mother tried to calm her. My stepmother's jaw was set tight though she seemed less shaken than anyone. I'd always admired that about her—her ability to weather any storm and still remain steadfast. It was one of the reasons my father had made her his queen, though he'd loved another at the time.

"Klara," Dannik said. "*Nik.*"

"I'll go with you," I repeated, forcing my gaze away from my brother's eyes.

"With one condition," came Sarkin's voice, oddly detached, as his arm clamped down on my forearm, pulling me forward. I had hardly caught my breath as he said, "Zaridan must approve of you first."

My feet stumbled underneath me as we broke through the line of riders at the edge of the clearing, who parted for us. And then Sarkin pushed me forward and I skittered to a halt before his dragon.

My breath whooshed from my lungs as her low rumble of a growl met my ears. I slowly craned my neck back to meet her eyes, and time seemed to stop. Her power was awe inspiring… and I knew, with utmost certainty, that she could kill me in an instant. In the gleam of her black scales, I could almost make out my reflection.

"If she doesn't kill you where you stand, you will live," came

Sarkin's voice, soft as silk though it nipped at my spine like the edge of a blade. A chorus of low laughs came from his riders.

Zaridan slowly lowered her head until our eyes were nearly level. I could smell her—earthy like the wildlands after a storm. Of underground rivers in deep caverns and of damp, black soil. Her horned head was five times as large as my entire body, and when she exhaled a warm huff, my hair blew back from my face, exposing my scar.

"And if you live, Klara of Rath Serok and Rath Drokka," Sarkin continued, his voice sharpening, "then I will make you my wife."

CHAPTER 4
KLARA

Like a shadow of the night, Zaridan moved. She prowled closer, surprisingly graceful for a creature so large. The weight of her limbs shook the earth, small little quakes that ratcheted up my heartbeat.

When I'd woken this morning, I hadn't thought it was a possibility that I could die this night. But looking into the golden, glowing orbs of a dragon's eyes, *feeling* the heat radiating off of her like a furnace, and inhaling the warm air of her breaths, the space between us shared…now it was a very high possibility. Perhaps even likely.

"Klara, get back," I heard Dannik order in a voice he very rarely used. The voice of a king, unyielding and cold.

"To interfere would mean your life, Dakkari," came a female's voice, one of Sarkin's riders. Zaridan whipped her head to regard my brother, a warning growl rumbling in her throat. Behind her, a mighty tail, spiked like a sword, thumped into the ground, making me jump.

Panic flooded me.

"Stay away. Trust in me, Dannik," I called out, my voice shaking, my hand trembling when I raised it. I couldn't see my

34

brother, but at my voice, Zaridan slowly returned her focus to me, and I felt some of my nerves leave. I took a step forward. Then another. Then another, drawing myself away from the others, from my family.

I continued walking until Zaridan was at my back and the night was swallowing me up. I felt her begin to prowl behind me, sniffing the air, the sounds of her scales rustling together like leaves in the harvest season as they blew violently with the winds.

My heart was a caged little monster, beating against bones. I thought of the archives, of the smell of parchment. I thought of the wildlands, those moments of quiet when I snuck through the gates, when I could be free, when I knew no one was watching, no one was whispering, when I felt like I could breathe.

I let out a sharp exhale just as the dragon at my back did, so hot it felt like fire, and the scar down my face throbbed as I gritted my teeth.

"Why did you do this to me?" I whispered to her.

Another rough exhale.

Zaridan shook the earth as she circled. As she passed at my side, I regarded her. The long muscled sleekness of her body was like a serpent's, her obsidian scales gleaming even in darkness. An unyielding harness was strapped to her body, secured in the notches of the joints of her wings. It was decorated in silver, eye catching yet well worn.

Behind me, I heard footsteps. He'd followed. When Sarkin's own heat was at my back, I felt him wrap his hand just underneath my throat, his grip loose. He tilted my chin back.

"Look into her eyes so she might see you, *aralye*," he commanded me. He smelled like her, I realized. Of beautiful earth. "So she might know you again."

Again? I thought, the world swirling.

My eyes connected with Zaridan's. I saw the black pupils narrow until they became like slits. The gold in her eyes danced like flames, and I felt Sarkin's thumb caress the spot on my neck where my heartbeat was thumping wildly. Over and over, back and forth.

Then something strange happened. The repetitive brush of his calloused thumb made my heartbeat slow. I began to time my breaths with his touch as Zaridan studied me, as she thumped the ground with her limbs and tail. I sensed the restlessness building in her, a ball of energy that was beginning to grow. I saw her scales begin to move, creating a rustling murmur that sounded almost like a voice.

No, a *song*.

A beautiful, ethereal song.

Behind me, Sarkin murmured, "*Sy'asha.*"

There was quiet awe in his tone.

I felt a calmness descend through my body. The smell of her and Sarkin, the light wind of the wildlands stroking through my hair like fingers, winds that my ancestors had once felt drift over their own cheeks, and the sound of that song filling me…this moment felt like a piece of fate slotting into place.

I didn't understand it. It felt so pure, so destined that I felt palpable fear take root in my chest, gripping me tight. I began to realize that I knew nothing at all.

Zaridan reared her head back, but instead of unleashing the red fog, she roared to the night sky, so loud and thunderous that it shook my bones. For a moment, the night seemed to blacken further, and I wondered if even the stars were trying to hide from such a fearsome creature.

Sarkin released me. He circled me just as Zaridan had done, and when he stood in front of me, all I saw was him and looming golden eyes of the shadowed dragon behind him.

His hand brushed my hair back. I felt him trace the curling edges of the scar on my face.

I couldn't read the reticent expression on his face. It was both perplexed yet resigned.

"Very well. It will be you, then," came the softly clipped

words. I caught an unmistakable edge of disappointment. "For reasons I cannot see."

I was already beginning to shake my head, panic rising. *There must be some other way,* I thought.

"Say your goodbyes to your family and your homeland, wife," Sarkin ordered, his hand sliding away from my face, already beginning to walk back to his riders. "We leave for Karak at dawn."

Shock rooted me into place like a tree, sinking me deep until I wondered if our goddess' earth could just swallow me up entirely.

"And Klara," Sarkin said behind me, "I advise you not to try to run before then."

The dragon huffed out a sharp breath, her scales rustling, though they no longer made her song.

"Zaridan has your scent now," he told me. "There is no where we will not find you."

CHAPTER 5
SARKIN

"Think they'll attempt to retaliate tonight?" Feranos asked me, sliding off Vorna's back, and his Elthika leapt to the sky, disappearing into the dark clouds above. Zaridan was above us as well, circling, surveying, waiting. She grew impatient so far from home.

"No," I answered, turning my gaze back to Dothik, the glittering city I'd once dreamed of seeing in person as a child. The Dakkari's capital was impressive, though I was disappointed. Fantastical stories never mixed well with a true reality.

Dothik looked tired. Tired and unwelcoming. The middle of this continent was dry, hot, and drab. I didn't know how most Dakkari lived here, how they lived on the inhospitable wilds of this place. The West Lands of their country, with its lakes and hills, held more promise. It reminded me more of home.

"For all the *Dothikkar's* faults, I don't think he's a fool. Neither is the heir," I continued. I was sitting on the ledge of a mountain to the west of the city. We were camped on the other side for the night. How Feranos had found me was a mystery. "The Hartans learned to kneel to the Elthika. The Dakkari will learn to do the same."

"The Elders will not be pleased that instead of a heartstone, we come home with a Dakkari princess," Feranos warned.

"I always deliver what I promise, don't I?" I asked, cutting a look over to him.

"But the heartstone—"

"Is but *one*," I finished, cutting off his words. "One dying heartstone. That's not what we need. We must be patient, for a little longer."

Feranos went quiet. "The princess?"

"Yes," I said. "Zaridan knows what she's doing. I might not understand it fully quite yet, but I'm beginning to. I trust in my Elthika more than anything, just like any Sarrothian. Wouldn't you trust in a mate Vorna chose for you?"

"Yes," Feranos said, his voice hushed in its quiet reverence. "I would."

Unlike Feranos, I'd never believed in fate…but after today, I wondered if I'd been wrong. I'd heard my dragon's song—the *sy'asha*—and I remembered the dizzying jolt of my future wife's words.

I have seen your forests of heartstones. Perhaps you're greedy for just one more.

She thought us greedy? She was wrong.

We were *starving* for mere scraps.

There was ancient Elthikan magic here—I could feel it. The heartstones had infused their power into this land. It breathed life into this place, cultivated itself in its sons and daughters. It flowed in the rivers, it enriched the soil, it was in the wind that blew from the north and in the waves that crashed against the cliffs in the south.

One thing was clear to me, however. It was diminished here too, just as it was in Karak. The Dakkari didn't seem to realize what would happen when that power was depleted entirely.

But we did.

"I still think we should take the heartstone, Sarkin," Feranos said, shaking his head. "We should *try*, at the very least, to take it to the Arsadia. To see if it will take."

"No," I said, the word sharp and firm. I inhaled a long breath, looking back to Dothik. "One thing we know about the Dakkari is they are a spiritual people. To take the heartstone is to offend their goddess. They will never forgive it. It once belonged to great kings here. Let it rest and die here. We won't need it soon anyway. And forging a path in peace is easier than in blood."

"The Hartans know that," Feranos said, his low laugh echoing along the mountains. I heard the great gust of wings overhead from our Elthika.

I inclined my head. "And if Elysom's council decides that we conquer this territory for Karak…well, by then the Dakkari will already be kneeling."

"Sometimes I forget how you are," my friend said suddenly. "It's been too long since you've had a challenge. You get restless without one."

With a grin, I look back to Dothik. I wondered which glittering turret my future *wife* was in. I wondered if she would sleep this night. That restless part of me—the one Feranos spoke of— almost wished she *would* run…if only so I could hunt her down.

"Get some rest," I ordered my second rider. "The journey home will be long tomorrow with the storms coming in."

Feranos nodded…yet he didn't move.

"The scar on her face, Sarkin," he finally said, quietly. "I've never seen a bonding mark like it. You…are certain?"

Not for the first time, I wished I could open my mind to Zaridan. But it was one of the powers that had been lost to us with the depletion of the heartstone magic. I wanted to ask her *why*. Why this female?

"No," I said, the truth escaping my lips with a harsh breath. "But my Elthika is. She's never led me astray."

I met Feranos's worried gaze.

"And she won't now."

"*If* Zaridan is wrong, you know what would happen," Feranos said, his tone careful and hushed, like we would be overheard or that I might take offense. Because he knew. He might've been one of my oldest friends…but I was still his *Karath*. His king.

My jaw ticked.

"I won't lose the citadel. And I won't lose the horde. Not with Zaridan at my side, not with you, not with the riders. Elysom wouldn't dare take it," I rasped.

Feranos inclined his head. "Your aunt only looks for opportunities to take it from you. I don't mean anything by it, Sarkin. It's nothing you haven't already thought yourself."

"We've weathered worse," I gave him, letting the words slide because I knew they came from concern. "Haven't we?"

The corner of his scarred lip turned up. "Yes, *Karath*, we have."

"This will be no different," I said, nodding at Dothik in the distance. "Their dying heartstone stays. I will complete my duty as promised and in full. Once and for all, I'll silence Elysom."

"And this time you get a pretty little wife out of it."

My mood soured, and I scoffed.

Standing, I tapped at my inner wrist, at the black cuff that emitted a sound undetectable to our own ears. But I heard Zari respond, approaching.

"In title only," I rasped. "You saw her. She's not strong enough to stand at my side, much less bond with an Elthika of her own. The Sarrothian will never accept her as their true queen."

Besides, I'd never intended to marry. Ever.

"Then why—"

"Because Zaridan knows we can *use* her," I said, looking at Feranos's perplexed expression. He would need to know eventually. "She knows where there are more heartstones."

"Truly?" Feranos asked quietly, going still.

I nodded.

"So let Dothik have their dying one. We will have more than we know what to do with soon enough. And then no one on this planet—not the Dakkari or the Hartans or the Selkavars—will ever be able to stand against Karag power again. Our home will be protected and secure for the rest of our days. That is what I want."

Zaridan circled overhead before landing on a ledge along the mountain cliff.

"I won't stop until it's done," I promised.

CHAPTER 6
KLARA

It was still dark on the wildlands when I stepped beyond the East Gate. Sarkin—or his horde of dragons—were nowhere in sight, and for a brief, dizzying, silly moment of relief, I thought maybe he'd changed his mind.

Dannik was beside me, stoic and stiff. He'd barely said a word as he walked me to the gate. It felt like a death march.

Last night, he'd come to my chambers. He'd begged me to leave Dothik—he'd even had a group of our father's *darukkars* at the ready, to shuffle me across the wildlands and hide me among one of the outer hordes. He would speak with the Karag, he'd promised. He would make Sarkin Dirak'zar change his mind; he would offer another female in my place. He only needed time.

I'd denied my brother. It wasn't only Sarkin's threat, that his dragon had my scent now and they would find me anywhere— and likely destroy everything in their wake, including whoever sheltered me.

It was also Zaridan's song. That pure moment last night and the sense that I was right where I was meant to be.

I had to do this even though I was terrified. Even though I didn't know if my new life would be atrocious or kind at the hands of my new husband. What life awaited me with the Karag? What would I find across Drukkar's Sea?

Like Vienne, the white-haired sorceress, my ancestor…I'd had dreams all my life. Visions, I assumed. I'd seen an alien place, one I'd never been able to find replicated in the archives. I'd seen the dragons. A forest of heartstones. And what of the stories my own mother had told me all her life? *Her* visions? Of things she couldn't possible know?

It was all connected. I *knew* it. Finally I would have the answers I'd so desperately sought for over a decade.

Dannik had been right—our last heartstone *was* dying, fading with every passing day. Soon Arik's sword would dull and tarnish, a great legacy beginning to rot with it.

What if I could find more heartstones across Drukkar's Sea? Heartstones had saved us against the red fog. If we had none left, what would save us against the Karag if they came with their dragons? If they unleashed their *ethrall* on the capital, on the hordes, on the outposts? Nothing would stop them from conquering Dakkar when we didn't have the power to fight back.

My father and his queen might not've wanted me. Alanis might've sneered every time I walked passed her in the palace. They might've deny my bloodlines…but Dannik was right. I had the blood of great Dakkari and humans alike running in my veins, and I had a *duty* to my people. This was my home. It was all I'd ever known.

So, when I stepped out onto the dark wildlands and didn't see Sarkin or his dragons, I was both selfishly relieved *and* disappointed.

It was short lived, however. As the first rays of the sun began to lighten the sky to a soft purple, I saw a dark mass flying from Bekkar's Shield—the mountain range to the west.

The group that was gathered beyond the East Gate was larger than I expected. Dannik and myself. My father and the queen. The high priestess of the temple, with her keen eyes that narrowed on me, as if loath to let me go. A few of my father's council. And guards. Many, many guards.

There were archers along the walls, and I thought their presence was laughable.

"I know you're angry with me," I said to Dannik, far enough away from everyone else that I spoke freely. I had a trunk of clothing at my feet, everything I owned, and a leather satchel strapped to my back, a dagger nestled within its confines. "But I don't want to say goodbye like this."

Dannik let a breath loose. He stepped in front of me, blocking my view of the grouping of dragons that were drawing closer and closer in the rising sun. I wondered what they called a formation like that. Surely the Karag had a word for it.

"I will find a way to bring you home," my brother vowed quietly. "Whatever it takes. The *Vorakkar* are riding in from the wildlands to meet with us. We are forming a plan to—"

My brow furrowed, and I gave him a half smile, reaching forward to grip his shoulder. "Dannik. You saw what they can do. The best plan? It's to understand them, to learn about them. It is not to attack blindly. To sail across the sea, searching for an uncharted continent that is home to powerful creatures who can wipe us out in a mere moment."

"I told you that I would protect you. I promised it to your mother," Dannik confessed softly.

My heart squeezed. "What? When?"

"Before she was sent away. She made me promise, Klara. I have broken that vow already."

A stab of affection mingled with grief made me stand on the tips of my toes and press a kiss to his cheek. I embraced him.

Into his ear, I whispered, "Trust in me, brother. Zaridan gave me this scar. She gave it to me when I first dreamed about her, when I was just fifteen. And I have dreamed about her ever since."

Dannik stiffened beneath me, even though I didn't tell him

about everything else I'd dreamed. The other dragon, specifically. The ones I'd seen even before Zaridan.

I pulled back, looking up into his eyes. I grabbed his arms, squeezing tight, though my voice was steady and unyielding. "I *am* afraid. But I know that this is my purpose. I have been preparing for it nearly my whole life. Let me go with them. Political marriages are made all the time, throughout our history—you know that. Father knows that better than anyone. Let me go as a daughter of Dakkar because maybe it will soften the Karag's will against us. Maybe we can negotiate as allies and not as enemies. We cannot stand against them, against their dragons' power. This is the only way. It might even be a mercy."

Dannik stared down at me, turmoil swirling in his golden eyes.

"I always thought you would make a better ruler than me," he finally said.

I heard the gust of the dragon wings before I felt the earth's might tremble when one landed. The other nine remained in the air with their riders, circling overhead. When Dannik stepped to the side, I saw Zaridan, gleaming black and undeniably beautiful in her strength, illuminated by the rising sun.

My eyes caught on Sarkin's, watched as he ran his palm down her wide neck. He swung his leg over, dismounting expertly with a long jump down in front of her left wing. He landed in a crouch and then rose.

I'll ride a dragon this morning, came the sudden thought, so unfathomable that it didn't quite feel real until this very moment.

My chin rose when he approached. Sarkin's eyes narrowed on my brother, a curl of black hair drifting in front of his left eye when Zaridan gusted her wings. I heard Orak—one of my father's council members—make a distressed sound. I got the impression Zaridan had done it on purpose.

I watched Sarkin assess the clearing, flickering from me to the group behind us, to the archers on the walls and the locked East

Gate. Not that it mattered. He'd been in the market yesterday. He knew another way to get into the city. There were rumors of tunnels beneath Dothik, tunnels that King Arik had once used. Perhaps those?

I wondered how long the Karag had been among us. Since their very first dragons had been spotted? How long had they been gathering information on the Dakkari, waiting for the perfect moment to strike?

And why did that strike happen to begin with me?

"Sleep well, *aralye?*" he asked, his tone gruff and mocking, raising his brow.

"Perfectly," I lied. For once, my dreams had been strangely quiet.

Those beautiful eyes dropped to the trunk at my feet. "Where do you think you're going to put that?"

My hand tightened on the strap of my brown leather satchel. "It's my clothing."

Sarkin made a sound in the back of his throat. "It stays. Let's go."

Dannik stepped forward and Sarkin's eyes cut to him. The icy chill in them had me reaching out to squeeze my brother's wrist, a warning in my own gaze when he looked over at me.

Sarkin looked behind me, directly at my father, assessing the distance he'd put between them. I could almost hear his thoughts. He didn't think highly of the *Dothikkar.*

"At least you, heir, can look me in the eyes," Sarkin said, voice rising as he looked at my brother. "Tell your father we will be in contact soon."

"What is it that you'll be in contact about?" Dannik growled.

"Our terms" was all Sarkin said, and I could feel my brother's frustration.

"Fuck your terms. If you hurt her," Dannik said, his voice so quiet and deadly that even Sarkin stilled to regard him, "I won't care that you have your dragons at your back. I won't stop until I find you, Sarkin Dirak'zar."

The slow spread of Sarkin's grin made me hold my breath. I felt my brother's temper snap. Zaridan's wings gusted again, and I wondered if she could feel the palpable tension in the small clearing.

"Enough," I said quietly, stepping forward in front of my brother before a brawl began. Sarkin's eyes fastened on my own when I looked up at him. "I'm ready. Let's go."

Did I catch a hint of surprise? I couldn't be certain as nerves began to rush, making my limbs shaky at the realization of what I was about to do. I hadn't cried once since last night, and I refused to now…but all I wanted was to curl into a little ball on the wild-lands and sob. I was leaving my home, where I'd been with my mother, where she was buried. Leaving Dannik, the city, the archives, Sora—who I wouldn't get to say goodbye to, all my research, the comfort of my routine. My quiet morning walks along the Spine. My dusky evenings sneaking out on the wildlands.

Sarkin took my chin in his grip, turning my cheek to peer down at my scar. I swallowed loudly, discomfort swirling. I'd pinned back my hair this morning, leaving my scar on full display. And there was a reckless part of me that wanted everyone to see it. I'd hidden it away behind the curtain of my hair for years because it made *others* uncomfortable.

Now? I *wanted* my father to see it, who'd once loved my mother but couldn't stand to look at me. My stepmother, who'd only ever hated me because I threatened everything she'd built. The *Laseta Kalliri*, the high priestess, who I assumed had always known about my abilities and had just been waiting for her own perfect moment to take me away to the North Lands. Now I had a strong suspicion Dannik had helped protect me from her grasp.

Sarkin's thumb brushed the bottom edge of it, the marking

that Zaridan had left on me. He recognized it. And I wasn't a fool —I knew it had something to do with my being taken away.

The mark throbbed under his touch, making me flinch.

His lips pressed, and for a moment, he looked furious. He grabbed my waist, pushing me toward Zaridan, and I nearly stumbled into her. Standing next to her front clawed legs, as thick as tree trunks in the Ancient Grove, I craned my head to look at the dragon, my mouth bone dry in my fear and awe.

She huffed out a hot breath as I looked into her slitted eyes of gold. Zaridan moved, lowering her left wing, and I watched Sarkin ascend it before seating himself in the worn mount with the silver catches.

Looking back at Dannik, I tried to give him a small smile, but I feared it came out as a grimace.

"Strength," he reminded me, the soft word meant for me drifting over the distance between us.

I inclined my head, my gaze catching on the trunk at his feet. Another part of me I'd leave behind, clothes I'd lived in every day for years. It felt...wrong. Every part of me was being stripped away, bit by bit.

"Ascend," Sarkin bit out, voice cold and cutting. "We need to leave. *Now.*"

As if I were outside of my body, I felt myself move. Zaridan's wing was surprisingly steady, like unyielding earth, beneath my feet, a testament to her strength. The climb was steep, my footing uncertain, the weight of my satchel at my back throwing me off balance.

I heard Sarkin's sharp, impatient exhale when I nearly stumbled, catching words under his breath that I didn't understand.

Zaridan breathed deeply, lifting her wing, and I cried out, landing hard on the mount, right into Sarkin's side, my satchel nearing falling off my shoulder. My face was burning with fear and mortification, knowing my family had witnessed the pitiful scene. I wasn't used to being so on display, but I could feel dozens of eyes directly on me.

"Sit behind me. Find your balance and hold my waist tight. If you fall, you're dead. Remember that, princess," Sarkin rasped. The mounting saddle was as hard as a boulder between my thighs, though I guessed it was marginally better than Zaridan's scales. For a moment, he said nothing as my arms wound around his body, digging into his unyielding strength.

My breath was coming out in quick gasps and pants…and we weren't even off the ground. Overhead, I heard the others flying.

"Learn quickly," Sarkin said. His voice might've been quiet, but there was no mistaking the menace in it. "The Sarrothian will never accept you otherwise."

Those words sounded like a promise.

With that, Sarkin's hand tightened on two black tethers hooked into place.

"*Thryn'ar.*"

I felt Zaridan's body respond to his command. She seemed to hum to life, vibrating in her unmistakable power. Heat rushed. I swore I could feel her heartbeat, and for a moment, my fear was replaced by awe.

I felt her launch from the ground. One moment we were stationary. The next, the air was hurtling around us and we climbed higher and higher at a steep, terrifying angle. My stomach dropped at the unfathomable speed, the pins in my hair whipping out immediately.

The wind was so loud that I couldn't hear myself scream.

But then we leveled out. Already I was panting and could barely hear over my pounding heartbeat.

"You'll leave your own scar on me with those claws," Sarkin grumbled when the world quieted again. I was gripping him so tight I was surprised I *hadn't* drawn his blood.

Yet I didn't loosen my grip. I didn't care if I hurt him.

When the other nine dragons fell into formation around us,

with Zaridan in the lead, though flying lower than the rest, I couldn't help but look behind me.

There was Dakkar. In all its expansive, wild beauty. In the rising sun, I'd never thought it looked more beautiful. The mountains, the plains, the river that ran toward the coast from Dothik…

Outside the East Gate, my brother was a mere speck on the earth, growing smaller and smaller by the moment.

And I *knew* then…this was how the Karag saw us. Mere specks. How could they not on the backs of their mighty dragons?

I swayed, going dizzy. I couldn't wrap my mind around the height. I imaged myself falling. How long until I reached the ground?

"Turn forward," Sarkin ordered me.

In front of us was Drukkar's Sea, glittering and seemingly endless.

My future lay beyond it.

The moment we crossed the threshold of the continent's coastline, flying past the jagged cliffs and rocky shores beyond Bekkar's Shield…I couldn't stop the tears that dripped from my cheeks, though the wind whipped them away mercilessly. I imagined them landing in the sea below us.

Though Sarkin had ordered me to turn forward, I disobeyed him.

My heart ached as I watched my homeland become a mere speck behind us too.

CHAPTER 7
SARKIN

The storm hit hard in the late afternoon.

Levanth, my navigator wing, had been tracking the storm system through the night—I knew she'd barely slept. And just as we passed over where the Dakkari's sea met our own, the dark clouds turned the day into night, just where she'd predicted.

Purple lightning pierced the sky open, and with every bolt, I felt Klara's hand tighten further into my abdomen. I envisioned dark bruises tomorrow morning from her grip alone, even worse than the ones I'd received in rider training all those years ago.

The rain that pelted us slowly made her grip slicken, the mount getting wet. Her clothing was unsuitable for riding, the soles of her boots slipping across Zaridan's scales.

When my Elthika veered suddenly, narrowly missing the bolt of a lightning strike, Klara slid. I caught her panicked gasp, even in the deafening roar of the wind and rain, and felt her hands scrambling for anything she could find in her desperation—my vest, my thighs—her dull claws digging.

Quickly, I twisted, grabbing her by the arm as her legs kicked to try to right herself, hanging off the side of the mount. Her eyes were wild with fear when I met them, and I kept a grip on

Zaridan's tethers with one hand while I tried to prevent my future wife from toppling off the back of my Elthika with the other.

"Stop fighting me!" I growled, irritation making me snap. A child could ride on dragonback better than her. A child would know how to lean with an Elthika in flight, when to brace their thighs, when they could relax them. "Stop fighting her!"

Zaridan veered sharply to the left, giving Klara more control to right herself.

"Fuck," I said through gritted teeth as I blinked the rain from my eyes. "Come here!"

I let go of Zaridan's tethers, tightening my inner thighs to keep me rooted into the mount, and twisted in my seat. Klara was shaking, soaked through, and I grabbed her by the waist, lifting her easily.

The beginnings of a screech left her when she found herself dangling in midair over the side of Zaridan, which I promptly quieted by dropping her between my legs.

"Brace your thighs and hold this," I growled into her ear, finding her hands and guiding them to the leather-wrapped curved bar that ran across Zaridan's mount. The bar was a little too large for her small palms, but she gripped it like her life depended on it—which, in her mind, very well might've been the case—her knuckles going white.

She was shivering, and I pressed down into her back, her bulky and rigid soaked satchel meeting my chest. The afternoon was dark. I had wanted to reach the citadel by midnight, but she wouldn't last until then. Not in this storm.

I searched the wing for Feranos, finding him flying below. On my cuff, I pressed the small ridge and a single light flashed out, beaming toward him. I saw his head jerk up in response, pulling on the tethers to guide his Elthika's ascent.

I tapped out my message on my cuff, a series of lights flashing, a language only riders would know. He flashed two back, and I watched him maneuver up toward Levanth to relay my message to the rest of the wing.

It was nearing evening when I finally spied the coastline of Karak in the distance. Klara was still trembling. She'd refused to eat the travel rations or drink from the water skin I'd tried to press into her hands. She'd refused to let go of the stabilizing bar, and I felt a pitying discomfort burn in me, knowing I was the cause.

When we passed over Karak land, I leaned over and thumped my fist against Zaridan's side three times. The hardness and strength of her scales felt like striking metal, the reverberation going up my bones, discomforting to me, though she'd barely feel it. She knew the signal, however. I felt the response in the powerful swing of her tail as she began to circle back, searching for a suitable clearing.

Around us, the rest of my wing continued on to Sarroth. They had another four hours of flight to reach our horde, but they could withstand a week of this weather before it would start to wear. The Dakkari princess—currently hunched over Zaridan as low as the mount would allow, her eyes squeezed tightly shut —could not.

Zaridan shook the earth when she landed on a rocky cliff at the edge of a forest. The trees shook with the boom, leaves rustling brightly like chimes, and then it was silent, save for Klara's ragged gasps.

"Let go," I ordered her, my voice coming out rougher than I'd intended. Her knuckles were still white on the bar, her shoulders trembling.

Reaching forward, I pried off her palms before sliding off Zaridan's side, landing on the stone ledge hard.

"Jump down. You need to get warm," I ordered. When she didn't move, irritation shot through me. "*Now*, princess. I don't need you dying on me of wind chill before we even reach the citadel."

"Then why even take me?" she snapped, her head jerking toward me, tears in her eyes making them glassy. The whites of her gray-colored eyes—a human trait, I knew, belying her ancestry—were bloodshot, red veins shooting them like roots of a tree. She was furious, even wet and shivering and frozen in place on Zari's back. Her voice trembled from the cold as she added, "*You* wanted me. *You* wanted this. What's even the purpose?"

Peering up at her, I observed as she tried to calm down. Taking deep breaths, slowly in, slowly out, life returning to her limbs.

"Jump down," I ordered again, though I made an effort to keep it soft, when it was not in my nature to try to give comfort. It still came out harsh, even to my ears. "You need to get warm. You do realize that, yes?"

Her lips pressed. After a beat of silence, she nodded and slowly swung her far leg over the mount, though it caught briefly on the bar, nearly causing her to lose her balance.

I growled, stepping forward. "Be careful!"

"I know," she snapped.

My brows ticked up, and for a brief, startling moment, I had the urge to laugh. She *did* make an amusing sight, all sodden and annoyed.

Zaridan huffed, and the movement made Klara slide. I caught her small gasp before she was falling—

I snatched her before she hit the ground, grunting with the force. She was ice cold. And in my arms…surprisingly small. For a moment, I couldn't help but take the opportunity to study her.

It was the first time I was seeing a Dakkari this close, though I'd studied their continent, their language, their culture, their cities and outposts extensively since I'd been in rider training. Even before then, as boy in my small farming village, I'd ask anyone I could about the Dakkari.

Though she wasn't *quite* a Dakkari, was she? They'd mixed

their bloodlines with humans over the course of the last two centuries. She *looked* human—small, vulnerable, and weak.

So small, I thought again, my eyes tracking down the front of her body when I placed her on the ground. She had no tail, as if she was a rider. Short limbs, smooth flesh, dressed in worn brown pants and a green embroidered tunic saturated from the storm. Not unlike any other female, though I had the unyielding impression that she was…*soft*. Unhardened to this life.

And easily broken.

I couldn't have picked a worse wife.

She wouldn't last one riding season. The Sarrothian horde would never accept her. It was laughable.

Though…as she stared back at me in this strange moment of quiet, I could concede she *was* pleasing to look at, scar and all. Beautiful, even, with her smooth—albeit wind-stung—skin, upturned nose, round face, and full pink lips. The tips of her ears were subtly pointed. *Different.* She possessed a soft beauty so unlike what Karag valued, and I found the contrast oddly…

And her eyes. Gray and luminous, I felt like they could sear straight through me. I'd never seen a match to their color.

Intriguing.

I had the discomforting sense she was observing me in a similar way, all careful curiosity, and I released her quickly, stepping back. I tapped on Zaridan's wing, which she lowered, and I walked up to untie a thick satchel, throwing it down before I went to the second one.

When I returned, I said, "Go wait under the tree line. We'll stay here for the night and wait out the storm."

CHAPTER 8
KLARA

A short while later, after we'd found a drier spot within the protection of the forest, Sarkin pulled out what looked like a black rock from a leather bag, wide and round at the bottom but tapered toward the top.

It was gleaming and smooth, but inside…I caught a glow of red.

I was trying to ignore the throbbing pain my entire body was in. Every small movement ached and burned, my muscles screaming in protest. My skin felt chafed and raw in every place my clothing hadn't covered it. Between my thighs, I knew the skin was bloodied and scraped from Zaridan's unyielding leather mount. My palms were beginning to blister from where I'd gripped the bar.

"Is that a dragon egg?" I asked in disbelief, trying to keep my teeth from chattering and my limbs from shaking…because it *hurt* to shiver.

Sarkin's gaze flashed up to mine, and I watched him place it on the forest floor. It sizzled on contact when it met the damp ground, steam rising, but it did nothing to dull the red glow within.

"No," he replied.

I waited for him to explain, but he said nothing more. In my curiosity, I walked forward, gritting my teeth as I bent down, but I wanted to get a closer look. The heat it was radiating was unfathomable.

"Don't touch it," he growled. How had he? It should've burned him. "Undress."

I gasped, straightening quickly, feeling a searing ache follow. "*What?*"

From the other pack, he tossed me a bundle of clothing. "You can't get warm in those clothes."

The material in my hands was heavy but soft. A pair of thick trews, well–broken in, and a long-sleeved black shirt. Simple and without decorative embellishments, so unlike what my people wore.

But they were dry. That was all that mattered.

Gazing around the clearing, I saw a tree wide enough to offer me privacy, and I walked—gingerly—to it.

The forest we'd landed in was lush and damp, the floor covered in a soft dark blue moss. The trees' trunks were smooth and black, leading up to thick, curling branches laden with velvety leaves, a kaleidoscope of different colors—dark greens, blues, and purples. I imagined in the daylight, or in the golden glow of a sunset, this forest would be breathtaking.

Strange flora illuminated the forest, bushes and shrub and vines glowing. For a brief moment, I thought they were *heart-stones*, my hopes for Dakkar coming true. But instead, it appeared it was the stamens of the blooms themselves, glowing a light blue at their very center, and disappointment swept through me.

Though I still had hope. I'd dreamed of heartstone forests. They had to be here.

"Don't try to run," came the dark warning, though Sarkin's tone was nonchalant. "There are worse things in here than me."

A chill went down my spine, the beauty of the dark forest

suddenly turning ominous. Quickly—as quickly as I could—I undressed. Inspecting my inner thighs briefly, I winced when I saw they *had* been scraped raw, little beads of red blood already drying.

The thought of asking Sarkin for help—because he'd likely scoff at me, that telling disappointment entering his gaze—made me pull up the fresh pants, dry and clean, though they were much too big. I took the belt from my own clothes and tightened it around my waist, keeping the material from falling. I pulled on the shirt next, hunching over to shield my breasts just in case Sarkin poked his head around the tree trunk.

When I emerged, I saw Sarkin had a sleeping roll laid out. The outside was leather, but the inside appeared to be lined with black fur.

Alarm went through me, but I ignored the sleeping roll…for now. Instead, I slowly lowered myself down to the moss nearest the glowing egg. The heat had already dried it out there, and I sighed, feeling the warmth begin to seep into my chilled skin. I laid out my soggy clothes and satchel next to it, knowing they'd be dry by morning, even through the chilly night. I wasn't worried about the satchel. It was made of *bveri* leather, and I'd made sure the seams were tight.

Across from me, Sarkin tossed over a pouch of dried meat, followed by a heavy water skin.

"Drink, so I can go refill it at the stream," he ordered, watching me, as if daring me to disobey. Now that I was dry and getting warm, I *was* thirsty. And starving.

"What about Zaridan?" I asked. We'd left her on the cliff, though I'd heard her take off shortly after.

Sarkin paused, his hand stilling in midair as he ate his own rations. "She'll be fine."

I nodded, taking a long swallow, drinking until I nearly emptied the whole skin. Then I ate all the rations in the pouch, acutely aware of the burn of his eyes on me all the while. When I was finished, he handed me a thick slice of red-colored bread, the top dotted with what I thought were black seeds.

I polished that off too, wiping my lips with the edge of my thumb when I was finished.

"Where are we?" I asked when the silence stretched uncomfortably long. "In Karag? Is that what you call this land?"

"Karak," he corrected, watching me. "Do I make you nervous, princess?"

He had his legs drawn up, his arms wrapped around his knees. A slice of the bread was dangling from his hand, and he brought it up to his lips for another bite. He was the picture of perfect ease, and I felt on edge.

I watched his strong jaw as he chewed.

"Of course you do," I said quietly. His chin tilted back. Surprised? "Did you expect another answer?"

"I expected you to lie," he said, finishing the last of his meal. "Most would."

"I have nothing to gain from lying, only losing a bit of my pride," I answered. "After today, that's long gone with you. So what do I care?"

A gruff sound left Sarkin's lips. A laugh? Perhaps as close as he'd come to one with me.

"What do you want with me?" I asked, cutting straight to the question that had been circulating in my mind since last night. Since I'd seen the red fog stream from his dragon and thought how bleak our future would become. Since I'd tasted the bitterness of the *ethrall* wind its way down my throat, constricting it tight.

I had a million questions racing in my head—questions I hoped I could find the answer to in being here.

Tonight, however, was not the time or the place to ask them. Even I knew that, but I wanted to see what Sarkin would say.

"I want to use you."

Hearing the words felt worse, somehow. They were honest, at

the very least, but they really drove home how *powerless* I truly was with him.

"For what?" I asked carefully.

"For many things," he rasped. A jolt went through my belly. "But mostly to find the forest of heartstones you spoke about."

Dread spread.

"But…but you have that here. You *have* them, don't you? You know where it is!"

Had I misunderstood entirely?

"We have a good supply," Sarkin replied, his eyes fastened on me tight. "But Karak is vast and our kingdoms are wide spread. Heartstones get depleted quickly because of the Elthika."

I'd been very, very wrong.

Quickly, I asked, "How do you know I wasn't lying?"

Sarkin grinned, and the sight was so startling that I nearly gaped. "Tell me that you were, *aralye*. I would love to hear that."

His mockery was plain.

"You believe me so easily? I'm a stranger to you! You were at our gates and demanding the one source of power we had left to protect ourselves from things like *you*. Our last heartstone. I would have said anything to make you leave."

"Ah, but you said the *wrong* thing, Klara of Rath Serok and Rath Drokka," he said. "And now you're here. Under *my* control. I know you weren't lying."

"How?"

"Because of that scar on your face," he replied simply, gesturing toward it, eyes fastening on it.

"And what would that prove?" I asked quietly, my heart leaping in my chest. Even though the burn of despair and disappointment nearly seared me from the inside out, there were other reasons why I'd agreed to come with him. For answers. Finally.

I merely thought it ironic that he was intending to use me for heartstones…just like the priestesses had wanted, just what my mother had tried so hard to shield me from for the entirety of my life.

"It proves that you possess Elthikan power," he told me. "It proves that you can cross realities in dreams, an ability the Karag have long had."

"If that's true, then you don't need me," I pointed out. He wasn't telling me something. "One of your own could find the forest."

He glanced down briefly at the glowing stone between us.

"Elthikan power is unpredictable. It manifests in different ways," he replied simply. "It's been a long time since we've heard of one with your ability. And I am not foolish enough to ignore a gift that has landed right at my feet."

"So you took me," I finished. "To use my ability to find you more heartstones."

"Precisely."

"Then why threaten to make me your wife? That's entirely unnecessary."

"*Threaten?*" he repeated. Sarkin's brow dropped, his expression amused yet foreboding. "You don't know the Karag at all. But you will."

The warning in his voice nearly made me shiver.

"Get some sleep," he ordered, gesturing to the fur roll as he stood, just as I heard a rumble of thunder in the distance. "Let's see what you dream of tonight, *wife*."

"Where will you sleep?" I asked. Even I could hear the trepidation in my voice.

"Worried?" he asked, the question sounding clipped.

"I don't trust you."

He smirked. "Good," he said. "But luckily for your sake, you're one of the last things I'd want to fuck right now."

My spine stiffened, a harsh exhale escaping me at the crassness and ugliness of the words. No one had ever spoken to me like that. It was like getting dumped over the head with a bucket of ice water.

"Get some sleep while you can, princess. We leave as soon as the storm ends," he said, snatching up the empty water skin next to me. I watched as he prowled off into the darkness of the forest, no doubt to search for a water source.

He really had no fear that I would try to leave.

And unfortunately, I thought as I slid into the fur roll, wincing at my aching muscles and the burning between my thighs, *I'm in no position to even try.*

CHAPTER 9
KLARA

I hadn't quite known what to expect when I'd heard Sarkin mention "the citadel." But we'd been up before dawn, the storm breaking in the night. And just as the sunrise peeked out over the horizon, we flew over a deep mountain valley, a twinkling river winding its way at the very base.

At the very end of the valley was a tall, jagged mountain though I could see decorative markings etched into its face even from a great distance. Reliefs carved into the rock of Elthika, their tails curving around the mountain like an embrace.

Below that mountain, spread out among rolling hills that rippled out toward flat land was a city. A towering stronghold made of gray stone overlooked it all.

That was the citadel, I figured, my eyes widening at the sight. Momentarily, I forgot my fear, riding on Zaridan's back when I could feel every muscle of my own body ache in protest. Momentarily, I forgot my pain and the fact that my legs felt like needles were pricking into my flesh over and over again.

I was awestruck. In the rising sun, it was beautiful, the land lush and vibrant, so unlike the wildlands of my own homeland. The river of the valley—which cleaved the city into two—led to a wide lake in the distance, and even there, I saw structures dotting close to the shore. It was a sprawling, expansive city…and Sarkin was its king?

"You call *this* a horde?" I asked. "It's larger than Dothik."

I didn't think Sarkin would be able to hear me over the rush of wind.

But he responded, "Sarroth. The stronghold of the South Lands."

"A stronghold against *what*?" I couldn't help but question.

He didn't answer me.

Instead, I heard a dragon's roar. No, not quite a roar. A call. The gust of wings funneled toward us, and I saw three Elthika flying overhead in formation. Beneath me, Zaridan responded. I could actually *feel* the way her lungs expanded before she mimicked the sound, bright and trilling into the sky, so unlike the deadly and powerful roar she'd unleashed in Dothik.

This was power, I realized. Not to control a creature that could decimate an entire civilization. But to ride with one. To bond with one. To feel that power and trust they wouldn't use it against you.

Was that how the Karag felt? Dannik's words returned to me, how he'd said they'd had no fear. This was why. What was it like? To feel so certain in your safety, knowing that no danger could ever compare?

Beyond the mountain, I could see Elthika flying. I watched as one latched into the side of the rock face, disappearing into a hidden entrance. My lips parted. *Their* home?

As we neared Sarroth and began to fly lower, heading straight for the citadel, I heard horns sound from below. Perhaps to herald Sarkin's return? Squinting over Zaridan's side, I ignored the great distance to the ground, ignored the way it made me feel dizzy, because I wanted to see it all. I *needed* to.

Karag milled around throughout the city, even this early. The horns were placed at regular intervals along what I assumed was the main road, set up on small platforms, and I wondered if this was their only purpose.

The city likely held a smaller population than Dothik, but it was certainly larger in size. It was widespread to accommodate the Elthika, I realized, eyeing a dragon casually perched on a wide ledge that overlooked crop land on the outskirts.

The structures and homes were grouped together, like they made up smaller villages within the larger city, all connected to a wide, winding road. Like the Spine in Dothik. The road crossed the river at the bridge before spiraling up the hills on the other side, dotted with smaller structures, smoke rising from a few. Nearest the citadel, the structures were more tightly packed, even multiple stories high. I thought I spied spaces for markets, training grounds, and shops along a paved road.

I've seen this before, I realized, jolting.

The citadel itself was separated from the main city by a steep, winding incline. It was nearest the mountain, the back section abutted against it. It was smaller than the *Dothikkar's* palace in Dothik and much less opulent, but I had the sense the citadel had been standing for much, much longer. There was longevity in the lines of its structure, made up of solid columns and gray stone. There was a timelessness to it.

As we got closer, I saw the stone of the citadel's facade also had etchings of Elthika, like the mountain above it. A history, perhaps, one I was itching to inspect and study.

What surprised me the most were the sprawling gardens at the back of the citadel, however. Zaridan flew over the stone keep and circled around, beginning her descent to land. It was a massive area, meant to accommodate multiple dragons, I thought, judging by the empty stone slab that led off the citadel's back gates. There was even a private training ground nearest the mountain.

But beyond the stone slab was a large plot of land, filled with overgrown shrubs, trees, vines. At the very back of the garden was a smaller structure, similar in architecture to the citadel but kept apart.

Zaridan landed on the stone slab, surprisingly graceful for one so large. Just then, one of the three Elthika that had accompanied us to the citadel landed—an Elthika and rider I recognized.

The other two continued on, circling back toward the main city.

Behind me, I felt Sarkin dismount. I would never admit it to him, but I'd felt safer flying with him at my back. I'd felt more protected, and I was silently grateful that he'd changed our positions for the rest of the journey.

"Get down," he grated from below. I bit my tongue, my lips pressing together. Even being the outcast of the royal line in Dothik, I hadn't been ordered around this much in years.

I huffed, but instead of sliding off Zaridan—I wouldn't give him the satisfaction of watching me struggle to dismount—I reached over and tapped at the joint of her wing, just as I'd seen him do the night before.

Triumph and relief went through me when she extended it in response. I hid my wince when I swung my leg over, my limbs feeling like boulders, and then carefully navigated down the flattest part of Zaridan's wing, taking my time though I felt the burn of Sarkin's eyes.

When I stepped off and looked up at him with mild smugness, he was studying me—his expression neutral, his jaw clenched. He wasn't glaring, at the very least, and I thought I almost caught a *hint* of approval.

Sarkin broke our gaze to retrieve the satchels, and as he did, I felt Zaridan's stare. When I moved my head, I bit the edges of my tongue, regarding her carefully. Once, she'd been my nightmare. I'd feared sleep because I'd feared she'd kill me in my dreams. But now I wondered if I'd had it wrong. She hadn't hurt me. She'd marked me. Why? To lead me to this place?

She'd showed me Sarroth before. I'd caught glimpses of the river, of the city, though they'd been like wisps of memories, uncertain and blurred. She'd showed me…but for what purpose?

And what of the other dragon that haunted my dreams?

Sarkin stepped between us, and I felt like I could breathe again. He placed his hand on her wide snout, inspecting her eyes, turning her this way and that way like he was a concerned parent.

Then he murmured something in the Karag language, which sounded like beautiful, soft whispers, so unlike the harshness of the Dakkari tongue.

I watched the exchange, rapt and intrigued, though it felt oddly like spying. *They're bonded,* I thought. What was that like? The Dakkari revered the *pyrokis*, our great, powerful creatures that rode across the wildlands with our hordes. But this felt different. This felt fated.

Sarkin ran a wide, calloused palm down her snout, raising his chin as he stepped back.

"*Thryn'ar esh lyiss,*" he said. "*Sen endrassa.*"

"*Thryn'ar,*" I whispered under my breath, studying the way Sarkin's lips formed the words. He'd said that word before, and so I memorized it. "*Esh lyiss.*"

Zaridan pressed low to the ground, her muscles bunching, power in every small, minuscule movement. Then she launched herself into the sky, the gust in her wake nearly knocking me backward.

A pair of hands righted me, and I looked over my shoulder, startled, only to find Sarkin's rider there. His dragon followed Zaridan, leaving the three of us standing near the back gate of the citadel.

He released me, then approached Sarkin, leaning forward to murmur something into his ear. I caught the way Sarkin's mouth tightened briefly before he nodded.

Then the commotion came behind me—footsteps and chattering voices. My movements were limited given the stiffness of my limbs, but I still stepped back, seeing a small group of Karag approach.

They were all of differing ages—some old, some young. Some were dressed in rich purple or dark green robes, others were in more fitted clothing, dragon scales stitched into them like a plating of armor.

I could feel the burn of every one of their eyes, could feel the palpable tension in the clearing when they approached. I could feel them sizing me up, and one older female narrowed her eyes on Sarkin, Karag words tumbling from her lips.

Sarkin replied, his voice cold and unyielding.

Then her eyes snapped to me. In my language, she demanded, "You. Dakkari. What is it that you think you're doing here?"

I didn't react. With calm I didn't feel, I replied simply, "I believe I've agreed to marry Sarkin Dirak'zar."

A sound left Sarkin. All at once, the group erupted into chaos, and I took a step back in retreat, only to meet my future husband's unyielding hand, pressing into my spine, holding me in place.

"Coward," he rasped. A gasp left me, my back going ramrod straight as my neck turned sharply to regard him. Those swirling eyes were looking at the group, and I thought I caught a hint of gleeful malice in his gaze. He liked to see them in disorder? Who were they? "Never run."

"I wasn't," I gritted out. "I haven't, have I?"

His eyes cut to mine. "No. You haven't, princess."

"What is the meaning of this?" the older female demanded, stepping toward us. She was dressed in light purple robes that brushed the stone. "Sarkin. This is reckless, even for you."

Sarkin's thumb brushed up my spine. Once. Twice. I blinked quickly.

"I'm honored you traveled all the way from Elysom to meet

my new bride," Sarkin replied. "But you came in vain. We leave for the Arsadia at dawn."

More travel? I thought in dismay, feeling my body painfully throb in response.

"On Muron, you will not," she snapped. "Elysom has forbid this union until we can make contact with—"

Sarkin stepped forward, blocking my view of her.

"I am a *Karath*," he growled. "You do *not* choose my wife. Or have you forgotten your place, Aunt?"

His…aunt?

"You stubborn bastard," she said quietly, so quietly that I thought the rest of the group couldn't hear. The words were meant only for Sarkin. "You couldn't stand it, could you? You never liked to be told what to do. By *anyone*."

Behind her, I noticed a long tail sweep the stone. So the Karag did have tails…just like the full-blooded Dakkari. So why didn't Sarkin? Or any of the riders I'd seen? My eyes swept to the group behind her. Most of them had tails as well, save for a handful.

"Only when they were wrong," Sarkin corrected, his voice just as low, and I had the strangest sense I was stumbling onto some very rooted issues between the two Karag. His aunt scoffed as Sarkin stepped forward until they were only an arm's length away. "Elysom gave me two *mysar* commands to repay what my father did. I have now fulfilled them both. The last of the Dakkari patrols are over. I have secured a wife of my own choosing. Elysom will no longer give me orders. My freedom is mine, as is Sarroth's. Don't forget that. Or you *will* answer to Muron's wrath."

My lips parted, hearing a heated passion in Sarkin's voice that I hadn't expected. No longer cold or detached.

"You disgrace the Karag to choose a wife such as her. And you know it," his aunt returned. *Never run* was what Sarkin told me.

Well, she wasn't backing down either. "The council *will* decide on this once we return to Elysom."

"It's already done," Sarkin rasped. His aunt froze, a glare forming. "Zaridan has accepted her. I heard the *sy'asha*. An Elthika's song is more powerful than any binding ceremony in this mortal life. But you wouldn't know that, would you?"

The *sy'asha*?

An Elthika's song?

Immediately, I knew what he was referring to. That moment on the wildlands, outside the East Gate. It seemed as if Zaridan's scales had whispered, a song only we could hear. It had been mesmerizing, lulling. I still remember the heat of Sarkin at my back, the brush of his thumb across my neck, the rhythm and softness of it.

My breath shuddered out. What was he saying? That we were already *married*? Because of that singular, unexpected moment?

"You still have to go to the Arsadia to bind it," she said quietly.

"Which is why we leave at dawn," Sarkin answered, and I could hear the smugness in his tone. "Or will you try to have her killed before then?"

I stiffened.

"Don't tempt me," his aunt replied, her tone clipped, her eyes practically burning holes into Sarkin's head. The hostility between them was even greater than my stepmother's hatred of *me*.

"If you try, you will have three kings to answer to for her death. One old, one new...and her husband," Sarkin replied. I swallowed, my breath shuddering out of me. One old...my father? One new? He must've meant Dannik. "She is of royal blood. Dakkari, yes, but ancient lines all the same."

The aunt's glare cut to me. "What is your name, Dakkari?"

My tongue felt stuck to the roof of my mouth. A long moment of silence passed. Even the group quieted behind her, waiting for me to speak. It was discomforting, I realized, to give my name so freely to strangers. But this was the Karag way, I remembered.

Names should not be hidden, Dakkari. Names should be feared. Those had been Sarkin's words. A part of me liked the sentiment.

"Klara of Rath Serok," I answered, "and Rath Drokka."

Murmuring went through the rest of the group. Were they the council she had spoken about? Advisors to her? Or to Sarkin?

"The *Dothikkar's* daughter," the aunt said, her tone cold and measured. Her eyes—yellow as gold—swept me up and down, calculating. They fastened on my face, and I felt them touch on my scar. Her lips parted and she moved forward. When she reached for my face, I heard the whistle of a blade. Sarkin's reflexes were quick, a dagger at the ready, glinting in his grip. She paid it no mind, as if this were a common occurrence.

For all I knew, it was.

"Watch yourself, Kethra," Sarkin warned, tone low.

"Will you spill my blood here for the council to see?" she answered. "Just as your father did to your mother?"

I sucked in a sharp breath, but then her fingers pressed into my scar. Her lips parted, her brows rose.

"I see," she breathed, eyes narrowing. Then Kethra laughed, the sound booming as she took a step back. The sweep of her tail brushed my ankles when her back turned. "Such an unremarkable girl to bear such a mark."

A pit lodged itself into my belly. Was I to be shunned here too? Cast aside? Looked down upon? I was a long way from Dakkar, and still…my problems would be the same?

"I hope you know what you're doing, Sarkin," Kethra snipped.

She stalked away, her strides short and clipped. A few members of the group followed until only a couple lingered.

A dark-skinned male stepped toward us, his blue eyes regarding me before fastening on Sarkin. He inclined his head briefly, his eyes closing. When he opened them, he touched silver markings below both of his eyes, the right, then the left. He touched the middle of his forehead and then gestured to Sarkin.

"*Karath,*" the male said.

"*Endrassa,* Gevanth," Sarkin said, pressing his fingers to his own forehead. A Karag sign of greeting, I assumed.

The male's voice was booming and rich when he said, "And thank *you* for riling her up. It will be a long journey home now."

"Difficult to break old habits" was what Sarkin replied. He stepped forward, clutching Gevanth's outstretched forearm with his own.

"It is when you don't try to break them," Gevanth replied. "She would know that better than anyone. You have more in common than either of you would ever admit."

"Blood is blood," Sarkin rasped.

"I'll need your patrol report. The council will call a meeting once we have it."

Report…on my home? On the Dakkari? To find weakness?

"I'll send it" was all Sarkin replied. "I'd ask you to stay and rest, friend, but with all due respect, get out of Sarroth. I have enough Elysom problems. I don't need a dozen more staying in my citadel."

Gevanth laughed, gruff and short. "Kethra, I'm sure, is already on dragonback to Elysom."

"Then make sure she stays there," Sarkin returned. "I meant what I said, Gevanth."

"I know," the male replied, inclining his head. His eyes cut to mine, I felt him observing my scar, and then he turned. Without so much as a goodbye—not that Sarkin seemed to want one—he left, the last of the council leaving with him. Until the stone terrace was cleared out, save for myself, Sarkin, and his rider, whose name I still didn't know.

"That went well," the rider declared, the sarcasm dripping from his tone.

"Next time," Sarkin said, "keep the citadel gates locked. They can rot outside for all I care."

"I was as surprised as you were."

"How did they know?" Sarkin growled.

"I've been trying to figure that out. A watch, perhaps. On the south coast. But we've had no reports of riders crossing our territories."

Sarkin sharply exhaled. "Elysom always knows things they shouldn't. And you know how that usually happens? A weapon. But now we have our own."

My spine snapped and I frowned. "I am not yours to use."

"That's exactly what you are," Sarkin answered, so dismissively it made my hackles rise. "Mine to use however I see fit."

Impossible male! I thought, frustration making my jaw grit. I was tired, hungry, and so sore I didn't want to move.

"Why don't you just knock me out so I can dream for you?" I asked, my voice intentionally sweet.

Sarkin came close, dropping down until our eyes were level. He brushed his thumb across my scar and murmured, "Tempting. Should I?"

The rider cleared his throat as I glared.

Sarkin rose. He gestured to the far corner of the garden, to the small structure I'd seen tucked along the stone of the mountain.

"Your accommodations, princess," he said. "Enjoy the bed while you can. We leave at dawn, and we'll be staying in wild territory. Just like your hordes and *Vorakkar* of old."

"If you think that scares me, you're sorely mistaken. I grew up in a horde," I said, my chin raising. "On the wildlands of Dakkar."

"But you've never seen wildlands like these," he said quietly, studying me as if surprised by the discovery. Softly, like a lover, he murmured, "That I promise you."

CHAPTER 10
KLARA

I was surprised that Sarkin left me on my own, though I shouldn't have been. According to him, Zaridan had my scent. She could find me anywhere. And I believed that. I was trapped without the bars of a dungeon, held tethered and leashed by his dragon.

Not that I had anywhere else to go. I'd agreed to this. And on the journey to Sarroth, I'd vowed to myself that I would take advantage of this surreal situation, to learn whatever I could about the Karag, to learn about the Elthika, and to learn about my purpose here.

Because I had a purpose here. Sarkin had made that clear. But I wasn't going to explore that purpose for *him*. It was only for me. To answer the questions I'd had for years. To understand the strange stories my mother had whispered about for my entire life.

Something greater was happening now. I was no longer in control of my own fate, and I accepted that.

When I stepped inside the small structure, I saw that it was clean, if spartan. Perhaps it had belonged to a groundskeeper… whoever had once tended to the overgrown garden swallowing it up.

The inside comprised of a simple room with a raised bed—just like in the *Dothikkar's* palace, though I preferred a nest of furs on the floor like in the hordes—a high table, chairs, and a stone hearth on the opposite side. There was a room off the back wall, and when I inspected that, I saw it was a washroom with a sunken-in bathing pool flush with the floor. It was steaming, already filled with water. I'd never seen one so large.

Immediately I stripped off, lowering my satchel to the ground gently. The walls in here were a black stone, so polished that I could see my reflection in them. I saw dark bruises across my flesh. Around my shoulders where the satchel had dug into them, the force and velocity of dragon flight punishing. Bruises in my abdomen from where I'd hunched over the harness, a round metal knob pressing into it. My palms were raw and blistered. Between my thighs, the skin was so hot to the touch, chafed and irritated.

My whole body hurt, and when I stepped down into the steaming pool, I nearly screamed as the water met my wounds. But after the initial searing pain passed, I breathed out a sigh of relief, the heat beginning to loosen my sore muscles.

It was only morning, and yet I felt like I could sleep away the day and night. My eyelids began to droop, my neck lolling back.

When I woke, my skin was puckered and pruned, but I was still so incredibly tired. I crawled from the bath, blotting at my wet skin with a black cloth I found, and managed to stumble to the bed. Sunlight streamed in through the windows, bright and merciless, and I collapsed onto the thin blankets.

It wasn't comfortable by any means, but that didn't stop my eyes from sliding shut. As the cool air drifted over my drying skin, I thought, briefly, it felt like a calming touch. It felt nice.

I slept.

The forest floor was glowing. It looked like an iridescent mist was sweeping and swirling across the ground, but when I crouched and pressed my fingers into the earth, it was cool and damp. The sounds of the forest were hushed. There was a reverent quiet here, a divine peace. I scarcely dared to breathe in fear I would disrupt the balance.

Trees surrounded me, towering canopies dripping with white leaves threaded with blue veins. The tree trunks were thick, as wide and immovable as the gold statues that dotted Dothik. Above me, the sky was dark, and I knew this was a dream.

Only it felt different. It felt *real.* I'd always been aware when I'd been dreaming. I'd always been aware of what was happening in the moment, but I'd never experienced *this.*

It felt like I'd been dropped inside a forest. I touched my skin, realized it was still bare from my bath. I was naked in a dark forest, but I no longer felt the stiffness and soreness from riding on Zaridan. I felt no pain at all.

When I smoothed my hand over the trunk of a nearby tree, it scraped against my palm, the texture rough.

Wake up, I thought, suddenly alarmed. Because this was *too* intense. I'd only ever seen snippets of places in my visions. They'd always been blurred at the edges, never clear. They'd been manageable that way because a part of me could always write them off as imagination.

This was different. When I breathed, I could *smell* the decay of leaves and the earthiness of the damp soil. My nipples puckered tightly when a stray breeze funneled through the trees, and I suppressed a shiver, rubbing at my arms.

There was a bright spot just below my feet, glowing underneath the topsoil. I crouched down, my heart booming in my chest like a horde drum.

I began to dig, my fingernails scraping at the earth, the fragrance of the dirt hitting my nostrils. Deeper and deeper I dug until—

The glow of a heartstone, the biggest I'd ever seen or researched, illuminated a horned beetle I'd uncovered, which immediately wiggled its way back into the wall of soil, disappearing.

A soft exhale left me, and I reached down to smooth my fingertips over the heartstone. It was rooted into place. I realized it was attached to the roots of the *tree*. Like fruit on a vine. The roots were pulsing with light, giving energy to the heartstone, giving it life.

The tree?

Dazed, I stood, tilting my head back to inspect it carefully. Why was it so familiar? I'd seen it before, hadn't I? But what I couldn't determine was if it'd been in a dream or not. Had I been here before?

A headache bloomed behind my left eye, and I hissed, pressing my fingers to my brow bone hard.

Overhead, I heard the unmistakable wings of an Elthika, and my neck snapped back, my throat exposed as I scanned the sky through the thick canopies. Zaridan?

No, I thought, seeing the familiar flash of silver scales. It was *him.*

"Wait!" I cried out, sudden desperation pushing me into a sprint, following it. My feet dug into the soft soil, slipping on slick leaves, and I nearly stumbled over thick, exposed roots. "Please! *Thryn'ar…esh lyiss!*"

It was the only Karag I could remember, and I had no idea what it meant. But maybe—

The dragon roared but never stopped. My heart throbbed in time with the pounding of my feet, and I tried to keep track of the dragon overhead, narrowly running into a wide tree and dodging it at the last moment.

"Wait!"

I needed to know why I'd been seeing this dragon in my

dreams for decades. It had to *mean* something, just like seeing Zaridan.

The forest gave way to an open cliffside. Beyond that was endless ocean, glittering in the moonlight, and I felt a flash of despair in my chest as I watched the silver-scaled dragon fly farther and farther away. Out of my reach. Again.

Before I reached the cliff, I heard, *"Klara!"*

All at once, the dream ended abruptly, falling away like a veil.

Wind was whipping my hair and exposed skin, cold and icy, the pain of my body returning in a dizzying rush. Below me was an endless drop down to Sarroth. It was pitch black, save for a sliver of a crescent moon overhead—

"What are you doing?" Sarkin's roar came from behind me. "Wake up, Klara!"

I gasped, feeling my feet slip on the edge of a cliff when I turned to the voice. For one breathless moment, I met Sarkin's wild gaze as he sprinted to reach me...

But then I was tumbling over the edge.

My scream was silent as I scrambled violently, thrashing my limbs and arms, trying to find purchase on anything. I managed to grip the ledge of a rock, my palm splitting over a rough edge, accompanied by a piercing stab at my side.

Animal sounds escaped me, terror making me gasp, trying to find air.

A dragon's roar reverberated against the mountain, and I felt the rush of wind. Zaridan?

Sarkin's appeared, reaching down for my hand.

"Take it!" he demanded.

But my bloodied grip was slippery. I felt it slide.

"Klara!"

Then I was falling.

CHAPTER 11
SARKIN

I didn't hesitate. Hesitation got someone killed more times than not. And I wouldn't allow Klara to be one of them.

I dove off the cliff after her. I trusted in Zaridan's positioning, but Klara wasn't skilled enough to be able to mount an Elthika in midair. It was a maneuver that took new riders years to master, and dozens had died in the process.

The drop down the cliffside to the base of the mountain wasn't long, and I didn't have much time to catch her. She was flailing in midair, a silent scream on her lips. I tightened my limbs close to my body to increase my speed, and when I was close enough, I saw the wild panic in her eyes.

Our bodies crashed into one another's, and she scrambled to hold me. I gripped her so tightly that nothing would be able to pry her away, not even death.

"Brace," I shouted, seeing Zaridan out of the corner of my eye, trying to match our speed as best as she could before beginning to angle underneath us.

She swooped. I held my breath, tightening my thighs.

And when we landed on her back, we landed *hard*. I acted quickly, moving Klara into place. She was gasping, the breath had gotten knocked out of her, but I kept her pressed down on Zaridan's back, locking my legs around her body and snagging the tethers.

I didn't allow myself to feel relief until Zaridan guided us back to the citadel landing. She extended her wing, and I snagged Klara's waist, feeling her tremble uncontrollably as I got us back onto solid ground.

The anger rose, hot and bright, but I kept it masked, especially when I saw the wetness of her cheeks.

"Fool," I rasped, but I didn't think the harsh word was directed at her. She was completely naked, but I swept her up into my arms because I knew she would collapse if she tried to walk. Her hand was bloody and a long gash was along her right abdomen.

I strode into the citadel, quiet and dark at this time of night. Marching up the left staircase, I took us to the highest floor, my private wing, and kicked open the door to my quarters.

The blue fire was still burning in the hearth. I sat her on the table, disentangling her hands where she held me tight.

"I need to get bandages," I informed her.

"For what?" she whispered, her eyes wide and glassy. She was in shock.

"For your wounds," I replied, trying to keep my voice gentle. Her blood was *red*. Not black. Like human blood? I didn't know why that fact fascinated me.

"I was dreaming," she said quietly. "I never…I never saw the edge."

"I know," I said, restlessness eating away inside my chest. I left to retrieve a healing pack from my washroom.

With my newfound privacy, I let out a deep, rattling breath, striking the wall repeatedly with one of my fists until the dull ache of it helped to calm the maelstrom in my chest. The bones throbbed. I never should have left her alone. It had been an oversight. One that had almost gotten her killed. My pride had almost cost her her life.

And I wouldn't allow it to happen again.

Despite the desire to keep her at arm's length, she was *my* responsibility. And the moment we sealed the bond in the Arsadia, she would be my damned *wife*.

The fear in her eyes when she'd tumbled over the edge…I would never be able to shake that. It was my punishment. It was forever imprinted in my mind, like so many terrible, unshakeable memories. Like Haden getting thrown off his Elthika, rejected after the first flight. Like Tyzar's mournful roar when my father had sent him away. Like Kyavor with his grim expression as he'd told me my parents were dead.

When I returned to Klara, I observed her sitting on the edge of the table, and my guilt only tripled. Her body was bruised not only from the fall but from riding. I'd pushed her too hard coming here. I'd been a young rider myself once, long ago. I remembered the pain so intense I couldn't sleep no matter how exhausted I was. I remembered the brokenness.

This wasn't me. Where was the honor in punishing her like this? And was that what I'd been doing? Punishing her for a decision *I* had made?

When I stepped up to her once more, I cupped her face in my palms, forcing her to meet my eyes.

"Are you all right?" I asked softly.

To my surprise, she nodded. "Yes."

She'd seemed to have calmed when I'd been retrieving the kit, whereas my restlessness had only amplified.

"Do you have a blanket?" she asked.

My gaze trailed down her body. It was no time to admire her curved lines, the fullness of her breasts, and her soft belly and hips…but I would've had to be blind or dead not to.

"Let me tend to this first," I informed her, controlling my physical reaction to her. It had been much too long since I'd had a female underneath me, I decided. She was soft and warm. She smelled like *naro* blossoms on a hot harvest day, and I gritted my teeth, swallowing down the sudden need I felt. I wasn't surprised by my reaction. Adrenaline and frustration were often coupled with lust. But finding this maddening Dakkari princess beautiful was entirely inconvenient. It would pose its own set of problems.

The gash along her side wasn't too deep, but she didn't even hiss when I cleaned it with a cloth.

"Why are you naked?" I rasped.

I caught a flush of redness of her cheeks. Fascinating.

"I was too tired after my bath. I went right to bed," she answered. Her arm came up to shield her breasts, the other falling in her lap. She had no hair between her thighs, and my nostrils flared. I forced my gaze away. "Why are *you*?"

That brought out a small huff from me. When I looked down, I saw that I was, indeed, naked. I'd forgotten. Which made my half-hard cock all the more alarming.

"I was asleep," I answered, watching the way her eyes flickered everywhere *but* me. "Does it bother you?"

She didn't answer. Perhaps the Dakkari were shy about such things, whereas the Karag were not. I had to remember that my new bride was not of my kind. We couldn't be more different.

I stepped away, snagging blankets off the bed. One I tied around my waist in a neat knot. The other I handed to her, which she spread over her lap quickly. I watched as her long, graceful fingers caressed the soft fur, and I cleared my throat, hunching down to inspect the gash above her ribs.

Once it was clean, I applied salve and a clean bandage. I'd patched up my own wounds more times than I could count, so I worked quickly. When I finished, she wrapped the blanket more tightly around her body, and I took her bloodied palm in mine, blotting it.

It was quiet between us, the energy in the room charged.

"Heartstones are like seeds, aren't they?" she asked softly. I paused, casting a long, assessing look at her. Her eyes flicked back and forth between mine. "Or maybe not like seeds. More like… fruit of a tree."

"They are both," I murmured. "They used to grow in a place called the Arsadia. Heartstones were planted to grow *thalara* trees. And then the trees created more heartstones at their root systems."

"Used to grow?" she asked, catching my misstep. "They don't now?"

My jaw tightened.

"Is that what you dreamed?" I asked. "Is that what you saw?"

Our faces were close. I could see golden strands in her very human eyes.

"Yes," she admitted.

"Where?"

"How would I know that?" she said. "Besides, it wasn't so much a location as a realization. I was being shown. I've seen the trees before though. At least…I think I have."

"The *thalara* tree," I told her, stilling. "You've seen it in Dakkar?"

"If you call my homeland Dakkar, I wonder what you call the entirety of this planet."

"Easy. Thikana," I replied. "And our nation is Karak."

She sighed. "We call our *planet* Dakkar. You call it Thikana. Who is right?"

"Does it matter?" I wondered. "It might only matter to off-worlders."

"You've kept to your side of the world and we've kept to ours," she said. "But no longer. We can speak the same language. We seek the same thing. And right now, I can touch your skin and feel that connection with you when before it hadn't been possible."

My heart jolted when her fingers pressed to my inner wrist. I hissed out a short, surprised breath, finding the touch maddeningly sensual. Her voice was husky and soft. Mesmerizing.

"So when our two nations collide, when our two cultures become intertwined, what would we call our planet then?"

I met her quizzical gaze.

"Thikana," I answered finally.

She chuckled, the sound beautiful and musical. I didn't join her, however, and her laugh slowly died.

"I see," she said, but her tone struck me as sad when she saw I was serious. "No room for negotiation with you?"

"History will tell you, *aralye*," I said, spreading cool salve over her cleaned palm, the jar clinking when I replaced the cap, "that the dominant race creates legacy."

"You are a dominant race because of your Elthika," she pointed out.

"And why do you think the planet is called Thikana, then? And not Karak?" I questioned.

Her lips pressed together.

"No Karag will ever deny the part the Elthika have played in our good fortune," I told her. I tipped up her chin so she met my eyes. "But no other race has bonded with the Elthika like the Karag have. No other race has *dared* to try. Does that not deserve your respect, now that you have been on the back of Zaridan? Now that you have seen her capabilities firsthand and felt the humbling awe of your own fear entwined with her might?"

"Are you fearful every time you fly with her, then?" she asked. Clever girl. "Even after all this time?"

"Of course I am," I said. Surprise flitted over her face, as if struck that I'd admit to it. What she didn't understand was that *all* riders would. "If you are not, you do not respect your Elthika. But you will learn that concept in time. Sarroth produces more riders for the Karag than any other of our nations. If you are to be the Sarrothian queen, you will learn that fear better than most.

Your people will expect it of you…and they will never accept you otherwise."

A soft exhale escaped her.

Tonight had proven what I'd needed to know. Tonight had proven why I'd trusted my instinct with Klara, why I'd made a split decision the moment I'd seen her scar—the bonding mark of my own Elthika, meant for me to see.

Tonight I'd woken in a strange state from a dead sleep, feeling a pressure at the base of my neck. I didn't know how to explain it, but I *knew* it was Zaridan's call, though I'd never felt anything like it before. That ability—that bond with an Elthika—had been long lost with the diminishing power of the heartstones. It might not be until the next generation, possibly even two, where riders would feel that connection again…and that was only if we were able to find more heartstones.

But I'd felt it tonight. I'd felt Zaridan's restlessness, and it had driven me immediately from bed, sensing that something was wrong.

Zaridan had saved Klara's life, not me.

Klara had been on Karak soil for no time at all, and already I felt a blooming connection with Zaridan that hadn't been there before. Tonight had proved to me that *this* was the right choice. Despite what I wanted, Klara was an important piece in helping to restore Karak to what it had once been.

Zaridan knew that. Now I did too.

But it was my own oversight that had nearly cost Klara her life. What would we have lost if she'd fallen tonight?

"Do you often wander in your sleep?" I asked, my tone harsher than I expected. "Sarroth is an elevated city, especially the citadel."

"Tonight was the first time," she said, watching me wind a bandage around her palm. "Another reason to fear sleep, I suppose."

The words were quiet. They made discomfort wiggle in my chest.

"No need to fear it anymore," I said, blowing out a sharp breath.

"Why?"

I met her eyes before packing up the healing kit, pleased that her wounds were cleaned and tended to.

"From now on, you'll sleep with me. I'll tie you to me at night if I must," I informed her. Her lips parted, a red, enticing flush coloring her cheeks. "Let's rest now. Even after the events of tonight, we still leave for the Arsadia at dawn."

CHAPTER 12
KLARA

"Stay with Zaridan," Sarkin ordered me. "We'll make camp here for the night."

He left me sitting on the back of his dragon, but I was too exhausted to protest. I could feel others' eyes on me, a sensation I'd been well acquainted with back in Dothik.

A thrum of sudden longing went through me, a cutting ache. I missed my home. I missed my life. I missed Dannik and Sora, the quiet of the archives, walking the Spine early in the mornings when the city was still sleeping, and the desolate beauty of the wildlands in the evenings. The soft wind curling through my hair like Kakkari's touch.

Tears started swimming in my eyes, but I refused to cry. I was just tired, I reasoned. We'd traveled all day, with only a single break in the middle. Ever since I'd left Dothik four days ago, I'd had very little time off Zaridan's back. Last night, at Sarkin's citadel, had been my longest respite, and it had been a restless one. It was punishing…but everyone else around me was used to this.

The rider horde was studying me as Sarkin walked away. I could feel it. I'd felt their eyes on me all day, even mid-flight.

They were sizing me up, trying to determine if I would be a hindrance…dead weight.

Zaridan hummed underneath me, and I tapped on her wing. She extended it, and I maneuvered off her back. When I didn't stumble and thereby make a fool of myself in front of Sarkin's horde, I breathed a sigh of relief.

Which quickly morphed into a sharp inhale as I took my first step. *Ignore the pain,* I coached myself. I hid my wince, my legs numb, my back throbbing.

To distract myself, I asked a passing male, "Can I help you with that?"

He was a rider, though I knew he wasn't one of Sarkin's prime group—the ranks and orders of which I still didn't quite understand. He was carrying two buckets of water, heading in the direction of a small group of people who were preparing fresh meat for the traveling horde.

His eyes narrowed on me. "No," he grunted.

Then he walked past as if I hadn't spoken at all. My throat felt tight, embarrassment taking root. I walked a short distance away, determined to make myself useful even though my entire body screamed in protest.

The camp was a flurry of life and activity. I heard the Karag language being spoken, jovial laughs, and orders being barked. I got the attention of a young female who was going around refilling waterskins.

"Can I help you with that?"

She frowned. She gave me a strange look, mumbled something in the Karag language, and then pushed past.

I felt the prickle of Sarkin's gaze on me, and when I looked up to meet it, he had his chin tilted back, regarding me over a fire that had already been built *on the earth.* Something a Dakkari would never do. Fire should never touch the earth. It was an insult to Kakkari.

But you're not in Dakkar anymore, I thought sadly.

Sarkin was speaking with his commander, the one who'd flown with us from Dakkar, the one who'd been present on the terrace yesterday. Feranos, I'd determined his name was, hearing it lobbed around at various points throughout the day. That was another thing that was strange—to know the given names of horde members that I'd barely even spoken to.

Why did I feel like I had something to prove to him? To these people?

Because they won't accept you if you don't, I reminded myself. Sarkin had said something similar to me last night. Just because Sarkin intended to make me his queen, it didn't mean the Sarrothian would welcome me with open arms.

But this was my life now. This was where I would live. I wanted to be accepted by them. I wanted to be comfortable with them, like I had been with our own horde, growing up on the wildlands of Dakkar. The horde had been like a family. A strong community of people, working together. When my mother and I had moved to Dothik, it had been like losing a limb.

"Let me help with those," I said, reaching out to touch pelts that an older female was distributing. She jerked the pelts away, and I stood there, reeling and mortified, as she turned her back.

I spun on my heel back to Zaridan when I felt the tears sting my eyes. The last thing I wanted was the horde to see me cry. I wouldn't be able to stand that.

"It's just been a long day," I whispered under my breath. "It'll get better."

Gingerly, uncaring who saw this time, I sought comfort next to Zaridan. I didn't think I would be able to stand a rejection from Sarkin's dragon too…but Zaridan accepted my touch. She lifted her wing so that I could maneuver next to it, steadying myself with her at my back as I slowly slid down her side, close to her forelimbs. She was sitting, her wings curled almost demurely around her, and I could feel her radiate heat. Her head was raised, observing the encampment just as I was, a quiet sentinel on the edge of the forest.

Though my shoulder protested, my hand spread up to her side, feeling her chest rise and fall with her powerful breaths. Watching the Karag mill around the darkening camp, I whispered, "*Sen endrassa.*"

It was what Sarkin had murmured to her. By his tone and body language during that moment, I figured it was a term of respect.

A rustling filled the clearing, a sound I'd heard before though it was quieter. Zaridan's scales. The sound was like a song.

Sy'asha, Sarkin had said when we'd heard a similar thing on the wildlands of Dakkar. I'd heard that word again when he'd spoken with his aunt upon landing in Sarroth. He'd told her he'd heard his Elthika's song and that it was more powerful than any binding ceremony.

I wondered what it meant. *Sy'asha.*

I noticed the clearing go quiet. Most of the Sarrothian horde stopped, freezing in their places, to regard Zaridan. To regard *me* as her song weaved throughout the entire encampment.

With the sudden attention of an entire horde, I swallowed thickly and dropped my hand away, straightening my spine. My stepmother had always hated when I slouched, even when sitting.

I thought I had done something wrong, but when I sought out Sarkin's gaze once more, I thought I spied *approval* on his features. His brows were furrowed, full lips pursed. The fire highlighted the sharpness of his face, and from this distance, it appeared as if his eyes were pitch black, like a starless night.

"*Tarosh,*" he barked out suddenly, and the horde jolted into movement again, though I still caught whispering and long glances cast my way among the different factions of the horde.

A short while later, as the activity began to die down, and as the delicious scent of cooking meat and bubbling broth filled the clearing, a female approached me. I'd noticed her before because I thought she looked more Dakkari than Karag, with her slighter build and straight black hair. Her skin was dark, and unlike the Karag riders, she had a tail, like any full-blooded Dakkari might. But her features resembled the Karag, straight and sharp, all hard, cutting lines with very little softness.

She had a rounded chin, though, which only sharpened when she smiled at me. I was not used to being smiled at by the Karag, and so I blinked at her, almost in disbelief.

"Hungry?" she asked. She stopped a good distance away from Zaridan, who turned her broad head to regard the new female. She chuffed out a sharp breath, lifting her wing slightly. The female approached, and I realized it was because the Elthika had given her permission.

I struggled to sit up taller, my back against the unyielding hardness of Zaridan's scales. But given the coldness of the Karag's reception to me, I still vastly preferred them. At least Zaridan's body was warm, seeping into my skin and sore muscles.

"Meat, broth, and bread," the young female added, crouching before me to lay the tray she'd brought on my lap. "The delightful meal of travel. Though maybe you are used to it."

"What do you mean?" I asked softly.

"I had heard rumors you lived in an actual Dakkari horde." She dropped her voice like it was meant to be a secret.

"Oh," I said, giving her a small quirk of my lips, warming to her. Maybe she just wanted to get intel for her Karag friends, but it was the first time a Sarrothian was actually speaking with me—willingly—so I didn't mind. It was no secret. "I grew up in a horde on the wildlands."

"And where is that?" the girl asked.

"Well…everywhere," I answered truthfully. "The wildlands of Dakkar are everywhere. Hordes move from place to place, tracking different game throughout the seasons. *Wrissan* herds to the East Lands, *bveri* in the North. We would travel three, four, five times a year if necessary."

The girl listened to me, seemingly rapt. Perhaps the Karag were as curious about the Dakkari as we were about them. But I didn't think they feared us like we did them. There was no need for it with creatures like Zaridan at their backs.

Her tail swept over the ground, my eyes catching on it. Curiosity got the best of me when I said, "May I ask you a question? But I hope it won't offend you."

The girl quirked a brow. "There is very little that would offend me. Why ask permission? It wastes time. Just ask."

"Why do you have a tail when others do not? I've noticed that the majority of the riders don't."

Including Sarkin.

"*You* don't have a tail," she pointed out.

"No," I said. "But that's because many of my ancestors were human. And I don't think that's the case with the Karag."

She drank in that information slowly. I didn't know what she thought of that, but she said, abruptly, "Riders have their tails cut off. It is called the *thryn'rosh*. The final commitment."

I froze. "What?"

"Many do when they are young, for riders from the ancient families. Blood borns, we call them. They get off easy. Some don't even remember it. But others, who came into riding or who were not meant to, like our *Karath*, get them cut off during the oath-taking ceremony, as a sign of their dedication and honor to the Elthika."

"That's…that's…"

Barbaric? Was that the word I was going to say?

But who was I to judge? Given the old *Vorakkar* trials of our own people, the insurmountable obstacles and tests of physical strength and how well one could withstand pain.

"It's the Elthika's plating. Trust me, it's for the best. My oath-taking ceremony is next season. I'll be glad to get rid of mine. I'm so worried sick almost every flight that I've begun to strap my tail down my outer leg."

"Plating?" I asked.

"You might have noticed on Zaridan," the girl said, jerking her chin back at the Elthika. "The way her scales overlap near the beginning of her tail. Our own tails can get caught there if a rider isn't careful. During flight, it can get ripped right off. You can bleed out on the back of your Elthika. Many have died that way. It happens."

For the first time, I was *glad* not to have a tail, when I'd been teased about it mercilessly, growing up in a horde.

I hadn't noticed the plating on Zaridan, but I would surely look for it now. Not that it mattered—I'd been riding in front of Sarkin, his strong chest pressed to my back.

"Do you think that you'll miss yours?" I asked, the question popping out before I could stop it.

The girl grinned, a small chuff of laughter falling from her. "I haven't given it that much thought. But I suppose I will. I'll learn to live without it though. I heard the first couple weeks, you're off balance."

Across the clearing, I watched as a female rider—one of those who had traveled to Dakkar—approached Sarkin. Her hand touched his arm, and he turned to regard her. They spoke briefly and then he nodded, following her—alone—into the darkness of the forest beyond the clearing. I didn't know why, but I felt a pinching in my belly, watching them disappear together, how closely they walked next to one another.

Then I couldn't help but notice Sarkin's rider's reactions. Their shared looks, smug smirks.

I swallowed, jerking my gaze away. When I met the girl's gaze, I knew she'd seen it too. She gave me a soft, knowing smile. "You don't have to worry about *that*. That's long been over."

So there had been something?

I shouldn't care. Then again, I'd witnessed my stepmother's bitterness for over ten years. She'd been humiliated when my birth had been discovered. It had been a mark against her, an insult that she had never recovered from.

That was the only reason, I argued silently, that I felt a lump in my throat, watching her and Sarkin go off alone.

"This marriage is happening because he threatened to kill my people," I found myself saying. My tone was matter-of-fact, almost soft. The Karag female blinked, her brow furrowing. "I don't mistake what this is."

But it bothered me that others might. That I would turn into my stepmother, that despite all of her strength, despite her good family name, everything she'd accomplished...it could still be tarnished at the hands of her husband.

That was why I could never blame her for her hatred of me.

I'd made the air between us tight and uncomfortable. "I'm sorry," I breathed. "I didn't...I didn't mean it quite like that."

"The *Karath* is a good leader," she told me. "Any of us would be glad to follow him. He is bound in honor as well. It includes *all* vows made, even to you." She dropped her voice. "I'm sure it's overwhelming. I'm glad I'm not you, to be honest. Thrown into a new life as you were."

I swallowed, turning my head to regard the edge of the forest where Sarkin had disappeared before I forced myself to look away.

Though it was strange to ask, I realized that I could. "What is your name?"

The girl smiled. "Sammenth."

Pretty name. I wondered what it meant.

"I'm Klara," I said. "You've been kind to me. I won't forget it."

She looked down at my untouched tray of food. "The Sarrothian, I know, are a difficult people to connect with. They don't like outsiders. And they certainly don't like outsiders who will become their queen."

"Then why, Sammenth, have you been so kind to me?" I asked, trying to understand.

"Because I know what it's like to be an outsider," she confessed. "I am not a true Sarrothian. Half of my ancestors were Dakkari."

A jolt went through me. I heard myself exhale a sharp, small breath.

A million questions bubbled in my mind, but I kept my lips firmly pressed together. I would scare her away if I bombarded her with questions.

Instead, I asked a single one. "How?"

"Sammenth!" someone called. A group of riders were looking at her expectantly, one waving a loaf of bread in the air. They were all young, I noticed. Their faces unlined by the seriousness and intensity of Sarkin's riders. *Novice riders?* I wondered.

There was eagerness on Sammenth's face when she turned back to me. "We'll talk again, and I'll tell you. I promise. Eat now. And rest. We have another long travel day tomorrow."

And before I could protest, she stood and walked back toward the group, stretched out on their sides or sitting on tree logs they'd pulled from the forest around us. Sammenth grinned, gladly accepting a bowl of broth thrust into her chest. She pushed off a male from the log, who toppled over with a sharp laugh, and took his seat.

She'd learned to be accepted. A Dakkari...just like me.

I could scarcely believe it. But how that was possible, I didn't know. Though I had my suspicions...guided by the stories my mother had told me all my life. Fantasy stories, I'd always thought. But ever since her death...I'd begun to see them as truth, especially as my own gift had manifested quicker and stronger as I'd aged.

"Finished eating?" came the gruff question.

Sarkin appeared, peering down at me and my full tray of

food. He crouched, snagging my bread, bringing it up to his lips and tearing off a bite.

"Have *you*?" I returned, raising a brow when he dropped the bread back onto the tray. I studied him, looking for unkempt clothing or any laces undone.

His chin lowered to regard me. "What?"

"It's nothing."

"Your tone implies otherwise."

I didn't want to talk about this, especially since I didn't even know what I was feeling. "How did the Dakkari come to be here? In Karak?"

Sarkin exhaled sharply. "They came on ships. Long ago. There were hordes along the southern shores for nearly a century. I figured you would have known."

My jaw dropped. "Of course not. There's no record of it in our archives."

"Ah, but *you* knew, *aralye*, didn't you?"

My nostrils flared. His hand reached out to grip my chin, studying me, his eyes flickering to my scar.

If not for this scar, he never would've looked at me twice, I realized. It was because of this scar that I was here.

And perhaps I should've been grateful for it because he'd been ready to use the *ethrall* on all of Dothik.

"Finish eating. We're sleeping up on the cliffs tonight."

I gaped. "Why?"

After last night? Was he insane?

"Zaridan won't sleep on the earth, and I'm taking first watch. Since you sleep with me, you go too. No exceptions."

CHAPTER 13
SARKIN

"What is that you need to watch out for?" came Klara's quiet question.

I'd been observing her as she stood by the edge of the cliff, my eyes taking her in as I would an opponent...or a lover. Watchful and careful and hungry.

She turned to regard me with those light gray eyes. Her hands were clasped demurely behind her back. Her hair was plaited into a neat braid, wispy tendrils of it having escaped on the flight up here, which framed her soft features. I spied the small tips of her pointed ears peeking out, distractingly delicate. I couldn't see her scar from this angle. For the first time, I wondered if I'd stolen her from a lover in Dothik. A mate.

Good, came the sudden, stray, and surprising thought. I was used to feeling possessive over things I considered mine, but I hadn't expected those uncontrollable feelings to extend to *her.*

She's my responsibility. That's why I feel this way, I reasoned.

When I quirked a brow, she asked, "You said you were taking the first watch. For what?"

I grunted, tearing into the chunk of bread filled with meat.

Flying always made me ravenous even though Zaridan was doing most of the work.

"Elthika," I answered.

Her brow furrowed. "I don't understand. I thought the Elthika were friendly to the Karag."

"Bonded ones, yes," I answered, my nostrils flaring in slight frustration. She was like a child, wasn't she? She knew nothing of our kind, of our race. But I needed to have patience with her, which was never a strength of mine. "We are nearing the northern border into Elysom's channel. The East is Elthika territory. The Sarrothian have territory there too, but it is still wild land and under Elthikan rule."

Klara turned fully to regard me, the moonlight illuminating the scar—Muron's mark—on her face.

"We are in the outer lands," I told her, sweeping my hand toward the view she'd been admiring. "The Elthika that live in this territory are not bound by traditional Elthikan law. They are the dragons that have forsaken it, and as such, it is dangerous territory to be in for very long. Zaridan does have sway here, as does Levanth's. But that will only extend so far if we overstay our welcome."

"So much to learn," she said softly. Her spine straightened. Her chin rising. "But I'm up to the task. I was a scholar in Dothik, you know."

I snorted. "You think your scrolls and books will help you here?"

"No, perhaps not. But my need for knowledge will," she answered, surprising me. I heard the quiet confidence in her voice.

"Are you not frustrated by your lack of it?" I wanted to know.

"Of course I am. But I know that knowledge comes slowly. It is absorbed and savored like a wine. It might be tempting to chug it down, to quench that unyielding, maddening thirst, but in order to understand something fully, with the appreciation it deserves… knowledge, complete knowledge, demands patience. And even then, it is ever changing. That's what my mother always said."

I had stopped eating to regard her, her words holding me like a vise.

"It will frustrate you to know then that your soon-to-be husband has never read a book in his life," I lied, to see what she would say. "The Sarrothian pride themselves on physical and mental strength, unshakeable honor, and willpower. Perhaps you would have been better suited for a nobleman in Elysom."

When I'd first met her in the marketplace in Dothik, she'd had a book then. Had been aghast when I'd dared to touch it with my *filthy* hands, coated in Zaridan's scale dust.

"Knowledge is not always about books," she replied, her eyes shining in the darkness. She *was* a beautiful woman, the surprising *want* curling in my belly. "You have far more knowledge than I—I'm sure of it."

I frowned. "Knowledge is what you pride yourself on, and you give that achievement to me so readily? Why?"

"Because knowledge is like…love," she answered, a soft smile curling her mouth as she settled on that particular word. "It should be freely given. It shouldn't be a selfish thing."

Her words struck me and held on. Like she'd plunged her fist into my chest, wrapping her little fingers around my shriveled heart, squeezing tight.

Discomfort swam in me. Karag didn't speak of such things so freely. Though perhaps the Dakkari did.

"You said Zaridan holds sway in this territory? What did you mean?" she asked, stepping toward me.

The Elthika in question was perched to the far left, curled up and resting along the cliff edge. But the spikes of her ears, which usually flattened against her skull in flight, were perked and twitching at the slightest sound.

Klara leaned against a rocky boulder, crossing her ankles in front of her as she regarded me. The pose lengthened her legs, encased in her tight trews. I couldn't help but look. Did her cheeks pinken because of it?

"Zaridan is one of the remaining descendants of Muron," I said softly when I swallowed, feeling familiar pride swell up in my chest as I looked over at her. "One of the ancients."

"Muron?" she asked quietly, her eyes shifting back and forth between mine. I saw it then…her passion for knowledge. The need for it. The most surprising thing of all was that it lit a fire in my belly. It was an attractive trait in a mate, one I'd never given much thought to before.

"*The* ancient," I answered, holding her gaze. "The Elthika revered him like a god once. His bones make up the stretch of a northern peninsula—a sacred place for the Elthika."

"Does Zaridan look like him?" came the unexpected question.

I nearly laughed. "It's difficult to say," I said. Then I tilted my chin back and said, "That scar on your face…that is the mark of Muron. Zaridan's line."

Klara's hand touched the scar on her cheek. "How can you tell?"

"Muron led a battle once against an enemy faction of Elthika, to bring order to their race. An impossible feat. His dragon horde was severely outnumbered, the odds against them. So the stories go, he was struck by lightning during battle and the scar it made was permanently imprinted onto his body, right over his heart. The strange thing is that the lightning didn't hurt him—it made him stronger. A heartstone gift. It was the first recorded moment of *ethrall* being used in our history."

Klara's lips parted, but otherwise she was frozen in place along the boulder.

"You call it the red fog. We call it *ethrall*. But they both are rooted into the power of the heartstones, and that power grows like the boughs of a tree. Wild and untamed. It manifests in different ways, like your gift," I said, nodding at her. "That day, that heart-stone power flowed through Muron. He alone, when many of his brothers and sisters had already fallen, defeated the enemy faction with *ethrall*. Suddenly a new order of Elthikan rule came to be. But Muron's scar never faded. It passed to his descendants. You can see it on Zaridan, even from here. On her back flank."

Klara's breath hitched, and her eyes sought it out eagerly. They widened on the familiar mark. "But...then why did Zaridan pass it to me?"

The question of the millennium, I thought. Why would Zaridan cross into dreams to find a Dakkari princess and mark her as mine? As *ours*?

"Only she knows," I said instead.

"And you listen to her without hesitation?"

"Yes," I answered. "And she listens to me. That is the nature of a bond with an Elthika."

"Even if you cannot communicate?"

"Oh, but we do," I told her, brow furrowing. "Your hordes rode on the backs of *pyrokis* for centuries, yes? To this day, they still rely on them, yes?"

She nodded.

"And would you not argue that the bond between a *pyroki* and their Dakkari rider is strong? Perhaps they cannot communicate with words, but you communicate with everything else within your power. With the Elthika, it is the same. You learn to hear every unspoken thing in the beat of a heart. The gust of a wing. Elthika can make a seemingly infinite number of sounds, strung together in different ways. Just like language, like words. You learn to listen closely. They are far more intelligent than us, and so they listen closely too."

Klara stared at me. "Like the *sy'asha*?"

My chin tilted back. "Yes. That is one way they will communicate. Effectively, at that."

"And what does it mean?"

I wasn't certain I wanted to tell her yet. But I didn't see the point in deceit when we would soon mark our marriage in the Arsadia, deep within the temple of Lishara.

"It is the song of an accepted bond," I said. "Zaridan accepted you, on the wildlands beyond Dothik. She gave you her song. I am her rider, and that bond can never be replaced. But she has taken you under her protection, given you her oath, which all Elthika must do with their rider's chosen mate."

"Oh," Klara whispered. "And…has an Elthika ever rejected a rider's mate?"

My lips slid up in a rueful smirk. "All the time. Elthika are possessive creatures, even more so over their riders. They do not accept outsiders easily. And if a rider does not have his Elthika's *sy'asha* for their intended mate…it is not a circumstance that ever ends happily."

I swallowed, my eyes running up Klara's form carefully. "Zaridan gave you her song upon meeting you," I said quietly.

"Is that…rare?"

"Rare?" I repeated. I shook my head, standing to stretch. Klara's neck craned back to meet my eyes. "It has never happened before in our history."

She said nothing at first.

"I suppose that means you are well and truly stuck with me," she finally said.

Silence dropped between us. When I glanced over at Zaridan, I saw that her head was raised, peering at the both of us from her place on the cliff, no longer hiding that she was listening to our conversation.

Stepping forward into Klara, I brushed the tendril of hair away from her scar, remembering the jolt I'd felt in the market-place in Dothik when I'd first seen it. How it had felt like all the air had been sucked from my body, a strange sense of familiarity and knowing making the city sway. As if I'd been there before. As if I'd been *remembering* her.

Heartstone magic was an unpredictable, dangerous, and powerful thing. Klara of Rath Serok and Rath Drokka was at the root of it all.

She cleared her throat when the silence stretched too long between us, lowering her cheek so that my touch slid away.

"You, um, said that Zaridan has sway here because of Muron. What of the other Elthika? Levanth's, was it?"

"Levanth is one of my riders," I corrected. "The navigator wing, I'm sure you remember."

She stilled. "Ah. The female you went into the forest with tonight. Alone."

That made me straighten, hearing an odd note in her tone, one I recognized from earlier. "What?" I asked quietly, irritation beginning to burn in my belly. I couldn't stand cowardice. "Would you like to ask me something?"

Her lips pressed together. Then her mouth opened. "Everyone saw."

"Nothing happened," I rasped, stepping closer, lowering my head until our eyes were parallel. "I am not only a *Karath* of the Sarrothian people, Klara, but also the lead commander of a rider horde. You think I would do something like that when I have given *you* my vow?"

"I don't know you, Sarkin," she whispered. "I have no idea what you would or would not do. I know nothing of the Karag. Nothing of the Elthika. I know what I saw. And I saw your own rider horde react in a specific way when you went off with her. *Alone,*" she said again. "Into a dark forest. What would you have me think?"

Bright anger tightened in my chest. The dishonor she thought me capable of…it was maddening!

"I know these forests better than most, Klara," I snapped. "Levanth needed my help locating the closest stream for our water supply. I showed it to her so she could direct others to it, and then I returned to the camp. To *you*."

A sharp breath left her. "*Oh*."

"Let me ask you this," I began, trying to keep tight restraints on my temper. "Do you expect your husband to be in your bed alone? To never stray? Even given the circumstances of this marriage?"

Her brow furrowed. A spark of her own irritation shone hot in her eyes, and the mere sight tightened my abdomen. "How could I even begin to answer that? There's too many factors to—"

"Your heart's reaction, then," I exclaimed, my voice beginning to rise, pressing my hand to the thundering beat of her chest. Her eyes widened. "Don't think. Give me an answer. Now!"

"Yes," she breathed, glaring. "Yes, then."

"Tell me why."

"Because I'm the child of an affair, of a broken sacred vow, spoken before Kakkari!" she retorted. "It hurt a lot of people, *including* me."

Shock went through me. My lips pressed together, and I leaned back, understanding dawning.

"You...you must have known. You've been watching us for a long time."

"I didn't," I confessed. "We were there to observe, not to ask questions that would get us exposed."

To the Karag, especially the Sarrothian...her birth would certainly cast Klara in a bad light if the truth got out. The Sarrothian were a regimented people, almost to a fault. Rarely did they see the shades of gray in this life. They saw right or they saw wrong. And if you fell onto the wrong side of that divide...it would take you years to be seen as an equal again.

Memories were long, unshakeable things among the Sarrothian.

I would know that better than anyone.

"Then we are in agreement," I finally grunted.

Her lips parted in disbelief. "What? Agreement about *what?*"

"We arrive to the Arsadia soon. We will seal this marriage, and I expect you to uphold your oaths to me, your *husband*," I said. "Just as I will to you."

Realization was dawning over her expression.

"Levanth and I were involved *once*. When we were young, not old enough to know better, and never since. But I trust her with my life, just as I do with all those in the *kya'rassa*—my rider horde," I told her. "Believe me or not. That is for you to decide. But do not accuse me on a whim when you know nothing about what I value."

Klara held my eyes. She must have heard some truth in my words because she said quietly, "I'm sorry."

"The Elthika," I began, matter-of-factly, "mate for life, and so they choose carefully, if at all. They never stray from their bonded mates. It creates unnecessary division within a legacy. It is not *romantic*, Klara, so get that out of your mind. A mate bond is logical, bordering on cold, and it takes discipline. The Sarrothian believe what the Elthika believe, more than any other Karag might."

Did I spy a flash of disappointment? "I didn't know," she said.

"Now you do," I said simply, releasing her and stepping away.

I'd laid it out for her. I didn't want her to think this would be a passionate, consuming union between us. Perhaps she had wanted a marriage like that. Perhaps she had wanted a love like in her precious history books, of the *Vorakkar* of old and their mates...but she wouldn't find it with me. I wouldn't allow that. Love was a distraction and nothing more.

Better to disappoint her now so she knows exactly what she's committing to before the Arsadia, I reasoned.

"Anything else you wish to address?"

She rubbed at her forearm as a cool breeze made her shiver. "How...how do you expect your people to ever accept me?"

I inhaled a slow breath. I shouldn't have been surprised by her oddly vulnerable question. My chest even gave a little twist, my instincts telling me to comfort her. I'd watched her get rejected by numerous Sarrothian tonight.

"Klara," I said, waiting until she met my eyes. I spied sadness there. Loneliness. And it made even more discomfort wiggle in my chest. "Don't get discouraged by the horde. And tonight… you handled it better than I expected."

She snorted, crossing her arms over her chest. "By slinking back to Zaridan?"

"Who presented you with her *sy'asha* for *all* the horde to hear," I growled. She blinked and then looked over at my Elthika. "She honored you tonight, and she knew exactly what she was doing."

"But why don't *you* do that?" she asked. "If I'm to be your queen and you leave me so quickly to my own devices, as if you cannot *wait* to get away from me, what image does that present to the Sarrothian?"

"Klara," I bit out. "The horde values *strength*. I'm doing you a favor, whether you see it or not. They need to see you stand on your own. They *need* to see that you are comfortable with Zaridan, that she respects you to obey your commands. And this is only the beginning."

"You…you've been calculating out how they see me," she realized softly. "You planned this. It was a test?"

"An opportunity," I corrected. "I won't lie to you. You *are* an outsider, a Dakkari—who no one will trust because they know you are not loyal to me or to the Sarrothian."

She opened her mouth, her brow furrowed.

"It's the truth," I rasped. "Because given the choice, this very moment, would you not turn your back and return to your true home? If I promised to release you from a marriage and no harm would come to your people? Wouldn't you wish to be back in Dothik by tomorrow? We could leave right now."

"You don't know what I would choose," she argued softly, and

I stilled at the surprising *honesty* I heard in her voice. "There are many reasons for me to be here, and some of them don't concern you at all. Or your people."

"That may be the case, but it proves my point. None of your reasons are out of loyalty."

She didn't answer, just raised her chin slightly, as if in challenge. And I felt the burn of her sass curl straight to my cock.

Much too long since I've had a female, I thought, irritated.

"Let them see your strength," I rasped. "This rider season will be tough on you. But as queen to the Sarrothian, there is deep-seated expectation that you cannot ignore. And the first test will be your strength and your willpower. You're much too small and weak to claim an Elthika of your own."

She sputtered, her eyes wide. "Excuse me?"

"But they will never accept you if you don't, so…you will have to claim one regardless."

Her jaw dropped. "*What?*"

CHAPTER 14
KLARA

"You need sleep," Sarkin growled into my ear once I descended down Zaridan's wing. I nearly cried in happiness when I stepped foot on the earth. Nearly fell to my knees too, every muscle in my body on the verge of giving out.

"Don't worry about me," I said, though I felt the heaviness of my eyelids threaten to close.

"I told you—you don't need to fear sleep. You think I'll let you wander away again?" Sarkin argued. "I don't make the same mistakes twice."

I believed him. And yet…I'd barely slept since the night I'd seen the heartstone forest in my dreams. We'd been traveling to the Arsadia for the last two days and nights. We'd stopped again last night, at the edge of a vast, wide lake that tumbled down into a waterfall. Even though we'd flown up to yet another cliffside for Zaridan's sake, away from the camp, I couldn't relax enough to rest and I'd been too exhausted to speak.

"I'll be fine," I informed him, my voice firm when I met his eyes. I'd been cranky too, irritation and anxiousness a constant companion today during our flight. I was tired of being hungry. I was tired of my body burning and aching with every step. I was tired of being tired.

For the foreseeable future, I wanted to stay in one place.

And it looked like I would finally get my wish as my eyes fastened on a *horde* spread out before us, vast and sprawling and on solid ground.

"Please tell me we'll be here for a while," I pleaded quietly, nearly stumbling into Sarkin when we took our first steps away from Zaridan. He frowned, reached out to steady me, and the heat of his hand felt so good against my back. Like a hot stone, loosening the soreness of my body.

"We will be here through the riding season," he answered. "Yes."

Relief and a twist of dread warred within me. Ever since I'd learned that I was actually *expected* to claim a dragon of my own, riding on the back of Zaridan had taken on a new trepidation. I'd begun to study other riders, sizing up their build and strength, only to realize that my future husband had been correct in his assessment...

I *was* small and weak compared to them. Perhaps I shouldn't have spent so many years tucked into the quiet folds of the archives, where my only form of physical activity was walking the Spine of Dothik in the mornings and evening and pulling books and scrolls out from high places.

The Sarrothian were like the *darukkars*—the horde warriors —I'd grown up admiring. Only they held themselves in the strictest regard and were uncompromising in their work. Watching them interact among the camp, I saw they worked tirelessly and without complaint, even after long days on dragonback. I felt like a child compared to them, and I'd endeavored to hide my pain even more, to bite my tongue when I'd been on the verge of asking Sarkin for a reprieve.

I didn't want them to think me weak. I couldn't allow that.

Before my very eyes, I saw a horde. Only it was in a much different place, on an entirely different continent. And considering we'd crossed over another ocean today to reach the Arsadia, I wondered if I'd just stepped foot onto the *third* continent of my life. How many Dakkari back home could say that? None that I knew of, despite the mystery of the hordes along Sarroth's coast long ago.

It might've been a horde, but it was a Karag horde and there were very stark differences to that of a Dakkari one.

"This is a permanent outpost," I noted, realization hitting me when I saw structures that resembled the stone *solikis* in the Dakkari outposts, the permanent villages spread across the wildlands.

"*Lysi,*" he rasped, and my lips parted as our eyes met. *Lysi* meant *yes* in the Dakkari language. It was an odd sensation, hearing that word here, hearing it fall from his lips…but I liked it. It felt comforting, even if it only highlighted how far away from home I truly was. "The mountain village. We call it Rysar—the Sarrothian outpost in the Arsadia."

"Rysar," I repeated softly.

Unlike the domed tentlike structures called *volikis* in a Dakkari horde, here there were taller structures, made of a dark gray-blue textured stone that had marble streaks of black running through it like a river, glittering in the lowering sun. Not unlike the little home that was nestled in the wild gardens behind Sarkin's citadel in Sarroth.

Some of the stone buildings even had carvings in them like the citadel's, depictions of elaborate Elthika and Karag alike. Some homes were flat to the earth, others raised slightly depending on the elevation of the land, the entrances of which could be accessed by winding staircases.

In the distance, behind the horde was a tall mountain, much like in Sarroth. The top of which I couldn't even see because it disappeared in the cloud covering. A gentle mist was floating, the air damp and alive here, which likely accounted for all the dark blue and green moss I spied.

To the east, I saw a circular building, taller and larger than any other here. To the west, I saw what I thought were training grounds, a vast section of the forest cleared away. Many of the riders' Elthika were perched there, resting after the long journey. Others had already flown up into the mountain or had flown north, swooping in the sky as if pleased to be home.

Flying over the Arsadia, which was what the Karag called the Elthika's homeland, I saw that it was a lush and vibrant place. Sarroth had been covered in deep, dark forests and mountainous valleys that gave way to rivers flowing out toward lakes and coast-lines. As we flew farther north, the landscape had shifted subtly. There were open plains or vast hilly country surrounded by some of the tallest mountains I'd ever seen in my lifetime.

And here in the Arsadia? It was covered in forested land, but there were also open plains we'd flown over. At the base of this mountain, it was almost like the Trikki back home. A lush rain-forest, giving way to tumbling waterfalls and vibrant life.

I couldn't *see* the waterfall, but I heard it—the sound of rushing water violent and powerful. I wondered if that was why the air was so damp.

It smells good here, I thought. Wild and fresh and alive.

"This is a *saruk*," I noted softly, peering up at Sarkin after I'd observed all that I could from this vantage point. "Perhaps we are not so different after all."

"Perhaps."

"People live here permanently?" I questioned, confused about that small detail, but it was obvious that Rysar was inhabited year-round. People milled about, welcoming the rider horde like they were old friends, helping them with their supplies. One of the novice riders, who was friends with Sammenth, went up to someone I thought might be his mother and pressed a kiss to her cheek before embracing her hard.

My heart twisted, longing going through me at the beautiful sight they made.

"Yes," Sarkin said. "I live here nearly half the year. For the rider season and the mating season."

I stilled and asked carefully, "The mating season?"

Sarkin leveled me a hard look. "For the Elthika." He waved his hand to the east of the horde. "The hatchery."

Amazement shot through me, momentarily making me forget about the pain in my body and the way I was attracting the attention and whispers of the horde as we passed by. A millions questions bubbled up in my mind.

"Ah, ah, *aralye*," Sarkin said, surprising me, his hand still on my back, guiding me down a stone pathway. Was my curiosity so evident? "My priority is not to answer your questions this night. It is to get your wounds checked and get you rested, so I can attend to my *saruk*, as you call it."

"I don't have any wounds," I lied.

He snorted with derision. "You forget so easily that I was once a new rider myself."

"I'm not a rider," I said quickly, a large part of me still rejecting the idea of what was expected of me.

"Yet you will be, Klara. Your instruction begins in the morning, which is why you need to sleep tonight."

I sucked in a deep breath as we started up an incline. "You cannot be serious."

"I am deadly serious," he replied, cutting me a sharp look. "And I never say anything in jest when it comes to the Elthika. You'd best remember that."

"Can I not have one day to rest, Sarkin?" I asked, stopping in the middle of the pathway when the muscles in my legs tightened so painfully that they began to spasm. I clenched my jaw. "*Please*," I whispered, so onlookers wouldn't hear my pleading.

Sarkin studied my features, those colorful eyes flitting back and forth. I wondered what he was looking for.

Finally he nodded. "Very well. One day of rest. Instead of your instruction beginning tomorrow, we will go seal our marriage bond in the temple of Lishara."

My eyes widened. "Is there a rush to do that so soon?"

I would be *married* tomorrow?

Sarkin shrugged. "And I ask you, why wait? I want this done. I have an oath myself to Elysom that I am eager to see through."

I remembered him mentioning that to his aunt. Something about *mysar* commands, whatever that meant. Elysom, I knew, seemed to be the governing body of the Karag, and his aunt was on the council.

"My mind is made up, and it will not change," he added, his voice lowering as our eyes held. "I have chosen you as my wife, Klara. Waiting will not change that."

My heart gave a frantic skip, my lips parting. The *shock* of hearing those words…they pleased a primal part of me I'd never known I'd needed calmed to begin with.

But, with the exception of my mother and Dannik, I had never been chosen by anyone. Even my own blood. My half sisters, my father…they had all turned their backs on me at the urging of my stepmother, and I had felt their rejection and sting for years. In Dothik, I had *never* felt like enough. For any of them. I'd been a disappointment. A painful reminder.

So to hear Sarkin say that he had *chosen me* and that it would not change…those words filled a desperate, gaping ache in me, one I hadn't realized was an incredible, lonely void.

"*Lysi?*" he questioned softly, tipping my chin up with his calloused index finger.

I blinked, reality returning in a rush. I'd been staring at his exposed neck, tracking small scars there, as I processed his words.

"*Lysi,*" I whispered.

He nodded, pleased, though my thoughts raced. Before last week, I had never given much thought to marriage. I had filled my days with the pursuit of research and knowledge, to try to better understand my dreams and my mother's own stories. I had always had an obsession with the dragon riders from across Drukkar's Sea, ever since I'd seen one fly over Dothik when I'd been only twelve.

In the span of a week, my life had altered and shifted so drastically that it was hardly believable.

"What is it?" Sarkin grunted, urging me into a walk once more.

"This time last week, I was…" I took in a deep breath. "I was walking home in Dothik after a day in the archives trying to understand *this*. This place. Your people. What it all meant. I've given over a decade of my life trying to make sense of this. And I'm beginning to realize that it might have been a waste. Because I don't understand anything at all."

I'm wholly unprepared for this, and that frightens me, I thought, but I left that thought unspoken.

"But you will," Sarkin said. An easy answer to a complicated worry.

Tears ushered into my eyes, but I tried to blink them away quickly, lowering my head as we passed a group of onlookers. Sarkin nodded at them when they called out a greeting. After we passed, I looked up, noticing that we were heading toward the back of the horde, toward a structure that I knew must've been Sarkin's home here, given the intricate carvings on the facade. It was small, but it was overlooking the entirety of the horde, perched on a small hill, the pathway leading up a gentle incline.

My muscles screamed in protest as I walked up. But when we reached the top, I couldn't help but turn. The sun was setting over the forest, and my lips parted in disbelief. I saw what I hadn't been able to see over the structures of the horde or the forest beyond.

We were high up. The Arsadia, it seemed, had dramatic

changes in elevation. *Now* I saw the waterfall. I saw the thick white plume of water billow next to the east of the forest and not far from what Sarkin had called the hatchery. Water from the mountain was running down toward the horde, where it pooled into a wide, sparkling river before rushing down a steep drop, into the depths of the forest below. While the forest that surrounded the horde was at our elevation, I saw vast wilderness stretch out beyond us in deep valleys as far as I could see.

"It's beautiful," I breathed. In the distance, I saw mountain ranges, wild Elthika making dark figures in the sky, miles and miles away. I knew we weren't far from the coast, but I couldn't see it from this vantage point.

And it would be my new home.

Footsteps clattered on the pathway, and when I turned my gaze forward, I saw an unfamiliar male waiting for Sarkin's permission to approach. He was tall and broad, his arms crossed behind his back. Not a rider, though, because I saw the sway of his tail behind him. But a warrior perhaps? His build was certainly similar to one.

"Go inside and rest," Sarkin ordered me. "There's hot water for a bath. I'll send someone with food and to look over your wounds. Then I want you to sleep afterward—no questions tonight. Do you understand?"

His tone set my back straightening. "I'm not a child."

His lips curled slightly in a humorless smirk, one that made my belly flutter and dip, which was quite quizzical and maddening.

"Syndras will watch over this entrance, so don't fear sleep tonight," Sarkin replied, nodding at the Sarrothian, who inclined his head at me, though his eyes were narrowed, curious.

"Where will you be?"

"There is always much to be done when we return to the Arsadia," Sarkin told me. "I likely won't return tonight. I'll collect you in the morning."

And with that, he turned his back, passing Syndras briefly, his head bending low to say something I couldn't hear.

He didn't turn back once.

CHAPTER 15
KLARA

It's every bit as stark and cold as I thought it might be, I thought, sighing, gazing around Sarkin's Arsadian residence with a critical eye as I soaked in the hot bath.

The home had a familiar layout as the one outside the citadel. A raised bed with no fur coverings in sight. A round table with bench seating, similar to the taverns in Dothik, but this one was made of a shimmering material that resembled dragon scales.

There was a tall black cabinet opposite the bed, and I knew, from my first inspection, it held clothing and nothing else.

The washing area was at the very back of the home and only separated by a sheer gossamer curtain, which seemed utterly useless. The washing tub was sunken into the ground and the most opulent thing in the home. It had running water, for one, no doubt due to the waterfall so close in proximity, but what amazed me was that the water rushed out hot from the metal pipes. Once I'd stepped into the bath, after the first initial sting of pain as hot water had met my chafed, inflamed skin, I'd sighed happily. I never wanted to leave the confines of the bath again.

I leaned my head back over the edge, sitting on the submerged ledge that ran along the inside, and closed my eyes. I must've dozed off because the next thing I knew, there was a loud creaking from the front metal door and a stranger's voice filling the room.

I gave a little shriek of surprise when I saw an unknown female enter.

"What—what…who are you?" I stuttered, slinking down underneath the bath water, my heart thundering in surprise.

"I apologize," the female said, though her tone was bright, no remorse heard. "I didn't mean to startle you awake, though I am glad I did. It is incredibly dangerous to fall asleep during baths, or has no one ever told you that?"

I blinked, watching as she set down a tray of hot food, opening the various dishes' lids with a flourish, as if expecting me to be impressed.

When she looked at me expectantly, I cleared my throat and said, "That looks…delicious," though I couldn't see it all from this angle.

"Come and eat," she ordered, patting the bench chair as she pulled out something else from the black satchel looped over her shoulder. "I am your food delivery *and* your healer tonight. You can call me Ryena."

My heart was returning to its normal pace. Right. Sarkin had said he'd send someone.

"Ryena," I repeated, thinking she looked familiar but not able to place her face. She hadn't traveled with the rider horde, had she? No, I decided a moment later, observing her clothes. They were loose fitting, made of soft hides and breathable fabrics. Her boots had mud caking the very tips—at least I hoped it was mud.

She nodded. "I am one of two healers here in the village, though my specialty is hatchlings and not future queens."

She laughed at her own joke, but it died when I didn't join her.

"Hatchlings?" I asked under my breath, brow furrowing.

"Unfortunately for you, our other healer is currently stitching up the leg of a young boy who thought it would be a good idea to try to jump off the waterfall, at the daring of his friends," Ryena explained. "What are you still doing in the bath? Come, come. Eat, so I can get some medicine applied to your rider burn."

Despite her being a stranger, there was a no-nonsense and urgent tone in her voice that had me obeying. I stood, water rushing off me as I climbed out of the bath, wincing as cool air rushed over my skin.

"You poor thing," she tsked, eyeing my bruises and inflamed skin. "That is why you will *never* catch me on the back of an Elthika if I can help it. I like my feet firmly planted to the earth, don't you?"

"Yes," I said, a sharp breath exhaling from me when she dug into her satchel once more. I watched as she pulled out a jar of pink-colored paste and a thick roll of what I thought were bandages. My injuries from my cliff fall were still healing, the skin puckered after my soak. "But I thought many Karag preferred to be riders."

"I never understood the appeal," she confessed, "though I am a minority in that feeling. My sister, on the other hand, very much ascribes to it."

It hit me then, why she looked familiar.

"You're Sammenth's sister," I said, pulling a thin cloth around my body to dry it as I padded toward the table. She looked at me in delighted surprise. "I thought you looked familiar, and I couldn't place why."

"We share a father," Ryena told me.

"So you're...you're Dakkari?" I asked. Or at least part Dakkari, I thought.

"Through our father, yes, though even his line has been mixed with Sarrothian blood," she replied. "There are still a couple Dakkari villages along the outer borders of the South, much to Elysom's annoyance. They keep to themselves for the most part, but they are there if you know where to look."

"I still can't believe there have been Dakkari here, all these years, on your shores," I confessed, my legs giving out underneath me with the weight of that knowledge after the day I'd had. Luckily I was close enough to the bench that it caught my fall. Ryena rounded toward me, wielding that strong-smelling jar of salve. "Everything we know…everything we thought we knew about the world has been completely challenged by your people."

"I imagine it would've been quite the shock, seeing those first few Elthika," she gave me. "I grew up in a Dakkari village with my sister, and there aren't many wild Elthika down there. I remember my first time seeing one, I nearly wet myself." I laughed in surprise, in the dry delivery of those words. "And then it's even more frightening when you see one up close."

Ryena raised her eyes—red eyes, Dakkari eyes—to my face. I watched her pupils track over my scar, and her lips pulled slightly. "The rumors are true, then. You really do bear the mark of Muron."

I still didn't quite know what that meant, but all I could do was sit still as Ryena tugged the cloth away, baring my naked body. The bruising was purple today, and between my thighs, it was a raw mess. Even Ryena winced.

"Did the *Karath* see this?" she asked.

My cheeks flamed. "Of course not."

When he'd patched me up the night I'd fallen off the cliff, my thighs had been firmly *shut*.

"You best be careful," she warned. "We don't need this infected, especially since your instruction is beginning soon. The salve will help a lot though. One of my own making when Sammenth was going through the beginnings of her rider training. She said it was the only thing that helped her heal quickly," she told me, pride in her tone.

I smiled. Both the sisters, I noticed, had an openness about them, a kindness that I hadn't quite found in any of the other Karag I'd come in contact with in the last few days.

"These will heal fine though," Ryena told me, cocking her head and applying gentle pressure to the lacerations across my ribcage. She held out the jar. "You want to do the honors?"

I nodded, taking it from her gratefully.

"Keep it," she told me. "Put some more on in the morning too. I'll speak to the *Karath* about getting you more protective clothing for riding." She picked up my hide trews, poking her finger through the hole the friction had made. "These obviously won't do. He should know better…but the Karag believe that the quicker the skin thickens up on the inner thighs, the easier it will be for a rider. Pain now, relief later, or so they say. It sounds better spoken in Karag."

I swallowed as I dabbed my finger into the salve before spreading it on my inner thighs. I hissed at the sting, but it slowly gave way to a pleasant, numbing warmth.

"They're not wrong, I suppose," Ryena continued, getting the bandages unraveled. "The skin will toughen with repeated trauma and irritation. Not that I agree with the method."

I listened to her voice, finding it a much needed distraction as I spread the stinging paste…though when I got all the skin covered, only a couple breaths went by and then I was blissfully numb. The skin didn't throb. The pain melted away.

"Thank you," I breathed, closing my eyes in relief.

Ryena looked at me. "You should tell him next time. You should not have to withstand this. There is no pride in pain."

For the Sarrothian, that very much seems to be the case, I couldn't help but think.

I helped her wrap my inner thighs with the thick swaths of clean bandage. Once they were covered, she urged me to eat, though I was too tired to properly be able to appreciate it. She set out yet another jar of the paste for me, leveling me a look that said, *You'll need this—trust me.*

"I'll check on you tomorrow, but otherwise, rest. Sleep well, Klara."

"*Kakkira vor, Kerisa*," I said quietly. Dakkari for *Thank you, Healer.*

She paused at the threshold of the door, giving me a knowing smile. She nodded.

"*Veekor*," she ordered back to me. In Dakkari, it meant *sleep*.

With that she left.

Once I'd eaten, with my wounds tended to and my body clean, I found a fresh tunic from Sarkin's cabinet, which ended at my knees, and then pulled the thin blanket off the bed. I curled up on the hard floor to sleep.

And for once, I dreamed of nothing.

I was woken by hands and an angry-looking Sarkin, his face illuminated by the hearth I definitely hadn't lit, a flickering fire that changed colors—from blue to gold to purple.

I tensed when he pulled open my thighs, and I kicked out at him. "What are you doing?" I exclaimed groggily.

He held them open, my tunic shoved up to my stomach, his calloused hands on my calves. He whispered a curse under his breath, and I looked between my thighs, saw the bandages had already bloodied through the night.

Sarkin unwound them, and when I tried to fight him, he growled, "*Faryn*."

I stilled immediately, a primal part of me obeying whatever it was I heard in that tone. I recognized that word. It was the word that had made Zaridan pull back her *ethrall* on the wildlands outside Dothik.

I assumed, now, it meant *stop* or *cease*.

"I found blood on Zaridan's harness. Dried *red* blood," he growled. "Then Ryena came to tell me. So why didn't you?"

When the bandages fell away and he saw the red streaks, angry and chafed, he whispered out a rough curse, sliding back to lean against one of the stabilizing poles at the foot of the bed, one long leg stretched out in front of him.

"Do you think me such a monster than I wanted you to suffer through *this*?" he asked, angrier than I'd ever seen him as he glared.

His head leaned back against the pole, and he blew out a rough breath before bringing his hands up to rub at his tired, no doubt wind-stung eyes.

"I didn't want you—or your riders—to think I was weak," I mumbled, coming fully awake.

When his eyes crashed to mine, I realized that I was sprawled out on the floor, half-naked, with my legs spread wide. I struggled to sit up and close them.

"Don't," he rasped. "We should reapply the salve anyway. It's been a few hours."

He dragged his body up, graceful and strong, crossing to the table and snatching one of the jars off. He was uncapping it as he returned, crouching in front of me.

"I'll do it," I said quickly, embarrassed.

He only growled. It was a warning, making me bite my tongue. I'd never seen him like this. I was used to him being in control, bordering on stoic and cold.

"Open, Klara," he commanded, and I didn't dare disobey him.

With a loud swallow, I slid my legs apart, turning my head to the side as he slid the paste across the skin. The numbness had worn off, the flesh sensitive again, and I sucked in a breath. His touch never paused. It was methodical and careful. Even...gentle, which I hadn't expected.

When I turned my head back, our eyes met briefly. The moment felt charged, the tension palpable. It was a strange sensation, to be in pain and yet…his touch was making me feel warm. His touch was a distraction.

His nostrils flared, something flickering in his eyes, making them so molten I nearly gasped. With a soft curse, he finished, leaning back on his heels, and I reached for the roll of bandage before he could, wrapping my upper thighs again.

"Again I find you on the floor," he said after a long, lengthy silence had passed.

"But at least I was sleeping this time," I returned.

He was referring to the night in his citadel. When he'd brought me back up to his private quarters to tend to my wounds and then he'd tied our ankles together with a long cord so I wouldn't wander away in sleep. Only I hadn't been able to sleep that night.

Sarkin had. But I hadn't even joined him in the bed, finding it too intimate. The cord had been long enough that I could perch myself on the plush chair near the bed as Sarkin had slept. But after a couple hours, I had moved to the floor to *try* to sleep.

"Is sleeping in my bed really that deplorable?" he questioned, his voice sounding tired.

My brow furrowed. He didn't understand.

I'd never slept beside a male—that was true.

"It's not that. I like to sleep closest to the earth as I can," I told him, drawing my knees up to my chest gingerly.

"Why?"

"Because Kakkari is the earth," I answered.

"Your goddess," he said, a subtle realization dawning in his tone. "I hate to tell you this, *aralye*, but we are high above valleys and forests here. A few feet above that, in a more comfortable bed, will not make much difference."

"I know," I said, with utmost patience. "I saw where we are. But this," I started, spreading my hand next to me to touch the floor, "reminds me of home. Of living on the wildlands, when my mother was still alive. It…it brings me comfort," I confided.

Sarkin regarded me in the low, flickering light. It was quiet here, I realized. So incredibly quiet. Beyond the walls of the stone structure, I could hear nothing. Not the whistle of wind or a dragon's cry.

"I feel rooted. I feel safe," I added. "Connected to something greater than me. My people are of the earth and your people are of the sky. Isn't that strange?"

His expression was unreadable, but the intensity in his eyes nearly made me shiver. Out of curiosity, I would give a lot to hear what he was thinking.

"You can't sleep on the bare floor all night," he finally said. "It's Arsadian stone, sourced from the mountain behind us."

I watched as he crossed to a chest, one tucked away against the wall, between the bathing area and the table. He pulled pelts, furs, and intricately woven blankets from within its depths.

When he returned to me, he spread them out beside the bed as I shifted to the side. A cozy little nest of furs, just like in a horde.

My heartbeat had picked up again, skipping. A part of me had expected him to scoop me up and place me in bed instead of going to the trouble of making me one.

Then my mouth went dry, a sharp inhale whistling when he kicked off his boots, unclasping his flexible armor of his dragon-scale vest, slipping the metal hooks off. When his bare chest was exposed, I heard the heavy thud of his vest as it fell to the floor.

I'd seen his chest before, though I'd still been half-traumatized from my near-death fall. But now...I admired it as it gleamed in the soft light, the muscles creating hard planes and deep shadowed valleys. The body of a warrior.

"I'm going to bathe," he said. "Sleep."

He turned as he tugged off his trews. My face felt hot, my heart a rapid thud in my chest when I caught the flash of his firm backside, a telltale silvery scar where his tail had once been.

I thought about what Sammenth had implied, that Sarkin

hadn't been destined to ride an Elthika, and I wondered what she'd meant by that.

When I heard the splash of water and Sarkin's deep, contented sigh, I bit my lip. The desire to watch him bathe was surprisingly overwhelming, my curiosity making my hands twitch.

Sometimes it was easy to forget that he was a mere mortal like the rest of us, even though his drive and discipline seemed otherworldly. Over the last couple days, I'd witnessed firsthand the respect he wielded among his riders. He was magnetic in his command. I could understand why he'd risen to the rank of *Karath*, but I found myself wanting to know *how*. Why. I wanted to know *him*.

I tried to sleep, but it wouldn't come, as distracted as I was with the delicate sounds of water. In my mind's eye, I imagined him washing, running those calloused palms over his scarred, warm, firm flesh. I squirmed in the furs, pushing my hair away from my neck when it felt too hot. Yet beneath my stolen tunic, my nipples were pebbled tight.

I hadn't given much thought to what a marriage to him—and the loyalty that he expected—would mean. Sex, obviously. Siring heirs as a Sarrothian queen would be expected, wouldn't it? Though I didn't know about legacy here, if the horde passed down through bloodlines or if their leaders were chosen in other ways, like the *Vorakkar* of Dakkar had once been.

"I can hear you thinking, princess," came his roughened voice. "I thought I told you to sleep."

He'd emerged from the bath, and though I couldn't see him from my vantage on the floor, with the bed blocking my view, I heard him drying himself off with a cloth near the table of my half-eaten food. Scrubbing it through his wet hair roughly.

"I had been sleeping so nicely before I'd been rudely awakened," I reminded him, though there was no bite in my tone.

"You should've told me about the severity of the rider burn," he responded easily. "Then I wouldn't have had to."

I huffed out a sharp breath just as he rounded the bed. I blinked quickly, catching a shadowy glimpse of bronzed flesh. Naked bronzed flesh. And there was something in his grip. A leather cuff?

"What are you doing?" I squeaked when he dropped down beside me. On the floor. In the nest of furs and blankets he'd made me.

"Sleeping," he answered. Without asking—the high-handed male—he dragged my ankle toward him, securing the leather cuff. This cordage was shorter than the one he'd used at the citadel and on the clifftops the last two nights—though I hadn't slept once on our journey.

The other cuff he attached to his ankle, and he tugged on the strength of the cord, testing it.

When he was satisfied, he let out a deep sigh and fell back beside me. And I fought with everything in me not to inspect his body with hungry curiosity, my skin practically buzzing with the need. I'd seen statues of naked men before…but none had ever quite looked like Sarkin. I'd also seen plenty of naked bodies in my lifetime. Most Dakkari were not shy about nudity, but I'd grown up more sheltered than most, even when we'd lived on the wildlands.

"*Shy'rissa,*" came the tired word. "Sleep," he translated.

I felt the heat of his body, making me even warmer. The tug at my ankle was oddly…comforting.

Yet it felt like a grip too. It was impossible to ignore.

"You're…you're…"

"Naked?" he asked, voice groggy. "This time tomorrow night, you'll be my wife. You will get used to it. *Shy'rissa.*"

Well, when he put it like *that*…

There was a swooping sensation in my belly when he

murmured those words, like I was falling off the edge of the cliff all over again.

"*Veekor*," I whispered.

"What?"

"*Veekor*. It means *sleep* in the old Dakkari language."

Sarkin shifted. Above us, I watched the flames from the fire in the hearth flicker along the walls. If only to keep my gaze off him.

"*Veekor*, then," he rasped.

I hid my smile when I turned my head.

"*Shy'rissa*," I said.

CHAPTER 16
SARKIN

"*Today?*" Mazra asked, her eyes nearly bulging out of her sockets. "*Karath*, surely you can't mean—"

"Today," I said, my tone final. "She begins her rider instruction this week. I want Lishara's blessing before that happens."

Mazra wrung a dirtied towel in her hand. "I—I—"

Behind her, her kitchens were already bustling, the Karag under her command obeying her like they would me. Mazra was a force of nature when she wanted to be.

"There doesn't need to be a grand feast, Mazra," I told her, reaching forward to squeeze her arm. The older cook took great pride in her ability to throw celebrations for the horde. She had been slowly preparing for one, to celebrate our return to the Arsadia…but she hadn't expected to throw a wedding feast with little notice. "A simple meal would suffice."

"Of course there needs to be a feast!" Mazra said, her head snapping up, frowning in her confusion. "Oh, on Muron, *Karath*, there will be a feast."

Feranos had been watching this exchange with a raised brow, but he kept his tongue firmly behind his teeth.

"We don't have any decorations though. No banners, no spark showers," she lamented.

I placed my hand over hers when it began to wring the towel too tightly. I wondered if she wished it were my neck, for giving her such little notice that I would take a wife today.

"This is an outlier circumstance, Mazra," I told her. "I'm sure you understand."

She blinked. Her lips were pursed, and I studied the lines that extended from the corners of her mouth. Mazra had two emotions that I'd seen: displeased or jovially happy. Never anything in between.

"I'll do my best, *Karath*. But…you will not even allow witnesses?"

"No," I said firmly. Impatience cut through me, and I tried to tamp it down. Of course the horde would want to be involved. Of course they would be curious, I reasoned. I would only marry once, after all, and it was a rare thing indeed for an Elthika—especially one such as Zaridan—to give her blessing to a rider's mate so swiftly. My people wanted to know *why*. They wanted to know everything they could possibly glean about Klara, this strange hybrid Dakkari human from across the sea.

I left Mazra shortly after, hearing her bark orders at her cooks, given she had to prepare an entire wedding feast for the horde by tonight and it was already late morning.

"Do you not think it an insult to your bride to not allow witnesses? To throw together a quick ceremony like this? Your horde wants to celebrate you, Sarkin. This will be a new age for us all," Feranos reasoned. "Perhaps you should put this off until—"

"I only need you as a witness so that I can send the confirmation to Elysom," I told him. "Everyone else will simply be a distraction. It is not meant to be an insult to her. I just want this *done*."

Feranos blew out a sharp breath as we walked toward the field.

"I will send the Dakkar scouting report alongside your letter of confirmation that we received Lishara's blessing from the temple," I told him, seeing Zaridan waiting for us, her black scales gleaming in the warm afternoon sunlight. I turned to Feranos. "Two *mysar* commands fulfilled. Then we will be rid of Elysom's influence. For good. Free of…"

The shame, I almost said. Or perhaps *free of my father's complicated legacy,* which had almost cost me my future.

But Feranos was an old friend and he knew what I meant.

He inclined his head. Understanding and acceptance were in the line of his shoulders, in the glint of his eyes. "*Karath.*"

My title, falling from his lips was an agreement. A reminder of who I was to him, despite our longstanding friendship.

Tracking the sun in the sky, I was eager to leave. It would be long hours until we reached the temple of Lishara, though the weather was on our side. A surprisingly bright and warm day, warm enough to dissipate much of the moisture in the air from the falls.

"I'll scout ahead," Feranos told me, walking toward his Elthika, Vorna, on the other side of Zaridan. "Meet you there."

When I approached Zaridan, I placed my wide palm on her snout, running it up until my fingers encountered the long notch of a nearly invisible scar. Zaridan seemed on edge this afternoon, her head constantly raising into the sky, searching, her ears perking and twitching with something unheard. She only did that when her sibling was near.

"Do you sense him here?" I asked quietly. Lygath. Another Vyrin, another descendant of Muron, and Zaridan's hatchling brother. "He must feel you're near."

Zaridan's eyes burned into mine, and I patted the side of her wide jaw, feeling her hot huff of air rustle through my hair. Her pupils shifted over my shoulder, and I turned.

There, Klara approached, led by the two females—Bezeth and Yar'la—I'd put in charge of her earlier this morning.

My nostrils flared, and I turned to fully regard her, Zaridan straightening at my side, standing proud and tall. My heart quickened in my chest.

Adorned in the ceremonial hatchling-scale dress, Klara was a sight to behold. The material flowed over her body like a gentle waterfall, skimming and caressing her lovely, soft curves. Hatchling scales were sheer but nearly indestructible, shed from young Elthika as they grew and a valuable resource among the Karag. They reflected in the late-morning light, shimmering with iridescence with every step Klara took, going from soft blues to bright silvers to gentle purples.

Half of her hair was pulled back, secured with an intricate braid and interwoven with dragon scales and silver clips. The rest of it ran down her back, a dark tumble of wild waves that made me want to bury my hands in it.

She was so unlike every Karag beauty I'd ever seen. The Sarrothian valued physical strength in their women, all hard lines and striking forms. Yet Klara was small, weak, and…*soft*. There was not a single hard edge on her body, save for the harshness of the scar on her face, but it made me squeeze my fists together at my sides, trying to fight the urge to explore every pleasing inch.

It was an inconvenient thing, I realized, to be immensely attracted to one's own wife. Especially when this marriage was meant to be a transaction—both a fulfillment of a command from Elysom *and* a way to help my people secure more heartstones. It was meant to be a cold, logical decision. Only the fire that sparked within me at the mere sight of her was proving to be the opposite of that.

Fuck.

As if hearing my thoughts, Zaridan snorted. Closer and closer, Klara approached, and she shyly met my eyes when she stopped in front of me, Bezeth and Yar'la falling away when I waved my hand.

My gaze tracked down the line of her body as she shifted. There was a large group of my horde gathering on the outskirts of the field, curious and wanting to see us off. I hadn't announced the marriage, but I'd shared the news with a few individuals instead. Like fire, it had spread. I hadn't walked anywhere this morning without catching the whispers.

"The dress was not the practical choice," I grunted.

I'd left out two garments for her to choose from this morning. One had been this dress. The other had been a much more logical choice of pants and a fitted tunic, meant for a dragon rider.

"Then why give me the option?" she asked, quirking a brow. Clever female.

"Because I knew which one I would rather see you in," I informed her, keeping my voice low. The reckless part of me, the *old* part of me I had stuffed so deeply down, surfaced as I added, "And it wasn't the practical choice."

Klara's pink lips parted on her sharp inhale. Our gazes held. Thin woven straps made of delicate silver chains were looped around her shoulders. They were the only thing that held the dress up. I thought about how easy they would be to snap with a quick tug.

"It is very pretty," she said quietly, giving me that shy smile again that made me clench my fists. "So very impractically pretty that I couldn't resist."

I should've told her that she looked beautiful. That was what a groom would say to his bride, wasn't it, on the cusp of their wedding blessing?

But I didn't, the gentle words stuck in my throat. I'd noticed that Klara was still walking gingerly, and I knew that her thighs were likely freshly bandaged, that she could not ride Zaridan as she had been.

Instead, I pinched a wild wave of her hair between my fingers, rubbing the silky strands between them. When I stepped closer, a plume of soft fragrance met me. The scent of wild blossoms that grew along the edge of the falls, along the cliffside. I thought it likely Bezeth had given her a gift of her prized soap.

"Is it far?" Klara asked softly.

"No," I said, dropping her hair. I leaned down, scooping her up into my arms before she realized what had happened, the trail of her scale dress fluttering around my legs as I turned toward Zaridan.

She sounded breathless. "What are you doing? Your horde…"

Would some disapprove that she would not be riding Zaridan properly toward the temple of Lishara? Yes. Did I find it in myself to care at this moment? Not really.

"Your rider burn will never heal if you irritate it so soon," I reasoned. She was so light in my arms. "The quicker you heal, the quicker you begin rider instruction."

That shut her up.

"I've been thinking…maybe I'm just not meant to ride," she said softly. "Perhaps there are other uses for me around the *saruk*."

"The *saruk*?" I asked, snorting. "No. A queen needs to bond with an Elthika. In order to bond, you must learn to ride. That is the way. I will hear no arguments about it. Besides, it is not nearly as difficult as you might think. Once that happens, then we can discuss other duties for you."

She sighed, and I got the distinct impression that she was biting her tongue. *Good.*

Zaridan lowered her wing to the cheers and cries of my people, which lifted into the air behind us. She practically preened with all the attention, tossing her neck and straightening. I shook my head with her pride, though I was used to it.

Klara's cheeks were a little pink, whether from our closeness or the cheers, I couldn't be certain. I slid easily into the leather seat, draping Klara over my lap so she would be sitting sideways, her small feet dangling.

"Like this?" she asked quietly, sounding worried. "Are you sure it's safe?"

"You think I would let you fall?" I asked, furrowing my brows, frowning.

Her hands were clutching my long ceremonial vest. Unlike hers, mine had been crafted from Elthikan scales, hard as Arsadian stone and completely impenetrable by man-made steel. The only thing that could pierce scales were claws.

As she pondered my question, her grip loosened slightly. I took up Zaridan's tethers, having replaced them this morning when she'd come to the field at dawn, waiting.

"No, I suppose not," Klara finally relented. "I'm no use to you dead."

"Don't say that," I immediately growled.

Her words were meant in jest, but my chest squeezed tight, wondering if she believed there was truth in those words. I supposed I hadn't led her to believe otherwise, and yet...I wasn't a cruel monster, intent on using her up until there was nothing left. Did she think me one?

She didn't tell me how much pain she'd been in, I reminded myself.

"Zari," I called out, to distract myself, to escape the mad pumping of my heart. "*Thryn'ar!*"

In its literal meaning, it meant *unleash* in Karag. To feel the effects of that word, one would understand why. At its core, however, it was the command for a bonded Elthika to fly, and so the two meanings were interchangeable. To fly was to unleash oneself, untethered to this world.

The ultimate freedom.

Zaridan drew on her power, her muscles tensing and contracting beneath us like an intricate machine, and when she unleashed it, launching herself into the sky, the cheers from below were nearly as loud as the sudden rushing of the wind.

I didn't have to guide Zaridan. She knew exactly where we were going. Instead, I focused on Klara, wrapping my arm around her back in support as she turned her face into my chest to shield her eyes.

My aunt had been right. I'd never enjoyed being told what to do. I detested it. I had always forged my own path, my own way. I made mistakes along the way—it was a certain thing—but like I told Klara, I didn't make them a second time.

Only with her, there would be no second chance. I'd meant what I said. I took the marriage vows as sacredly as my bond with my Elthika. Klara had Zaridan's song, her blessing. As far as I was concerned, the bonds were already tied between us. This ceremony in the temple was only a formality.

I turned my gaze north, over the Arsadia in all its wild beauty, thinking of the *mysar* command the Elysom council had given me to marry. Elysom wanted the South secured—Sarroth secured. A part of that included a queen. Heirs. They'd thought I would refuse. Perhaps my aunt had even counted on it so they could install another to lead *my* people, my territory. She knew I'd never wanted to marry—I'd made that perfectly clear in the years I'd been a *Karath*.

And perhaps taking a Dakkari queen had filled me with a strange, rebellious, vindictive thrill. But with Klara in my arms...

This is it, I realized, nostrils flaring.

She would be a very large part of my future.

I needed to make the best of it. A strong legacy required respect. We might never love one another...but we could respect one another at the very least.

Perhaps we could even be *content* with one another. Stranger things had certainly happened in our history.

And so, I decided right then that after our marriage was

sealed in Lishara, I would treat her as my wife, in the truest of forms.

On the back of his descendant, flying toward our future, I vowed it to Muron.

CHAPTER 17
KLARA

Zaridan landed at the edge of a wide, glimmering lake in a hilly valley. Overhead, I heard Elthika. *Wild* Elthika, I realized, my heart giving an excited but alarmed jolt. When I looked up, I saw an entire horde of them flying overhead, passing us as they flew west.

"Where are they going?" I asked Sarkin, still in his arms as he guided us down Zaridan's wing. I craned my head past him, if only to watch them a little while longer. They *were* beautiful. Beautiful and awe inspiring in their power.

"There's some nesting grounds toward the western coast," he told me. The ringing in my ears from the wind was slowly dissipating. That had been a pleasant ride, if only because there had been very little pain. And with Sarkin holding me, I'd felt surprisingly safe. I'd *enjoyed* it. I wondered if, with time, I *would* come to enjoy riding an Elthika.

I just had to get over this pesky rider burn first.

And the teeth-gritting ache and soreness in every muscle of my body. No wonder Sarkin and the rest of the riders were so well *built*. Riding an Elthika was deceptively difficult and required a level of physical strength and endurance that I wasn't certain I'd ever be able to possess.

"Where are we?"

"The temple of Lishara," he told me.

I frowned, looking around with curiosity and confusion. "I don't see a temple."

He set me down into the spongy, bright teal grass. It was long, brushing up toward my calves, and feathery light as it swayed in a gentle breeze. The lake was sparkling in the lowering sun. It hadn't been a long journey, but it hadn't been short either. I had no idea where we were. How far away we were from the horde, but I knew that my stomach was rumbling with hunger. It warred with my nerves, however, and eventually my nerves won out, quieting it.

I noticed that Zaridan was oddly still, though her ears were twitching. A dragon appeared overhead, a familiar one, and it circled until it landed behind us. Feranos, Sarkin's commander, dismounted, nodding at us both as he approached.

Sarkin went to Zaridan, murmuring words I couldn't understand in Karag, but then I watched as the Elthika stalked to the lake line, stepping within.

"Come," Sarkin told me. The hairs at the nape of my neck rose, my flesh tingling. There was something here. I could sense it. It felt like…Bekkar and Arik's sword. Deep below the palace in Dothik. That quiet humming of power and magic.

He led me to the edge of the lake before pulling me into the water until it lapped at my ankles.

"A mate bond's blood," Sarkin said softly, "with the blessing of their Elthika. That is what opens the temple. That is why you cannot see it. Yet."

My brow furrowed when he pulled one of his daggers, my heart giving a mighty thump at the sight of it. Yet I watched as Sarkin cut his palm, black blood welling up. His hand dropped, and I watched the blood drip into the lake, blooming like an ink splatter on parchment over the still surface.

He went to Zaridan.

"What are you doing?" I breathed, watching him use his dagger to slide underneath one of her scales, one on her chest. Zaridan blew a sharp huff but otherwise didn't move as Sarkin plucked out the scale, nearly as wide as his palm. Onyx black and thick.

"Elthikan magic was once the most powerful thing in existence," Sarkin told me, holding the scale up to me. I saw a small drip of shimmering silver blood coating the edge. *Elthika* blood.

He tapped the scale, and the drop fell into the lake.

The blood seemed to create a larger ripple than was possible for something so light. There was a sensation of electricity in the air, as if a storm was coming. I could smell it. It felt like a humming, the land coming alive.

Like…heartstones.

Feranos's Elthika stomped his forelimbs, his tail swinging, and yet his rider didn't move. He watched us from his spot on shore, a decent enough distance away that I wondered if he could even hear us.

"Once, there was plenty of it," Sarkin continued, approaching me. "It bled from everything in this land. You could smell it in the breeze, feel it pulse in the earth. But our ancestors—and their Elthika—became greedy. They used it to create technology beyond what we thought was possible, advancing our nation forward at lightning speed, using it to protect our borders and crush any enemies that thought to take it from us. They consumed too much without replenishing, and so that power slowly died."

"The heartstones," I realized. Behind him, Zaridan began her *sy'asha*, and I inhaled a sharp breath, hearing her beautiful song as the humming grew louder and louder, ripples coming from the center of the lake, as if…as if something was *rising*.

"The way the story is told, it's said that the first Elthika, Mokag, cried tears of loneliness, wishing for a mate and a companion to share his long life with," Sarkin told me. I met his eyes, drawn by the tale, *hungry* for it. "And from his tears grew trees. *Thalara* trees, laden with powerful heartstones at their roots. With the magic of those heartstones, Lishara came to be. The first female Elthika, Mokag's mate."

Understanding went through me.

"And this is her temple," I said softly.

"Where she died," Sarkin corrected me, his eyes briefly leaving my own to look out over the lake. "Where they died together. The temple was built much later, with the same technology that nearly wiped out our heartstones, but…you can still feel the Elthikan magic here. Only here, in a sacred place, on sacred ground, does it still thrive. You'll see why."

My heart was throbbing in my chest, beating itself against bone, but I wasn't afraid.

He held out his hand, and I remember what he'd said. *A mate bond's blood.* I gave him my palm, and he made the cut quick and clean with a slide of his dagger. My red blood spread into the veins of my palm, and I leaned down, pressing my hand into the lake, watching the blood drift around it like a red fog.

I huffed out a breath at the sight, a connection of a distant memory…and then rose.

The lake began to tremble at our feet.

"Sarkin," I said, alarm going through me, stepping toward him. Zaridan's *sy'asha* only grew louder and louder. The stomps of Feranos's Elthika made a steady beat, like drums. Like music.

Something dark was rising out of the water, sending larger waves our way. The bottom hem of my dress was soaked. Soon, the lake lapped at my mid-calf.

With parted lips, I watched a stone structure rise from the lake. A single doorway.

An entrance, I thought. Thunderous booms echoed across the water, rippling out around the valley, hitting the tall mountains to the east and ricocheting it back. The sound of rushing water came next, sliding off the stone but also tumbling into the black mouth of the arched entrance, the inside pitch black, leading down into a hidden tunnel below the surface of the lake.

Carvings were etched into the stone. Of two Elthika—Mokag and Lishara, I knew.

Then it went quiet.

Sarkin's warm hand went to the small of my back, and he walked me toward the entrance through the lake. The water never deepened, and I realized that there was a road, a pathway beneath our feet that led us straight to it.

I marveled that if we had flown by this lake, it would have looked like any of the others I'd seen. There was nothing from above that had marked it as otherworldly, and yet...

This had been created with the technology that Sarkin had spoken of? Or was this magic, in its simplest and purest of forms?

Perhaps they are one and the same, I thought.

Sarkin stepped through the mouth of the doorway first. I looked over my shoulder, at Zaridan, who was regarding us from the shores of the lake, a scale missing, revealing dark gray, unprotected flesh underneath. Her sacrifice. Feranos was walking toward us, intent to follow us into the temple.

"Klara," Sarkin called. When I turned, I saw there were stairs and he was already halfway down them. "Come."

I took a deep breath, then followed.

CHAPTER 18
SARKIN

Deep down below the lake lay Lishara's temple. The stairs led to a small chamber, circular in size.

I led Klara down until we were both at the threshold of the room. Behind us, Feranos entered, but he would stay in the shadow of the stairwell, solely a witness to the short ceremony, if only so he could report to Elysom that we'd received Lishara's blessing. He would not speak. He would not interfere.

Making a circle around the room were five carved stone pillars, each glowing with a heartstone, imbedded within. In the center of the pillars was a small pool of water. Each of the pillars had a single vertical line carved into them, leading from the ceiling of the chamber. Water from the lake trickled down there before running around the heartstone like a stream. The carved channel guided the water directly to the floor. There, five little rivers ran from the pillars to the pool of water, pouring within it at a steady rate.

As such, the small pool was infused with the power of all five heartstones. All five ancient heartstones—the *arasykin*, as the Karag called them. Once, this land had been riddled with them.

Now these were some of the last in existence, and they would forever remain in this place. Any who had tried to steal them before had met a terrible end. A cursed end.

"Heartstones," Klara said in awe, moving to the closest pillar, her lips parted. The bottom half of her dress was wet, clinging to her skin, and nearly transparent. I forced my eyes upward, coming to stand at her side as she gazed at it.

The blue, glowing light lit up her face beautifully, illuminating Muron's mark and making her gray eyes sparkle like the iridescence of hatchling scales.

"I've never seen so many," she said in awe, raising her hand, gingerly, as if afraid to touch it. "I hear their whispers."

A chill went down my spine as I watched her. I could feel the pinch of magic here. It had always made me uncomfortable, as unused to it as I was. But all dragon riders of old had felt the bite of magic. It was only the newer generations that were unfamiliar with it.

Her fingers pressed into the face of the heartstone, water streaking off it, and a small stream ran down her arm. I watched closely and saw that the heartstone throbbed a bright blue, momentarily illuminating the entirety of the dark chamber, like the sun had filled it.

Klara gasped, and she tugged her hand away quickly.

"But these are different," she breathed, meeting my eyes. They were troubled, unfocused.

"You can feel that?" I asked quietly.

"I can *see* it," she said, shaking her head.

"These are ancient heartstones, the same heartstones that Mokag, the first Elthika, used for his beloved mate. We believe their power will never be depleted but never again will we see their equal. Not in our time. Not ever."

"I think you're right," she said quietly, meeting my eyes. When I looked down to the ground, I saw that our blood, still a slow drip from our palms, had entered one of the streams at our feet. Zaridan's scale was still hot in my hand. Within it, I swore I could feel her heartbeat. "Do you feel that?"

There was a palpable energy in the air. It infused this whole land, truthfully. It was what the old world would have felt like. A constant *awareness*. A constant presence of magic.

I wasn't certain I would've liked it, had I lived in an earlier time, though I supposed I wouldn't have known otherwise.

"Yes," I replied, though I wondered if Klara could feel it more strongly than I could. There was no denying her connection with Elthikan magic. Some beings were more sensitive to it, a gift in and of itself.

Klara swayed, and I reached out to steady her.

"Take my hand," I told her, and she gripped it without protest, the heat of our cut palms coming together. "This will be quick, and then we can leave."

It should be quick, I amended silently.

For it was nearly impossible to judge what would happen next.

"We are here for Lishara's blessing," I told her, guiding her to the pool in the center of the stone-pillar circle. Here, the light was blue, all of the heartstones pointed toward this very place. It even felt warm, like the touch of the Elthika goddess herself. "But I must warn you, her blessing can be unpredictable."

"What do you mean?" Klara asked, her eyes going to the basin of water at our feet and Zaridan's scale in my hand. "We drink that?"

I inclined my head. "Scholars from Elysom have their different theories. They believe Lishara blesses a mate bonding with what they need, not what they want. Sometimes it is a gift of patience. Other times, a gift of…fertility."

"That's…that's fascinating," she whispered, eyes wide before they turned to the pool, assessing it in a different manner, her brow furrowing, her mouth pinched. Had that been her expression in her precious archives, surrounded by her mountains of tomes and scrolls?

Klara the Curious, I thought, feeling a surprising pinch of affection for her.

"Has anything bad ever happened?" she wondered next.

"A few times," I told her.

"Like what?"

"If Lishara does not approve of the mate bonding, she sickens the pair with the water," I told her.

"Oh," Klara whispered. "So there's a chance that she might not approve of us?"

"Yes," I told her.

"Let's find out, then," she said, turning her eyes up to meet mine. "*Lysi?*"

I knew that word meant *yes* in her old Dakkari language. I felt my lips tug up, but I fought to keep my expression neutral.

"*Lysi,*" I said softly, crouching to scoop up some of the water in the sacred pool, using the curve of Zaridan's scale like a shallow bowl.

When I rose, I saw that Klara's eyes were on the water between us, watching as the remnants of Zari's blood mixed within. She would be part of Klara now, no matter the outcome of this.

"Whatever the blessing is, *aralye,*" I began, seeing her eyelashes flutter as her eyes flicked up to me, "do not fight it. Whatever she gives us, we must see through."

She nodded. The chamber felt like it was one giant heartbeat, throbbing in time with mine, with Klara's. The energy and heat of the heartstones was a distraction, the magic trailing up my skin like a touch, weaving into my lungs with every breath I took.

I brought the scale up to my lips first, holding her gaze as I took the first drink. The water was pure and crisp, icy cold. I held it out for Klara. After a slow inhale, she nodded, as if to herself, and her lips met the edge of Zaridan's scale. I slowly tipped it back until she drank the remainder, then I threw Zaridan's scale into the pool. The final offering.

We waited. And waited. I could hear when Feranos shifted on his feet in the darkness of the stairwell, ever patient.

"I—I don't feel anything," she said finally, frowning. "Do you think it worked?"

Then the air in the temple seemed to heat, like a fire had been lit.

No, not in the temple, I realized a moment later. In *me*.

At first, as heat seared me, I thought that perhaps Lishara *had* rejected our mate bonding. Perhaps she had rejected us and given us sickness instead, a fire raging through us as punishment.

Only, as my heartbeat began to throb in my throat and Klara's cheeks went flushed, a wildness in her eyes as she slowly started to realize what was happening too…I knew it wasn't sickness.

Lishara had given us a blessing.

Only…it was one of desire.

I stumbled over to one of the pillars, pressing my hands against it as lust and need ripped through my body, otherworldly and oppressive. I nearly bellowed with it. I breathed deep and ragged, resting my forehead against the cool stone. Its touch felt *good*, though it did nothing to help calm the storm within me.

Dammit, I cursed silently. This wasn't meant to happen. This was—nearly—the last thing I had ever expected.

I could *smell* Klara. I could smell her tantalizing and lush arousal bloom within the small chamber, mingled with the cool, earthy dampness of the temple. It was dizzying.

Fuck. I hated magic. *Detested* it because it only proved how out of control one could be in their own destiny.

My earlier words came back to haunt me. *Whatever the blessing is,* aralye, *do not fight it. Whatever she gives us, we must see through.*

"Sarkin," came Klara's gasp, more of a mew. A plea.

And *fuck me*, it was needy and full of want. My cock thickened in such a rush it was almost painful. Every throb of my heart, every breath I took of her arousal burned in my belly. Blood rushed, pounding in my ears until it was all I could hear.

"Feranos," I growled. "Leave us! Now!"

CHAPTER 19
KLARA

What is happening? I thought, feeling my core throb and heat as want and desire rode me hard.

I heard Feranos's quick retreat from the stairwell and knew that Sarkin and I were alone in Lishara's temple.

"Sarkin," I cried as a wave of punishing lust rippled through my body, leaving my knees shaky and me panting. The trigger had flipped in me so quickly it was frightening.

Elthikan magic was once the most powerful thing in existence, Sarkin had told me.

I felt it now. I believed it. Only I hadn't expected to feel it in *this* way.

I heard a growl, dark and rumbling. It sounded animalistic, like it rumbled from Zaridan instead of the Sarrothian male who, I realized, was now my husband.

My mate.

For a lifetime. Because nothing would break these bonds now —only death.

The thought should've sobered me, but all I felt was pulsing anticipation as I watched Sarkin stalk toward me. I felt every step reverberate in my chest, even as fear stabbed inside like a dagger.

I felt the heat of his body before he ever touched me, and I nearly cried out in relief when he did.

His hands slid over my body, and I arched into him shamelessly, like I was a puppet and he was controlling my strings. I had no experience with males…not like this, though I'd devoured the erotic books in the archives. There was a whole tome written about sex and how it celebrated our goddess Kakkari. There were instructions inside, sketches and drawings, and I'd brought it home too many times to count in my endless curiosity, feeling an exciting thrill every time as I'd pored over the delicate pages.

He was my husband now. I figured I might as well explore this new, enticing sensation with someone. And since he'd demanded it be no one else, it would be *him*.

Underneath his ceremonial vest, I knew there was endless bronzed skin, hot and carefully crafted and forged like a weapon. I nearly whimpered, my fingers going to his vest, wanting to see it. *Needing* to. I imagined digging my nails into him, liking the idea of marking him. *Mine.*

"*Aralye*, listen to me," he rasped. His hands came into my hair, and I swore I could feel his touch in every last strand. My scalp tingled, then my neck, a whole body shiver racking its way down my body until it vibrated between my legs.

I squeezed them together. "Is this…is this normal?"

"We can fight this," he told me. The words seemed plucked from him, harsh and guttural.

"Gods, no!" I thought, a scream in my mind, only it took me a moment to realize I'd cried it out loud. The room echoed with it. The damp, stone walls of Lishara's chamber seemed to pulse like it was a living thing. The heartstones glowed brighter until everything was cast in a soft, ethereal blue. "Don't ask me to. *Please*. I can't."

"You'll hate me for this," he argued. "After."

I was shaking my head, desperation nearly making a sob rise

in my throat. "I won't. I *promise*," I pleaded. "Touch me. Gods, Sarkin, *please!*"

Sweet relief burst inside me when his hands slid from my hair down my neck, his thumbs brushing over the thunderous pulse of my neck. One moved up to rub against my bottom lip, and my tongue darted out, catching the edge of his warm skin, eliciting a low, rumbling groan from him. Heat flooded between my thighs, the dress I was wearing felt so heavy, it was suffocating. The texture across my skin was becoming unbearable. It scratched and raked against me.

Too sensitive, I thought. *Need it off.*

I gritted my teeth when Sarkin dragged his hand down the length of my side, and I gasped, arching into the stroke of his touch across my breast. When had they ever felt so sensitive? I thought I might be able to come just from him petting them.

"*Fuck,*" he hissed, feeling my nipples pebble against the material. His thumb dipped on the underside of one, thrumming it upward, and my legs shook. I was wound up so tight, *too* tight. His head dipped, and my eyelids fluttered close, a shiver racing up my spine when he rasped into my ear, "I can't decide if I should try to have at least some restraint with you. But I fear it's too late for that, princess."

"I'm firmly against restraint at this point," I gasped out.

I heard his whispered curse in my ear. He spoke something in Karag, something I couldn't understand. Then I felt the bite of his teeth on the sensitive flesh. My hands flew to his shoulders, just as his felt like they were everywhere. All at once.

"*Lysi,*" I cried, the word echoing around the chamber. *Yes* in Dakkari. "*Hanniva.*"

Please.

"You're going to make me come with those sweet little words, *aralye,*" he hissed. "Say it again. Beg me again."

"*Hanniva,*" I whimpered. "*Hanniva, rei kassi.*"

Please, my mate.

I felt something unleash within him at the words, which I knew he understood. This was what I'd never experienced before. Had I ever thought I would beg a lover to touch me? Had I ever thought to hear Sarkin rasp those naughty words across my skin?

No. And yet it felt natural between us. There was no shame in this. Only *want*.

His hands flashed to the straps of my dress, and he snapped the thin, delicate chains with little effort.

"I have thought only about doing that since I first saw you in this damned dress," he grated.

He tore at the dress, but luckily whatever material it was crafted from—and I strongly suspected they were a kind of dragon scale—it was durable and strong. He didn't rip it in his ferocity, but he did pull it off quickly, tugging it over my hips with a swift jerk. It pooled at my feet, leaving me naked and exposed.

Sarkin's nostrils flared, those dark eyes skimming over every inch of me. He went behind me, his hand drifting across my waist. I heard his whispered curse, coupled with a soft groan. I sighed when I felt his hands stroke down my bare back and then bit my lip when they cupped my rounded backside, when they squeezed in appreciation.

"Perfect, *aralye*," he murmured into my ear, pulling me back against him. Against my lower back, I felt the unmistakable outline of his cock, hard like Dakkari steel and impossibly hot, even through his trews.

The heat between my thighs was growing unbearable as impatience nipped at my spine. Sarkin seemed to feel it too because his touch grew even more possessive, his fingers digging into my hips hard as he brought me back to rock against his cock.

Against my back, I could feel his heart. It matched my own thunderous beat.

He spun me around, and the intensity in his gaze was nearly a glare. His motions were quick and purposeful, his hands beginning to tug and untie the laces of his trews.

"Get my vest off," he growled. "Need to feel you against me."

My fingers flew to the silver catches, but my hands were shaking in my need. I only got two undone by the time Sarkin kicked off his boots and pants. He was silent as he ripped at the material, the silver clasps flying across the stone. My hands were on his chest before he even shrugged off his vest, fingers digging into the solid, warm muscles of his pectoral. I brushed them over his hardened, flat, dark nipples, eliciting a sharp inhale from him.

Then my hands were everywhere, roaming, exploring. My inner thighs were still wrapped, but the tops of the bandages were getting soaked with my need.

I moaned when I felt his fingers brush my sex. It was like a zap of lightning went through me, and I nearly drew his blood when my fingernails dug into his skin.

"*Fuck.* You're dripping for me, Klara."

I couldn't say anything but "*Yes.* More!"

My hips rocked against him as he touched me. My face lifted, wanting to feel him everywhere. His eyes were watchful though wild. If I didn't know any better, I would say he even looked furious in his intensity.

"That feels so good," I moaned, drunk on his gaze.

Sarkin's gaze flicked to my lips. Just as his thumb brushed over my sensitive clit, making me jump and gasp, he took advantage. His head lowered and he captured my lips in a fierce kiss.

His lips were soft and warm. My head spun. I breathed into him, feeling his tongue stroke against my own, a deep groan building in the back of his throat. His hard cock was pressed against my soft belly, his hand between my legs, playing and strumming me like an instrument, and I felt thoroughly claimed by his kiss.

My knees gave out, but he caught me, holding me up with little effort, and before I knew it, I was up in his arms. His lips never left my own though I felt the loss of his touch between my thighs.

When my back met stone, I realized he had me propped up against one of the heartstone pillars. The trickle of lake water ran over my body, little tendrils that felt like faint touches, stroking over me. A stream spilled over my shoulder and ran over my nipple, making me squirm against Sarkin.

He released my lips, biting his way down my jaw and over my throat. He sucked and kissed me there, and a shiver raced up my spine, the chamber spinning. How could I be so incredibly *sensitive* there?

I was loud, crying out uncontrollably from his wild kiss, one of my hands gripping his shoulder and the other diving into his thick, wavy hair, the strands silky and surprisingly soft.

I want to feel it tickle between my thighs, came the wanton thought, and even more arousal dripped from me. There had been a salacious image in my book of just that. I'd been curious ever since about what that must feel like.

His lips trailed down my neck and went straight for one of my nipples, sucking on it hard, making my back arch off the pillar. He lapped at the heartstone water that skimmed off my nipple, his tongue darting out to flick the sensitive peak. Around the room, I could hear the whispers, the beat and pulse of them growing louder and louder.

It might have been Lishara's presence here...or it might've been Kakkari's.

Maybe they are one and the same, I thought.

"Gods," I breathed, my brow furrowing, looking down at Sarkin with a half-lidded gaze. I wasn't scared or frightened of what would come next. I didn't care if there was pain. All I knew was that I needed him inside me. I needed to feel him, hard and possessive and wild, joined with me in the most primal of ways. "*Hanniva!*"

I felt the press of his cock between my legs, the slick head brushing over my entrance.

"Wrap your legs around me. Tight," he growled, his voice dark and deep, nearly unrecognizable in his lust. His hands came to my waist, hitching me up and holding me securely as my legs wound around his hips, my ankles locking around his back.

I was shamelessly exposed, and when I looked between us, I saw his cock. My lips parted, the first pinprick of doubt going through me, wondering if we would fit. A moment later, I realized it didn't matter. We *needed* to, or I would die from this agony, this "blessing."

The head was bulbous and slick. With parted lips, I saw a bead of shimmering pre-come push from the slit at the tip, and I nearly whimpered as it rolled down the side. His shaft was impossibly thick, but it was the heat that radiated off him that surprised me the most.

Just like full-blooded Dakkari males, I saw his *dakke*. The swelled bump above the root of his cock. I wondered how that would feel when we were joined, pressed and pulsing against my clit.

"*Sarkin,*" came my needy voice.

"Is this what you want, *aralye?*" he rasped, running his slick tip over my clit.

Stars burst in my vision, the back of my head hitting the pillar, my neck exposed. I felt his mouth go to my nipples, and when there was a telltale flutter between my legs, I thought, panicked, *I'm going to come.*

"Yes!"

I felt the burning sear of him as he pressed into me, my eyes flying open at the sudden pinch.

How will he ever fit? I lamented.

"Tight," he said in a low tone. "Too tight."

"Don't stop," I begged when I felt him retreat. "No!"

"Believe me, princess, there is no threat of that *ever* happening now," he grated. The muscles in the column of his throat were stretched tight, his jaw gritted, his body shaking with the needful energy I sensed just under the surface. Untapped. Waiting to be unleashed.

I gasped, feeling him push back inside.

Too much, too much, I thought silently, feeling when he met the burning resistance of my inner muscles.

He retreated again.

"You'll have to take me, Klara," he rasped, looking into my eyes, one of his hands lifting to grip the back of my neck.

His lips pressed against mine, and I kissed him back eagerly, becoming addicted to his taste and the sweep of his tongue. The back of my throat tingled with the sweetness of it.

"I'm sorry," he breathed into me.

With that, he pumped his hips once, hard and swift, until he was seated fully and deeply inside.

I tensed around him, but my need drowned out the retreating pain. Lishara's blessing had softened the edges of pain already—I hardly felt my rider's burn or the ache and pull of my muscles. Nothing else mattered except this. *Us.* Right in this moment. I would handle the consequences later.

Sarkin's groan reverberated into my chest, as closely as we were pressed together. I'd hardly dragged in a deep breath before he pulled back…thrusting even more deeply again. His *dakke* pressed against my sensitive clit, and I gasped. I could feel the pulse of his heartbeat there, the sensation indescribably intimate.

My teeth chattered together, feeling only a brief bloom of pain that slowly melted into heat, spreading between my legs. I felt so full of him. That strength and unleashed power between my legs felt *incredible.*

And when he unleashed it? When a warning growl ricocheted up his throat, momentarily drowning out the whispers I heard in the chamber and I felt his pace begin to quicken between my thighs?

I didn't know if I would *ever* be the same.

There's no going back now, I thought.

CHAPTER 20
SARKIN

Lishara's temple chamber was filled with the sounds of mating. The slap of flesh, driving and primal. The sounds of desperate moans and satisfied growls.

I felt Klara's nails dig into the backs of my shoulders, and in my *want*, I wished she would do it harder. I wanted her mark on me, just as I wanted to see my mark on her. I wanted to look upon it days from now, to remember this ache and wildness that was nearly too punishing to feel real.

There was no warning when Klara climaxed around me. Her scream was silent, but I felt her body twitch before going strangely still. I felt the tension of her muscles contract, tightening and tightening.

And then she was clenching around me, a desperate cry filling my ears, enticing me to join her. The tight, hot grip of her sex almost made me lose the last edge of my desperate, perilous control.

But I wasn't *nearly* done with her, and so I fought the pull with gritted teeth, momentarily retreating from her body when the orgasm faded, soft little pulses making her body shiver.

The chamber air felt chilled against my hot flesh. When I

looked down at my cock, I saw the way it shimmered with her come. Just the mere sight had me squeezing my fingers tight around the base in an effort to calm my arousal.

My cock bobbed against my abdomen when I lifted Klara away from the pillar. I was harder than I'd ever been in my entire life, on the verge of coming after just a few moments. When had I ever felt *anything* like this? This possessive, maddening *need* for a lover?

It's the blessing, I argued. It was only logical.

Though, in the back of my mind, I also knew from experience that you couldn't fake sexual chemistry like *this*, even with magic.

Klara was open and sensual, demanding. Everything I desired in a lover…though I strongly suspected she'd never been with another male before.

"Need more," she gasped. "*How?*"

I kissed her, feeling the warmth of her body pressed so tightly against my own. She was soft where I was hard, giving where I was unyielding. *Perfection.* The slide of her skin made me shiver.

I lowered Klara to the ground, near the shallow, sacred pool, using her dress to soften the stone as I positioned her into place. On her hands and knees before me, I felt a rumble of pleasure and satisfaction. Her body was beautiful. Soft with generous curves that begged for my grip. So unlike the Karag lovers I'd had before.

When I entered her from behind, I gripped her hips hard, and I heard the scrape of her nails against the stone floor. I heard her distant, desperate cry through the rushing in my ears. When I started again, my hips pumping into her own, I found I couldn't stop.

There was something erotic in knowing that I was so much stronger than her, knowing she was submitting to that strength. A tantalizing thrill went through me, knowing she would take whatever I gave her, knowing she would need it as desperately as I did.

I moved a hand to her upper back, pressing her into the floor, making her back arch and her hips raise. And when I slid inside so deeply, hitting a spot that made us both cry out as black spots burst in my vision, I didn't know if this moment would *ever* be enough. How could it ever be enough?

I felt my *syn'ra*—which I knew the Dakkari called a *dakke*—press into her ass on my next thrust, the wickedness of it making my sac draw tight. If I wasn't careful, I would come easily.

"I wish you could feel this," I growled, briefly leaning down to nip at her shoulder, pressing my lips against her skin. "How good you feel, *aralye*."

She nearly felt *too* good.

When I felt water lap around my knees, my brow furrowed, momentarily cutting through the haze of pleasure. I'd pounded into her so hard that I'd pushed us both into the shallow pool, scraping our knees against stone, pain we couldn't feel. Beneath the surface, I saw the shimmer of Zaridan's scale and felt the tendrils of heartstone magic reverberate up my spine. It made my jaw tighten, and I imagined that I could feel the strokes of magic up my skin, not entirely comfortable, but it only added to the sensation of being connected with Klara.

Her gasp sounded when I drove deep again. The splash of water sounded as her back arched and her hands clamored for purchase against the shallow floor of the pool.

"Yes, Sarkin," she keened. "*How*…how can it feel like this?"

Her voice was a choked cry.

"I don't know," I admitted, lowering myself down over her back, our bodies pressed together. She arched into me, as if needing to feel the heat of my skin even more than was possible. "Going to come, *aralye*! I can't withstand this much longer."

"Come!" she pleaded. "You're going to make me come again too."

I gritted my teeth, my abdomen swooping with those delicious words. *Fuck.* She was perfect.

"I can feel them," she breathed. "*Everywhere.*"

I knew what she meant, even though the knowledge brought a shiver up my spine. We weren't alone here. And Lishara demanded we see her blessing through. Klara was sensitive to their influence, could feel things I likely couldn't, though I gleaned a fraction of what she felt.

One hand went beneath her, finding her wet and slick and hot where we were joined. My thumb pressed into her clit, gently strumming in time with my thrust, and a choked sob tore from her throat. Her body went tight again as my pace increased, and I felt her clench around me as her pleasure ripped her in two. A desperate cry left her lips. A constant growl was reverberating up my throat, vibrating our bodies.

A tight bundle inside me was unravelling. I chased that aching heat, pouring my strength into my thrusts, hearing her orgasm echo in the chamber.

"*Hanniva!*" she cried.

Please!

My thrusts faltered, becoming choppy as my come sizzled up my cock. I bellowed my release, the orgasm being wrung from my body, squeezing and punishing. *Elation and ecstasy.* It stole my strength, my limbs shaking as the sacred heartstone water splashed all around us with my erratic thrusts.

And when it was over, I was spent, dragging in ragged, deep breaths. Beneath me, Klara was holding herself up on shaking arms, and I groaned, dragging her upward to take the weight off her. Her back was plastered to my front as we kneeled in Lishara's sacred pool. My arm was wrapped around her waist like a vise, keeping her in place even as she trembled. Our breaths slowed, but I knew she could feel the wild beat of my heart against her shoulder.

Still seated deep inside her, I felt her inner walls squeezing me, trying to draw out every last drop of my come. Still.

"I can feel you," she whispered. A soft sigh escaped her, like she was pleased about that. "It's nice."

I could only grunt. I was beyond words, my tongue heavy like a boulder in my mouth.

I hissed when I dragged my length out of her, lowering my hips. I was still half-hard, and we both watched as our combined come dripped into the water. I lowered my forehead until it touched the nape of her damp neck, breathing her in, while I tried to catch my breath.

The worst of the desire was fading with the orgasm. Control was slowly starting to return. But with it came realization of what I'd just done. With it came the pinching prick of shame.

Slowly, I unwound my arms from around her and kept her steady as I rose. Water sluiced off my body, and Klara turned to look over her shoulder at me.

My lips pressed together, seeing her glassy, half-lidded eyes and reddened lips from my kiss. Kneeling in the pool, naked, she looked like every erotic fantasy I'd ever had come to life.

But when I helped her stand, I saw her knees were red and raw from scraping on the stone. I caught a brief wince when she stepped from the water, likely a twinge between her thighs, coupled with the sting of her rider burn. The bandages were soaked with water.

Anger rose. Not at her. At myself. When I handed her the dress, silently, I did it with more force than I realized, the broken chain of the strap whipping at her exposed skin, making her flinch.

Which only made me angrier. The chamber walls felt like they were closing in on me, the darkness now oppressive, only lit by the glow of heartstones. And as I tugged on my own pants, catching Klara looking at me out of the corner of her eye, I caught a streak of pink blood on my cock. And I remembered.

"You were untouched?" I asked quietly.

I forced myself to meet her eyes, though I knew my expression was tight. This was wrong. It was all wrong. I hadn't wanted this and neither had she. But neither of us expected for *this* to have been Lishara's blessing. Or else...or else I might've waited to bring her here, even if it had delayed my *mysar* fulfillment to Elysom.

"Yes," she said quietly, her tone suddenly uncertain. Because I was acting like a cold bastard and I knew it.

Hearing her confirmation felt like one more strike against me. I'd been rough, unable to control my lusts. We'd both enjoyed it, yes...but this hadn't been either of our choices. This had been forced on us with magic. And the self-loathing that I'd hurt her, that I could've been gentler, that I could've *stopped* this ran deep.

I didn't *hurt* females. Ever.

"Get dressed, Klara," I said quietly, doing everything I could to control my tone, to keep it steady and even so I didn't scare her.

"Are you...are you angry with me?" she asked.

I turned from her, squeezing my eyes shut as I shrugged on my ripped vest. Because I'd torn through the clasps in my need to feel her skin against mine.

"No."

She didn't say anything else, and I listened to the rustle of her hatchling-scale dress as she pulled it on while I tried to regulate the maelstrom of emotions swirling in my chest.

And as we left the chamber, ascending the darkened stairwell that would lead us back above ground to the lake, I realized...

She was my *wife* now.

Queen of the Sarrothian, of my people.

And once reason returned, once the reality of what had just happened hit, she might hate me.

When we made it back up to the lake, I guided us down the

path, water lapping at my ankles. Zaridan, Feranos, and his Elthika were waiting in the grassy area beyond the rocky shore.

My commander eyed me carefully as we approached, his brow raising. When his eyes darted to Klara behind me, it took everything in me not to growl and step in front of her, to shield her from his view so soon after we'd mated.

Which was new…

The feeling of animalistic possessiveness sweeping through me, discomfort threading through my veins at the thought of him so close to her after what had happened in the temple…it didn't sit well. And Feranos was one of my oldest friends.

I stepped up to Zaridan. I placed a palm on her snout, briefly glancing at her missing scale, the flesh exposed. Her sacrifice for this ceremony and for her rider's bond. It would grow back, though slowly, and it would never be as strong as the scale that now lay in the bottom of Lishara's pool. Over time, the heartstone magic would slowly dissolve it, and Zaridan would forever be part of this place. But she would also be forever vulnerable.

Behind me, Feranos asked, in Karag, "Is everything all right?"

"Yes," I replied, tone clipped, making it clear I wasn't in the mood for further questions. Feranos went silent, and I turned from Zaridan to peer over at Klara.

She was uncertainly hovering by Zaridan's wing. The straps of her dress were ripped—my doing—and she was holding it up so the bodice wouldn't slip. She looked like she'd just been…well, fucked. Well and truly fucked. Her hair was wild, the ends dripping. Her cheeks were flushed. I saw the dark marks on her neck where I'd nipped and bitten and sucked. When she walked closer to Zaridan, she limped.

And self-loathing tore through me all over again, knowing that I'd only added *more* pain to her body. Klara didn't meet Feranos's eyes, and it was then I realized I wasn't making this better. I was making this worse for her.

Get her back home, back to comfort, I told myself. *Then you can figure out how to fix this.*

Because whether I liked it or not, she was my wife now. My responsibility. We were bonded until death, tied now with the blood of my Elthika and with Lishara's blessing.

And as her husband, it was now my duty to protect her. To make her feel safe, even if she didn't feel safe with *me*.

"Let's return," I said, going to Klara. I scooped her up into my arms, watching her blink in surprise, and she met my eyes. Some of the buzzing under my skin calmed when she looked at me, when I felt her comforting weight in my arms and scented myself on her skin.

Ascending Zaridan's outstretched wing, I prepared to bring my wife *home*.

CHAPTER 21
KLARA

The wedding feast that night was an uncomfortable affair. At least for me. Sarkin's horde pretended that they didn't notice their *Karath*'s brooding silence or me fidgeting at his side, at the head of the long table that had been set up during our absence.

It was a beautiful night. Balmy from the waterfall and warm. A bright half-moon was hanging overhead, surrounded by a smattering of stars. It brought me comfort to recognize the constellations. Bekkar's Sword. Tanniva's Hand. Dakkar history and story, plastered in the night sky, even though I'd never felt further from home than I did right then in my new one.

Nearly all of the village was in attendance it seemed. Brightly colored banners and ribbons had been hung from various buildings. Tall silver torches lit up the pathways, casting a golden, beautiful glow in the night. The food smelled amazing, though I hadn't yet tried any of it, my stomach cramping from the palpable tension pouring off my now husband.

I listened to the chatter all around me. Sarkin's riders had long given up trying to speak to him, and we'd been left on our own at the head of the table. Part of the horde and yet separate. As if everyone could feel the tension between us, they all kept to themselves, seemingly determined to enjoy the feast, which was meant to be a celebration of our union. So why did it feel like a mournful wake?

There's no reason why I can't enjoy this party even if Sarkin is sour on it, I thought, taking a deep breath, catching sight of Sammenth and Ryena, both laughing with a small group next to one of the trees that made up the edge of the vast forest. The trunk was wide, protected with a cushioned board, and I watched as they played a game, flinging daggers at the target. The object being whoever struck inside the four circles drawn at random areas of the map won points.

Wine was flowing, darkly colored and rich. My own goblet was half-empty. I wasn't used to drinking fermented fruit, but the Karag produced a delicious brew. I wondered what they used and if the process differed from Dakkari wines. The Karag ones weren't as sweet, though they were rich and smooth. And dangerously easy to drink.

Emboldened by the wine, I stood from my seat, catching the sharp jerk of Sarkin's head when he turned to regard me.

"I'll be over there," I informed him, not quite meeting his eyes as I gestured toward the tree.

He regarded the group briefly, seeming like he was on the verge of saying something, but all he did was sharply incline his head, as if I needed permission…which I didn't.

There was a part of me that was angry. A part of me *was* mourning. Because for brief moments in Lishara's temple, though those moments had seemed beautifully and breathtakingly endless, I'd thought that what Sarkin and I had shared had been *special.* I'd felt connected to him in a way that defied everything I knew.

And he'd taken that away.

He'd retreated, becoming even colder than he'd been to me before. I thought that before we'd left this morning, we might've even been on friendly ground. We'd understood what needed to happen. It wasn't as if sex would've *never* played a part in our marriage. I assumed the question of heirs would eventually need to be answered.

But now?

Our relationship felt more tangled and uncertain than ever. I thought…maybe he *regretted* what had happened. The harsh sting of that realization hurt more than I thought it would.

My body still ached from when he'd been inside me…and he'd never felt further away. Perhaps this was the real Sarkin. Not the male who'd kissed me passionately and squeezed my ass in appreciation, possessiveness pouring from him with every touch.

I nearly shivered just thinking about *that* Sarkin. A part of me was worried I'd never meet him again. It wasn't fair. To dangle *that* in front of me, a sublime prize I'd never known I needed, and then to snatch it away, leaving me reeling and confused.

I squared my shoulders as I approached the laughing group, even though nerves tangled through my chest. Would this be another rejection at the hands of the Sarrothian?

No, I thought, determination rising. I was Sarkin's wife, now. They couldn't deny that, and I needed to start demanding their respect. I would not be rejected, walked over like I'd been in my father's palace, for the rest of my life. I refused. I was their queen now. I might not have had their full respect yet—I apparently needed to bond with an Elthika for that to happen—but they had to recognize that I wasn't going *anywhere.*

This was my home now, whether I liked it or not.

And so I needed to *make* a home for myself here. I needed to demand it in my own way. Because Sarkin certainly wouldn't do it for me.

I could feel the burning sear of his eyes on my back as I approached the group. Sammenth noticed me first, and her smile widened, though her gaze tracked to Sarkin first over my shoulder.

"Can I try?" I asked, nodding at the tree trunk. I used to be a good shot, but these targets were small, the weight and balance of these strange daggers uncertain. And I hadn't practiced on targets in years. It used to be a fun pastime when we'd lived on the wild-lands. Though, truthfully, I had practiced endlessly because the young Dakkari boys in my horde had taunted me that I couldn't *ever* possibly hit a target.

"For a price," Ryena chimed.

My steps faltered uncertainly. "And that is?"

She pushed a half-full goblet into my hands. "Drink up, *Sorrina*. Those are the rules to enter the competition. No one plays without at least one goblet of wine in them."

My brow furrowed, taking the goblet from her hands, the wine nearly sloshing over the sides. "*Sorinna*? What does that mean?"

Ryena's head inclined briefly. "It's the Karag word for *queen*."

I blinked, a shot of nerves going through my belly, and I felt no less than a dozen pairs of eyes on me. Even behind me, from those not in the immediate circle of players, including Feranos, who peered at me carefully. Only he suspected what had happened in Lishara's temple, and I was proud when I didn't feel my cheeks heat under his cautious scrutiny.

Perhaps he suspected the worst.

I didn't drink the full goblet. After even just a sip, Ryena seemed satisfied enough, and I traded her for the first dagger. It was slim but heavy. The hilt was etched with decorative markings, the eyes of an Elthika peering back at me, two red gemstones glittering.

"I'll challenge the *Sorrina*," came Sammenth's voice. She grinned, stepping up next to me. "And I warn you, the Sarrothian are a competitive people."

"So are the Dakkari," I returned. "Perhaps that makes you doubly so."

Sammenth's smile widened.

"We'll see how you fare. I imagine there's little time for

dagger throwing in the *Dothikkar's* gilded palace," came a voice. A female, one of the novice riders, I knew. Her sly smirk was coupled with her narrowed eyes, watching, waiting for a reaction.

I didn't let her subtle jab get to me. I expected to be poked at for a while. I was an outsider, even if I was their queen. But did they believe I'd lived a privileged life, wealthy and wanting for nothing? I'd been happy with my mother on the wildlands, true. But even after I'd been forced to live in the palace, it had never felt like my home.

Instead of responding, I took another sip of wine, the dagger loose in my hand at my side. I twirled the hilt, getting used to the balance in my palm, and I set the goblet down on a nearby stool.

"Hit the middle of the marks?" I asked Sammenth, eyeing the target. In the archives, on particularly dull days when my research was frustrating and I needed a distraction, we'd done something similar with the tips of ink quills, weighted with heavy coins. Half the challenge was figuring out the weights and balances of each quill, which had all been unique.

She nodded. "Stand there. Behind the tether."

There was a long braided rope of black, worn leather lying perfectly straight at my feet.

I caught the stray, quiet voice from the novice riders. "Bets for if she makes it?"

No one said anything, and I felt my lip press. Again I ignored it. If this had been a Dakkari horde, they would've been silenced for daring to disrespect the *Morakkari* of their horde king. Perhaps they'd even be sent back to Dothik or given *pyroki* shit-shoveling duty for the rest of the season.

But I'm not in Dakkar, I thought, straightening my spine. *And my husband doesn't care what his riders say about me.*

A difficult truth, but one I would need to swallow.

I brought the dagger up, pinching the silver, cool blade between my fingers.

"I'll bet against," came the voice.

"We all would," came another grumble.

"Shut it," came Sammenth's hiss.

I let the dagger loose, swift and sure. I'd never felt more certain about anything, actually, and so when it hit the tree with a dull thud, the pointed blade stuck *directly* in the middle of the first target, I wasn't surprised.

But everyone else was silent. Even behind me, it seemed like the noise of the celebration died down. Because they'd been watching too? Was Sarkin?

I was happy because it reminded me of living in the horde. Sneaking onto the training grounds with my two friends at midnight, when the horde had been quiet, the whistling of daggers in my ears as my friends had sparred with wood poles as swords.

A simpler time, I thought, a stab of longing and nostalgia going through me. If I'd returned to the *voliki,* our domed tent that I'd shared with my mother, with cuts from the daggers, she'd only shake her head, a smile playing over her lips. She'd known the importance of freedom. She'd longed for it her whole life. It was why she'd chosen to live on the wildlands. She'd always told me that Dothik had made her feel caged.

I couldn't help but think that she would've *loved* riding on the back of an Elthika. Because what could feel more freeing than that?

"Do I go again, or is it your turn?" I asked Sammenth.

She was staring at me before a wide grin split across her face, a laugh following. She'd had a few goblets of wine, her cheeks dark in color.

"You go again, I insist," she replied. She presented me with another dagger, pulled from her belt, the weight nearly identical to the first. When I looked down, I saw the Elthika carved into the hilt had blue gemstone eyes, and I wondered if the first dagger had been Ryena's. Twin daggers for the sisters. A gift?

When I let her dagger fly, I was a hair off the very center but still within the boundaries.

"I changed my mind," came one of the rider's voices. "I'll bet on the *Sorrina.*"

By the end of the competition, I'd run through all the opponents, even Feranos, who'd nearly beaten me at the very end. My arm was sore, however, the muscles still protesting from flying to reach the Arsadia. I was pleasantly buzzed, flushed with wine, since I had to take a drink with each new opponent.

Sammenth and Ryena were sitting together on the ground, the younger sister leaning her head on the healer's shoulder. I was perched in a stool, which had been procured for me. The dress I was wearing—another that was a similar style to the one Sarkin had ripped off me earlier—was comfortable and loose. Perfect for the warmer evening, considering the wind was blowing the waterfall mist in the opposite direction of the horde.

A small portion of the group had trickled away—including Feranos, who was speaking with Sarkin—though a large portion of the novice riders remained. A few older Karag were lingering on the outskirts of the group under the pretense of offering us food, though they hovered close, listening to our conversation with barely concealed interest.

I was being interrogated. A stream of rapid-fire questions from the Karag riders.

Where did you learn to throw like that?

When I'd lived on the wildlands in the horde of Rath Drokka...my great-uncle's horde.

What was it like living in a horde?

Perfectly simple, though many times I'd wished to stay rooted in one place.

Is it true that Dothik is made of gold?

No. Only the statues.

What happened with the red fog? Is it true that the heartstones defeated it?

It was then I realized that the Karag knew much, much more about the Dakkari and our history then we'd ever thought possible. They knew our currency, our language, even the *Vorakkar* of our history.

How long had they'd been watching us? Studying us? Because I was beginning to realize it had been for much longer than when the first Elthika had been spotted along the coast of the West Lands. Perhaps that had been the first time the Karag had *wanted* us to know that they watched us.

With that thought, I looked over my shoulder at Sarkin. He was still speaking with Feranos and another older Karag male that I didn't recognize. I couldn't help but think he looked more relaxed than he had earlier. Perhaps it had just been me that set him on edge. He even smiled at something the older male said, inclining his head, as he sipped from his silver goblet of wine.

Slowly, the interrogation tapered off, the novice riders starting up a new game of daggers, leaving just Sammenth, Ryena, and myself.

And I finally found the time I needed to ask the questions that had been burning in me for days.

"How is it that the Dakkari came to be here?" I asked both of them. "When? All this time, we never knew about the Karag. But you knew about us all along, didn't you?"

I had my own theory. Well-formed from things my mother had said over the years, pieced together shortly after I'd received news of her death. No one had ever believed me. Worse yet, no one had ever believed *her*…except me. My research in the archives had proven fruitless except for one bundle of old journal entries I'd uncovered one day. A Dakkari talking about sea travel, of navigating beyond the Teru Gulch. He'd gone on about the importance of littering the land with "seeds" to strengthen us.

No one knew how the entries had come to be placed within the archives because there was no record of them. Even Sora had rolled her eyes when she'd read them, tossing them back to me, telling me I'd have to be a fool to believe any of it. Sora had believed the author to be "half-mad."

Then again, many had considered my ancestor, Davik of Rath Drokka, to be half-mad, when in reality, he'd had a gift of Kakkari. So I hadn't placed much value in Sora's dismissal.

"Hundreds of years ago," Sammenth said, shrugging her shoulder as she raised her head. "Three hordes of them landed on the south coast during the age of Krovag."

"Krovag?" I asked. My heart leapt. *Three* hordes? My theories were true.

"Oh, one of the ancients," Sammenth added, seeing my confusion. "We keep track of our centuries by which Elthika is in power. Krovag was a great leader, though he passed the title on when his rider died of old age. He thought it time to give his rule to a new bloodline."

Endless questions sprouted. The Karag spoke of the Elthika like they were a kingdom themselves, with laws, a governing body, and a society of their own.

Focus, I thought. I might not get another chance to ask these questions for a while.

"And these three hordes, they were *actual* hordes? With *Vorakkar?* Horde kings?"

"I suppose," Ryena replied. "But by the time that the Karag discovered them on their shores, it had been many years. They had multiplied, become one. They called themselves Rath Darok."

"Then how do you know it was three hordes that landed on the shores?"

"Our grandmother told us before she died. Some of the Elders still pass down the old stories," Ryena said. "There are still many who live in the old Dakkari territory in the South. That's where we were born," she said, bumping shoulders with her sister. "Many Karag live there too. Many of mixed blood, just like you."

"But you don't know the names of the original horde kings?" I asked, my shoulders lowering in dismay.

Sammenth frowned, as if trying to think back, but shook her head, "No. Those names would have been lost long ago, especially since the Dakkari are so strange about names. We only know the name of the horde that they became."

Names should be feared.

That was what Sarkin had told me outside the East Gate of Dothik.

Perhaps he was right. Because then names might've been remembered instead of forgotten.

The lost hordes.

That was how I'd always thought of them, in the quiet of my mind. And now they truly were. Lost in history and memory.

"Why are you so interested in these hordes?" Ryena asked, her voice sleepy and relaxed from the wine. "I mean, despite the obvious. I know it must come as a shock to learn, as it likely was a shock to learn about the Karag or to see an Elthika for the first time."

I took a deep breath, taking another sip from my goblet.

"During the third *Dothikkar's* reign, he decreed a law that all *Vorakkar*, the horde kings, would need to bend to Dothik's rule. Those who rebelled against him were said to have been banished...but *where*? Some tomes say *banished*. Others say *executed*. A few scrolls say *left*. That's the thing about words. They can mean so many things," I said quietly, my tone wistful. "The original account is lost, and the original meaning of the words have been twisted until it's difficult to determine what really happened. But there were three hordes that refused to bend their will to the *Dothikkar*. Three. And it was like they just *disappeared* from history."

Sammenth was peering at me carefully.

"I believe they left the shores of Dakkar," I said quietly. "I believe they sailed across Drukkar's Sea until they found land. A new home, to begin again. Free. All of this is unproven, of course, and I'm no stranger to the scholars in Dothik laughing at me. But my mother believed what I believe. And I believe they came here. Knowing that there is Dakkari blood here proves that. Now I know *how*. But there's still so many questions."

"And many of them might always be unanswered," came a familiar voice. "Especially tonight."

Sarkin.

When I turned my head, I saw he was standing just at the edge of the clearing. There was a mark on his neck, from my own nails, I remembered, the skin just beginning to heal. I felt my body grow even warmer from the sight, coupled with the wine.

Sammenth and Ryena straightened in the presence of their *Karath*.

"You have an early morning tomorrow," Sarkin told me. "You need to be well rested. Let's return home."

Home.

I hadn't forgotten about my training beginning, though I had hoped for another day of reprieve. It seemed I wouldn't get that.

I stood, swaying lightly, and Sarkin stepped forward to take my wrist, pulling me so that his hand was at my back and I was tucked close at his side.

I waved goodbye to Sammenth and Ryena, realizing that Sarkin was right. I'd waited over a decade for answers. Would I be satisfied if I never answered all of them?

I might not have a choice, I knew.

"Are we friends again?" I asked quietly, peering up at Sarkin as he led us away from the dwindling celebration. We passed an older male, snoozing at the table, still laden with food.

In the quiet of the horde, Sarkin said, "You are not my friend, Klara. You are my wife."

"I can be both," I said, a little drunkenly. "We can build this to last, you and me, and I think being friends would certainly help. Don't you think?"

Sarkin stopped in the middle of the pathway. We were alone, everyone either in their beds or still at the feast. "Is that truly what you want?"

I thought about Lishara's temple. The magic I'd felt there. The raw passion, the ache, the frenzy of it. Of Sarkin's lips at my throat, his cock deep inside me, my nails digging into him as I'd needed *more, more, more.*

"Yes," I said, a little breathless, feeling a flush come on, and I hoped that Sarkin just thought it was from the wine. "That's what I want."

Sarkin said nothing.

And we walked back to his—*our*—stone dwelling at the top of the village in silence.

It didn't feel like a truce at all.

Yet…right at the doorway, as I turned to look back over the celebration one last time, I heard the quiet words: "I can be your friend, Klara."

I looked up at him, hope springing in my chest. A stray breeze pushed a wavy lock across his forehead as his dark eyes burned into mine.

"At least, I can try," he amended, brow furrowed.

I figured that was as good as I'd get tonight.

"Friends," I agreed.

CHAPTER 22
KLARA

"This is a jest, surely," I said quietly under my breath, seeing the small group assembled just inside what Sarkin called the landing field.

It was the field to the west of the village, the same one we'd left yesterday for our ceremony at Lishara's temple. Only now there was only a single Elthika in the field, sleek with scales of shimmering blue.

A familiar male was standing in front of a group of young adults. No older than eighteen or nineteen. Hell, one of them appeared to be a teenager.

"You will learn with them," Sarkin informed me, his arm brushing my shoulder when we stopped on the outskirts of the fence. "*Lysi?*"

He was using my own language to try to charm me?

I wasn't in the mood. Thanks to the wine from last night's celebration and my poor decision to continue drinking it with each new opponent, my head was throbbing, my jaw tight.

The rest of my body wasn't faring so well either. While the majority of the rider burn between my thighs was healing—I could at least walk without feeling like the skin was chafing and

179

raw—I was acutely aware of new aches, courtesy of Sarkin and the blessing that his dragon goddess had bestowed upon us.

In my bath this morning, I'd uncovered bruises from his fingertips, tender red marks where he'd nibbled and sucked, and a sharp ache between my thighs whenever I moved a certain way.

And now…it was my first official day of Elthika riding training.

"I'll be training with children?" I asked softly, eyeing the group, eleven in total.

"Yes, and you have some catching up to do," Sarkin informed me unhelpfully, making my head pound even further. "They've already been in training for five weeks."

I shot him a look. I had the distinct impression that Sarkin enjoyed poking at me when I was so obviously grumpy.

"I trust that you'll handle it," he told me. "I have to fly north today."

"Why?" I asked. I had noticed he was in his riding leathers, but since I knew very little about his daily life—or that of the Karag in general—I hadn't thought much of it.

"Patrol" was all Sarkin said. When I waited, he added, "There was an Elthikan stronghold along the northern coast of the Arsadia. We received word from another *Karath* that they appear to have left."

"You want to investigate why," I guessed.

He inclined his head.

"Does it have to do with the heartstones?" I wondered.

"Perhaps," he said. "There are so few now. The heartstone's energy is like the sun to them. They need it. They will instinctively seek out wherever they feel their energy. At least the remnants of it. That's why we saw that Elthikan horde by Lishara's temple yesterday. They are new to the territory. And whenever hordes start encroaching…well, Elthika are notoriously territorial and will defend their land if necessary. The *Karaths* fear another Elthikan war with so many dragon hordes living closer and closer to one another."

Again I was reminded that there was *so much* to learn. My gaze went to the familiar male, standing tall in front of the group of young riders, his hands clasped behind his back. Last night I'd seen him speaking with Sarkin when I'd been talking with Sammenth and Ryena. That was why he'd looked so familiar.

Was he to be my instructor? If so, perhaps I could begin my Elthikan education with him, one I desperately needed, as long as he wouldn't mind my endless questions.

"I didn't realize that there were territory disputes and politics among the Elthika themselves," I said. How would I be able to cram in a lifetime of education as quickly as possible?

To anyone else, it might've seemed daunting. To me, it was a worthy challenge. I felt a spark of determination light up my chest. Part of my reason for coming here was to *learn*. To understand the Karag and the Elthika. They were one in the same…but also apart. The Karag didn't own and care for the Elthika. Not like the Dakkari hordes with their *pyrokis*. There was a very special and careful relationship between them. And I was beginning to realize that the Elthika were a race all their own, one that worked in tandem with the Karag, not *for*.

Given what I knew, I could understand why the Karag revered and respected them. Why they spoke of them in such a particular way. There was a healthy mixture of understanding and fear. Because if you feared something, you respected it. Sarkin had alluded to that once.

"Go," Sarkin urged, pressing his hand to my low back, the heat seeping into the stiff material, and giving me a nudge. "I'll be back after nightfall."

It was just after dawn, the Arsadia encampment quiet behind us, especially after the celebration last night.

"Be safe," I told him, giving a small smile. His eyes flicked to mine. "We're doing all right at this friend thing, don't you think?"

It was meant to lighten the mood between us, which still felt a little stilted and strange.

But the moment I said the words, I thought of us at Lishara's temple, flashes of sensations—pleasurable and intense—returning to me.

What was worse was that I could *see* Sarkin thinking the same things, remembering the same things.

I cleared my throat, cheeks going warm, and Sarkin let out a growl—one I had the impression he hadn't meant to make—before taking a step away.

Last night, though he'd slept on the floor with me, in the bed of furs still haphazardly slung onto the ground, with our ankles tied together again, we'd both made an effort to stay as far away from each other as possible.

"I'll return tonight" was all he replied, and I couldn't help my sigh when he finally turned away.

There was a group of riders that had assembled—Sarkin's main wing—down the pathway. Levanth was among them, and I felt my throat go a little tight, blinking when I saw her smile at him in greeting.

She said something to him I couldn't make out, and I heard his responding chuckle. Jealousy burned in my belly, discomforting but real. I hadn't expected it to bother me so much. He was my husband now—we were bonded together in his culture and mine.

So why did it bother me that another female—one I knew he'd had a romantic history with—could make him laugh and smile?

You're being ridiculous, I thought, shaking myself, and I resolutely turned around. Of course she would make him happy. They were old friends and riding partners. I was just a stranger he'd made his queen.

"Ah, *Sorrina*," came the voice. I looked up, giving the group of riders and my instructor an uncertain smile as I stepped toward them. Their faces were so serious. One, a girl with stern lips, even looked me up and down, as if sizing me up for competition. "The *Karath* told me you would begin instruction today."

"You can call me Klara," I said, joining the group, realizing that even though they were over a decade younger than me, most still towered over me.

The male shook his head. "I will call you Acolyte, for that is what you are now."

I nearly gulped.

"You may call me Kyavor," he said. "I'll be your riding instructor. Now, fall in line with the rest of the acolytes."

I swallowed down the sudden knot of nerves in my throat, suddenly apprehensive about what the day would bring.

"Yes, Kyavor."

By nightfall, it hurt to even move and Ryena was patiently and courteously listening to my whining as she mixed together more salve. Sammenth, on the other hand, was trying to stifle her laughter.

"And then the look she gives me," I said, my eyes wide, a soft chuckle filling Ryena's home, which she shared with her sister when she was in the Arsadia. "You'd think I'd committed a grave atrocity against her."

"Vyaria is a blood-born rider," Sammenth informed me behind her sly smirk. "She'll be harsh, even to you. During rider training, rank doesn't matter. You're all equal. It'll be her one and only chance to chastise her queen, and she likely knows it."

"I noticed she doesn't have a tail," I said quietly. "The majority of them don't."

"Most are blood borns. It's the easiest way into rider instruction, especially with Kyavor. He's one of the greats. Even the *Karath* from the North will send his acolytes to be trained by Kyavor some years, if they show any great potential."

Vyaria, the blood-born rider, had nearly sent me scurrying from the training grounds in shame that afternoon. I'd been partnered with her to do practice mounts. Kyavor had placed an Elthika harness—with no extra padding—on a boulder in the very center of the river. Off of a ledge that jutted out near the stone, we were expected to jump onto the saddle and secure ourselves into place.

With the rushing river, it was our partner's job to ensure that we didn't get caught up in the current if we missed the mount. One time, I swore that Vyaria had been debating whether to throw me the tether to save me before I'd tumbled over the waterfall's edge. Only at the very last moment had she thrown me the braided leather.

"Well, this blood-born rider wants to kill me," I deadpanned.

"Ahh, I miss the afternoons of river mounts," Sammenth said, her tone wistful. "When you've barely enough strength to hold on to the harness, much less fight the current. One of the acolytes during my year went over the falls. They don't put the net out yet to catch the riders. He was unconscious for the rest of the day."

I nearly shuddered, remembering my fall off the cliffside in Sarroth. If I thought I'd been tired after riding Zaridan for nearly three days straight, I'd been sorely mistaken. My limbs felt like jelly. I was scared to stand up in case my knees gave out.

And tomorrow! Gods, how would I ever survive?

"Finished," Ryena announced, spooning the last of the fresh salve into the jar for me, the reason why I'd come in the first place.

"*Kakkira vor,*" I murmured. "Thank you."

"I'll have more ready for you tomorrow," she promised, patting my shoulder. "Try to stay alive until then. Or at the very least, try not to let a little acolyte murder you."

"She wouldn't murder me," I said. At least I didn't truly believe so.

"She just wouldn't save you if she could," Sammenth cackled, snickering. "On Muron's strength, I don't miss rider training."

"You're still *in* rider training," Ryena pointed out.

"I meant I don't miss the training before I bonded with my Elthika," Sammenth amended. She looked at me. "It gets better, I promise. During training, all riders are equals, including the blood borns who come from a long line of riders. No favor is given. The instructors don't make it easy—they don't believe in that. Hardship creates mental fortitude, discipline, and willpower. All are necessary to bond with an Elthika, and all are necessary to become a rider for the horde."

"And bonding…how does it happen?" I asked, sliding my elbows onto the table.

"At the end of the season," Sammenth said, nodding at her sister when the healer brought her a cup of steeped tea, "the riders who are of age are taken to the Tharken cliffs."

"Of age?"

"Yes, eighteen years and above. You can be in rider instruction as young as twelve though, you just can't participate in the *illa'rosh.*"

"At Tharken?"

Sammenth nodded. "It's a mountain range, northwest of here, where unclaimed Elthika gather during the silver moon. You're given the opportunity to bond with an Elthika of your choosing, but they must choose you too. That happens during the first flight. You have to claim an Elthika—without a harness, mind you—and if they accept you, they won't throw you off their backs so that you plummet to your death. It's called the *illa'rosh.*"

My chest squeezed. My first thought was that Sarkin—or Zaridan—wouldn't let me be thrown off and fall…but I wasn't so sure. In order to fully be accepted as queen of the Sarrothian, I *had* to bond with an Elthika. If I was rejected during the first flight…that would make me the queen of nothing. I would lose the respect of Sarkin's people.

I would lose *his* if I had it at all.

"How many have been rejected?" I asked, not entirely sure I wanted to know the answer.

Sammenth shared a look with Ryena. The healer set a cup down in front of me, steam curling from the top. She'd told me the tea would help with muscle aches, to help with the pain that would undoubtedly come tomorrow.

"Plenty," Ryena said. She shook her head, a shiver working its way up her spine. "When Sammenth wanted to be a rider…I swear, I couldn't sleep for years until she bonded with Orelle."

Orelle must've been Sammenth's Elthika.

"The *Karath*'s best friend, when they were younger, was rejected during his first flight," Sammenth said quietly. "Sarkin had to watch him fall. That, I imagine, is worse."

"What?" I whispered, shock rooting me into place on the bench.

"That's not our place to talk about," Ryena said sharply to her younger sister.

Sammenth breathed in deeply, flashing me a small, apologetic smile. "No one in my *kya'rassa* was rejected." I remembered that word. Sarkin had used it once. It meant *rider horde*, though he'd used it to refer to his best riders, the ones he'd chosen, the ones he trusted to keep the entire horde safe. "It happens less than you think. The Elthika are choosy about their riders, but only a few rejections end in a death fall. Most will return the rider to steady ground. The Vyrin…those are the ones you need to be careful of if you select one."

"The Vyrin?"

"It's a name for the ancients, though they aren't truly old— not in years at least. They are high-ranking Elthika from strong bloodlines. Zaridan is a Vyrin, for example. Vyrins can afford to be very particular about their chosen rider. They're the ones that are dangerous during a first flight."

"And…Sarkin's friend," I began, "he tried to bond with a Vyrin?"

"Not only a Vyrin. With a direct descendent of Muron," Sammenth answered.

A jolt went through me. "But Zaridan…"

"Yes," she replied, inclining her head at me. "He tried to claim her brother."

"Zaridan's brother killed Sarkin's friend?"

Sammenth's quiet was answer enough, and my brow furrowed, lowering my gaze to the steaming tea.

I took a small sip, the taste bitter, though Ryena had tried to sweeten it with a thick syrup that reminded me of *kinu* berries.

"How tragic," I said softly.

"The *Karath* understands that these things happen. You cannot control an Elthika, just like they cannot control the Karag," Sammenth answered. "What happened to his friend *was* tragic but not surprising."

"And it never should've happened in the first place," Ryena cut in, giving Sammenth a long, lingering, stern look. "Enough now. Drink your tea. Both of you."

"Yes, Mother," Sammenth grumbled, but I caught the stray flash of her smile. It was obvious the sisters were close, though Ryena did take on a more parental figure between the two.

I thought of Dannik, a stab of longing to see him, speak with him going through me. I wanted to tell him not to worry. I wondered if such a message was even possible. I wondered about Sora, thinking how I wished our last interaction hadn't been so tense.

Then I wondered about Sarkin, thinking over the new tiny bit of information I'd gleaned tonight. I couldn't imagine how helpless I would feel watching someone I cared about falling to their death.

I remembered the look in his eyes that night when I'd fallen over the cliff at his keep in Sarroth. I remembered how he'd dived straight off, without hesitation, to save me.

Every night, he firmly tugged the strap that connected our ankles, like he needed the extra assurance it was tight.

Now I couldn't help but wonder if he was remembering his friend while he was trying to protect me. The only place I could fall off here was the waterfall, and I'd have to navigate the village carefully to find it. We couldn't stay tethered in sleep forever.

Under Ryena's watchful gaze, I took another dutiful sip of my tea.

And I realized that in addition to the Karag, to the Elthika, of which I knew very little about, I could add my husband to that growing list as well.

CHAPTER 23
SARKIN

Klara gasped when she came awake, seeing me lingering above her.

"Get dressed in your riding clothes and come with me," I told her.

"You're back," she breathed, still groggy. "I'd dreamed…"

"What did you dream?" I wondered, stilling.

She shook her head. "Nothing of the heartstones." She blinked the bleariness from her eyes. "Is it still night?"

"Yes. We just returned. Hurry."

Klara didn't question me, only slid out from beneath the furs, as I tried not to skim my gaze over her legs. As I remembered the way they'd tightened around my hips in Lishara's temple. I still had her little claw marks down my back. This morning, I'd looked at them in my reflection for longer than necessary.

I decided to wait outside as she dressed, and when she joined me in the cool night air, I led her to the landing field.

"Are you going to tell me where we're going?" she asked, more awake now, though she kept her voice a hushed whisper. The horde was quiet, slumbering.

When we reached the landing field and she saw Zaridan waiting there, her confusion only doubled.

"Kyavor told me you had difficulty mounting today," I informed her.

Her lips parted in realization, blinking as I swore I caught a flash of embarrassment on her features. "That's not... It was... You're keeping watch over me?"

"You are at a grave disadvantage, Klara," I informed her, rubbing at my tired eyes. I'd been on dragonback all morning, day, and night, trying to track down the missing Elthikan horde, with no luck. I was tired and wanted sleep. But this was important, and I needed her to realize that.

"I'm not training to be a rider, Sarkin," she said softly. "That's not my purpose here."

"But it is your duty to claim an Elthika of your own," I said, my tone inviting no argument. "You don't have to ride well, Klara, but you do have to master the basics if you want a mere *chance* at succeeding. Most Sarrothian riders begin practicing mounts when they've barely begun to walk."

"Is that when you started?" she questioned, going to Zaridan.

The ease with which Zari lowered her head to press into Klara's palm should've been maddening...given how much challenge the Elthika had given me during our bonding process.

"I was not a blood born," I told her, leaving it at that. "So I know how difficult it is to catch up during instruction...and I even started training at fourteen. You're over a decade older than your peers."

"I know," Klara grumbled, and I didn't know why that cranky tone tugged on the corners of my lips. "You don't have to remind me. I know how out of place I am among them."

"That's not what I meant," I said, softening my tone. "The silver moon is only a month away...but there are already signs that the Elthika are migrating to the Tharken cliffs, where the first flights take place. You were told about those?"

"Yes, from Sammenth," she said.

I should have been the one to tell her, I realized, recognizing my failing. She was the first Dakkari to step foot onto Karag soil in centuries. Of course she would have no knowledge of these things like we did about them. We'd been watching them for decades. Even now, there were Karag on Dakkari soil and they were none the wiser.

Know your enemy. Conquer them before they conquer you.

That was one of Elysom's commands, etched in silver on their capital building in their pristine coastal city.

But the Dakkari weren't our enemy, were they?

"The first-flight choosing might happen before the silver moon with how restless the Elthika have been lately," I said. "That's what I'm saying. So you need to be as ready as you can be. In addition to your lessons with Kyavor, I'll be training you at night as supplementation. *Lysi?*"

Klara blew out a sharp breath. "Do I have a choice?"

"No," I told her truthfully, honestly. "You might be my wife now, Klara, but I will not be easy on you. I will be *harder* on you than Kyavor would be."

"You're worried about me," she said quietly, realization threading through her tone. "You wouldn't be doing this otherwise."

I said nothing.

"You don't think I have it in me to claim an Elthika of my own," she guessed next.

My silence felt long and harsh.

"I see," she said quietly. She looked down to the ground, her hand never leaving Zaridan. "I suppose I cannot fault you for that. And I know I'm no good to you dead."

My brow furrowed, my body jolting.

"I told you before—don't say that," I growled.

"It's the truth," she said, shrugging a shoulder. "Let's at least be honest about it, Sarkin. You need me because you know that

I'm your best chance at finding more heartstones for your people and for the Elthika. And in order for that to happen, to remain here, your people have to accept me. You'll do everything you can to ensure that. I'm not a fool; I'm actually very practical. I know what's at stake, just like you know there are other reasons why *I* want to be here."

The restlessness in my chest grew. Did she really think I was as cold as that?

Of course she does, I thought, shame spreading. I'd never done anything to show her otherwise. Navigating this with her *was* difficult. Uncertain. I felt out of my element. As *Karath*, I was in control at all times. With her, I'd never felt so untethered.

I'd *always* been detached from my lovers, given what I'd experienced growing up. When they drew too closely, I pulled away. I recognized that part of myself. But Klara was my *wife* now. Just that thought alone brought dark pain rising. I shouldn't have been surprised that I was struggling to let her in.

I thought this all while knowing that my mother was only *one* of the wounds that I kept buried deep, enclosed in the unyielding tomb of my chest. How long would it be before Klara wiggled herself inside? How long would it be until she saw the depths of my grief, the scared boy who feared love?

"I haven't been fair to you," I said quietly.

Her breathed hitched. "What?"

"I'm not *easy*, Klara. I know that," I admitted. "But I do believe in you. If I haven't told you that before, let me tell you now, in no uncertain terms. I *believe* that you can do this, *aralye.*"

"You do?" she asked. My chest squeezed when I heard the quiet hope in her voice.

"*Lysi*," I said, inclining my head at her. "I would not lie to you about this."

She took a deep breath as she studied me. I would've given a lot to hear her thoughts at that moment, wondering what she thought of me, wondering what she saw.

Then she flashed me a surprisingly bright smile. "What will you have me do tonight?"

Her quiet determination was impressive.

"You will practice mounting a real Elthika tonight," I informed her, knowing the best way I could show her I cared was to do everything I could to ensure she succeeded. "No harnesses in rivers. That's for children."

"Where?" she asked, trying to hide the mild apprehension in her tone.

I jerked my head up at the mountain behind us. Her neck craned back to take in its spectacular size.

"There."

"Again," I said, voice even and calm with my hands tucked behind my back.

She'd been unsuccessful for the last hour, and I could see the overwhelming fatigue on Klara's features. What impressed me, however, was that she never gave up. Even when she tried to hide the way her arms trembled from the strain of pulling herself onto the harness, over and over again, or the way she swallowed her fright and fear with every leap off the cliffside onto Zaridan's back.

We were high up on the cliffside, intentionally so. Despite what she might've believed, being higher allowed more time to recover her if she happened to topple off Zaridan. If she tumbled off one of the lower cliffs, there wouldn't be enough time to react before she met the ground. She was wary of heights, I'd realized, which never boded well for a rider. Most Sarrothian overcame that fear very young, but she was a Dakkari. One with the earth, not the sky, as she'd pointed out to me the other night.

I hadn't realized what a hindrance that would be to overcome.

"Sloppy," I assessed after I watched her make another

attempt, this time barely sliding her leg over the harness, causing her to grapple for the stabilizing bar in a panic.

She was huffing as Zaridan hovered close to the edge of the cliff. She rested her forehead briefly on the bar as she tried to catch her breath.

Though frustration was rumbling in my chest, I knew there was a delicate balance of when to push and when to rest. If I pushed her too hard tonight, she wouldn't perform well with Kyavor come morning, perhaps losing out on vital skills.

"Enough for tonight," I said. "*Faryn,* Zari."

I heard Klara insist, "I can keep going."

"No," I said. Her back hunched, her eyes catching mine. I backed up a few paces and then launched off the cliff, landing behind Klara in the harness.

"You do it so easily," she observed in defeat as my hand came to her waist. Our bodies jolted forward as Zaridan gusted her wings, circling away from the mountain and back down toward the village.

"I've had years of practice," I said into her ear, my lips brushing the sensitive flesh, my tone coming out gruffer than intended, and I caught her shiver. "Remember that. Today was your first time."

"I'm not used to doing things *not* well."

When Zaridan landed back on solid ground, I thought of Klara's dagger tossing at the celebration feast. She'd surprised even me.

"Patience," I said. "We'll continue tomorrow night. This is one of the most difficult skills you will need to master, and it is the foundation of riding."

"How long did it take you?"

My second attempt, I thought. But I didn't tell her that, not wanting her to get discouraged. I'd studied Elthika riders closely when I'd been young. I used to watch them for hours in our village outside Sarroth, long after the sunlight had faded, more as an excuse not to return home than anything.

Most importantly, I'd grown up with an Elthika, even though I was not a blood born.

"Long enough."

"Gods," she groaned. "You're lying to me. That's exactly what someone would say when it took them no time at all."

"You're being ridiculous," I grunted, tapping on Zaridan's joint, feeling the vibration as she extended her wing for our descent. "I never pegged you as a pouter."

"I'm not pouting," she argued.

"You just don't like failing," I finished for her. "I hate to tell you this, *aralye*, but you will fail more than you will succeed when it comes to the Elthika. The sooner you accept that, the easier time you'll have. Do not focus on perfection. Focus on consistency. Think like this instead: There is no right way to ride an Elthika. All that matters is that you *can*."

Klara was looking up at me, her lips parted, as we both stepped off Zaridan's wing, onto the earth.

"All that matters is that I can," she repeated softly, and I saw her consume those words. "I can work with that."

"Good."

Then she sighed, bending down to stroke her fingers over the moss-covered dirt.

"If I fail during the first flight," she began, "will you or Zari let me fall?"

I flinched, the reaction her words brought forth. A flash of Haden's face flickered to life in my mind, the fear and realization I'd seen, and I squeezed my eyes shut, momentarily trying to dispel that harrowing image.

"What?" I said carefully.

"Never mind," she breathed, her fist clenching into the earth in finality, as if squeezing that worry away. "The soil is so rich here. So full of life."

I was still frowning when she stood. Between us, she held out a clump of dirt. I could smell it, the damp musk.

"I hadn't noticed."

I'd always been too busy looking at the horizon. Not the land.

"My people believe that the same power that created the red fog in the Dead Lands, the fog that almost wiped out our entire race, had happened before. Nearly four hundred years ago when the *mrok illa* star was shining in the sky," she said, her eyes rapt on the dirt, pressing her thumb into it.

I hadn't heard that, nor had our spies or scouts ever mentioned anything like it.

"It was a disease in the soil, leeching the life out of the land, sickening everyone. Or perhaps it was a heartstone curse," she said. "Maybe once, the earth of Dakkar was like *this*. But we don't have beautiful soil like this back home."

I remembered Dakkar. While it held a wondrous, raw beauty, the wildlands could be desolate and punishing. It was a particular way of life, and I marveled that Klara had grown up living it.

After last night, there were stories milling around the horde about her, mostly positive, which boded well. After her dagger display and the questions the acolytes had peppered her with afterward, it was becoming apparent to the Sarrothian that they had perhaps misjudged her.

As had I.

She wasn't a spoiled princess who'd had an easy life. She'd grown up like many of my own people and not without her own challenges. But questions of her lineage would undoubtedly rise. She was the child of an affair, one of the highest dishonors among the Sarrothian, and I knew that many would not look kindly upon that, even if Klara herself had had no part in it. She was marked by it and would be forever.

The Sarrothian could be a judgmental people, one of the things I'd hoped to change when I'd taken over command of the territory. But one could not erase centuries of preconceived notions.

The rest of the Karag viewed the Sarrothian as a rigid, unyielding people. But it made trade more difficult, negotiations more tense. It would benefit us to be more open to outsiders. Perhaps a large part of that change could come with Klara.

If she can bond with an Elthika, I knew. That one sacred oath that the Sarrothian expected above all else.

It wasn't enough that Zaridan had given Klara her *sy'asha*. It wasn't enough that I'd chosen her as my wife. It wasn't enough that Lishara had given us a blessing at her temple—the memory of which was still a constant reply in my mind, a constant erotic reminder.

Klara dropped the clump of earth she'd picked up, wiping her hands together. I cleared my throat, the night returning to me.

To Zaridan, I said, "*Sen endrassa.*"

She made a sound like a half groan, half purr, energy being pulled in from the ground all around her before she unleashed it, catapulting up into the air.

"What does that mean?" she asked, watching Zaridan fly, tracking her toward the mountain.

"It is a term of respect, appreciation."

"Like a thank-you?"

"Yes," I said.

"And where does she go? She sleeps in the mountain? Does she have a family of her own?"

"Zaridan? No. She has chosen no mate and, as such, has no brood."

"Are all the Vyrin like that?"

I cast her a look as we walked back toward the horde. It seemed she'd learned much today. "When you get to be as advanced in your years as the Vyrin, when you have made a name for yourself among your kind and wield the power of *ethrall*, with all of its responsibilities, you have the luxury of being particular."

"Are mate bonds not seen as desirable among the Elthika? I would think it would strengthen them."

"They do. But equals are hard to find among the Vyrin. And they would never settle for less than their equal."

Klara looked up at me, and I could see what she was wondering. If I considered her my equal and…vice versa.

My spine straightened at the thought, frowning.

"Zaridan's brother…"

"Lygath," I told her.

"Lygath," she whispered, and a strange look came over her face. "Where is he now?"

My jaw tightened. "He is near. When Zaridan is present in the Arsadia, he is always near."

"And what is he like?"

"Unyielding" was the immediate word that spilled from my mouth.

"I'd…I'd heard that…" She trailed off, as if uncertain how to form the words.

I made a sound of derision in the back of my throat. "Though the Sarrothian pride themselves on being principled, they sure do like to talk."

"Ignore me," she relented. Her cheeks pink, embarrassed. "I'm sorry."

Briefly, I debated telling her. It wasn't a secret. In the end, I couldn't stomach it. Not right then. "I don't enjoy talking about it. Don't take it personally."

She nodded and thankfully remained silent on the subject. There was a sudden restlessness building up inside me, despite my fatigue. Brought on by the memory of Haden? Lygath? It started slow, like an itch beneath my skin, but it made my heart race. My pace quickened too, like I was trying to escape it, drawing nearer and nearer to my home. *Our* home, I realized.

"Did you find the Elthika you were looking for?" she asked instead.

"No sign of them," my voice clipped, which she tried to ignore.

"Is that a bad thing?"

"Not yet."

We walked the rest of the way in silence as my restlessness grew. When we reached the steps that led up the door, I stilled, and Klara looked back at me with confusion.

"I'll post a guard out the door tonight," I told her. But the thought of going inside with her, feeling the heat of her skin next to me on the furs on the ground, the strap around my ankle, surrounded by walls...I couldn't bear it.

"You're not coming in?" she asked, her lips frowning. "Sarkin, I'm sorry about—"

"It's not that," I growled. It was *exactly* that. When I caught the flash of hurt on her face, I couldn't stand it. Frustration and self-loathing cut through me. I'd wanted to move forward with her, but like I feared, there were many wounds that kept her away. "And *please* understand, Klara...this...this isn't about us. This is *me*. And only me. Go. Sleep."

This was why it had always been easier to be alone.

Now I feared I could *never* be right for her. That I could never be what she needed me to be.

"And where will you sleep?" she asked.

"I won't. I'll see you tomorrow night for another session with Zaridan."

Then I left, heading toward the spray of the waterfall, trying to get Haden's face—and Lygath's roar as my friend had fallen— out of my head.

CHAPTER 24
KLARA

"Uncoordinated," came Sarkin's growl. One of his favorite critiques whenever I launched myself on the back of Zaridan, limbs flailing.

I was dripping in the wet night air. I'd come to learn that depending on the direction of the wind, the nights were either cool and damp or warm and only slightly humid. Tonight it was warm, but the humidity mingled with my exertion until I was constantly wiping my slipping palms on my pants.

"You're not locking your legs when you land," he told me when I walked off Zaridan's wing again, his gaze cool and assessing. His arms were crossed over his chest.

"I'm *trying*," I argued, hunching over, dragging in breath. "I don't have that much time to make the jump!"

Zaridan was so massive that she temporarily had to tuck her wing that was closest to the cliffside during the drills, using her other to keep herself airborne. Otherwise she'd be too far away for me.

Today Kyavor had pushed us on endurance. We'd run for miles over the terrain, dodging through thick forests and crawling over any boulders we could find, even if they weren't in our way.

It was a good way to get a feel for the surrounding land that rippled away from the village—the Arsadia *was* quite beautiful—but I couldn't appreciate it enough given how out of breath I'd been, on the verge of losing my morning meal.

The archives in Dothik hadn't exactly afforded me the physical endurance of the average Karag rider. Perhaps if I'd still been living on the wildlands, it would've been easier.

I'd been in instruction with Kyavor—and Sarkin—for the last four days.

And Sarkin still hasn't returned to bed, I couldn't help but think. I didn't see him in the mornings or afternoons. He only came to collect me during the evenings.

"You perfected it with Kyavor yesterday, didn't you?" Sarkin asked, letting me catch my breath. I could feel his eyes on me in the darkness as Zaridan flew away from the cliff briefly, stretching her wings. It was an exercise for her too, to keep herself stationary, just underneath the ledge of the cliff.

I thought back to the river exercises. Even my grumpy little partner, Vyaria, had been begrudgingly impressed when I'd nailed the harness landings three times back-to-back.

"Yes," I answered, a swell of pride making me straighten. I wiped my arm over my forehead.

"You're frightened," Sarkin guessed.

I bit my tongue. He didn't have to tell me that.

"I see it. The hesitation, right before you jump," he said. "Every single time. Get it under control, Klara."

Irritation made my lips press together. "Oh, I had no idea it was so easy. Thank *Kakkari*, I'm cured!"

Sarkin blew out a sharp breath at my sarcasm. "We're done for the night."

Even I could see his exhaustion. His *kya'rassa*, his most trusted riders, had been on patrol for days on end. I knew he'd had a meeting with the *Karath* of the North yesterday too—it was all anyone could talk about.

"We'll take a break from mounting," Sarkin said. Both relief and worry filled me. "Tomorrow we'll practice commands and control on Elthika-back."

"We haven't reached that yet in our lessons with Kyavor," I said.

"Then you'll have an edge," he snapped, and I nearly drew blood with the way I was biting my tongue. "But I assure you all those riders already know what I'll be teaching you."

We were both on edge and tired. I didn't protest as we flew back toward the landing field. It was the same every night. Sarkin would walk me back to our home, and then he would leave me there. I didn't know where he went or where he slept. All I knew was that every time I watched Sarkin walk away, I felt another little prick deflate something in my chest. Hope?

Tonight, though, I had a plan. This couldn't continue. There was a strange tension between Sarkin and me, one that had truthfully started after Lishara's temple, but one that had only grown since I'd hedged the conversation toward Lygath all those nights ago. Ignoring it hadn't made it any better.

My whole existence in Dothik had been ignored except by my brother and Sora. I didn't want to be ignored here too and certainly not by the Karag male I'd attached myself to, bound in blood and heartstone magic.

I watched Sarkin disappear, heading toward the waterfall again, and I took a deep breath before following after him. Past the quiet stone dwellings on the outskirts of the horde and the lined pathway that led to the entrance of the hatchery.

When I rounded the corner of a dwelling, I lost him and I frowned, trying to see where he'd gone. Then, right at the edge of the waterfall, which was barricaded with a stone wall, I noticed a break in the blue shrubs that grew alongside the cliff edge. A small set of stairs was carved into the side, leading down the length of the falls. From the top, I could just make out Sarkin, disappearing into the darkness below.

Where is he going? I wondered.

Carefully, I climbed down the slick, narrow steps, noticing how high up we were from the base of the waterfall. The forest to my right sloped gradually downward, but wherever Sarkin was going, it seemed like its own hidden cove, separate.

I stayed within the shadows when I reached the bottom, the sound of the waterfall helping to mask my steps. I half-expected to find Levanth here—that had been my fear, even though Sarkin had assured me otherwise—but it was only him.

It was the base of the waterfall, the stream of torrential water pouring down into the base of the lake, though it wasn't as deafeningly loud as I thought it might be. Around the lake, to the right, the forest was high overhead on a rocky hill. But on the other side of the lake, I saw flat land, a dense jungle of wild trees just beyond.

Sarkin was nearly undressed when I maneuvered to the bottom step. His head jerked quickly to regard me, eyes narrowing in carefully concealed surprise, and I couldn't help but admire the dimple on the side of his firm ass, the muscle there carefully defined.

Likely from years of Elthika mounts, I thought, my breath going a little shallow when I saw the swing of his softened cock when he turned to regard me.

He waited for me to speak as he dropped his pants onto the smooth rock floor that led into the lake. He was standing there in all his naked glory, confident and certain as he met my gaze in silence.

"I've been thinking," I called out, my tone casual, as if I hadn't just followed him and stumbled upon him naked at the edge of a waterfall. Though my voice did sound a little high pitched, and I cleared my throat, dislodging the lump there.

"By all means, please continue," came his dry tone.

With the nerves bundling in my belly, I had the insane urge to smile.

"We don't know much about each other," I said. "And I think we should change that."

A rough exhale emerged from Sarkin. "I'm not in the mood to talk, Klara. But you're more than welcome to join me as I bathe."

There was an edge in his tone as he jerked his chin toward the rippling lake.

"You don't think I will?" I asked, my voice rising so he could hear me over the rushing of the walls.

He didn't reply. He really was in an awful mood tonight—broody, quiet, like he'd been at the wedding celebration feast.

I thought of how he'd been that first night we'd trained together. When I'd pressed about Lygath, he'd shut down, but I couldn't stop remembering the panic that flitted across his expression that night. He'd been *so* close to opening up to me.

Maybe I just need to be patient, I thought.

I pulled at my clothes when his back turned. I watched him enter the water as I stripped off my sweaty clothes, reasoning that it wasn't anything he hadn't already seen before, even if it made me feel even more vulnerable than what had happened between us in Lishara's temple.

When the scar on his lower back disappeared beneath the water, I stepped forward until the waves lapped at my toes. My nipples were pebbled tight, the cool mist from the waterfall feeling amazing against my flushed skin and my exertion from the day's training sessions. For a moment, I closed my eyes, savoring it.

"What are you doing?" he growled, having turned to find me naked on the edge of the shore.

Yet…his eyes were on my breasts as I walked into the lake, and my heart skipped a few beats when that gaze *lingered.* I'd never really given much thought to my breasts before, but the way Sarkin was eyeing them? I'd say the appeal was definitely there.

He ran a hand down his face as I drew closer. His gaze only lifted to my face when the water lapped around my neck and I treaded water toward where he stood.

"Since we are learning about each other," I started, "one thing you should know about me is that I don't like other people saying I can't do something."

"I didn't," he replied. "Did you hear me say that?"

"It was implied."

"Is that how you learned how to throw daggers so efficiently?" he asked, eyes narrowing on me. "Someone told you you couldn't?"

"Actually, *yes*," I answered. "That is exactly what happened. A boy who lived in the next *voliki* over dared me I couldn't hit the center target. He thought I was too weak."

"The same is obviously not working for your mounting lessons," he pointed out.

"Yet," I shot back. "Gods, give me *time*, Sarkin. I've been practicing for less than a week."

I heard what went unspoken. I was running *out* of time. Even with my success in the river yesterday, it was obvious I was still way behind in skill among the acolytes.

"You're right."

I nearly jerked at that. "What?"

Sarkin splashed his face with water, scrubbing at his tired eyes. Had he been coming here every night? But where had he been sleeping? Certainly not down *here*.

"You're right, Klara," he said again. "I forget that you are Dakkari. That the first time you've encountered an Elthika, up close, was the shadow moon. I've been pushing you too much. I know I have. It's only because I'm trying to help you."

"I know that," I said quietly, feeling my heart pick up speed in my chest. His words made me soften toward him, and I swam closer as I blinked the spray of the waterfall from my eyes.

"This is unprecedented," he continued, gesturing between us.

"A Sarrothian king taking a wife who hasn't yet claimed an Elthika. It's never happened before in Sarroth's history. Perhaps in one of the other territories, yes. But *never* in Sarroth. That is why I'm hard on you. I have to be."

I still remembered the solidness of his body against mine. I still remembered how it felt to dig my hand into his back, gripping the obvious strength of his shoulders, threading my fingers through his hair as we shared each other's breath.

Underneath the water, my hands curled until my fingernails made little half-moons in my palm.

"I understand," I said, my tone coming out a little breathless, almost sinking beneath the water.

"What do you want to ask of me?" he began, when the silence stretched and it was apparent I wasn't leaving.

"Where have you been sleeping?"

"I told you," he said, fire sparking in his eyes, "that I take my vows seriously. Despite…"

He was angry at what I was implying.

"Despite?"

He huffed out a breath. "Despite that we do not love each other. Despite that we barely know each other."

"I'm trying to change that."

He stilled. "The former or the latter?"

I flushed, but I hoped the darkness of the night hid the worst of it. Quickly, I said, "The latter, of course."

He relaxed in obvious relief, and I didn't know why I felt a thread of disappointment tighten within me.

"There are empty dwellings in the horde," he told me. "Sarroth is vast. The majority of our people don't travel with the horde. Only potential riders and those who choose to split their time between the Arsadia and our homeland. As such, there are always places to sleep here in Rysar."

I nodded, believing him.

"Don't ask me again," he continued, walking closer to me,

making my heart pick up pace. "I keep my promises, Klara, even to you. It's an insult for you to continue to question my honor to our union."

"I won't," I whispered. He couldn't possibly hear me over the falls, but he inclined his head in acceptance nonetheless. Raising my voice, I asked, "Why bathe down here, then?"

I swore the edge of his lips quirked up. "Because I like it down here. It helps me focus. The wildness."

"The wildness *helps* you focus?"

"For someone like me, yes."

"You strike me as a very structured kind of person, one who doesn't welcome surprises."

"Then you have me all wrong. Or maybe you're correct. Maybe this is who I am now, who I've needed to become," he informed me, those eyes reflecting the silver light of the moon. I went a little dizzy looking into them, my legs treading water faster, despite my aching muscles. "Once, most would have called me reckless. Actually, everyone would have."

A familiar feeling of intrigue pulsed through me like my own heartbeat. It was like the feeling of a brand-new book, one I'd never seen or touched before, but one that held so much promise. That giddy excitement as you peeled back the cover, as you thumbed through those first few pages of delicate parchment.

"But we're not talking about that tonight," he added, leveling me a raised brow that had my hope deflating once more in my chest.

"Then what are we talking about?"

I held my breath as his eyes dripped down the column of my throat and to the rippling water lapping just above my breasts. He wouldn't be able to see them underneath the dark water, but merely knowing that he *wanted* to sent a dangerous thrill through me. My legs momentarily stopped treading water, and the lake came up to my lips, wetting them.

"I want to talk about *you*," he said.

CHAPTER 25
SARKIN

"Me?" Klara asked.

"Tell me how you got your scar. About your dreams."

Her hand reached out from underneath the surface of the water to press her fingertips to the mark.

"You recognized Zaridan because you've seen her before," I said. "You told me that."

"Yes," she told me. "I started having dreams when I was young. They started slowly, easy enough to write off, easy enough to disregard as a child's imagination."

"But you saw the same things, over and over again," I guessed, knowing that that was the case for Karag who exhibited power like Klara's.

"An Elthika came to Dothik when I was twelve. We'd just returned from the wildlands, two days before. After that day, the dreams started happening almost nightly. In one of them, I remember Zaridan slashing out at me, and I woke up with my face bloodied, screaming."

Discomfort curled in my chest. "You were just a child. You must've been afraid."

"Yes," she admitted, her eyes darting back and forth between my own. We were close enough that every so often, I felt her knees brush my legs as she kept herself afloat. How easy it would be to reach out and hold her against me. "But it was my mother who was most afraid after that."

"Tell me why."

I had my suspicions, but it was different than hearing her perspective. During our scouting missions and from the reports of our spies, we'd learned the Dakkari priestesses of the North Lands were snapping up anyone who showcased just a hint of magical ability. They were feared. They had the authority, under the *Dothikkar*, to take whomever they pleased.

"It's complicated," she said, her lips quirking in a sad smile.

"Help me understand, then."

She blew out a rough breath, looking over the darkened, rippling water of the lake. I watched as her eyes tracked beyond the edge of the shore, going into the forest.

"I am descended from not one but two powerful females who exhibited Kakkari's gift. The ability to wield heartstones, to feel their power and channel it. A human woman named Vienne, queen to the Mad Horde King, Davik of Rath Drokka, was my ancestor. She was the sorceress who used heartstone magic that unleashed the red fog over the Dead Lands, trying to save her husband."

"And the other?" I asked, though I knew.

"Kara of Rath Serok. Who I'm named after. The first hybrid of our history, who wielded not one but two heartstones during the battle that defeated the red fog," she said. Her eyes lifted to mine. "The *ethrall*."

My lips pressed together.

"As such, everyone in my line has been scrutinized by the priestesses very carefully. We don't know much about heartstone magic, but we do know it can pass down through bloodlines."

"Does that mean your mother had a gift as well?" I wondered.

"Yes," she said. "She did. She had visions, like me. Hers didn't happen in sleep though. They could happen anytime, so she had to be careful. She had to be mindful about who was watching her."

"And what did she see?"

"She called them the lost horde kings," Klara told me, a sad smile on her lips, but her voice was strong and proud.

"The Dakkari who landed on our southern shores centuries ago," I guessed.

"I can only assume," Klara said. "She saw this place too. We are both connected to Karak, to your homeland. No one believed us, of course. Then again, I had to be careful with who I told because I didn't want to attract the priestesses' attention. It was difficult enough being in Dothik. I felt like they were always watching."

"That's why you wanted to know about them," I said, inclining my head. "It proved you right. It proved that your mother knew a truth that no one else did."

"People called her crazy," she said. Though she tried to hide it, I saw how it still cut her. "They called her mad, just like they called Davik the Mad Horde King. They dismissed her. Part of why I dedicated my life to research and knowledge was to prove that she wasn't."

I could see the love she had for her mother.

"What happened to her?" I asked, straying even closer. She bobbed under the water when her legs faltered, and I reached out to grip her waist. Her lips parted, but she slowly relaxed into my touch, trusting that I wouldn't let her slip beneath the surface.

"My mother grew up in a noble family in Dothik…because of her bloodline. She and my father, they'd known each other since they'd been children. They'd grown up together, loved each other. But he married another, one who helped secure him his throne. My mother might've been from a noble family, but they were poor. My father's wife wasn't," she said. "Their affair continued for *years*, until my mother found out she was pregnant with me. She knew the queen wouldn't accept that. She feared retaliation, knowing I would have a legitimate claim to the throne, especially because of my other bloodline, and so she left. My great-uncle was a horde king. He extended her a home, and she took it. I was born on the wildlands. I grew up on the wildlands."

"Did she ever tell you who your father was?"

She shook her head. "My mother kept a lot of secrets—that being one of them. There were rumors. Children could be cruel growing up, repeating things they'd heard their parents whisper about. I never believed them until my mother told me herself."

"I'm confused," I admitted. "Why did you both return to Dothik then? Especially if she was trying to keep you safe?"

"My great-uncle died," she said. "The horde collapsed. We had nowhere else to go, but my mother had family in Dothik, who helped us get established. We got a small room above a tavern in the market district. My mother worked there. The dreams became more frequent, and when I woke that night with this scar…that's when she got even more scared."

"Your father found out you were in the city. He found out about your birth," I guessed.

She inclined her head, and my fingers tightened on her hips.

"He actually wanted me back then," she said, a sad smile crossing her face. "But I think he just wanted to feel attached to my mother in some way. And I was that link to her. He was furious that she'd hidden the pregnancy. When I was fourteen, he had me come live in the palace. Maybe to punish my mother—I don't know. But she made a deal with him, or maybe even the queen. Something I could never truly figure out. But I went to live with them…and my mother was sent away. To the *orala sa'kilan.*"

"The priestesses," I knew, understanding finally dawning.

"One year later, I received news that she was dead."

My jaw tightened, a knot forming in my belly.

"She was always so scared of the priestesses. Ever since our heartstones were wiped out, they'd been trying to create new ones. With the power that some Dakkari manifested, that's what they would use—using people like power sources," Klara said. "But more times than not, it would kill them. That's what happened to my mother. She was used for her power, and it killed her. And the worst thing is that I think that was the deal. She willingly went to the *orala sa'kilan* so that I would be protected from that fate."

It was a tragedy. Pure and simple. What the Dakkari were doing to their own people…it was pointless. Heartstones couldn't be *created*.

"She gave her life to keep me safe in Dothik. I don't know the extent to which my father knew. I do know he loved her—he wasn't seen for weeks when we heard of her death—but he became cold to me after that. Like he could barely stand to look at me," she said. Her eyes were glassy with a film of tears. "I just wish we'd stayed on the wildlands. We were happy there. Safe. Maybe she'd still be alive."

"I'm sorry, *aralye*," I said gruffly, my chest tight from the tale. "I didn't know."

She wiped under her eyes and then splashed her face with water. She gave me a half-smile, trying to dispel some of the tension between us.

"It wasn't all bad," she told me. "Dannik protected me. I met my friend Sora. I was content in the archives. I was content in my research, though more times than not, it was frustrating. But it gave me purpose. It made me feel connected to my mother."

I remembered her brother, Dannik. By our reports, he would overstep the eldest daughter and his father would instead pass the throne to him. Would he make a good king? That would remain to be seen, but it had been in my report to Elysom.

Did it soften me toward the Dakkari male? Knowing he'd watched over his sister?

Perhaps.

I'd seen how protective he'd been over her outside the East Gate. Knowing what I knew now, my estimation of him increased. Because he hadn't *needed* to love Klara. It would have suited him better to have ignored her, like some of her own family had, no doubt.

"Heartstones cannot be created," I informed her. She stilled under my grip. "They are not *made*. They are grown."

"With the roots of the *thalara* tree," she guessed. Her own visions had proved that.

"Yes," I said. "It's terrible what your priestesses are doing. Pointless and terrible. Then again, most things are when it comes to power and fear. Together? That's a deadly combination, especially in a group of people with unchecked authority."

She inclined her head. "Do I get to ask a question now?"

It depends on what it is, I thought immediately. Then I felt shame. She'd been honest with me. More open than I'd thought she might be. But I was used to the Sarrothian, who kept their emotions close and their tongues behind their teeth more times than not.

She wasn't anything like a Sarrothian. She couldn't be more opposite.

"Yes," I said instead.

"Is Dakkar in danger from an attack by the Karag?"

That wasn't the question I'd expected. But she'd perhaps wondered why I'd been poking about her history. Did she think I'd asked about her family, her mother, her father because I was trying to glean information?

"Make no mistake, Klara," I began, "the Karag have been monitoring the Dakkari for decades."

"Spying, you mean."

"Call it what you want. But the Karag do not make it a habit of entering a war with neighboring nations without reason. And certainly not unprovoked."

"But you want the heartstones."

I blew out a breath, adjusting her slightly so that she was more in the crook of my arm, her naked side brushing mine.

"We were *spying*, as you call it, because we were trying to establish if there were heartstones worthwhile to try to take."

"To steal, you mean," she corrected again, quirking a brow, and I huffed out a sharp laugh.

"I prefer *negotiate for*."

Klara laughed, the sound carefree and beautiful. For once. It was the first time I'd heard her laugh like this.

"We believe that an ancient Elthika took the heartstones and dropped them over different nations. There are reports of other heartstones all over this planet. Dakkar isn't the only race that has possession of them."

She straightened in my grip at that. "Why would an Elthika do that?"

"To share power," I answered. "To give it freely. To start wars. To hide them. To grow them in different soils to see if they had different effects. Who knows. I've heard all theories. But the one thing that is never in disagreement among Elysom's scholars is that it was an Elthika's doing. Long ago."

"We believe that they are gifts from our goddess, Kakkari," she informed me, gazing up at me with those warm, seeking eyes. "I like our explanation better."

I felt my lips curl slightly, and I hid it by looking away.

"The Karag don't believe in gods or goddesses, do you?"

"We believe in our Elthika," I answered her. "And our bonds with them. That's all we need to know."

She didn't argue with me. In fact, she accepted my simple answer, inclining her head.

"How long will we be in the Arsadia?" she asked.

"Until after the *illa'rosh*, after the riding season is complete," I told her. "Why?"

"I would like to do my own research on the lost horde kings. Sammenth and Ryena told me about the villages where they grew up. I was hoping to talk to some of the Elders, to see if I can record their knowledge, their stories before they're truly lost forever."

"If you make your bond with an Elthika, you can do whatever you want as queen," I answered her.

"Truly?" she asked.

"Did you expect a fight from me about it?"

"Well…*yes.*"

"Fulfill your oath to the Sarrothian, Klara," I started, dipping my head down so our eyes met, "and you can do whatever you please."

A determined spark lit up her eyes. "I'll do it, then."

I didn't hide my smile this time. "If that was all I needed to say, I wish I'd done it long before now."

"That's why we should learn more about each other," she pointed out, though she kept her smug satisfaction at bay. "Don't you agree?"

I grunted.

"Though I haven't truly learned much about you tonight," she added with an assessing look.

I grunted again.

"And you won't tonight," I said. "Now stop talking, wife. Let me enjoy my wildness in peace."

"You won't tell me just one tiny thing?" she pressed.

I bit out a sigh. She *had* been open with me tonight, had answered my own questions without complaint.

I swallowed down my discomfort when I said, "Do you know how a Sarrothian *Karath* is chosen?"

"No," she said, a little breathless, like she couldn't believe her pressing me had actually worked.

"They are taken from a pool of the best acolytes and riders for the territory when the position becomes open, either when the previous *Karath* dies or relinquishes his position or is removed."

"Removed?" she asked.

"By the Elthika," I answered, knowing that was how my predecessor had gone. "These choosings only happen once in a lifetime, maybe twice, if that. And it happened to fall during my rider season. Perhaps luck, or perhaps fate. One rider from each of Sarroth's villages is chosen and sent to the cliffs. Whoever claims a Vyrin more often than not comes out a *Karath*, though other riders can challenge them. In the weeks following, those challenges can seem endless, but not many are foolish enough to stand against a Vyrin and their chosen rider. Except other Vyrins."

I saw Klara process the information. And when her brow furrowed, I knew she was filling in gaps, what went unspoken.

"Haden was like a brother to me," I told her, swallowed deeply. "Going into the *illa'rosh* that year, he was favored to be the next *Karath*. We both tried to claim a Vyrin that year. Lygath rejected him. Zaridan chose me. Nearly all the acolytes died that year. I tried to save Haden…but in the end I watched him fall. And I was challenged relentlessly in the aftermath. Elysom allowed a law where I could be challenged for a full year afterward. There were many who believed I had murdered my own friend to claim the throne of Sarroth. So that's why I don't like to speak of it."

"I'm sorry," she breathed, and I barely heard her over the rush of the falls. What struck me was how *sad* she looked by my confession. As if she hurt for me. "Sarkin, I had no idea…"

"What's done is done," I said, steeling my voice. "That year taught me a lot. It was a trial, and I came out with the respect of my people. I *had* to go through it."

I'm glad I did, I thought. It made me a better *Karath* in the end because it taught me to trust very few and to build an Arsadian stone wall around me, allowing no one close.

"Enough for tonight," I told her, releasing her only when she began to tread water. "It's late. And you need sleep."

"Will you return with me tonight?" she asked softly. The question struck me as vulnerable.

I blew out a rough breath. There was a reason why I'd stayed away…but I realized I couldn't run forever.

"Yes," I answered. "I will."

CHAPTER 26
KLARA

In this dream, I was in another forest. I breathed in the scent of damp leaves and woody trunks. The soil was fragrant at my feet, so black it looked like Zaridan's scales. Low-hanging vines dipped into my view, and I pressed them aside, ducking underneath as I followed the path of what I thought used to be a riverbank. There was no water now, but the indentation of a stream still compressed the ground, rocks imbedded into the soil at the base of it.

This wasn't the heartstone forest I'd seen before. This place was unfamiliar and unrecognizable, though I did feel the hairs on the back of my neck rise, a gentle breeze blowing behind me.

At the end of the dried-up river, I saw it. A great, ancient tree, its trunk as wide as Elthika limbs. Its branches were black. I would have thought the tree was dead if not for a few white leaves peppering its twisting branches. The leaves appeared to have blue veins within them, glowing a dull color.

My lips parted, and I looked around the clearing for some hint of where I might be. I didn't have much time before I'd wake —anything could disrupt this moment—and I was seeing this tree for a *reason*. Dropping down into the bed of the dried stream, I began to dig into the wall at the base of the tree, my fingers nail scratching at the dirt. Quickly, I worked…and soon I was rewarded.

At the end of one root was a grouping of heartstones, though their light was dull. I counted five. A tree this big would have dozens of roots. How many heartstones could there be underneath the earth?

When I touched the root, I gasped, a thousand whispers pouring into my head. My blood pulsed in my veins. It was like being dragged under a roaring river. It was all I could hear.

I wrenched my hand away, stumbling back onto the earth, hitting the compacted, dry soil *hard*.

Staring up at the tree, now with slight trepidation, something nudged into my memory. A story. My mother's story, passed down from Rath Drokka's line about a whispering, bleeding tree.

My heart began to pound, so fast and quick that I felt it in my throat. I scrambled up the crumbling bank and went to the trunk, looking around for something sharp. I needed to know. Because that would mean…

I grabbed the first rock with a hard edge I saw. I touched the trunk, gritting my teeth when those voices filled my mind again. The tree was *warm*, like flesh and blood.

Blood.

I struck the trunk with the sharp edge of the rock. It was like striking a boulder, the strength of the tree reverberating up my arms, rattling my bones. I struck again, and a small piece of the trunk splintered off. I peeled it away.

The rock tumbled from my grip, and I walked back a few paces as the trunk began to bleed. A small trickle of golden liquid, rolling down the blackened bark.

Without another moment of hesitation, I ran. Underneath my bare feet, I cut my soles on rocks and exposed, spiky roots, but I didn't care. Nothing mattered in dreams except the memory of one.

I sprinted in one direction, praying to Kakkari that I'd chosen the right way. I could get lost in here. But I kept my sights on the constellations overhead, letting them keep my path straight.

My lungs burned. I was gasping with the exertion. Vines tangled in my hair. One whacked me across my cheeks, making it sting and burn, but I kept going.

And at last, even as the moon began to dip in the sky, I saw a break in the forest line. When I burst out beyond it, I stopped, panting, sweating, swinging wildly around to try to find a marker. *Something.*

In the shadowy distance, I saw it. The familiar stretch of mountains that I could trace in my sleep because my horde had once lived in the East for a season of *ungira* hunting.

The Dead Lands.

The outer mountain range that protected what had once been the Dead Mountain, where a race called the Ghertun had lived before they'd all been killed with a heartstone. A heartstone wielded by Vienne of Rath Drokka. My ancestor.

I sank to the ground, breathing in deep. I fell back as my chest heaved, staring up at the sky, my mind reeling from my discovery.

"All this time," I breathed.

All this time, the heartstones had been in Dakkar.

They'd been back *home.*

When I woke, it was quick. One moment I was dreaming of the Dead Lands…the next, I was staring at Sarkin's chest rising and lowering as he slept.

I was crying, I realized, and I wiped my face in the darkness with my palm. The discovery in my dream didn't make me happy or pleased. It made me sad. *Angry.* Because the priestesses had been using people as conduits for the last hundred years, trying to create a source of power that had been under our feet the entire time.

My own mother had died because of it.

I stifled a sob, feeling the urge to scream. Feeling the urge to tear down the *orala sa'kilan*, the priestesses' temple in the icy and desolate North Lands, stone by stone until it lay in ruins at my feet.

This level of anger was frightening. It wasn't *me*. But I'd been keeping my own grief suppressed for so long. This dream had unlocked a truth that I hadn't been ready to face.

Sarkin jerked in his sleep. Speaking in Karag, he moaned and his limbs flailed. He narrowly missed hitting my chin with his elbow. I rose quickly, pressing my hand to his chest. His brows furrowed in sleep, a bead of sweat rolling down his temple when he thrashed again.

"Sarkin," I called softly, shaking him. His chest was bare and hot. He'd gone to bed naked. "Sarkin, wake up."

His eyes flashed open, and he sat up immediately, the furs pooling to his lap. He pressed his hands to his face, rubbing over his eyes and jaw as my hand hovered over his shoulder.

He was shaking, I realized. Something twisted in my chest. Had our conversation about Haden and Lygath sparked this dream tonight? This memory? Or had he dreamed of something else?

"Are you all right?" I whispered, placing my hand on his shoulder.

He shook me off, and my hand hovered in the air as I bit my lip, trying not to feel the sting of his rejection.

"I'm fine," came his rough, tired voice, raising his head from his hands. He didn't look at me as he said, "Go back to sleep."

He's going to leave again, I thought, a feeling of dismay spiraling through me. Just when we'd patched up our holes. And I didn't want that. I didn't want to be left alone tonight, not when I'd just seen what I had in my own dreams. I wouldn't be able to stand it if he left. Maybe that was selfish of me.

But perhaps he needs this just as much as I do, I couldn't help but hope.

I touched his shoulder again, my heart picking up speed in my chest.

"Klara," he growled, turning his head sharply to regard me, a warning in his gaze.

I wouldn't be frightened away though. Not again. I knew this was only him trying to keep me at arm's length, trying to push me away when I'd witnessed a vulnerability. He only let his people see his hardened edges. But I was his *wife*. And he couldn't keep his guard up forever, not when we were alone. That would exhaust anyone.

I ran my hand up his shoulder, holding his eyes, and traced up his neck. His skin was damp, a thin sheen of sweat covering him from whatever it was he'd dreamed.

"I'm here," I whispered, my fingers making contact with the curled ends of his dark, thick hair. "I'm not leaving, Sarkin, and neither are you."

His eyes flickered, his pupils dilating further in the darkness. There was a small fire smoldering in the hearth, casting its multi-colored light into the room. We were still on the floor beside the bed, in a mess of furs, and our ankles were strapped together. Connected even in sleep.

And I wouldn't let him run from this. *I* wouldn't run from this.

His breath hitched when I scraped my nails across his scalp, curling my fingers into his hair.

"Klara," he murmured. A warning.

"I'm here," I repeated again.

Then I leaned forward, eager to feel him. I needed him to *ground* me. I needed to feel tethered to something.

Our lips met, and I felt the hot rush of his breath. Had I

surprised him? I felt the tenseness of his jaw when I brought my other hand to his face. I kissed him softly, just a light brushing of our lips, like I was coaxing him, like I was trying to tame him.

I wanted to comfort him. I wanted him to comfort me.

His shoulders trembled, and then he was kissing me back. It wasn't gentle. It was hard and claiming and desperate…and it was just what I needed tonight.

Our teeth clattered together, and then I was up in his arms before I could close my eyes. All the raw, suppressed strength I felt in the cords of his muscles made his motions quick and certain. I was in his lap, my legs wrapped around his waist, as I felt him grapple with the cord at my ankle, releasing us. Then his hands gripped me hard, digging into my hips as I clutched at his warm shoulders.

Liquid heat lapped between my thighs, distracting and frustrating.

"This is what you need from me, *aralye*?" came his gruff words against my lips.

"You're not the only one who dreams," I answered, squeezing my eyes shut. I licked at the seam of his lips, pulling a groan from him. "We *both* need this. Even you."

Sarkin huffed out a sharp breath, and then he was dragging up the tunic I was wearing. One of his. Another I'd stolen from his chests. He nearly ripped it off me, like he couldn't wait to feel our naked skin pressed together. Immediately, his head dipped and he sucked at my breast, hard and rough, as his hand went to the other. My head went back, a long moan falling from my lips when he pinched my nipple gently.

The heat and tug of his mouth made my eyelids flutter as the pulsing between my thighs grew. Between us, I felt his cock bob, and I reached down, wrapping my hand around the velvety shaft.

I'd thought about this far more often than I would admit. But what had happened in Lishara's temple had been permanently imbedded into my brain. And I now knew that the desire we'd felt for one another that afternoon…it hadn't solely been because of the heartstone magic and Lishara's blessing.

That same desire simmered the air around us now, and sweat dripped down my back. One hand was in his hair, holding his head to my breast, and the other squeezed around his cock, stroking gently as pre-come dripped over my palm. My fist bumped his *dakke*, that small, hardened bump at the base of his shaft, feeling it hot and throbbing like a heartbeat.

He wanted me. He wanted this. Maybe he'd been having the same fantasies.

His grip went even harder, and his hand came over mine, guiding his cock to my entrance. I lifted up, ignoring my obvious inexperience, only knowing that I was infinitely curious, that I wanted to learn and enjoy every new sensation sex created within me.

I felt the thick stretch of his cock slide into me. A pinching ache followed, but I moaned and rocked my hips down, biting my lip, ignoring the brief bloom of pain.

"Oh, *aralye*," Sarkin whispered, his brow furrowed. We were almost at eye level with me sitting in his lap, and I saw the exquisite, maddening ecstasy there. It almost appeared as if he was in pain as he tried to control himself.

"What does *aralye* mean?" I asked, something I'd wondered but never had the courage to ask. Not until this moment, when he was seated deep inside me, our walls down briefly.

His eyes were so dark they looked black. I could see myself in their reflection.

"Sweetling," he murmured, brushing a kiss over the bridge of my nose before trailing it across my cheekbone to my ear. "Darling."

"*Oh,*" I breathed.

I rocked over his cock, and he hissed. His lips returned, and when he kissed me, it was hard but consuming. Perfection.

His lips were a distraction, his wandering touch lighting me on fire. When he slid deep, I jerked, feeling him hit a spot inside me that made little stars spark in my vision as his *dakke* pressed to my clit.

"Right there," Sarkin rasped, a bead of perspiration falling down the side of his face.

I didn't know what possessed me, but I licked at it, tasting the saltiness, wanting everything he could give me as he stoked the burning embers between us.

"*Fuck,*" he breathed, his eyes on my lips. He kissed me again, this time more wildly, and his body jerked with his increased pace. "On Muron's blood, you drive me to madness, wife."

I found my own pace even as I explored his body. There was an urgency to our lovemaking, but there was also a patience to it. I took my time, stroking over scars and muscles as he was relentless with his teeth-clattering thrusts, sliding deep every single time. I touched his hair, brushed over his lips. He nipped at the tip of my thumb, watching me with that strained, intense expression, creating a new fire between my thighs.

He leaned forward, kissing and biting at my shoulder. His hands tightened on my hips, lifting me off him slightly so he could control the pace and the power of his thrusts completely.

Helpless and suspended, I gasped, wrapping my arms around his neck, like I was trying to hang on as he *unleashed* himself. Unleashed his power and desire and the rising frustration of the last few days. The uncertainty between us.

Maybe sex is the answer, I couldn't help but think. I felt more connected to him than I'd felt in Lishara's temple. There was a raw openness, a welcome vulnerability between us. This was what I'd craved. This was what I'd needed.

His *dakke* kept hitting my clit, making me thrash and moan in his arms. When his speed increased and he ground his hips against me, I felt my legs tighten around him and I held my breath for a brief moment.

Familiar heat exploded at my core, rippling and extending

out like waves to every part of my body. I cried out, digging my nails in his shoulders, and he captured that scream with his lips.

Into our kiss, he growled, "Going to make me come, Klara."

"Come," I begged. "I want to feel it."

That was all the warning I got. A violent breath rushed out of him, heaving his shoulders. His desperate groan felt like a victory as his hips jerked against me. He emptied himself into my clenching heat.

When it was over, I felt his cock throb and pulse inside me. He shuddered, our ragged breaths becoming one as we tried to catch them. We didn't move for a long time…him seated deep inside as his cock softened. Me with my face pressed to his neck, breathing him in. I felt our heartbeats flicker against each other.

Sarkin sighed, relaxing. A contented sigh. I stroked his shoulder, thinking it wasn't so bad to be married to someone you barely knew. Learning about each other would come with time. We couldn't fake *this*. This need.

"Did I hurt you?" came his question.

"No," I whispered. I wanted to smile. I felt lethargic and drunk off our lovemaking.

Gently, Sarkin lifted me, untangling my legs from around his waist. He laid me back on the furs, hovering over me. His lips parted, a sharp huff escaping him when he pulled out from me. I bit my lips, feeling sensitive but content.

Sarkin rose, and my gaze flicked up the perfect statue of his body. All hard lines and smooth flesh, he could have been created by an expert sculptor.

He observed me, running a hand over his face, over his reddened lips from my kiss. His eyes dipped to my own, then trailed down my naked body, over my peaked nipples—puckered from his sucking and bites—and then to the marks his fingers had made digging into my hips before finally settling between my thighs. I could feel wetness there, his come trickling out of me.

"Gods," he rasped.

"I thought you didn't believe in any gods," I teased in a whisper.

He shook his head. "You're beautiful, Klara. You know that?"

My brow furrowed. I didn't know why those simple words made me want to cry. No one had ever called me beautiful. Only my mother, when I'd lamented over my scarred face. But I'd certainly never been called beautiful by someone like Sarkin.

What made the back of my throat burn was that I knew he *meant* it. I could hear the honesty in his voice, the awe.

I'd never expected that from him. Not ever. And I was suddenly glad that I'd pushed when he'd tried to keep me at arm's length. I was glad I'd stepped across that boundary he'd drawn between us because if I hadn't, I never would've realized this.

"Thank you," I said. Shyly, I added, "You are too."

But I was certain that someone like Sarkin would've heard that throughout his entire life. He was one of the most handsome males I'd seen. And his mere presence alone was eye-catching and demanding.

His lips quirked at the corners, and he walked toward the back of the dwelling. I heard the splash of water briefly, and when he returned, he crouched between my thighs. There was a soft, damp cloth in his hands, and my lips parted, my cheeks flushing in realization, when he cleaned me off. The gentle way he stroked me made me bite my lip. I was sensitive, my belly sucking in when he teased at my clit.

When he was done, he wiped his softening cock before he returned to the furs, refastening our ankles together, always mindful.

I felt a little shy as I curled against him. His arms came around me. He was warm, his scent comforting and familiar.

"What did you dream of?" he asked as my eyelids began to flutter.

I blinked, some of my sleep escaping me with that single question.

"My mother," I lied. I didn't know what to do with the knowledge I'd uncovered in my dream tonight, but I wouldn't decide right now. "What did you dream of?"

"My mother," he answered, but his tone invited no extra questions. "*Shy'rissa.*"

I'm not the only one who hides things, I thought, closing my eyes.

CHAPTER 27
KLARA

"You want us to…what?" I asked, gulping.

Kan, another acolyte, snickered until Kyavor shot him a stern look.

"You heard me right, Acolyte," he said. "You first."

In the middle of the river, jutting out over the edge of the waterfall, was a narrow plank attached to what appeared to be a practice mount. The body of which had the wide curvature of an Elthika's back, a harness slung over.

What filled me with trepidation was that the metal plank was attached to a mechanism, of which Kyavor would be handling. He'd demonstrated it, flipping switches and pressing smooth buttons, cranking a handle on the side all the while. It caused the Elthika's mount to turn and sway, as if it were in flight.

While I'd been on Zaridan's back for more hours than I could count, Sarkin had always been there. All I'd had to do was hang on for dear life, his strong thighs encasing me, making me feel safe and secure in the air with him.

During this training exercise, I would be alone and dangling over the edge of the waterfall that, after navigating the staircase down its length last night, I knew was a steep drop.

"There's a net below, Acolyte," Kyavor said, as if reading my mind. "You don't need to fear falling. In fact, you will fall. Most do. Falling is a skill in itself that you will also need to master."

I was stiff with fear at *those* words. My nerves were even shakier given the crowd that this particular exercise drew.

Out in the river, when we'd been practicing our mounts, jumping from the small ledge, there had been a few horde members who would watch from the river's edge. Hatchery workers would eat their lunch and watch us too from their fenced-in enclosure.

But today? Nearly half the horde was gathered along the riverbank. Groups had spread out blankets, lounging in the sun because it was a nice, balmy morning. Some had even brought snacks, nibbling on bread and what I thought might be aged cheese.

And when I saw Sarkin strolling up with Feranos?

On Kakkari, I wanted the river to swallow me up.

"And I have to go first?" I asked, lowering my voice so only Kyavor would hear.

His brow raised. Briefly, his eyes flickered past me, no doubt spotting my husband among the crowd. His gaze returned to mine, and there was no mercy there.

"Yes," he answered simply. "You are the *Sorrina* to your people, are you not? Lead by example."

He had it out for me. Or maybe Sarkin had told him to go extra hard on me because I was severely at a disadvantage of my younger-but-more-experienced peers. With the exception of two younger riders—both blood borns who had been in instruction since they'd been twelve—nearly the entirety of my class would be entering the *illa'rosh*. Which meant competition would be steep.

I waded through the river, my boots soaking through, navigating to the metal plank, bracing myself when I turned my back to the river current. The plank was thick and sturdy but barely wider than my booted foot.

Briefly, I turned my head to regard Sarkin. He was standing along the riverbank, his arms crossed over his chest, Feranos at his side. I saw Levanth too, though she was speaking with Ryena.

This exercise would be child's play to a rider like her, a little voice in my head reminded me.

Sarkin reclaimed my gaze. I swore I could still feel the strength of his grip on my hips from last night. My breathing went even more shallow, thinking of his warm skin and the sweep of his tongue.

I'd fallen asleep in his arms last night, but I'd woken alone this morning. This was the first time I was seeing him since our lovemaking, and I found myself looking to him for comfort. For assurance?

He inclined his head at me, those dark eyes intense and watchful, and I took a deep breath.

"Everyone falls their first time," Kyavor's voice came, loudly. "That should make you feel better, Acolyte."

"It doesn't," I grumbled under my breath, inhaling deeply as I placed my slippery foot on the metal plank.

As I steadied myself, I looked out over the view from the top of the river. I could see endless forests, valleys, and majestic mountains. The sun was casting everything golden, highlighting every inch of beauty of the Arsadia. I thought of the quiet but dark archives, the whisper of paper and the murmuring of hushed voices. I wondered where I would rather be at this moment.

And with the memory of Sarkin's kiss and the knowledge that he thought I was beautiful…I thought that I wouldn't trade this view for anything.

Even if fear made me tremble.

I balanced myself, holding my arms out parallel, as I stepped fully out on the beam. Belatedly, I realized that most riders would have done a running jump mount, but it was too late for that.

Navigating the beam was easier than expected, and I was relieved when I dropped onto the harness, assuming the rider position—back straight but bent low over the Elthika's body, thighs tight and braced, and with a steady grip on both tethers. Riders could either use the tether or just keep their hands on the bar that ran across the harness. Sarkin had always used the tethers for Zaridan, however, and so I didn't think twice about reaching for them. Everything was wet from the spray of the waterfalls. Perhaps on purpose, to prepare for any situation on Elthika-back.

It was my mistake to look down. I went a little dizzy when I saw the drop and the rushing violence of the waterfall.

"Ready?" Kyavor called out.

I heard my own gulp over the noise, my hands tightening on the leather straps.

I can do this, I thought. *I have to.*

Kyavor's system of levers and pulls was a surprisingly intricate mechanism. The mount jolted into motion, the force and strength of which surprised me. My first thought was it *did* actually feel like riding Zaridan, but then panic set in when my grip began to slip.

My eyes flicked down the drop of the waterfall, my heart beginning to pound so fast and hard that it felt like a punch in my chest.

Stop, I wanted to cry out. Tears pricked the inner corners of my eyes, and it took everything in me not to plead to Kyavor. It would embarrass Sarkin. It would make me look weak in front of his entire horde…because word would spread like wildfire through Rysar.

My thighs slid, and I let out a little cry before I could stop myself, my hands scrambling to hold on to the tethers tighter and tighter. They were slippery in my grip. I released them, instead using the bar in one last attempt to hold on.

Kyavor was merciless with his machine. It was what I imagined trying to ride on the back of a wild *wrissan* felt like. He was *trying* to make me fall.

When my thighs slid off the harness when Kyavor tilted the body of the Elthika model, there was no stopping the fall. There was a part of me that *wanted* to fall, if only to end this. This fear, this panic. When my hands let go, I didn't know if it was willing or not.

I heard the collective gasp from the horde when I tumbled off the side. My gut dropped, an unpleasant fluttering beginning in my throat as my scream escaped me. I was freefalling, my thoughts wild, hands flailing out to try to grip something, to try to catch my fall. It reminded me of Sarroth, of tumbling off the side of the cliff. If Sarkin hadn't been there, if he hadn't caught me in time, I would be dead.

My eyes squeezed shut, willing the world to stop.

Please, please, please, I prayed. To Kakkari? I didn't know. To anyone—god, goddess, or Elthika—who would listen, more likely.

The net knocked the wind right of me. I lay there in disbelief, tears dripping out of the corners of my eyes, mingling with the mist of the falls as I stared up at the sky. Gasping. Trying to breathe. Trying to understand that I was *alive*.

My hands curled into the weave of the rope net beneath me, using it to stabilize me. The rough scratch of it felt comforting. I was halfway down the cliffside, and when I caught my breath, I crawled off the net, keeping my eyes up and not on the drop below me. I made it to the staircase that led back up to the landing on shaking legs.

Reality hit me. I'd maybe lasted a few seconds on the mount, though it had seemed a hundred times longer. Above me, I watched as Vyaria did a leaping mount onto the Elthika model, and mortification burned. I pressed my back into the cliff wall, watching as my partner easily maneuvered through the exercise, no matter what Kyavor threw at her. Her position was unmovable. I didn't see her slip once.

I heard footsteps on the stone steps. When I turned my head and saw Sarkin, I bit my lip, tilting my head back.

"Don't lie to me…how bad was it?" I asked, eyeing Vyaria.

"I told you before—your fear of falling will only hinder you. You must overcome it," Sarkin replied, making me blow out a breath.

"I can't go back up there," I breathed. "All those people watching…"

Sarkin came down the final few steps. I felt his hand come to my cheek, tilting my face up toward him. He was warm and solid. I wanted to reach out a hand to press against his chest, to feel his sturdy and stable heart, to let it ground me. But I didn't know if it would be welcome. So much was still uncertain between us, though last night had been a step forward.

"Is that a factor? The horde watching?" he asked.

"It doesn't help," I admitted, catching his eyes. Above us, Vyaria was still on the mount. *Clang, clang, clang,* the machinery went, bumping above the strong metal stabilizing plank. "I know I'll be watched more than others. And I don't like…I don't like being *bad* at anything. I don't like other people to see me fail."

"That is all riding is in the beginning," Sarkin told me. His eyes were beautiful in the shadowy light of the cliff. The mist from the waterfall danced between us, sparkling in the sunlight. "Everyone expects you to fail…until you don't anymore."

"I felt like I was watched in Dothik all the time," I admitted. "The bastard child of the king. Everyone was waiting for me to slip up. I've heard all sorts of things said about me, my mother. Horrible things. Here…the Sarrothian expect greatness because I'm now your wife. I hate…I hate being laughed at."

"No one is laughing at you," Sarkin said immediately, his tone inviting no rebuttal. "That's all in your head."

They were sweet words, meant only to comfort me, but I

knew the truth. If I couldn't master riding an Elthika, I would never be one of them.

"Come," Sarkin said, his grip trailing my face to take my hand. "You don't want an audience? We will train in private."

My brow furrowed. "What?"

"This exercise," Sarkin said, waving his hand above us, "is only that. It will help you prepare for the real thing, but it can never be a replacement for it."

There was resignation in his voice, which confused me.

"Where are we going?" I asked.

Sarkin led me up the stairs, and I braced myself for the eyes of his horde.

"To the Tharken cliffs," he answered.

My breath hitched. "But that's…"

"Yes," he answered. "I'll give you the real thing."

CHAPTER 28
SARKIN

We reached the Tharken cliffs by the afternoon, just as the bright sunlight crested over the tall peaks, and we could see the stretch of ocean that extended out toward where Elysom lay.

"It's beautiful," Klara breathed when we hovered in midair on Zaridan's back. I'd wanted her to see this. I found myself wanting to show her all the beautiful places of the Arsadia…even though *this* place also brought many memories with it, tethered tight to me like cuffs.

It was colder here, and even with the sun, there was still a gentle fog bank rolling in from the coast. Cloud cover weaved in and out of the peaks of the mountainous cliffs, reappearing and disappearing at regular intervals.

She might hate me by the end of this training session, I thought, gritting my teeth, my arms wrapping tighter around her.

I was hesitant to do this to her, but I knew it was necessary. Breaking one's fear was pertinent to success as a rider. Panic got you killed. Fear paralyzed you. Some might not've agreed with these methods, but I needed her to understand that there was truly *nothing* to fear. Not when I was here. Not when I was around. She was my wife. I would always protect her.

Even if I had be cruel first.

I urged Zaridan forward, weaving into the pass of the Tharken cliffs so that the tall mountains jutted on both sides of us. Like they were closing in around us.

"These cliffs will be covered with Elthika in a few weeks' time," I murmured into her ear.

"Is this where you saw Zaridan for the first time?" she asked.

"Yes," I said, sweeping my hand in front of her vision. "Just beyond this cliff here."

And where my friend fell to his death, I thought.

In the rush of adrenaline after claiming Zaridan, I'd flown too high with her during our first flight. When Lygath had thrown Haden off his back, I would've never been able to reach him in time, even with a death dive. If I'd stayed closer to the base of the cliffs, if I hadn't been so elated with my claim, Haden would still be alive.

During Klara's choosing ceremony, I would be at the very bottom, tracking her movements closely. Nothing would distract me. She had nothing to fear because…I'd learned from that tragic mistake. I would never make it again.

When I tugged on Zaridan's tethers, she stilled in midair again, her wings flapping rhythmically, keeping us hovering high above the pass below. Wisps of gray clouds floated around us, and Klara shuddered. Our clothes had dried from the waterfall on our journey here, but it was colder closer to the coast.

"No one is watching here," I told her. It was quiet, save for Zaridan's wings. The Elthika wouldn't start migrating to this territory for another two weeks. We were alone here. "All right?"

"Except you," she answered, shifting to regard me. I supported her back as she did. Her feet dangled over the harness with her turned to the side. "I don't want you to see me fail either. Most of all, you."

"That's inevitable," I informed her, trying to keep my voice gentle. "It won't make me think less of you, if that's what you're afraid of."

"Those are pretty words," she said, a sad smile on her lips. "But I'm not sure I believe them. You would care what your horde thinks of me. I'm aware of that more than you are."

I blew out a rough breath through my nostrils, steeling my spine. We swayed with Zaridan's movements. And we were here for a purpose, even if Klara might not understand it yet.

"When you fall, you want to give your Elthika time to catch you," I told her. "It's important to keep a steady mind and to think through it logically. Position yourself parallel with the earth, spread your arms and legs out wide to reduce your acceleration. Anything to give you drag. To give your Elthika time."

"Have you ever fallen?" she asked, trepidation rising in her voice.

"Many times," I said. "You can be unseated in countless situations. Last time I fell, we were flying home from the Arsadia two seasons ago. We encountered a storm just before we reached the mainland. Zaridan dodged a bolt of lightning, just like what happened to us returning from Dakkar, but I wasn't prepared. It was a sharp turn, I'd loosened my grip on the tethers…"

Her breathing went shallow.

"Falling is a normal part of being a rider. That's why you need to get used to it, Klara. Because the fear of it will get you killed if you panic," I said.

She looked focused at those words, like she was committing them to memory. It was how I'd picture her in her precious archives in Dothik, her expression determined.

I dragged in a deep breath.

"Remember what I told you before…I'm not your husband right now. I'm not your king. I'm not your friend. I'm your instructor. Whatever I do to you, I would do to any acolyte under my training. Do you understand?"

Her brows furrowed, a frown turning down her mouth. "Sarkin—"

"And falling can happen so quickly that you never see it coming," I said, gritting my teeth.

I grabbed Klara's waist—

And I flung her off Zaridan's back.

Her resounding scream of surprise and fear made everything in me rebel. I growled, restless. My first impulse was to immediately dive for her, just as I'd done in Sarroth that night. I felt wild panic *burning* in my chest. Not because I thought she was in danger. But because the last thing I wanted to do was make her feel so much terror.

Yet it was inevitable.

"Come on, *aralye*," I pleaded softly, watching her grow smaller and smaller below us. "Do what I told you to do. Focus!"

Zaridan's wings were flapping quicker, and she maneuvered her body so that the angle would be easier for a death dive. I'd done this exercise myself in the year after I'd become a *Karath*, in the year after Haden's death. I'd jumped off the back of Zaridan more times than I could count. She'd caught me every single time. I trusted her with my life. I trusted her with Klara's life. I would never have put her in danger if I had any doubt.

The Tharken cliffs were steep. We were high up in the clouds, but nonetheless, Zaridan began to circle downward, tracking Klara's fall.

And when I finally saw her limbs spread wide, when I finally saw her stop tumbling and somersaulting wildly in the air and she moved her body into a parallel position, I commanded to Zaridan, "*Sethra!*"

I pressed my body low against her back, locking my boots into place in the footholds, wrapping my fists twice around the tethers. The descent as Zaridan accelerated created that familiar fluttering sensation in my belly. I grunted against the force, tightening my leg muscles, shoving my inner thighs to the harness. The strength of the force was nearly enough to unseat me.

Closer and closer we got to Klara. Her speed had slowed now that she had control over her body, making it easier for Zaridan to come underneath her at a slight angle, matching her pace so the landing wouldn't be so rough.

When I caught Klara, all the air whooshed out from her lungs and she dragged in deep breaths, gasping. Zaridan immediately slowed, leveling out. By the time Klara was no longer struggling to breathe, Zaridan was hovering again, the wind quieting all around us. I could even hear the crash of waves along the cliffs of the coast, though they were miles and miles away.

"Klara—"

She was huddled against me in my lap, her legs dangling over Zaridan's side, but at the sound of her name, her head snapped up. Hot anger was written over her face, an expression I'd never seen before, even though tears were glassy in her eyes.

"*Are you fucking crazy?*" she yelled, pushing at my shoulder. "You could have killed me, you bastard!"

My shoulders lowered, a small breath escaping me in relief. I would take her passionate anger over cold and careful rage.

"And yet you're still alive," I answered, keeping my voice calm as my hand trailed to the small of her back.

"Don't you dare touch me!" she seethed, trying to shake me off even though we were on the back of Zaridan and she truly had nowhere else to go. "How could you do that to me? It was cruel!"

"Cruel, perhaps," I said, setting my jaw. "But necessary. You think I enjoyed doing that?"

She shook her head, words escaping her. Her hands came up to her hair, smoothing it down as her shoulders heaved and trembled. Her gray eyes darted around the Tharken cliffs. Her scar appeared even darker because her face was so pale.

"Klara," I growled. "Look at me."

Even though she was furious with me, she turned her head to meet my eyes.

"I will not have mercy on you because an unbonded Elthika will not during the choosing," I said, a fire sparking between us. "You need to be prepared for *anything*. You might think this was cruel. But believe it or not, I did this because I care about you."

Her chest was heaving as she glared, but I thought I spied a thread of understanding weave through her expression.

"And you can hate for me this," I added. "It was always a possibility that you might. But I will take that if it means that you know how to navigate a fall, that you have faith that you can be in control in a situation like that, should it arise. And it *will*. Yes?"

I tapped on Zaridan's wing twice, and she began to rise in the air. Bringing us back up to the top of the cliffs.

"What is there to fear, Klara?" I asked her, cupping her face in my palms. She breathed in deeply. "I will *always* catch you. So there is nothing to fear. I'm trying to make you understand that."

"And what happens if you're not there?" she asked through gritted teeth, blinking back her tears with a small glare. That expression made me want to kiss it off her.

"That is what we're doing here. To prepare you in case I'm not. But I can promise you, on Zaridan, on Muron, that until you have claimed an Elthika of your own, you will *never* be in danger if you fall. I did this exercise more times than I can count. Zaridan knows these cliffs like they are a part of her. She will never let you fall because I would never allow it. Do you understand?"

A rattled breath escaped her. She was still shaken.

"Because after this, *aralye*, that exercise that Kyavor had you do this morning, that seems like nothing, doesn't it?"

A sobbing laugh of disbelief escaped her. She turned her face out of my hands. We'd reached the tops of the cliffs again.

"Just because I laughed does *not* mean I've forgiven you," she felt the need to inform me.

I straightened. "I understand."

My hands lowered away from her. And I settled back into the role of her instructor, knowing that it would serve her best if I kept my emotions out of this. If I kept myself as cold and detached as I possibly could, even though she was my wife.

"Again," I ordered quietly.

She jerked, staring at me.

"What?" she breathed, already shaking her head.

"Again, Klara."

She stared at me, her shoulders lowering and rising more quickly, familiar fear entering her gaze. I wouldn't be satisfied until she no longer hesitated. She could be afraid—all riders held fear close—but I wouldn't be satisfied until she had control over that fear. I knew it would be an impossibility for today, but it was a start.

"Fall. Trust in Zaridan. Trust in *me*."

CHAPTER 29
KLARA

The sun was lowering in the sky, and I felt like I was out of my own skin. Like it was just something that had kept me contained my whole life.

My hair was wild. My skin sensitive and stinging. There was a ball of determination nestled deep in my belly. And I felt like I wasn't myself. I felt like this *other* thing. This wild being who threw herself off the backs of dragons, who'd looked at death as it had risen up to approach her.

My bones and joints were aching from the impact of Zaridan's catches. A permanent fluttering had taken root in my stomach, the force of the fall, and I wondered if it would ever go away.

There was another aching, wild thing in me though. An intertwining of frustration, anger, want, and gratitude. It mingled with the adrenaline, and I found that every time Sarkin caught me after another fall, it grew and grew.

His touch set me on fire. My body felt like it was a string, tightening and tightening, and I wondered what would happen when that string finally snapped.

I didn't know if Sarkin felt it too. The adrenaline. The building and mounting sensation of fierce need. I wouldn't have believed it, but in the last two falls I'd taken...I'd felt the fluttering in my belly move between my thighs.

When Sarkin caught me that final time, I knew I'd had enough. I'd willingly jumped off Zaridan over a dozen times that afternoon. I had been dismantled and then rebuilt with every last one until I was someone I didn't quite recognize anymore.

Sarkin's hands on me were as familiar as the sturdy, unyielding harness between my thighs and the sound of Zaridan's great wings.

That string of tension finally snapped when Sarkin murmured into my ear, "Good?"

A breath, or a gasp or a sob perhaps, escaped me, and I turned in his arms, swiveling in the leather mount.

My kiss was a desperate, aching, wild little monster. The thought of it—of him, his lips, his touch, his taste—had consumed me. *He* was a monster, one who cared about me, one who had pushed me off Zaridan's back to free me.

His kiss was immediate, his grip tightening on my waist. I was tugging at his clothes, fumbling with the clasps near the hem of his pants.

"Get them off," I pleaded, my voice husky and raw from the wind. I needed to feel his skin against mine. I needed to be grounded to something, or else I feared I would fall into nothingness. "*Kakkari*, please!"

Sarkin's growl was both a warning and a demand. He leaned over and thumped his fist along Zaridan's side three times. She veered, aiming for the nearest flattened ledge along the cliffside.

I moved my mouth, biting at Sarkin's neck, making him hiss, followed by a groan that had me squeezing my legs around the harness all the more forcefully. I couldn't find the relief I needed though. If I didn't have it soon, I was almost afraid of what would happen.

As sunset painted beautiful pastel colors over the Tharken cliffs and I heard the crash of waves from a faraway ocean, I felt a maelstrom of fierce need storming through every vein, rushing with every throb of my heart.

Sarkin timed our jump onto the ledge perfectly, and Zaridan left us, flying freely through the pass and disappearing from view. The stone was solid beneath my feet as Sarkin tore at my clothes. It was like a race to get us both undressed as quickly as possible. When we were naked, I crashed into him, crying out in relief at the warm stretch of his body against me, all solid muscles and tantalizing, arousing strength.

His mouth was hot like a brand on my neck, marking me with his teeth and tongue. My hands dove into his hair, keeping him there. He kissed and nibbled downward, seeking, before sucking my nipple between his lips. My moan echoed through Tharken.

"Need you now," I pleaded. I didn't want to be teased or kissed or petted. I needed him inside my body. I needed to feel the stinging stretch of him, the thickness of his cock keeping me rooted to the earth. "Sarkin, *hanniva!*"

"Take me in your hand," he growled. My fingers curled, my grip tight, and his hips bucked forward when I slid my hand down. "*Fuck, aralye.* I never thought…"

"Thought what?" I breathed, my eyes going half-lidded at the feel of him in my palm.

"Never thought it would be like this with you," he admitted, his brow furrowing in an almost angry expression. But I knew better now. "I thought Lishara's blessing was behind us."

I thought I understood what he was saying.

"This need feels almost worse," I confessed, running my fist down his cock again, my thumb swiping over the sensitive head, smearing his pre-come, making him grit his teeth. "How do you want me?"

He laughed, but it was low and humorless. "I want you in every way, Klara."

A shiver dragged its way up my spine like a slow touch.

"I'm afraid it will never be enough," he growled, glaring. As if it was my fault alone.

I kissed him again, and his tongue swept into my mouth. It felt like he was devouring me. Tingles started all over my body until I was trembling. The adrenaline was still pumping through me, still making me feel like I was flying.

"We're talking entirely too much," I said against his lips, the raspiness and urgency in my tone sounding like a little growl of my own.

He groaned, his hands threading through my hair. He pulled me back with a fist in my hair, my throat exposed to him, as our eyes connected. My breathing went shallow.

"Do that again—give me your little growl. Tell me what you want, princess, and I'll give you whatever you need."

"Make love to me, Sarkin," I pleaded.

His expression flickered. I saw his molten determination bloom, his hot, burning eyes roving down my body, as if he was envisioning everything he *would* do to me.

"Beg me with your little Dakkari word," he commanded, his thumb dipping between my legs, gentle and teasing over my sensitive clit. My thighs trembled.

"*Hanniva,*" I said. His eyes closed, and in my grip, I felt his cock pulse and harden even further, if that was even possible. "*Hanniva!*"

He pushed me up against the cliffside, my back against surprisingly smooth stone. The expanse of the Tharken cliffs was before us, a breathtaking view in itself, but all I had eyes for was my husband.

He moved me bodily, hitching me up as my legs wrapped around his hips. Reminiscent of our first time in Lishara's temple, only instead of a heartstone pillar, my back was against the cliffs.

We both groaned in satisfaction and relief when he slid deep inside without warning. I was open to him like this. I took him easily, with no resistance, my body wanting, *needing*. A desperate little thing, and it was hungry.

Our lovemaking was quick. Like falling off Zaridan, this moment felt like I was out of my body. I felt only sensations. I felt the drag of my hand across his shoulders. The tightness between my thighs, the pleasure rising with every bump of his *dakke* against my clit, rubbing against me with perfect friction and pressure.

I felt his lips at my neck. I felt his hot breath explode against my skin with every powerful thrust. I felt my legs tighten in time with the muscles flexing in his backside. My heartbeat was so loud it sounded like the great rush of Zaridan's wings.

When my orgasm hit, it blinded me. The whole world burst into starlight. My scream echoed throughout Tharken long after I'd unleashed it. Relief and ecstasy came. I wasn't aware that I was crying until after the most powerful wave of it was over. When I opened my eyes, they were blurry with unushered tears. Belatedly, I realized that Sarkin was groaning, his thrusts jerky and slowing as he gave me the last of his strength, as the lashes of his come filled me.

When it was over, I hugged him to me as tears dripped down my face. Again I felt the rapidness of our hearts against one another. Soon, as they slowed, their beats began to match.

Sarkin maneuvered my legs to the ground.

"What are you doing?" I whispered, not trusting my voice as I watched him slide to his knees before me.

I was shy when he parted my thighs, though I was curious. His thumb traced over my sex, and I jumped, biting my lip, anticipation curling in my belly.

In disbelief, I watched him lean forward, his tongue darting out as he lapped between my thighs. My lips parted, tingles exploding across my skin, my scalp prickling. When his tongue curled around my sensitive clit, I sucked in a sharp breath. He was gentle, rubbing his soft lips against the bundle of nerves, and

I started to pant. He was holding my gaze, those molten, multi-colored eyes watching every expression that flickered over my face.

He *liked* to see what he did to me.

My eyes closed as I felt desire bloom deep. This time it felt different. It felt slow, but it felt endless. It wasn't rushed or desperate. He licked and kissed between my thighs, lapping at our combined mess, the mess we'd made together, and he didn't seem to care at all how perfectly wicked that felt.

"Sarkin," I breathed, wanting him again, not thinking it was possible so soon. We'd barely caught our breath.

He rose and captured my lips. I sucked at his tongue, tasting what he had. My fingers dug into his shoulders, and his hands came up to my breasts, pinching at my nipples, making me arch into him.

"Again?" I gasped.

"Again," he growled. "We'll make camp here tonight. I'm nowhere near done with you yet, wife."

CHAPTER 30
KLARA

I'd only ever read about what it felt like to fall in love.

But as I sat between Sarkin's legs, looking out over the quiet darkness of the Tharken cliffs, with bright stars and a silver moon creating a kaleidoscope of beauty overhead, I wondered if this was what it felt like.

I was exhausted. The wild swings in my emotions that day were so vast that I wasn't even sure *I* believed them. All I knew right then was that we had a fire going, my belly was full and fed, we had a warm fur blanket draped over us, and Sarkin's arms were around me.

"Do you hate me for what I did today?" came his quiet question, his lips pressing against my shoulder.

We'd barely spoken in the aftermath of our lovemaking. We'd been ravenous for each other, to the point of obsession. Even after the moon had begun to rise, we'd still been going. Only after I'd begged for a reprieve, sore between my thighs, my eyelids drooping and my stomach rumbling with hunger, had Sarkin relented. He'd called for Zaridan with the black band on his wrist and retrieved his leather satchel. Supplies for our night, including a leather band that he would use to tie our ankles together before we slept.

"No," I answered, though I *did* take time to think about it carefully. He'd created a terror in me I wasn't sure I'd ever be able to forget. But he'd also given me a great gift. A gift of freedom.

He'd taught me what it felt like to defy death. He'd untied every last thread I had knotted inside me. He'd made me new.

I felt...*powerful.*

Was this what he felt like, bonded to an Elthika? This knowing, this sense of invincibility?

"You were worried about that?" I asked, turning my head to look at him.

"Don't misunderstand me," he told me carefully, reaching up to trace the curve of my face, his fingers running over my scar. "I will never regret what I did to you today. It *was* necessary. But I never wanted to hurt you."

My entire body hurt, but somehow I felt weightless.

"I meant what I said. When I first saw you in Dothik...I never imagined that it would be like this," he admitted.

Together? Was that what he meant? Us, naked, on the edge of a cliff?

"You knew who I was," I murmured, "when you saw me in the market."

"I had scouts on you, yes," he told me. "But I only knew you were part of the royal family, one of the *Dothikkar's* daughters."

"Was it always your intention to marry one of us?"

My gut churned, thinking that he could have easily demanded Alanis. Or Lakkis, the beauty of the family. I would have never known him like this.

If not for the scar that Zaridan had marked me with.

A sharp breath left him. His eyes darted back and forth between mine before dropping to my lips briefly.

"No," he answered. "I never had any intention of taking a Dakkari wife. You were a surprise. One I didn't foresee."

I turned more fully in his arms so we faced one another, placing my legs underneath his drawn-up knees.

"You mentioned that…Elysom gave you something called *mysar* commands. That marrying was part of them."

Sarkin's gaze flickered. "Are you asking me something specific? Or making a general observation?"

I thought he well knew what my question was, but I could actually *feel* a barrier being placed between us. I was desperate to stop it. I didn't think I could stand his retreat after today of all days.

"You are very rarely open with me," I said quietly, uncertain how he would take the words. His brows lowered, and I felt the way his muscles tensed, like he was on the verge of retreating. I gripped his wrist before he could move away, feeling his heat. "Is it so bad that I want to know you? That I want to learn about you? But this wall you keep up…it makes it nearly impossible."

Sarkin's shoulders lowered. He looked away from me, his jaw pulsing, his eyes scanning the darkness of the Tharken Pass below us.

"It's self-preservation, *aralye*," he told me. "And it is habit and has very little to do with you."

"But I'm your *wife*, Sarkin," I argued. "This, between us, is still so new…but I bonded myself to you. Doesn't that mean something?"

"And who is your loyalty to?" he asked.

"This again," I breathed, shaking my head. "We talked about this."

"If given the choice, would you not return to Dakkar? At this very moment? Leave all this behind?"

"Of course not!" I cried out, staring straight into his eyes. "And if you don't believe me, that's more of a testament to your loyalty than mine."

His expression shifted darkly with the words.

"How can we ever build anything if you believe I'm always

looking for a way back home?" I asked. "I don't know what else I can do or say to make you believe me."

But I am keeping something from him, I couldn't help but remember. And if I told him, would it only create more of a divide?

"Maybe I'll stop thinking that when you stop thinking of Dakkar as 'home,'" he said.

A sharp breath escaped me.

I didn't see a choice. If I kept it to myself, he would only have more reason to mistrust me.

I bit my lip. But then I gathered my courage.

"I had a dream last night. I lied to you. I didn't dream of my mother," I said.

His eyes sharpened on me. "What, then?"

I dragged in a sharp breath. But I figured this was the perfect place to tell him, away from the horde, trapped on a ledge, so we could actually *talk* about this without disruption.

"The heartstones," I said, meeting his eyes. "I know where they are."

His body went still. I didn't even think he breathed.

"Where?" he asked sharply.

"Back…in Dakkar," I said. I'd almost said *home.*

He dragged in a full breath, his shoulders rising. "*What?*"

"If my dream was true…but I believe it was," I added. "They are in Dakkar."

"Tell me," he said. "Everything."

The bitter thought in my head was, *But you never tell me anything.*

Still, I relented. I told him about the dream, about what I'd seen, the *thalara* tree in the middle of a forest near the Dead Lands.

"These heartstones were different," I finished. "They seemed *dulled.* Like the one in King Arik's sword. They're losing power."

"The tree is dying," Sarkin said, raking his gaze over my face. "The heartstones will die with it if we don't reach them in time."

"I figured as much."

"Why are you so certain that your vision is true? Have they ever been wrong?" Sarkin asked.

"Yes," I said, eyeing him. "Sometimes they're just dreams. The difficulty is dissecting which parts are true because sometimes my dreams and my visions can meld together. I know this one is true because…there have been stories circulating in my family's line for centuries. Ever since Vienne. Stories about a bleeding, whispering tree that gifted her a heartstone when she needed it most."

I took in a deep breath, wondering if he would be angry.

"Its location had been long forgotten, or perhaps purposefully kept secret, but the stories have always persisted. My own mother told me them, who heard them from her mother. She said it was an ancient family secret, that only those in the Rath Drokka line would know the truth of how Vienne found the heartstone that night."

"Why did you lie to me?" he asked next, after a brief lapse in silence.

"I don't know," I said quickly.

"That's not true. Tell me, Klara."

I took his hand in mine. His expression was intense, but he was *willing* to listen to me. "I feared what it might mean."

"And what is that? War?"

I inhaled deeply. "My own mother died—was murdered—trying to create these *rocks*. Seeds. Whatever you want to call them. I've watched my father give free rein to the priestesses in our North Lands. For greed. For power. The heartstones have done great things—twice that we know of, they've saved my people. But they've also created terrible things…and I know the Karag want them desperately. With the Elthika at your side, with the *ethrall*, I wasn't…I wasn't certain."

"And you think the Karag would fly to Dothik and slaughter

your entire people for the heartstones? Without a second thought?" Sarkin asked, narrowing his eyes on me.

"No! But you did unleash *ethrall* on my family to get me to do what you wanted," I argued, frowning. "Was it so inconceivable for me to have the passing thought that you might do it again, especially when the heartstones are involved? What you want most?"

Sarkin reared back, turning his head to the side, a scoff escaping him. I kept a solid grip on his hand, but I didn't need to fear him leaving. Instead, when he turned back to me, he pressed closer, cupping my face in his palms. He lowered his head until we were eye level.

"There is an enemy nation in the northeast of Karag. They called themselves the Hartans. A decade ago, only a year after I took over rule of my territory, Elysom called us to war. It took six months of battle until they bent a knee to us," he said. "Many died. On all three sides, since it was also a war against the Elthika. But war had been the *last* resort with the Hartans. We tried negotiations. Treaties. Trade pacts. We gave them a supply of heartstones for their own use, to progress their technologies.

"But they wanted *Elthika*. They wanted eggs, to raise them as battle-bred beasts, to control them, to use them. It's nonnegotiable for the Karag. The Elthika are not to be *owned*. The Hartans never understood that. Only after they attacked one of the outer villages in Grym, destroying a hatchery and attempting to steal the Elthika eggs there, did we declare our war against them."

I processed this information carefully and then asked, "Why not use the *ethrall* on them?"

"Because they used the heartstones we gave them to develop a new technology. It acted like a shield against the *ethrall*. We couldn't pierce it—and not all Elthika have the ability to use *ethrall*, only some of the Vyrin. Elysom's offering toward peace ended up prolonging a war that lasted months, one that could have been won in moments and saved countless lives."

"Then wouldn't you argue that the war with the Hartans taught the Karag to trust less, to not be so merciful?"

"I'm trying to make you understand that war only happens in extreme circumstances and usually on the heels of a horrendous act that cannot be forgiven," Sarkin answered, more passionate than I'd ever seen him, his cheeks flushed, a scowl on his face. "There are those in Elysom who believe that as long as the Dakkari have possession of the heartstones, there will always be a threat of war. That is why we've been watching you for the last few decades. Your people do not yet have the technologies that would be a great threat to us…but with time, you will."

"So you will take the heartstones away," I answered, his hands falling away from my face. "Now that you know where they are. You hoped they were *here*. But maybe there was a reason Zaridan marked *me*, a descendent of Rath Drokka. To lead you to the *thalara* tree, where my ancestor had once found a heartstone."

"Perhaps," Sarkin said, and I didn't know why I felt such a stunning throb of disappointment at the word. I couldn't help but rear back, but Sarkin took my hand, not allowing me to pull away. "But I like to think there was a greater reason."

A little pinprick of hope had me raising my eyes to his.

"And what is that?" I asked, my voice barely above a whisper.

He shook his head, a slight smile lifting the left side of his mouth. He wouldn't tell me. Instead, he sighed and leaned forward, brushing his lips against mine. I met his kiss hesitantly, but I met it nonetheless.

"The Karag have more honor than swooping into another territory and stealing something infinitely valuable, like common thieves," he told me when he pulled back. I felt the words across my lips as his eyes dipped to them. "I will need to take this information to Elysom. There will be negotiations. To destroy a *thalara* tree is a dire choice, but Dakkar will get their share. And yes, after my showing of the *ethrall*, your father might think twice about trying for more."

"And if he doesn't?" I couldn't help but ask. "If he argues that the tree grew in Dakkari soil, then it wouldn't belong to you and you would have no claim to it. You cannot deny that truth."

"There is the possibility, yes," Sarkin said. "Technically we have no claim to the heartstones. But we do need them. To create more. And we won't be denied them."

My belly dipped with realization. "Then it is very beneficial to you that you have a Dakkari wife, who is a daughter of the *Dothikkar*. Elysom will realize the gift you've given them even if they believe you'd first married me out of spite."

Sarkin scowled. "That's not what this is about, Klara."

"Isn't it? Will you use me in your negotiations to get what you want?"

"If I must, but no harm would *ever* come to you."

"But you would make my family believe that it might. My father might not care. But my brother would," I told him. "If you use me as leverage in your negotiations, then where is *your* loyalty to *me*, Sarkin? Or does it only matter when my allegiance is to you and only you?"

His expression was thunderous, the muscle in his jaw ticking.

"I'm not going to get into an argument with you about *hypotheticals*, Klara," he finally said. "It's pointless."

He didn't understand what I was trying to say, did he?

I shook him off. Suddenly I felt sad, a deep despair blooming in my belly. I still felt the heat of his touch on my skin, but I'd never felt colder.

We lapsed into silence. The night that had once seemed so magical and lovely now felt suffocating.

"Can we go back to the horde now?" I asked. "I don't want to stay here tonight."

I could feel Sarkin's frustration. "Klara."

"*Hanniva*," I said softly. *Please.*

Earlier I'd used that word to beg him to touch me. Now I used it to get away from him.

Sarkin's lips pressed together, but I saw his hand move. It went to the black cuff on his wrist, pressing a button on the side, one that he'd told me let out a sound we couldn't hear but Elthika could.

A moment later, I heard Zaridan's response, a muted roar, somewhere nearby, followed by the rushing sound of her great wings.

"Whatever you wish," Sarkin told me.

When he turned to pack up our supplies and put out the fire, I caught movement along the opposite cliff. My heart jolted when I saw the silvery scales flash in the light of the moon. An Elthika had been watching us.

It was him.

The one from my dreams.

I recognized him instantly, like a bolt of lightning had speared through me, sparking in my veins, making me straighten.

His great body moved gracefully as it flew in the pass, sticking close to the side of the cliffs. He was *silent*, I realized. Like a ghost. Like he had never been there at all.

With my heartbeat in my throat, I watched him disappear from view, diving deeper down in the rocky ravine until the darkness swallowed him up.

Gone. As quickly as I'd realized he was there.

When Sarkin turned, already dressed and hitching the pack up his shoulder, I thought about telling him what I'd seen.

"You should get dressed," he told me softly, handing me the clothes I'd fallen in over a dozen times. How long ago that seemed now.

With one last look down the darkened pass, I decided to hold my tongue.

Maybe I *had* seen a ghost.

CHAPTER 31
KLARA

The new bed was waiting for me when I stepped into our dwelling. There was a break in our training for the afternoon, and I wanted to escape the plethora of activity in the horde, opting instead for quiet and peace.

Gone was the simple pile of fur blankets and cushions we'd been sleeping on. Instead, there was a padded and plush cushion —the largest I'd ever seen and hand sewn with embroidered silver patterns—where Sarkin's raised bed used to be. On top were some of the softest pelts of white-and-brown furs. I sank down onto the cushion, testing its give, and spread my hand through the blankets.

It was heavenly.

Sarkin had done this for me?

I didn't want to get it dirty—I was caked in mud from the river and sweat—so I rose immediately, backing up a few paces to admire it more fully. A smile played over my lips. It was one of the nicest gifts I'd ever received, though admittedly, I hadn't received that many in my lifetime. But it was the meaning behind it that made it special.

There was a permanence about it. I'd told him that I'd like to sleep closest to the earth, to feel more grounded and rooted with our goddess, Kakkari. He hadn't complained once, though we'd been, essentially, sleeping on the floor.

Then my smile died into a sigh. I went to all the windows and opened them up, placing the sprig of a blooming vine across the high table, admiring the way it draped over the edge and the colors that the pink blossoms added. It was sunny and bright in our dwelling. I went to the ice box along the wall, pulling out an orb of fruit I'd learned was called slime fruit. The texture was more jelly than solid, but I enjoyed the subtle sweetness and the cool glide across my tongue. It was especially good spooned over Mazra's hot cakes, the grumpy cook always slightly pleased when I asked for one or two from her kitchen.

Unlike a Dakkari horde's *voliki*, Karag dwellings had small kitchens and hearths. Though there was a central cooking hub in the village and most of our meals had been brought to us, hot and delicious, I'd learned most households cooked their own food throughout the day, which accounted for the little gardens I'd seen next to many of the dwellings here. Families traded each other for meat and spices or worked for meals from the cooking hub, performing jobs and tasks around the encampment. The Sarrothian who lived here were free to hunt in the forests in the Arsadia. They hauled in their own water from the river.

It was a more independent lifestyle than the one I'd grown up in, but there was still a sense of community and belonging, which was achingly familiar. It was comforting.

I sat at the table, watching a ray of sunlight beam off the pink flower as I munched on my snack. The quiet was nice. To hear my own thoughts. To let my guard down. To not feel anyone's eyes on me.

The tension between Sarkin and myself this last week had already been tiring enough. Though, truthfully, I barely saw him, and if I did, they were only brief moments in the horde, usually around dusk, after his scouting party had returned. He'd been gone once on an overnight trip. To Elysom, I'd later learned, the Karag's capital city, situated on a small island west of here. Another trip had been made to the *Karath's* territory in the North. He'd finally located the missing horde of Elthika, but they'd taken up dangerously close to the Hartans' borders, so he'd gone on a scouting mission there.

Over the week, some of my anger had deflated. I realized that Sarkin couldn't possibly have been so calculated to take me as his wife for the purpose of using me *if* the heartstones were found in Dakkar. It was laughable…and if it were true, it meant Sarkin had visions of his own, which I highly doubted. I'd been hurt, yes. I still was. But I was determined to move on. I couldn't change that I was Dakkari. I couldn't change who my father was. Of course it would come up. Of course it would be used by the Karag as leverage. Sarkin would have little control over that, especially if it meant greatly benefitting his own people.

I just wished he could understand why it had stung. I just wanted him to acknowledge that. I just wanted him to acknowledge how hypocritical it was for him to question my loyalty when he would use me for the Karag's gain.

Yet…he hadn't. We'd been distant. He still slept beside me at night, though I'd only seen him once. He came to bed after I fell asleep and was gone before I woke. The only evidence that he'd been there at all was an obvious indentation and lingering warmth from his body in the mornings. Once, I'd woken in the middle of the night to find him sleeping, his arms wrapped around me. I'd lain awake, savoring the heat and scent of him, pressing my hand to his chest, before I'd gone back to sleep.

That had been the extent of our interactions.

There was a knock at the door. For a moment, a pulsing of hope went through, wondering if it was Sarkin, but then I realized he wouldn't have knocked on the door of his own dwelling.

I finished up the slime fruit and answered it, finding Ryena on the other side. The horde was bustling today, I'd noticed on my walk back home. I couldn't help but wonder why, but in the distance, I saw a decorative vine being hung near the flying field.

"Hi," I greeted, smiling. "Please come in."

When I stepped away from the door and let Ryena slide past, I saw her gaze go to the bed. Then she turned to me and said, "I'm just dropping this off for you. Sammenth wanted you to have some, but she's out on patrol right now with the *Karath*'s unit, much to her delight and much to my worry."

She'd grumbled that last bit, making my lips quirk, though I wondered if it was really all that dangerous, if I should perhaps be worrying *more* when Sarkin left.

"Oh," I said, tucking a strand of hair that escaped my braid behind my ear. My gaze dropped to the basket she was caring, a delightful aroma rising. "What are they?"

"The meat pies she told you about. Our father's own recipe."

"Right! The one she said might've been a Dakkari recipe."

"Precisely," Ryena said, folding back the cloth that kept them warm. "She pulled them from the hearth before she left. They're still warm. You want one now?"

"Yes, I'm starving," I told her.

She wrinkled her nose, seeing the spiky pit on the table. "Slime fruit not cutting it?"

"Not with Kyavor's training, no."

"I remember Sammenth cleaning out my ice box daily when she was in training. These will help weigh you down," she said. We both took a seat at the table. I'd left the door open, finding the breeze pleasant as it slid over the back of my neck. "How have you been?"

"Busy," I told her, taking a bite from the pie. It was really more like a ball, a flaky crust with a savory meat filling. The flavor burst over my tongue, and I nearly gasped.

"What?" she asked, smiling as she watched me.

"It tastes like home," I said quietly, feeling the sudden sting of tears rush in my eyes, and I was immediately embarrassed. Sarkin wouldn't like me calling Dakkar *home*, not to one of his horde members, and my hand dropped into my lap, gazing down at the small pie that tasted exactly like braised *wrissan*, marinated in *trilikki* pepper, that smoky spiciness blooming over my tongue. Comforting and warming.

Ryena's hand came to my forearm, and when I looked up at her, she was frowning. "What's wrong? If you need to talk, Klara, I'm here."

"No, it's...nothing."

Her sad smile was knowing. "I know what's it like. Maybe not like you do, but I watched my father get treated differently. Sammenth and I have always felt like outsiders, not so much here, but if we ever stepped beyond our village in Sarroth. It can feel overwhelming. I just want you to know you're not alone. You don't have to try to hide it."

I blew out a shaking sigh. I *was* touched by her concern and the meaning behind her words. But I didn't know how to tell her that Sarkin and I had been fighting about the relations between her people and mine, not without betraying my husband's trust or revealing my vision.

"*Kakkira vor,*" I said, giving her a small smile as I cleared my throat and blinked my tears away. *Thank you,* it meant in Dakkari. "I'm just a little homesick," I admitted. That wasn't a lie, but it wasn't quite the truth either.

She nodded her head. "I was like that when I first came to the Arsadia. I do miss Sarroth. You always miss home because that's where you have so many memories."

"Why did you decide to live here?"

"There are plenty of healers in Sarroth and the villages that dot around it. Here? Not so much. Plus, our hatchery is here. That's where my real interest lies," she told me, patting my forearm. "I miss home, but this is my home now. It's where I'm happiest, where I find the most purpose in my work. I still visit Sarroth, though I *hate* being on Elthika-back."

I took another bite of the meat pie, biting back a smile. Thinking of that day at the Tharken cliffs, of feeling powerful and terrified all at the same time.

Kyavor had been impressed with my overnight progress when we'd returned. My next turn on the practice mount *had* seemed laughably easy. Sarkin had been right about that.

"Sammenth tells me that you're turning out to be an accomplished rider. That you've even outshone some of the blood borns during training," Ryena told me. A prick of pride made my cheeks heat, but I took another bite to mask it. "Maybe Sarkin will let you join his unit."

"Oh no." I laughed. "That's the last thing I want. I'm not destined to be a rider. I only want to bond with an Elthika of my own, and then…"

I'd had the stray thought that had been growing more pressing with every day. Thinking beyond the Arsadia, thinking what would give me purpose in Karag. Ryena had said her purpose was here. I thought mine lay back in the South Lands of the Sarrothian territory.

"Then?"

"I'm thinking about archiving Dakkari history in Karak," I said. I'd told Sarkin once, but the idea had taken root and wouldn't let go.

"Oh," Ryena said, surprised.

"History interests me. Stories. It helps piece together a broader understanding of *being*. Of living. I've been thinking that when we return to Sarroth after the rider season, maybe I'll spend time at your village and the ones around it, to chronicle their stories, anything they might remember so that I can better understand my people who made Karak their home."

"That…that sounds like a wonderful idea," Ryena said, softly pensive.

"This," I said, holding up the food in my hand, "is what I want to understand."

"Meat pie?" Ryena joked.

I grinned. "Yes, I would like the recipe. Please tell your sister that. But…ultimately, what I want to understand is the melding of two races and everything that happened—the good and the bad—for that to be possible. I think that's important. If I don't, I fear those stories and those memories will be lost forever."

Just like my mother. The visions she saw of these people…I wished I'd asked her more about it. I wished I'd recorded some of our conversations. Now I only had my memory, and it was growing hazy. I hated that sometimes I couldn't remember my mother's face.

Ryena's gaze snapped to the open doorway, and I sensed his presence before I saw him.

"Oh, you're back early," I commented, eyeing Sarkin as he stepped more fully into the doorway. How much had he heard? "Ryena brought some meat pies that Sammenth made. Their father's recipe. Would you like to try one? They taste just like the skewers I used to get from the *wrissan* vendor in Dothik."

Sarkin's gaze was burning into mine, a soft understanding there, and I suddenly realized he'd likely heard all of our conversation.

"There's somewhere I'd like to take you tonight," Sarkin answered. "And yes, I would like to try one. Bring them—we'll have them for our evening meal."

"You want to leave now?" I asked, frowning, as Ryena stood, ready to excuse herself.

"No, after your instruction this afternoon. We can meet on the landing field at dusk. Dress warmly, *lysi?*"

He left, and I stared at the open doorway.

Ryena was smiling when she skirted the table. "You're going to see the starfall up close tonight," she said, her tone teasing. "How romantic."

I flushed. "The what?"

"The celebration tonight? The starfall? It's the time of year the

Elthika begin their migration to the Tharken cliffs. It marks the beginning of the end for the riding season. There will be a feast tonight to celebrate and to watch it happen."

"Then why don't we just stay with the horde?" I questioned, though it was more to myself, confusion swelling.

"Because he wants the best for his new bride," Ryena teased. "Enjoy it. It's a beautiful thing to witness."

CHAPTER 32
KLARA

We landed in a meadow after nightfall. The tall grass brushed at my ankles, and when I looked down, I thought the ground was glowing.

"What is this?" I whispered, crouching. I ran my fingers through the feathery light tendrils of midnight-blue grass and watched it light up beneath where my touch trailed.

"Starlight grass," Sarkin answered, watching as I swept my entire palm over a cluster. "It only grows here, in the Arsadia. We've tried to transplant it, but it always dies."

I looked up at Sarkin. "Because heartstone magic is still present here? Because of the temple?"

"We think so. Some believe there's hidden *thalara* trees in the Arsadia, that they still seep their power and magic into the earth, giving this place life, giving Elthika their vitality. But if there are, there are not many left."

I stood, watching the grass light up around the hem of my dress. Impractical to wear on Elthika-back, yes, but I had warm protective tights underneath, padding on the inner thighs, and the dress was loose enough to pull up toward my hips so it wouldn't be a hindrance. A soft shawl draped around my shoulders, and I held it to me tighter. I didn't know who had made my clothes, but they had been another discovery, another gift this last week. I'd pulled open the closet, intent to borrow another of Sarkin's tunic for the training session that day, and instead found the shelves brimming with soft colors and light materials. Dresses and shifts, ranging from formal to sleepwear, in addition to a healthy range of riding trews, thick-soled boots, and durable tunics sewn with Elthika scales.

I'd picked a dress I'd admired since I'd first seen it. A flowy shift dress, a deep inky blue in color, embroidered with silver thread. Simple but…romantic.

Sarkin was in his riding armor, as I liked to call it. Tailored riding trews made out of a thick but flexible soft leather, a black shirt that molded to his shoulders, and a vest of scales with silver catches. With his dark eyes and handsome features, he was every bit what I'd imagined a dragon-rider king might look like.

The basket of meat pies was hanging off my arm—cold now, but they would still be delicious—and Sarkin pulled down his travel bag from Zaridan.

Conversation between us had been nonexistent on the way here, ever since we'd left the horde just after the sun had disappeared into the horizon. The tension between us was palpable, and I felt a little silly in my dress, wondering if I'd misread the situation entirely. But why would Sarkin bring me here? Far away from the village, where there was a celebration in our absence?

The meadow was vast, giving way to rolling hills. A stone's-throw distance away, there was a glittering lake, small and still. The grass rustled around my legs as I followed Sarkin to the top of one hill, one that had a great view and vantage over the entire meadow.

"This is…" I started. *Romantic,* I wanted to say. Instead, I smiled, watching as Sarkin unrolled the blanket from the travel bag and laid it down on the hill, flattening the grass, though its light shone through the material. "This place is beautiful," I finally settled on.

There *was* a chill in the air, but my shawl kept the worst of it at bay. I didn't want to dirty the blanket with my boots, so I toed them off, feeling the grass tickle my feet.

Sarkin watched me as I stepped onto the blanket and lowered myself down, highly aware of his gaze and the fact that it had been over a week since he'd touched me, kissed me.

Since he'd knelt at my feet, my back against the cliffside, my body pulsing, and…

I blew out a shaky, nervous breath, and he came to sit beside me, our arms brushing, little sparks that nearly made me jump.

The silence stretched between us as we both looked over the meadow. The night sky above was shining, the glimmer of the moon picturesque. Everything about the Arsadia was beautiful.

I felt the earth tremble as Zaridan sat close by, her head raised to the sky as if in anticipation.

"What are we waiting for, exactly?" I asked. I thought we both heard the double edge to my question, reflected in the gleam in Sarkin's eyes.

"Every year at this time, there is a meteor event. The migration starfall. The wild Elthika will pass overhead. Right here," Sarkin informed me, gesturing toward the expanse above us. "They'll arrive at the Tharken cliffs by the morning."

A jolt of nerves went through my belly.

"It means the *illa'rosh* may happen sooner than we think," Sarkin admitted.

"Really?"

"We follow the Elthika. They tell us when it's time. They only stay at the Tharken cliffs for a couple weeks. Then they move on," he said. "You'll be ready. Don't worry. Kyavor has been keeping me updated on your progress. He's quite impressed with you."

A flush of pleasure momentarily dulled out my nerves. "I

suppose jumping off the back of Zaridan over a dozen times really puts thing into perspective."

Sarkin went quiet, and I cursed myself for bringing up that day. That night.

"When you…" I began, glancing over my shoulder at the Elthika perched to our side. "When you had your own choosing, when you saw Zaridan for the first time, how did you know?"

Sarkin brought his knees up, and he looped his arms around them as I watched the cords in his arm tighten and release.

"Among the Dakkari, there are recorded moments in your history where your own *Vorakkar*, your own horde kings, have claimed they've been led by your goddess, Kakkari. That a feeling of knowing came over them. I believe I heard it referred to as 'Kakkari's guiding light' once," he said.

"Yes, that's true," I said, knowing the exact accounts he was speaking of. "Arokan of Rath Kitala, one of the greatest horde kings of our history, specifically said he felt it when he saw his human queen, Luna, for the first time."

He inclined his head.

"Whether they felt it for their chosen wives or difficult decisions that needed to be made, it was there," he continued. "I believe that the Karag feel something similar, though we are not quite as romantic about it as your people. We believe they are deeply intuitive decisions that you feel with your own instinct. That perhaps they are even powered by heartstone energy at times, threading through the earth and into your body, magnetic or electrical impulses."

"I prefer the romantic view," I informed him.

He chuckled, low and soft. My shoulders relaxed, wishing I could bottle that richly warm laugh. "I thought you might."

"That's what you felt when you chose Zaridan?"

"Yes," he said. "I camped out on the cliffside for two nights until I saw her. I almost thought I wouldn't bond with an Elthika at all. The doubt was the worst because it made you desperate. That's what I think happened to Haden."

"I didn't ask because I wanted to talk about what happened," I told him, biting my lip, worried he might think that. I reached out to touch his arm, though my hand hovered above his skin, uncertain.

He reached out, snagging my hand immediately. He threaded our fingers together, holding tight. I looked down at the back of his hand, tracing over the scars that sliced over his flesh, and then I placed my other hand on top of his. I stroked the ridges of his knuckles and the bones of his wide hands.

"I know," he said, frowning over at me. "I didn't think that."

"What did you mean, then?" I asked. "You thought Haden was desperate?"

"Back then, Zaridan and Lygath were nearly inseparable," Sarkin told me. Out of the corner of my eye, I saw Zaridan's ear twitch at the sound of her brother's name. "You didn't see one without the other. But Zaridan and me…we chose each other that day. It felt like a bolt of lightning, like Muron's lightning, struck right through me.

"Haden watched from the cliffside as I took my first flight with her. He saw Lygath, not far away. We had already been there for a while. We were low on sleep. He saw me claim Zaridan, and he went after Lygath. I was too high up when I saw Lygath reject him. When I watched my friend fall to his death."

"I'm sorry," I whispered, my expression drawing tight.

Sarkin heard the pain in my voice, and he looked at me closely. He told me, "I've made my peace with what happened, *aralye*. Haden made his own choice. I could not have seen that outcome. I don't feel guilt anymore, but I certainly used to."

"It wasn't your fault," I argued softly. "Not at all."

"It's strange the tricks the mind can play on you" was all he told me. "But all of this to say…this time of year always bring these memories forward. This year more than ever."

Because of me was what went unspoken.

"If you don't want to do this, Klara, I would free you of this obligation," he said next. "There has never been a queen of Sarroth with no bonded Elthika, but I feel there *is* change coming for my people. Perhaps you can be the first."

He was…giving me a way *out?*

I breathed out a rough exhale. How easy it would be to tell him that I was frightened. That I was scared an Elthika might not choose me. That I would be an embarrassment to him, to the horde.

But I knew, as surely as I was afraid, that I would never be able to live with the decision to give up.

"I will go to the Tharken cliffs. I'll claim an Elthika of my own. That I promise you," I answered.

Sarkin dragged in a deep breath, making his shoulders raise. He nodded.

"There was a part of me that hoped you'd say no," he admitted. "Because at least I'd know then that you would be safe."

I jolted. But before I could say anything, I heard the distant flap of wings and a strange symphony of sound.

"They're here," Sarkin said, standing, pulling me up with him, scanning the sky. He turned and then said, "There."

He pointed in the distance, behind us. Next to the nearest mountain range, I saw a massive shadow moving toward us.

I gasped when I heard something sizzle musically in the sky and saw a bright white star shoot across the sky in a beautiful flash before disintegrating. "Was that one?"

"Yes," Sarkin replied, and I could hear the small smile in his tone. I could feel his gaze on me, watching me as I debated what to look at next—the sky for more falling stars or the horde of wild, unbonded Elthika that were coming straight toward us.

I settled on the Elthika finally.

Zaridan trilled, a sound I'd never heard from her before. It sounded like a call. It sounded delicate. She lifted her head high into the sky.

"*Thryn'ar,*" Sarkin commanded. The earth began to rumble, the familiar sensation of Zaridan pulling energy toward her, and then she launched herself off the ground to join the horde.

To join the celebration, I realized, moments later. Because that was what it was.

Hundreds of Elthika were flying together, very nearly blocking out the entire expanse of the sky as they drew closer and closer.

I watched them *dance.* They swayed and weaved in the moonlit sky, dipping and circling together, flaring their wings wide or gliding them close to their bodies.

And the music…

When I closed my eyes, I heard their song. It was like the *sy'asha,* the whispered song of their scales, only it was joined by trills and guttural bellows. The beat of their wings were like the sound of drums. They produced a symphony in the sky, echoing off the mountain ranges and funneling its way down the valley and meadows. It struck a chord within me, making tears burn in my eyes.

Before I knew it they were right overhead, the gust of their wings creating a storm of wind, whipping my hair, tangling my dress against my ankles. I tracked Zaridan, watching as she joined their dance, swooping overhead in a looping motion, making me smile. She let out a longing cry.

"She's looking for Lygath," Sarkin observed quietly, as if he didn't want to interrupt their song or the *awe* of this moment.

That breaks my heart, I couldn't help but think as I squeezed Sarkin's hand.

For long moments, we watched the hundreds of Elthika overhead, a special performance that I hoped I could see every year. We said nothing, but he kept my hand in his. Sarkin had gone out of his way to share this with me…I would never forget that.

Falling stars sizzled and glittered in the sky behind the Elthika, a magical backdrop that seemed too ethereal to be real.

When we finally sank back down onto the blankets, I was grinning, watching the Elthika continue their way due west. Toward the coast. Toward the Tharken cliffs. Zaridan was still flying with them, but I knew she would return to us before the night's end.

Sarkin was quiet, watching me, and I spied something in his expression that I'd never seen before. Something that made my skin tingle, awareness making me shiver. An expression that made my heart begin to throb in my chest, a caged little monster wanting to be free.

"Thank you for bringing me here," I said, a little breathless, feeling more of the wall between us chip away. "I'll never forget this."

The scales on Sarkin's vest rustled together when he shifted forward. He wrapped his hand into the wild tendrils of my hair. I was open to his touch, lifting my chin.

"I'm not any good at this," Sarkin's soft voice came, sounding almost amused, though I also heard a thread of frustration. "I've never needed to be. But I am trying, Klara."

"We can figure it out together," I said softly. "We have to."

"Ask me whatever you want tonight," he told me. "I'll answer your questions."

I tried to hide my surprise by curling my fingers into his wrist. "Really?"

"Yes. But I want to ask you something first."

"All right," I said, not denying I was a little nervous by the seriousness in his expression.

"Did you really believe that I would have unleashed the *ethrall* on Dothik?"

I blinked.

"You *did*," I reminded him softly, the question coming as a surprise though I answered swiftly. "Not for long, but you still did."

He grunted. "Did you think I would have let anyone die?"

"In that moment?" I said, meeting his eyes, squeezing his wrist. "Yes. I didn't know you then. I didn't know your intentions or how far you would go to claim what you wanted."

"And now?"

"No," I breathed, my brow furrowing at the restlessness I heard in his tone. "Now I know you meant the *ethrall* as a bluff. You knew exactly how long to let it linger. But even if I didn't give you what you wanted, you would have stopped it. You're a good leader to your people, Sarkin. You're honorable. You're fair. You wanted to frighten us, and you succeeded. But I know you wouldn't have hurt anyone."

He inclined his head, processing my words, and I spied relief on his features. Was this what he had been worrying about? That I thought him a murderous monster?

"I...I keep thinking about what we fought about at the Tharken cliffs," I admitted.

"Me too," he grunted.

"It was wrong of me to suggest that you would seek war with my people," I told him. "I'm sorry for that. But...they will always be *my* people, Sarkin. I will always think of Dakkar as home. It's where I was happy once, it's where I lived with my mother, it's where Dannik is. It doesn't mean I won't eventually think of Karak as my home too."

His tone was low when he admitted, "It was wrong of me to suggest that you choose."

"I've already *chosen*," I said, wanting him to understand that. "I won't ever choose to return to Dakkar. I'm *here* now. With you."

His swirled eyes—all the shades of bright golds, endless greens, and warm browns—flickered, his pupils widening. He was so beautiful that it hurt to look at him sometimes.

I pressed a kiss to his cheek to soften my next words, but they needed to be said. I wouldn't be able to forgive myself if I didn't say them. "But that doesn't mean I want to see my own people suffer. And at first, it hurt me to realize that you would use our marriage for your gain."

His sharp breath whistled, and he reared back to meet my eyes.

"Did you mean that?" I asked, swallowing the fluttering of my heart.

"You're not just a tool for me to use, Klara. You're my *wife*. And I am as bonded to you as I am to Zaridan."

"But I understand that this began as a kind of…political marriage," I said. "I'm highly aware that there is a benefit for you, taking me as your wife. Just as I'm aware that I can be an advocate for my own people, to soften your sharp edges toward them."

Sarkin tilted his head as the words bloomed between us. My hand slid down his wrist, following the ridges of his arm and up his shoulder. I stopped my exploration on his chest, feeling his breath rise and fall beneath my palm.

"Wives have swayed the minds of their husbands for centuries," I whispered. "It's an ancient understanding. I've been thinking about why I felt so hurt by our fight, and I think it's not so much the knowledge that you might use our union for political benefit but that I'd be kept out of that decision. There's nothing I hate more than being in the dark. Than being ignored or overlooked or cast aside. And I…I think…"

My cheeks went a little warm. Sarkin's voice was rumbly when he commanded, "Tell me."

"I think part of the reason why I chose to go with you was because you were the first person in a long time to actually *see me*," I confessed, my vision going a little blurry. "To look at me and see someone of value. To look at me like I was a puzzle you needed desperately to solve. I'd been numb for so long. I'd felt alone. Then you appeared out of nowhere with your dusty

Elthika-scale hands and your unrelenting *ethrall*. And it was like the flip of a page. A new chapter had begun. And suddenly I was forced to live again."

CHAPTER 33
SARKIN

"That's why I chose this," Klara said.

Again she was being vulnerable with me. Again I felt this resistance in me to give in.

"I gave you cruelty," I argued.

And you gave me beauty.

What had I really offered her?

"No," she said. "True cruelty hinges on your enjoyment of seeing someone suffer. I've witnessed that in Dothik, felt it within my own family. You would *never* want me to suffer, Sarkin. I know that."

I blew out a harsh breath, leaning my forehead against hers. "I've given you no kindness though."

"That's not true either," she said, her words brushing against my skin. "How could you think that?"

It's not enough, I thought to myself, feeling my heart thunder in my chest. I closed my eyes. This couldn't continue.

I made the decision, right then and there, to be better for her. Better for *us.*

She was soft and understanding. Forgiving.

I was cold and controlled. Unyielding.

I might not ever be the type of male she'd envisioned herself with. But I needed to try to meet her in the middle. Or else we would both be miserable. She might retreat back into herself, just like what she'd done in Dothik. I understood self-preservation better than most. I understood the toll it took.

All I knew was that it would be hell to see her like that. To see her a shell of the female before me now, with tears shimmering in her eyes and a soft, hopeful smile on her features.

Her mother raised her beautifully, came the sudden thought. But why keep that to myself?

And so I repeated the thought out loud, my voice gruff but certain, and I was rewarded with a radiant smile. I felt deep affection swell in my chest, a feeling that was becoming more and more difficult to ignore when it came to Klara. I rubbed at it, not sure I'd ever felt it so keenly, so heavily before.

"I wish I was more like her," she told me, pulling away to trail her fingers through the starlight grass at the edge of the spread blanket. We were whispering in the meadow like two young lovers who'd snuck away from a village to be together. "Growing up, my mother longed for freedom more than anything else. I've been having this overwhelming thought that she would have *loved* to fly with the Elthika. It would have suited her perfectly. She was brave and fearless. She savored moments, like she was memorizing every last detail. She was this warm, perfect beacon of wildness and joy. She had the loudest laugh in the entire horde. I remember her laugh so distinctly, even though I've begun to forget her face."

There was solemn grief mixed in with her soft smile as she spoke about her mother. I remembered my own. My mother's quietness, her distant love, her mental retreat from me. She *had* become a shell because her body had betrayed her. Perhaps she'd kept me at arm's length so that it would hurt less...when the inevitable happened.

I couldn't help but think that our mothers were opposites of one another…and they had both loved us in different ways.

"I hate most of all that she grew fearful," Klara told me. "She changed in Dothik, especially after my dreams became more and more frequent. Anything to protect me, to hide me from the priestesses' watchful eye. Their ever-watchful eye. I think I became afraid too."

Swiftly, I pulled her into my lap, catching her quick gasp, but I couldn't stomach the defeat I heard in her voice. I rolled until we were lying on the blanket, with her stretched out underneath me, her hair a wild, wind-swept halo around her head.

"Oh," she breathed, her eyes reflecting the falling stars above us as she looked at me.

I leaned down. She arched up, but I didn't capture her lips in the kiss I so desperately wanted to give her. Instead, my gentle words brushed her ear as I said, "You are beautiful…Klara Dirak'zar."

She sucked in a sharp breath, as I felt a sense of *rightness* take root within me, spreading through bone and vein. It was the first time I'd ever called her that. It was the first time I'd ever claimed her for my own line. *Our* line. The name our children would one day bear.

"Klara Dirak'zar of Rath Serok and Rath Drokka, queen of the Sarrothian. I hope you know how much of a rarity you are," I finished, pulling back so I could meet her eyes. She looked struck. Surprised. "And you were wrong on the wildlands outside Dothik that night. You *do* have a great name, and it will be remembered long after you're gone. And when you claim your Elthika, you will claim their name as well. You will be a fearsome thing."

"Thank you," she whispered. Her expression was serene. Her hands came to press into my chest, curling her fingers into the scales, and I wished it was off of me. I wished I could feel the naked press of her skin against my own. It had been too long already. "*Kakkira vor.*"

"I don't see you as a tool for me to use, Klara," I said again, risking this calm, pleasant moment to bring this thread of conversation back to the forefront. But I needed her to understand how I felt.

"Sarkin—"

"Let me say this so you never have to doubt again," I said, brushing my fingers over her scar on the side of her face. "You were marked for me. I believe in no god or goddess in this life except in my Elthika. She marked you for me. And I answered her call."

I felt her breathing quicken against my chest.

"We may never understand the Elthika. Not fully. They live on a different plane of existence from us. They draw their energy from heartstones, their power is like the sun to them. They are magical beings, gods and goddesses in their own right," I said. "And Zaridan led me to you. As a rider, you learn much from your bonded Elthika and they learn from you, more than you thought possible."

"What did she teach you?" Klara asked.

My lips quirked. "Patience and discipline. I was reckless once."

"I can't imagine that," she confessed.

I brushed my thumb over her cheekbone. "My purpose in saying this is that you were a gift to me, *aralye*. Not a weapon to use against your people. I will spend our lives learning from you, just as I have from Zaridan. My only request is that you continue to have some patience with me."

Her gaze warmed. She had that same struck expression, like she was seeing me for the first time.

Perhaps she was. For this was the first time I'd ever truly felt open with her.

"Of course," she whispered. "Of course, Sarkin."

"And I meant what I said earlier. You can ask me whatever you want, and I'll answer you."

She smiled. Leaning forward, she pressed a kiss to my lips, a chaste thing, but it made me restless for more.

"Let's just enjoy tonight," she said, her eyes trailing past me to look at the falling-star storm overhead. "Let's just enjoy each other. We have a lifetime to talk. And we have meat pies to eat."

I chuckled, though I'd be lying if I said a part of me wasn't relieved. Tonight was a first step in the right direction for us. As long as she understood I would take that journey with her, that was all that mattered.

"Sarkin."

"Hmm?" I asked.

"Kiss me," she whispered. "*Hanniva*."

My nostrils flared at that word like she had me trained. Before there was the possibility of her changing her mind, I captured her lips. I'd meant to kiss her gently, but whenever she said *please* in her language, it drove all reasonable thought out of my brain.

Her shuddered sigh drifted over my tongue, and I groaned.

"I love when you do that, *aralye*," I rasped, biting at her bottom lip. "When you breathe into me like that."

Her hands dove into my hair, our movements becoming hurried and possessive. The fire being stoked, those embers burning low. The sizzle of falling stars overhead and the distant sound of Elthika songs joined our soft moans and the rustle of our clothes. She tugged off the riding tights hidden underneath her dress as I nibbled my mark above her collarbone.

I rolled us so Klara was on top, her bare legs straddling my hips. Pushing the material of her dress up to her hips, I watched as she unclasped the catches on my pants, pulling my hardened cock free.

"Let me feel you, wife," I growled, hissing, my back bowing

when I felt her drag the head of my cock against her slick, hot entrance.

She rolled her hips down in one swift movement, and we both cried out. And as the stars fell around us, as the starlight grass glowed with the stroking fingers of an unseen wind, I watched my wife move above me. I watched the sublime pleasure cross her beautiful expression and listened to the music we made.

A song all our own.

And I thought, *How easy it would be to love her.*

Only, this time, I kept that thought to myself.

In the aftermath, long after it went quiet in the meadow, long after we'd nearly finished the meat pies in the basket, we were lying next to one another. Klara's hands were exploring me, tracing unseen things, her cheek pressed to my shoulder. I'd wrapped us up in the blanket to cover our naked flesh, shielding us from the worst of the chill. The rustle of grass around us felt calming. If I wasn't careful, it could lull me to sleep.

But we needed to get back soon. I was loath to leave this place though. There was peace here. And that peace felt like Klara in my arms, happy and sated.

We were connected here. I didn't want anything to ruin that.

Klara's fingers traced down my back, and I suppressed a pleasurable shiver. I felt them pause over the textured flesh toward the base of my spine, flesh that had never quite smoothed with time. It was where my tail had once been. For a moment, I thought perhaps she'd find it too strange, that she would pull away from me, shuddering.

Instead, her touch lingered. Why had I never realized how *sensitive* I could be there? I felt my cock begin to throb, a low growl reverberating up my throat as she stroked and explored the old wound. I couldn't help but capture her lips in a soft kiss. Her hot exhale floated across my tongue, making me crazed.

"You said I could ask you anything?" she asked against my lips.

The edges of my lips curled up in a lazy smile. I pulled away, knowing what the question would be. "Yes, *aralye*."

"Did it hurt?"

"Not so much in the moment. After…yes. Like hell. It's a phantom ache that takes years to shake. Sometimes I still feel it. Especially in the cold."

"Do you miss it?"

"No," I admitted, looking down at her in my arms. "All riders know how dangerous it can be. I was glad to be rid of it."

"That's what Sammenth said, that she would be relieved once hers was cut off," Klara said.

"I always knew mine would be gone one day," I told her. "I always knew I would be a rider. So, mentally, it was an easy transition. For others…it can surprise them, how traumatic it can feel. But it's our duty to adapt to the Elthika. Not the other way around."

She nodded against me, the fingernail of her thumb scraping over the scar, making me suck in a sharp breath.

"I'm sorry," she whispered, jerking her hand away.

"Mmm," I growled. "No, it feels good, *wife*."

"*Oh,*" she whispered, her eyelids going half-lidded at the purr in my voice. She smiled, and I didn't think she knew how seductive, how beautiful it was to me.

"Any other questions?" I teased, tracing the tip of my nose against her temple.

"Let me think," she said, her tone relaxed and languid. "Hmmm…what does Zaridan's name mean?"

I chuckled. "What made you think of *that?*"

She shrugged her shoulder, her hand returning to my back to

explore more of me, tracing over deep ridges of muscles and raised edges of scars. "You said I could ask you anything."

"That I did," I said, huffing out my lazy amusement. "Her name comes from a word that means *shadow. Zarikin.*"

"That seems fitting," she replied. "Did you name her?"

"No. She was first seen over a century ago," I told her. "I read the records in Elysom myself. A horde traveling to the Arsadia from the north. They typically pass over the Zarikin Mountains on their way here. That's where we believe she lived before I bonded with her."

"She lived there with Lygath?"

"Yes," I answered. "Or so the stories tell. The Elthika are nomadic by nature, much like your Dakkari hordes. But they do tend to return to one location more often than others, where, more times than not, they choose to nest. To hatch their young."

"But Zaridan never took a mate, right? Or had hatchlings of her own?"

"Not yet," I said. "The Vyrin are particular and stubborn, like I told you. As such, there are not many left."

She went quiet, processing the information.

"And Lygath?" she asked.

"What about him?"

"What does his name mean?"

"Ah," I murmured. "It means *ghost. Spirit. Wraithling.* If you ever saw him, you'd understand why. He's so quiet. He appears out of thin air sometimes. You never hear or see him coming unless he wants you to know."

"What?" she whispered, frowning, pressing up from my chest. Even I sensed the sudden, startling change that went through her. "Quiet, you say?"

"Yes," I said. "Why?"

"He's silver? A little smaller than Zaridan?"

I stilled. Silver-scaled Elthika were rare. "Yes."

"I—I think I may have seen him."

My heart leapt in my chest.

"*Where*, Klara?"

There hadn't been an actual sighting of him for *years*. He'd hidden from Zaridan, even.

"At the Tharken cliffs. That night, just as we were leaving. I—"

She cut herself off, looking down at her own lap, unseeing. She shook her head.

"What is it?" I asked, sitting up to cup her cheek with my palm, lifting her face so I could see her eyes. "You're sure you saw him?"

"Ever since she marked me, I've always seen Zaridan in my dreams," she told me. "But I've always seen another too. For even longer than Zaridan."

I jerked. "What?"

"I saw him in my dream when I went over the cliff that night in Sarroth. There was an Elthika flying over the heartstone forest, and I was running, trying to chase him down."

She shook her head as a knot lodged itself into my chest.

"I never imagined it was him," she confessed, looking at me. "But if that was Lygath at the Tharken cliffs, then that's the Elthika I've been dreaming of since I was a child. How can it be that I dream of both of them? Zaridan, I understand, if she was leading you to me. But Lygath?"

Karag who'd had gifts similar to Klara's had always said they'd seen their intended Elthika long before they ever claimed them.

Realization churned in me, but I didn't want it to be true.

"What does that mean?"

I couldn't lie to her. Not when we'd just begun anew.

"It means there's a very high possibility that Lygath is the Elthika you have a chance at claiming," I said. A fierceness rose in me. "But Klara, there is always a choice. Do *not* choose him. If you see him at the Tharken cliffs, choose another. Lygath might be Zaridan's brother, but he is dangerous and highly unpredictable. Most believe he cannot be claimed. Countless have tried. And like most Vyrin, he has no hesitation about killing riders if he thinks them unfit."

Her face went a little pale at the words. "You think he's meant for *me*? How is that possible?"

I shook my head. "Please, Klara. Tell me you'll be smart about your choice, that you'll keep a level head when the choosing comes. It draws near. I need to know you'll stay away from him."

If she felt the claiming bond with Lygath…I didn't know if anything I said would sway her. It was a powerful feeling and an undeniable truth.

"There has to be a reason I've dreamed of him for so long," she said softly. "Maybe this is it. Maybe Zaridan marked me not only for you but for him."

Fuck, it was entirely *likely*. The Elthika could see more than we could ever hope to see.

I closed my eyes, pressing my forehead to hers as I took a calming breath, to slow the sudden thundering in my heart. "Promise me you won't choose him."

"I can't do that," she said, honesty threading through her voice.

"Klara—"

"But I can promise I'll be smart. I'll listen to my instinct," she said, and I felt the warm press of her lips on the corner of my mouth. "Besides, if I fall, you promised you would catch me. Right?"

Suddenly the choosing loomed, distracting and menacing.

"Of course I will," I answered after a brief silence. "Of course. You never have to fear that."

I just wished I would never *need* to.

CHAPTER 34
KLARA

"Acolyte."

When I turned, running my arm over my forehead to wipe away the sweat, I saw Kyavor was looking at me as he lubricated the mechanisms on his practice mount, knee-deep in the river.

"You did well today," he said. I blinked, freezing for a brief moment, and Sammenth nudged me knowingly beside me.

"Thank you, Kyavor" was what I said in reply, inclining my head toward him.

Kyavor had put us through endless riding drills today on *his* Elthika, the blue-scaled one I'd seen the first day of training on the landing field. For the last few days, I'd been cramming in information on maneuvering the tethers—the leads—and practicing how to loop the tethers around an Elthika without a harness, which would be necessary during the choosing at the Tharken cliffs.

Wild Elthika were not trained…yet. Though there were many nonverbal cues that Sarkin used with Zaridan—like tapping her wing or thumping his fist against her flank or calling her with his cuff—those things were learned over time. Sammenth was still training with her Elthika. The horde—the warriors and scouts for

Sarroth—had to work meticulously to train their Elthika. I'd learned it took years, even with some of the Elder Elthika's guidance.

Me? I just had to get the basics down. I was no warrior, and I never would be. Just staying on the back of my Elthika was what I was most concerned with now. Well, that and actually claiming one.

Kyavor went back to working on his practice mount, which we'd done a run on before the end of the session. It was nightfall already. The torches around the villages were already lit, smoke wafting up from many of the dwellings as families cooked their meals for the evening. But training had been going on longer and longer this last week.

It had been a week since the starfall shower, since Sarkin and I had watched the Elthika migrate west. And every day since, there was a new sense of urgency in Kyavor and my peers. In *me*, most of all, because I was behind the young riders in instruction time, even with my supplemental nightly lessons with my husband.

Well, not the last two nights, I couldn't help but think. Sarkin had been away. To Elysom, he'd informed me, with a small group of his trusted riders, Feranos and Levanth included.

I knew why he'd had to go. To inform the council about the heartstones that we believed were buried in Dakkar. Decisions had to be made and quickly.

I only wished he hadn't needed to leave *now*, though I knew time wasn't on our side.

He might not return until tomorrow, but I knew that the moment he did, we would be leaving for the Tharken cliffs. The entire horde was waiting for his return with bated breath, travel packs ready to go. Many would come with us to make camp, to watch the *illa'rosh* as it unfolded.

Sammenth told me other riders, from various stretches of Karak, would also be joining the choosing this year, though they were staying in their respective territory's villages in the Arsadia. There were older riders too—some my age or even older—ones who were taking another shot at the choosing. I'd learned *anyone* could try to claim an Elthika of their own if they were of age, regardless of their instruction. But without it, it was a death sentence more times than not.

None of these things had done anything to quiet the steady rise of my nerves, as each hour passed, as each sunrise came and each moonrise followed.

"Where's Ryena?" I asked Sammenth.

"Hatchery duty," she replied. "Mating season is nearly here, so they are preparing."

The two sisters had become good friends to me the last few weeks. I felt like I was making a place for myself here...despite knowing that soon it would be time to return to Sarroth. Even Vyaria—my grumpy riding partner—had laughed at one of my jokes yesterday during training. It had felt like I'd won something, hearing it. The blood born had been difficult to crack. They were a different breed of Sarrothian, apparently.

It felt *good* to walk through the village and hear my name called out in greeting. Some would press food into my hand— urging me to keep up my strength for the choosing—and others would spare a few moments to speak to me or to eagerly show me their dwelling, giving me details of how they'd decorated it while I smiled and nodded.

They were a kind people once you barreled through their tough exteriors, I was learning.

Much like Vyaria.

Much like Sarkin.

Ryena and Sammenth had been different from the beginning.

"I'll never know everything there is to know about this place," I confessed. We meandered our way down to a quiet place along the rushing river. My body was exhausted. I was dirty and hungry, and I missed my husband, whose absence I had felt especially keenly the last two nights.

We were good. *So* good. When he left, it felt like a small loss, a lost limb.

I hadn't expected to miss him so much. I was surprised to realize how much he'd taken root inside me, filling up all my lonely places. When he was gone, I felt an aching emptiness.

"You'll learn," Sammenth assured me. "You've only been in Karak for…a month? That's no time at all. I was born here, and I still don't know everything. That's the beauty of it though. The exciting part of discovery."

I grinned. "That's how I felt at the archives. Every day there was possibility to learn something new. I just think I'm frustrated because I don't have the basic understanding of your people like you do. Of the Elthika. I don't even know when mating season is for them. Or how the hatchery works. Or what's going to happen at the choosing."

Sammenth smiled. "Well, that's easy. You see an Elthika you like, and you jump on their back. Done."

"I *meant*," I said, chuckling as I shook my head, "logistics. Do they drop you off somewhere? Do you share cliffs with the other acolytes? What happens if you go after the same Elthika? What happens if the choosing continues for days? Where do you *pee*? What if you don't bring enough food? What if a storm rolls in from the coast? What if all the Elthika are gone by the time we get there?"

"All right, all right," Sammenth said, looking at me in disbelief. "I get it. You're nervous."

"I'm not even nervous about falling," I admitted softly, blowing out a soft breath as I looked out over the river. Behind us, a group of younger Sarrothian—not the acolytes—laughed and chattered as they passed by. Kyavor was still methodically greasing his contraption in the middle of the river, and I watched little waves splash into his boots, though he didn't seem to mind.

"I'm nervous about disappointing Sarkin. Kyavor. You and Ryena. The horde."

"You *can't* think like that, Klara," Sammenth urged, taking my hand and squeezing it.

She reminded me of Sora, I realized. Open and courageous and extroverted and confrontational. They both never backed down from anything. I wondered how my friend was doing in Dothik, if Dannik had given her my goodbye letter, as he'd promised.

"You need to block all that out. Block out all those other worries," Sammenth said. "Where you'll *pee*? Really? It doesn't matter! You're in the *illa'rosh*! All of your focus should be on scanning those cliffs and waiting for your opportunity. The choosing can last days. The longest one lasted nearly a week. Most are over by nightfall. What happens, happens. You've prepared yourself. You've worked hard with Kyavor. You've worked even harder with Sarkin. You'll be fine, Klara, but only if you focus."

I hadn't told her about Lygath. I'd dreamed about him almost every night this week, but I hadn't told Sarkin. He wanted me to steer clear of the Elthika I'd seen in my visions for almost a decade. But I didn't know if I could. If the bonding pull was really as strong as everyone said, would I have a choice?

Sammenth sighed and then continued, "We ride out during the dawn. We'll reach the Tharken cliffs by the late morning. You can choose where you want to be, whether that's alone or with others. My advice? Go it alone so you're less distracted. Other acolytes might try to get into your head. And choose a place high up along the cliffs."

In case I fall, I knew. I listened to her carefully, cataloguing everything I could. "All right. What else?"

Sammenth looked up at the night sky, twinkling with beautiful constellations I recognized, as if trying to remember her time at her choosing. If it were me, I wouldn't be able to forget a single detail. "Keep up your energy with regular meals, but don't eat too much. If it's a longer choosing, sleep. If you're tired, you're more likely to make a mistake. The Elthika will move around. They're just as curious about you. Though watch out for their tails if they try to show off in front of you. They'll…preen. They like to be admired. During my choosing, one nearly whacked me off the cliff by accident."

I bit back a smile. "Anything else?"

"Yeah," she said, sighing. "Don't try to be a hero and go after a Vyrin. That's how most acolytes die."

My belly dropped with her words. I nodded.

"This was helpful," I said. "Thank you."

"Oh, and if you need to pee, try to do it *over* the cliff. The ledges are already small enough."

I laughed. "Noted."

"You'll know your Elthika when you see it, Klara. Don't worry."

"Did you feel the bonding pull when you saw Orelle?"

"Oh, yes," Sammenth breathed. "Heartstone magic, I think. Whatever is left of it. It's actually *wild* thinking about it. Some scholars in Elysom dedicate their whole lives trying to understand it. Me? I don't think it should be understood."

I licked my lips. "And have there ever been reports of a bonding pull that's been rejected by an Elthika?"

Sammenth frowned. "None that I've ever heard, no."

Relief went through me, however brief it was. That was promising at the very least. I watched as Kyavor finished working on the mount, packing up his supplies, and trudging out of the river. I knew he had a dwelling close to the landing field, and he set off in that direction after a small nod at both of us.

"Well…except for a disgraced rider," Sammenth amended, shrugging her shoulder. "But that happens so rarely."

"Disgraced?" I asked, brow furrowing. "An Elthika can decide to *leave* their rider?"

"If the crime, in their eyes, is terrible enough, yes,"

Sammenth said. "Only a few in Sarroth's history have ever had that happened. The last time it happened was, you know, to the *Karath's* father."

Shock wiggled into my breast. "What?"

Sammenth blinked, frowning. "To Sarkin's father. Tyzar rejected him after he stole the Elthika eggs? Surely you…oh."

My mind spun.

"Sarkin…he never speaks of his father," I said, feeling the obvious discomfort from Sammenth. "Or his mother, for that matter."

"I'm sorry," she breathed. "Ryena will be so angry with me. I thought you knew…because well, *everyone* knows. It's followed Sarkin like a disease his entire life."

"He told me…he told me he was challenged a lot after Zaridan. Because some didn't think he was fit to be a *Karath*."

"That's part of it, yes. Especially by Elysom. His aunt is on the council. His mother was her sister."

Suddenly it felt wrong to speak of these things. Sarkin hadn't brought it up, though he'd given me an opportunity to the night of the starfall. He'd told me I could ask him anything and he'd tell me. Since then, we'd just been…happier. I hadn't wanted to shake anything loose when we were finally on steady ground.

I heard an Elthika's trilling cry into the sky, a familiar one. I turned to look over my shoulder, my heart beginning to pound.

"Zaridan," I breathed, seeing her fly toward the mountain behind the village to rest. "They must be back."

I stood, suddenly eager to see Sarkin, despite what I'd just learned.

"Ryena always scolded me for saying too much," Sammenth said, biting her lip as she looked up at me from our place along the riverbank.

"I won't say anything to her," I promised.

"I really shouldn't talk so much," she sighed. "Go. Go find your husband. I'm sure you're eager to see each other."

"I'll see you tomorrow," I promised, waving at her as I left.

I looked for Sarkin for long moments but couldn't locate him. Thinking that maybe he'd already gone back to our dwelling, I went there, seeing that Sammenth had disappeared from the riverbank. I spied her walking down the path to the hatchery, likely to see Ryena.

When I reached our home, however, it was dark. Sarkin wasn't here yet. Nevertheless, I lit the hearth and the wax candles that dotted the dwelling, golden light spreading across the furniture and dark stone walls. I was filthy from training, thinking to wash quickly before Sarkin returned. I stripped off and hopped into the heated bath, nearly groaning my relief as I sat on the ledge that ran along the edges, the water lapping at my collarbones.

As I soaked, I thought about what Sammenth had revealed about Sarkin's father. A disgraced rider? I hadn't thought such a thing was possible. I wondered why he'd stolen dragon eggs. I remembered Sarkin mentioning the Hartans, wanting the eggs before a war broke out. Had that had anything to do with it?

And what about his mother? How did she play into all this?

Only Sarkin could tell me. I only wanted *him* to tell me. But with such little time left before the choosing—the realization that we would likely leave tomorrow, which spread icy worry in my belly—I thought it could wait.

I was so lost in thought, I didn't hear when Sarkin entered our dwelling.

I heard the quiet snap of the door bolting into place, and when I looked up, I saw him watching me through the gossamer curtains that separated the bath from the rest of the dwelling.

He held his travel bag and another bag, both of which he placed on the ground.

A sizzle of anticipation went through me as he approached, toeing off his boots, slipping off his vest, his tunic following. The laces of his trews were next as I felt my nipples pebble beneath the hot water.

Then he was naked, pushing back the curtain. The golden light made him look like a statue in Dothik of a *Vorakkar* of old. Perfectly sculpted, harshly beautiful, with a merciless expression.

"Welcome home, *Karath*," I said quietly.

"What a beautiful welcome it is, *Sorrina*," he answered, stepping down into the bath to join me, those swirling eyes never once leaving mine.

I licked my lips as I watched him approach.

"Do we leave in the morning?" I couldn't help but ask.

Sarkin reached me, sinking down to take me into his arms. I pressed my face to his neck. He smelled like Zaridan. Like salty coastal air and crushed leaves. I breathed him in harder as black Elthika-scale dust floated in the water around us from his palms.

"Yes," he replied. "I made sure to fly over Tharken on our way home. The Elthika are waiting. They are ready. We will leave at dawn."

I ignored the sizzle of nerves. I would worry about it in the morning. Nothing would change now.

"Then let's enjoy tonight."

"Yes," he rasped, pulling back so he could capture my lips. His hands roamed, and I arched into his touch, a gasp driving away all thoughts of the choosing. "Let me enjoy you, my *aralye*."

CHAPTER 35
SARKIN

My fingertips trailed down Klara's spine, skimming over the swell of her cheeks, making her twitch and shiver, making me smirk.

"Sensitive?" I asked, rolling into her in our bed, tugging her into the crook of my arm. How long it had been since I was so comfortable with a lover…

I thought it a blessing that I felt this way with my wife.

"Yes," she said. Though I couldn't see it, I heard her smile.

I smelled her hair, savoring this with her before the rush of the morning began. I rubbed my lips over the delicate—and sensitive—tips of her ears. I knew she needed to sleep, but I just wanted a few more quiet moments with her. We wouldn't get any during the *illa'rosh*.

"Why had you never taken a lover in Dothik?" I asked, a question I'd been curious about ever since learning she'd been a virgin in Lishara's temple. "Surely you had males vying for your attention."

Saying the words out loud brought a discomforting feeling with it. One I thought might be *jealousy*. It was strange and foreign. It made me feel restless, and I hated the feeling. By nature, I'd never been jealous over past lovers. Some had tried to make me so, but not once had they ever succeeded.

And now I was jealous over faceless Dakkari or human males who might have tried to seduce my wife into their beds, long before I'd ever known her?

It was laughable. And irritating because I was getting jealous over a hypothetical, not a truth.

"Most men stayed away from me," she said softly. "My scar kept many away. I'd learned most people don't like to look at it, so I'd tried to hide it a lot. Keeping my face down, not making eye contact, keeping to the edges. Never bringing attention to myself."

I jolted. To the Karag, scars were *meant* to be displayed. On females, they were considered attractive, alluring.

"I liked the archives. I never needed to hide there," she told me. "Though in a way, I guess I was. There were other males, but I could always see their true intentions. They wanted to get close to me to get close to my family. Dannik usually scared them off, and I didn't care for a single one."

"You never wanted to experience sex? To know what it felt like, being with someone that intimately?"

"I did," she said, her head lolling back onto my arm so she could meet me eyes. She smiled lazily. We'd made love twice—once in the bath, once in our furs. We were both sated, sleepy. "And now I do."

I chuckled. "Is it everything you thought it might be?" I teased gently, capturing her fingers when she traced my lips. I nipped at them with my teeth.

"Oh, yes," she whispered, all seriousness even though her eyes twinkled in the golden light of our dwelling. "No complaints at all."

I grunted.

"Do you wish I was more experienced?" came her unexpected question.

"What?" I asked, frowning, rolling onto my side more so I could see her better.

"I'm not bad at sex, am I?"

I scoffed. "You can't be serious."

"I am," she said, her tone earnest. "You're my first lover, Sarkin."

"And last," I growled, a delicious possessiveness curling low in my belly.

She smiled. "You're my first husband too."

"And last."

It looked like she wanted to say something else. Perched on the edge of her tongue, her smile dying as a shy expression overtook her teasing amusement. My heart picked up pace in my chest.

Come on, aralye, *what are you going to say?* I wondered, though I thought I knew.

You're my first love too was what went unspoken, a silent thing between us.

And last, I would inform her.

Klara swallowed the words, and I stroked my fingers over her exposed shoulder, feeling the softness of her skin, still warm from our bath.

"Because I'm inexperienced with these things," she said instead, going back to where the conversation had deviated. "I'm only acting on instinct."

"Then I will tell you, wife," I rasped, my lips replacing my touch, trailing them up her neck to her ear. A full body shiver racked her, a little gasping breath shuddering from her. "That you have only the most perfect of instincts."

And it's madness…wanting you this much, I thought, capturing her lips for a gentle, lazy kiss.

For the first time in my time as *Karath* to the Sarrothian, I wanted to lock myself away with her. Just for a little while. I didn't want to burden myself with Elthika migration or Elysom politics or the heartstones in Dothik or the preparations for the journey back to Sarroth.

Selfishly, I just wanted to stay in this bed with Klara. I wanted to fall asleep beside her and wake up to her, with no pressing obligation of needing to be anywhere else.

When had I ever felt like this before?

"I brought you gifts," I told her, pulling away from our bed of furs to snag the satchel from the ground near the doorway.

She rose onto her elbow, her full breasts on display. "Gifts?" she asked, hesitant but hopeful. Curiosity rose in her luminous and inquisitive gray eyes. "Really?"

"From Elysom," I said. "One day, you will see our capital city yourself. It is quite a beautiful place. But until then…"

I crouched down and dug into the bag.

Klara gasped when I pulled out a beautiful floor-length dress, made of silver hatchling scales with shimmering jewels sewed into the bodice.

"Sarkin, it's so lovely," Klara murmured, reaching out to touch the material. "I've never seen anything so fine."

"I thought you might want to wear this on Akymor. It's a special day in Sarroth—it marks the end of the Elthika's mating season, before they begin to nest with their eggs. I hold a celebration at the citadel for my *kya'rassa*, and there are small parties in each of the villages. I try to visit them all through the night."

She was staring at me, that shy expression on her features again. She looked down at the dress when her cheeks flushed, rubbing the material between her fingertips. "I would like that."

Satisfaction burned in my chest.

I pulled out my next gift. Her eyes alighted on the pair of them, jeweled hair clips, crafted of the purest of silvers.

"So you never have to hide your scar," I told her, thinking of what she'd just told me. "Especially not from me."

She sucked in a quiet breath, meeting my eyes. I thought hers went a little glassy before she blinked swiftly.

"Thank you. I…I don't know what to say. You spoil me with these pretty things," she said, touching the clips when I placed them in her palms, running her fingertips over the etched metal.

But pretty things didn't make her truly happy, did they?

I thought my last gift might though.

"One more," I said.

"More?" She laughed.

"I saved the best for last."

Her eyes nearly bugged out of her skull when I pulled an Elthika scale–bound book from the bottom of the bag.

"Sarkin," she breathed. "That's a…that's a…"

"A book?"

"Yes!"

I chuckled, knowing I made the right decision. Books weren't usually for sale in Elysom's collections, but I'd offered a price to a private collector, one he hadn't been able to turn down.

She reached for it eagerly, and I grinned, shaking my head when I saw her hands were trembling.

"Don't worry—I didn't get my filthy hands all over the pages," I informed her, thinking back to when I'd first bumped into her at the marketplace in Dothik.

"Oh, Sarkin," she breathed. *Now* she was actually blinking back happy tears as she carefully flipped open the cover, thumbing through the first few pages. "And it's in the universal language!"

"It's in both," I informed her. "It's translated from Karag— you can see the original text in the last half of the book. When we return to Sarroth, there is a scholar there who can help you learn to read it. Most of our books are written in our language or a blend of Karag and the universal tongue. It will expand your available reading material at the very least, learning Karag."

"Of course," she said, her shoulders rising with a deep, determined breath, as if she was ready to begin her tutoring now. "I'll learn it."

"It's a history of Elthika," I told her. "I thought it would be useful to you."

I grunted when she launched herself at me. I caught her around the waist, the book pressed between us.

She kissed me. "Thank you. *Kakkira vor.* I love it. I…"

Again she stopped herself, whatever she'd been about to say next, though we both heard it. Then she beamed at me.

"You shouldn't have shown this to me because now I don't want to sleep," she said, sighing, running her fingertips over the cover, the scales making a sound as her nails stroked over them.

I smiled. "How about I read you a few pages in the Karag language?"

"Would you?" she asked, brightening.

Her passion for learning, for knowledge, for books—so pure and loving—only made my affection for her grow all the more.

"Of course," I told her, taking the book from her grip gently. We lay back in the bed—I was getting used to sleeping closer to the ground, in a nest of furs. Klara's eyes ran over the foreign letters on the page, her head pressed into my shoulder.

Anything to get her to relax for tomorrow, I thought.

I began to read…because dawn would come much too soon.

CHAPTER 36
KLARA

"Remember," Sarkin murmured, his voice soft and hushed, even though we were alone on a ledge on the Tharken cliffs, "you don't have to do this, Klara."

"Don't tell me that," I said, my voice even. I went cold, even stoic, when I was nervous. From an outsider's perspective, it might've even seemed like I was bored. "I *can* do this."

He looked at me steadily. "I never thought you couldn't."

"Then stop giving me an out," I told him, deliberately trying to soften my words. "My brother always did that. He always tried to protect me. I loved him for it…but sometimes I wished he would let me stand on my own. When it came to my family. When it came to the *Dothikkar's* hungry court. Because they never respected me."

Sarkin inclined his head. There was understanding in his eyes. "Then go claim your Elthika, *Sorrina*."

But don't claim Lygath was what was unspoken between us.

He turned to call for Zaridan on his black cuff, but I snagged his arm. His hands dove into my hair when I stood on my tiptoes to give him a deep, long kiss. He breathed me in. I knew he would take Zaridan to the very bottom of the ravine beneath my ledge…just in case. But I also knew he wouldn't tell me that.

"My only fear is disappointing you," I confessed to him when I pulled away, blinking back the sudden tears that pricked my eyes.

"Then you have *nothing* to fear, Klara," Sarkin said simply.

A smile broke over my face, the first one that entire morning since we left the village at dawn.

"*Lysi?*" he asked, tipping up my chin.

My smile only widened at the Dakkari word, and I nodded, taking a huge breath, letting it fill my lungs, letting it ground me, even as high up as I was along the cliffs.

"*Lysi,*" I replied. "Go."

His eyes flashed down to my right hand, where the tether he'd given me this morning was hanging, as if in assurance.

His gaze connected with mine. We looked at one another for long moments, only interrupted when Zaridan swooped low overhead, all the other wild Elthika scattering away from her. It seemed to please her, their fear. Their reverence.

Sarkin said, "Tight core, brace low."

Then he jumped off the cliff edge, right onto Zaridan's back, my heart leaping in my throat. He made it look so easy, but he'd had years of practice. I studied his easy positioning, where he had his boots locked into place at the harness, now knowing how much leg strength it took to keep them there with the velocity of flight.

He was a beautiful, accomplished rider. I could appreciate that now.

Sarkin flew out of sight, circling down to the bottom of the cliff pass…

Then I was alone.

The Tharken cliffs had been transformed since Sarkin had brought me here. Wild Elthika were all over the cliff sides, latching their taloned claws into the rock face, clinging to edges and navigating more easily than I thought possible.

I was high up. Alone, as Sammenth had recommended. That morning, at dawn, I'd ridden with Sarkin and, seemingly, an entire horde of dragons behind us. Most of the village had come to attend the *illa'rosh*. They'd gone to the opposite mountain, which had an excellent view of the cliffs. There was a flat rocky surface toward the very peak, and many had set up camp, similar in appearance to a Dakkari horde. Domed animal-hide tents—though the Sarrothian used a dark cloth material—and communal cooking areas. There was an air of excitement, or jovial celebration, even though most of the riders in attendance had been deathly quiet during the initial meeting with Kyavor.

There were other hordes from Karak in attendance as well. Sarkin told me that the *Karath* of the North had made camp on the northern mountain, though I couldn't see them from the vantage I had facing south. The northerners had been here for a couple days now. Their *illa'rosh* had already begun. One rider had already taken a death fall, trying to claim a Vyrin—though which one, no one could say for certain.

I wondered if Lygath *was* here.

I know he is, came my next thought. I stood at the edge of the cliff, pressing my hand in the rock face of the mountain, peering down. The world swayed. I'd never been so high up when I *hadn't* been on Zaridan. Something about being stationary and looking down to a bottomless pit struck me as wrong.

The wind whipped my hair around my face, the tendrils that had escaped from my braid. From this vantage point, across the valley, I spied the telltale flash of Vyaria's blue-scaled vest when it reflected off sunlight. She was on the same ledge as Kan—her cousin—but many of my peers had chosen to be alone for the choosing. I saw others dotted around various points across the cliffs.

When I'd been searching for a suitable ledge with Sarkin, I'd seen other riders I hadn't recognized.

Blood borns from other territories, Sarkin had explained to me, his lips brushing my ear. *They'll be trying for Vyrins. It's best to stay away from them. They'll be ruthless.*

My heart lurched in my chest when I thought I spied a silver-scaled dragon across the valley, flying low. A moment later, he emerged out of sunlight and I saw that it was only a trick of the reflection off his scales. He was dark gray in color, and I watched as he circled back around one particular rider, sizing him up, as the rider's head swiveled, tracking him in the sky.

There was a roaring sound that came, emitted from a beautiful light blue Elthika.

In the blink of an eye, I watched as Vyaria took a running sprint off the ledge of her cliffside. My heart thundered in my chest, watching her aim for the light blue Elthika. Smaller than others around the Tharken cliffs, but regal nonetheless.

At the last moment, the dragon sharply turned, and my stomach lurched. "No," I breathed.

Vyaria landed on the Elthika hard but not cleanly. I watched with bated breath as my training peer grappled with her tether, digging her hands into the scales, trying to get a grip so she wouldn't fall off the edge. Kyavor had told us that certain Elthika might test their riders during the choosing. Was this what this one was doing? Or was she trying to reject Vyaria?

The Elthika banked until Vyaria was almost vertical, dangling from her chosen dragon with only a precarious grip on the edge of a few scales. The Elthika righted itself, and Vyaria used the momentum to swing herself up. I heard her cry of exertion, the strength and will it took, echo through the cliffs. I saw the slim flash of her tether as she swung it around the Elthika's neck, using the sliding metal hook to tighten it like a leash.

Vyaria got into a rider's position, even without the comfort of a harness. Everyone seemed to wait with bated breath, to see if the Elthika would accept her, return her to the cliffside…or let her fall.

The Elthika let out another roar, and I watched as they both ascended, flying higher and higher…

The first flight.

Cheers raised up from the other riders, dotted along the pass, and I breathed out a shuddering sigh, my knees feeling a little weak. *Everyone* was watching. The eyes of hundreds on one Sarrothian girl and one Elthika, taking their first flight together.

How many eyes will be on you? came the nasty thought, making my heart freeze with trepidation. *How many will watch if you fail?*

Just like that, Vyaria had claimed her Elthika. The first of our peers. And she'd only been on the cliffside for mere moments.

Sammenth had told me the choosing could happen quickly or could drag on until the Elthika decided they'd had enough and left the cliffs entirely.

Suddenly I wished that I felt the relief that Vyaria must've been feeling right this moment. How wonderful it must've felt, to know that what you'd worked hard for was just realized. That you could silence the fear.

I watched Vyaria and her Elthika until the sun blotted them out. I dragged in a deep breath, my eyes scanning the cliffside again, waiting, just like all the riders.

Be patient, I reminded myself. I knew the others might feel pressure now. They, too, envied Vyaria's relief, coveted her success. Would some try to claim their Elthika not because it was the right choice but because it was the easy choice?

My head craned over the side of the cliff. I couldn't even see the bottom, a steady mist was covering it. Mist that hadn't burned away in the sunlight because the shadows of the cliffs kept it protected.

There was no sign of Zaridan, but I knew they were there.

Somewhere. Sarkin would wait until I claimed an Elthika. Or failed. He would wait for as long as it took, patrolling the pass.

And so I waited too.

When I first caught sight of Lygath, he was cast in moonlight.

Night had fallen. I'd been sitting on the cliffside, my legs dangling over the edge, feeling the keen slip of time as the sun lowered and the moon took its place.

I was hungry. Tired. Thirsty. My eyes were burning from watching every Elthika that passed. And though I knew better, I began to think how easy it would be to try for one that flew too closely…

Over the course of the afternoon, I'd watched fifteen more riders claim their Elthika, and I watched even more rejections, though none had ended in a death fall. Those Elthika had returned their potential riders to the cliffside. One rejected rider had even tried for another…only to be rejected again. He was still waiting across the way. A rider could try for as long as there was an Elthika present at the cliffs, but I imagined it took great mental strength after a rejection, let alone two.

With every Elthika that was claimed, with the available pool dwindling and time passing, more rejections became commonplace, the riders growing desperate and impatient. So palpable, I could almost taste it in the air.

I tried to steady my constant nerves with every rejection. I was one of three remaining acolytes among my Sarrothian peers who still hadn't claimed an Elthika. The other two were among the ones who'd gotten rejected, though they continued to wait for another attempt.

I was likely one of the only riders who *hadn't* tried to claim one yet, except for the older blood borns from the other territories. But something had always stayed my hand. That flash of memory of Lygath, right here at Tharken. That searing familiarity.

Like Muron's lightning, just as Sarkin had described.

And so when I saw Lygath, bathed in moonlight, flying in the middle of the pass, I could even hear the astonishment from the hordes, still watching along the outer mountains. Sound carried oddly, and I could hear a smattering of their murmurings, even miles away.

Sarkin had told me Lygath hadn't been spotted in years. Yet here he was. Flying in plain view, as if he *wanted* to be seen, gliding along silently like his namesake. Appearing out of thin air like an apparition.

My heart began to thunder in my chest as shouts were raised among the remaining acolytes, the blood borns. They were here for a Vyrin, Sarkin had told me. And here was Lygath, prowling down the pass, a descendant of Muron himself.

They would die, came the stray thought, that realization stealing all the breath from my lungs.

If I didn't get to him first, they would die. I *knew*, deep in my bones, that I was meant to claim Lygath. It had to *mean something*. My visions, my dreams. I'd felt the bonding pull, hadn't I?

And so if I was meant to be Lygath's rider, he would throw off all others who tried to claim him. Just like he'd done to Haden. Would Sarkin catch riders who fell?

I wasn't certain. His priority was *me*.

My husband wouldn't be distracted—his focus would be unshakeable, tracking my movements, especially with Lygath so near after what I'd told him. I couldn't promise him that I wouldn't *try* to claim Lygath if the situation presented itself. Here it was…and Sarkin likely felt the frustration of my stubbornness.

As if on cue, I heard Zaridan's roar from the dark depths of the foggy pass. Lygath responded, his tail flicking, his movements becoming agitated, swinging his head to search for his sister. His distraction brought him within mounting distance to where another acolyte was waiting, not far down the pass from where I was situated.

"No!" I called out when I saw the sudden movement. The leaping figure, shadowed in the darkness until a piercing shaft of moonlight hit him, just as he was airborne. Lygath's head whipped to regard me, the piercing gold eyes cutting straight through me. Zaridan's eyes.

An acolyte—a male Karag, no one I recognized but either from the North or the East—latched onto Lygath's back.

The Vyrin roared, the sound jolting my heart in my chest. I watched in horror as Lygath swung his head, trying to dislodge the rider, diving low as he spun…

Which brought him directly into the path of another rider.

In disbelief, with my heart in my throat, I watched another rider launch himself onto Lygath, landing on his other side. Were they going to challenge each other for the Elthika?

They will be ruthless, Sarkin had said.

The sound that Lygath made caused the hairs on my neck to stand on end, anguish building in my belly. It seemed to quiet the entire night, making movement slow all around us. They swept right in front of me, so close that I could actually *smell* the Elthika. Earthy musk, like damp dirt on the wildlands after a summer storm.

A flash of knowing went through me, so certain, so *right*.

"Lygath!"

The Elthika's head swiveled at his name, and he veered, ascending into the sky while the riders on his back grappled toward a better mounting position, their tethers hanging off the side. I tracked them overhead, and then Lygath turned, descending quickly, spinning again, hurtling straight toward the cliff where I was waiting.

I felt the *boom* of the cliff, the ground shaking beneath my feet as the entire mountain seemed to tremble with the force of his deliberate impact. Lygath latched himself into the side of the mountain. When I craned my neck around, I only caught a glimpse of him before I heard the guttural cries.

Something flashed in the moonlight. Then another.

Two Karag males, plummeting toward their deaths, dislodged off Lygath's back when he'd rammed into the cliffside. The Elthika roared, and I could hear his talons scrape against stone. He catapulted away, flying down the pass before he started to turn, heading back toward me.

All I could do was watch the darkness swallow the two riders. A death fall. *Two.* The echoes of their cries went quiet, and I heard Zaridan's roar.

If I don't claim him, more will die, I thought.

Determination rose in me. My heart was rapid, beating so hard that it hurt, that it was difficult to breathe after what I'd just witnessed. The air was crisp, and it burned when I sucked in a sharp breath. I had to time it perfectly when there was no time at all.

Closer and closer, Lygath came. I backed up, imagining where I would meet him.

"*Klara, no!*" I heard dimly. Sarkin's voice, echoing up the pass. He knew what I was about to do.

Now! I thought.

I sprinted as fast as I could off the short ledge, launching myself into the air, the tethers grasped tight in my grip.

Wind rushed in my ears when I went airborne. For a moment, the Tharken cliffs went quiet. I felt the force of Lygath's approach more than I heard him.

Then I was *there*. His wings flashed before me, and I cried out when I landed on his back, the impact nearly stealing my breath entirely. *Tight core, brace low,* I thought, my teeth gritting as I drew in gasping lungfuls of air.

It was a clean landing, much to my surprise. But Lygath roared, and I actually saw a stream of *ethrall* escape him, bright red in the darkness of the night. Seeing it momentarily lost me my focus. My hands slipped, and I narrowly slid off his back. In a last desperate attempt, I tossed the tethers toward his neck, the sliding metal clasp *just* catching, allowing me to straighten as Lygath picked up speed, thrashing.

His movements dislodged the clasp, and I gasped when the tethers slipped through my grip.

"No, no, no!"

The tethers fell into the darkness below, a winding snake that vanished. The Tharken Pass swallowed it. I went low, acting on instinct, bending flat over his back, and I tried to reach up to grip the sharp, taloned bones that jutted up near his wing joints.

Lygath thrashed.

"*Lygath, hanniva!*" I cried. "It's me!"

He bucked again, whirling so fast, the force making me slide. I had nothing to hold on to, and he seemed determined to get me off him.

Confusion and despair outweighed my shock as I slid to the side…

The whole world tilted.

Then I was falling.

Lygath grew smaller and smaller above me, pumping his wings as he fled the pass, ascending higher and higher. He was silhouetted by the moon. That was the last I saw of him.

I was in a death fall. One I'd been well prepared for.

But I hadn't expected *this*.

Rejected by the Elthika I'd been certain was meant to be mine.

CHAPTER 37
SARKIN

"The last rider finally decided to end his *illa'rosh*," Kyavor told me. "He's being retrieved now."

"Who?" I asked, though my mind was elsewhere.

"Nirin," Kyavor said. "From the lake village. He wants to continue instruction through next year. To try again."

I inclined my head. "Blood born?"

"No, his father is a fisherman."

Then he would feel the rejection from an Elthika all the more sharply.

"Let him continue to train," I decided. "He can stay in the Arsadia for the year if he wishes."

Withstanding the *illa'rosh* for as long as he had, with a rejection, spoke for his mental strength. One day, he might make a good rider.

"I will. And all but two Sarrothian acolytes claimed an Elthika," Kyavor reported. There was hesitation in his voice because we both knew that one of those acolytes was my wife. "We will add ten new riders, ten new Elthika to Sarroth's horde."

"Get a report on the new Elthika," I said. "I'll have Levanth deliver it to Elysom in the morning."

Kyavor inclined his head, and I walked away, intent to find my wife.

It was two nights after Klara had taken the fall.

Finally the *illa'rosh* could come to an end, with only two deaths recorded. I considered that a success, though I knew the nightmares would come, as they always did. The two blood borns who had tried to claim Lygath...I had managed to save only one. The other had been too far away, just like Haden. I'd only narrowly been able to drop the surviving acolyte down to the pass floor before I'd needed to track Klara overhead.

The horde would pack up our encampment at dawn, and we'd leave for Rysar. The remaining wild Elthika had already begun their migration from the cliffs. Tomorrow this place would be as if the *illa'rosh* had never happened. Only...the territories of Grym and Kyloth had lost two of their acolytes, both blood borns, and their families would always remember this choosing. The first had taken a death fall before we'd even arrived to Tharken. Another Vyrin had apparently been scouting the area, and the acolyte had tried his hand.

My horde was celebrating the end of the *illa'rosh*. The fires were lit, the feasting had begun. It had been successful for Sarroth. But I felt this stone pit in my belly that I couldn't shake, knowing how much Klara was hurting right now.

There was a break in the celebration noise, a sharp knife cutting through it. When I glanced up the pathway, I saw Klara, walking with Sammenth. Klara had her head held high, but my fists clenched at my sides when I heard the quiet that had descended. The whisperings that started up in the festivities' wake.

I stepped forward, slicing a sharp look over to a group of younger riders, making them swallow their tongues. I approached my wife. The Sarrothian didn't publicly show affection to partners or lovers, but I pressed my lips to the side of her temple when I reached her.

Slowly the celebration carried on, though I felt dozens and dozens of eyes on us. Sammenth squeezed Klara's forearm, murmuring, "I'll find you later." And then with a careful look of greeting at me, the young rider fell away, into the fray.

Pulling back, I looked into Klara's eyes, seeing the way they flickered around the celebration before lowering.

"I thought I could do this," she whispered softly, "but I don't think I can. Not yet."

I nodded, taking her hand and striding away from the clearing. From other neighboring mountains, I heard the celebration of other hordes. I heard the telltale drums of the Grym territory and echoing laughter of the Kylothian fill the Tharken cliffs. The horde from Elarin had already departed.

Klara shivered, and I pulled her closer. I brought her to our domed dwelling, untying the laces at the entrance and holding open the flap for her to step through. I tied them tight, and the thick material helped blocked out all sound. Our tent was placed toward the back of the encampment, closest to the wide expanse on the mountain where the Elthika could land. It was separate, and I knew that Klara would feel safer here.

"What do you need?" I asked her, taking her into my arms.

"To not feel like this anymore," she answered immediately, her shoulders slumping even though her hands pressed into my abdomen. I couldn't stand the defeat I heard in her voice. "To not feel like everyone has turned on me. To not feel like an outsider again. To not feel like a failure."

"You're not a failure," I growled.

"I am," she answered simply. "You don't have to lie to me. I know what happened. I know what everyone saw."

I blew out a sharp breath. At least she was *speaking* with me tonight. She'd been withdrawn for the last two nights. Stoic and detached. She still showed her face, bravely, among the horde, though I knew she heard their biting remarks, their judgments. It was what I disliked most about my people. The Sarrothian frost, it was called. If they didn't know you or if they didn't respect you, they made you feel it like the prick of a dagger. Failure was a brand on your skin. And it took what felt like a lifetime to shake away shame in their eyes.

Klara was feeling it keenly. Just as I had once.

"Lygath was never going to accept a rider, Klara."

It was the wrong thing to say. Her head snapped up, but the burn of the anger in her eyes felt better than her quiet resignation. At least there was *life* in her now.

My nostrils flared. I wanted to stoke that fire even more, to shake her from this.

"I told you not to choose him. So why did you disobey me?"

"*Disobey?*" she breathed. "More riders were going to *die*, Sarkin!"

"And you would've been one of them!" I growled.

She reared back, stepping from my arms as she began to pace our dwelling. It was decorated sparsely and had a bed of furs at my request. Her booted feet treaded over the soft carpets that created a barrier against the hard mountain stone.

"I *felt* it," she cried out. "The bonding pull. I knew—*know*—that Lygath is meant to be mine. How do you explain that?"

I shook my head, feeling the tension build in my chest as I watched her pace. "Klara, there is always choice—I've told you. You might have felt the bond with Lygath; I won't discredit that…but sometimes an Elthika doesn't *want* a rider, no matter the pull. Lygath has always been one of them."

"Then why was he there?" she asked. "Why was he at Tharken if he didn't want a rider?"

"Zaridan," I answered, thinking it obvious enough. "They sense each other. He knew she was there. There is a bond in blood that cannot be denied, and it is the only bond he cares about."

Klara looked away from me. "I felt it so *strongly*, Sarkin. I thought…I thought that I could prevent the others from trying to claim him, from *dying* if only I claimed him first. I felt what they didn't. They want him because he's a Vyrin. I chose him because of what I felt. Because I've dreamed of him for years. I thought… I don't know what I thought anymore. All I can see is those two riders falling into the darkness and the sound that Lygath made when they latched into his side. It was…awful, that sound."

My heart twisted in my chest when I saw the drops of her tears roll down her face like translucent jewels.

"*Aralye*," I breathed, going to her, sighing. I took her shoulders and then wiped away her tears with the pads of my thumbs. "It's not your fault. Don't ever think that. They made their choice."

Coming from me, after what I'd experienced with Haden, I knew she understood what I was telling her. She *knew* it wasn't her fault, that she couldn't have prevented their falls. I'd been able to save one acolyte, but I knew she was thinking of the other.

"Don't take on that guilt," I ordered her. "*Ever.*"

"I'll try not to," she promised me. "But what do you recommend for the shame?"

I shoved down the urge to flinch at the words.

"I hear them talking about me. I feel their eyes," she said, looking down at the ground. "You're my husband, you're their king. What does that make me?"

"My wife," I growled. I cupped her face, lifting it so I could see her eyes. There was a lantern burning on the table, giving us a small glow of light. "The one I chose. The one I vowed myself to in Lishara's temple."

"And is that all I am to you?" she questioned softly, reaching up to place her hand over mine, though she didn't remove it. "Is that my purpose here? To be your wife? To warm your bed and smile beside you? To support you, to agree with you?"

I scowled. "Of course not."

"But that's what they want, isn't it?" she asked. "They won't respect me now. Because even though I am your wife, I am not their equal."

"You are their queen, and they will treat you as such," I argued, hating the tone in her voice.

"Only if I give them reason to. And when I fell off Lygath, they cast their judgments on me," she said. "This was my worst fear, Sarkin. *This* feeling."

I softened again when I saw her tears. I pulled her into me, and her face pressed into my chest.

"*Aralye,*" I murmured, restlessness stirring in my chest because I didn't know how to *fix* this. "I faced their fire too. Remember that."

Her shoulders shuddered. There was something I needed to explain to her, something I'd been avoiding, something she'd likely heard about in passing but hadn't asked me about. And it was something that would help her. That was all I wanted. To help her. To try to protect her heart and guard her against the horde.

"The Sarrothian's fire is a trial in itself," I continued. "But for me, it was doubly so."

"Because of Haden?"

"No, because of my father."

I felt her shoulders stiffen. She lifted her eyes until they met mine.

"Have you heard about him?"

"Briefly," she admitted, her tone slightly sheepish. "Only that...his bonded Elthika rejected him after he stole Elthika eggs. That he was considered disgraced."

My nostrils flared. "He was forever marked by that story. As was I."

"Will you tell me about it?" she asked when my pause lingered too long, uncertain *how*, or even where, to begin.

"Come," I said, leading her over to our bed of furs. She followed, our fingers intertwined, and only when we were comfortably situated did I continue with "There's more to the story."

"There usually is," she said. "I didn't want to hear about it from anyone else but you."

I pressed my lips to the back of her hand, feeling the softness of her skin.

"I will say this first because it is the ugly, tragic truth. My father killed my mother," I said, matter-of-factly, hearing Klara's gasp, "and then he followed her in death. It is not an easy thing to understand, but believe me, it was a mercy. And he did it because he loved her."

Her brow furrowed. I saw the edges of her horror but also the desire to understand.

"Everyone else believes a different story, however. One spread by Elysom. My aunt, my mother's sister, who you met at our keep in Sarroth, was responsible for the lie. Her and the *Karath* who came before me."

And I can never forgive them for it, I thought.

"I remember her," she said quietly.

Where to begin? I wondered.

"This story begins long ago," I warned her. "Tyzar was my father's Elthika. And they bonded in a strange way because my father was not a rider. He never trained to be one—he was from a farming family on Sarroth's outskirts, from a small rural village called Kaval. Where I grew up, in the same house he had."

Klara blinked, processing the information. I'd never spoken of my childhood, of my family with her before, but I could see her hunger for it, her *need* to understand. To understand pieces of me I'd kept hidden.

"He found an egg in a Sarrothian forest when he was young, rejected by the mother. He saw her drop it, and he went to look for it. It was still warm," I told her, thinking of the awe on my father's features when he used to tell me this story. "He took the egg, and he tended to it, waking in the middle of the night, every night, for new coals to keep it warm, until it hatched. My father and Tyzar never felt the bonding pull, but they were bonded forever nevertheless by choice. Tyzar chose to remain in Kaval with my father instead of seeking out his own horde, his own ancestors. And that's where they lived."

I could see her confusion.

"My mother, on the other hand," I said, "was from a wealthy family in Elysom. Stories of Tyzar and my father reached the capital. Many traveled to see them. It was an amusement for them, a poor farmer on the outskirts of Sarroth and his found hatchling. That's how he met her. Their love was a quick thing… like Muron's lightning, my father told me. He finally felt the bonding pull, but it wasn't for Tyzar—it was for her," I said quietly.

It was hard to reconcile the girl he'd fallen in love with and match her with my mother, who'd kept her emotions leashed tight, even toward me. It was my father who had shown me affection. Perhaps he'd been what she'd needed. Perhaps I was more like *her* than I realized, needing someone warm and open and loving. Someone like Klara to thaw me, to keep the frost away.

"I was meant to be a farmer too. Can you believe that?" I asked her.

A sharp huff left her. "No. Not at all."

"I was not a blood born. I was actually of the earth. Like you, like a Dakkari—born with cool, steady, unyielding earth beneath my feet. But I was always looking toward the sky. I loved Tyzar. I grew up on his back. And that's why I wanted to be a rider. That feeling when you fly, when you feel the whole world is open to you—*that's* freedom."

"It suits you," she commented, her eyes glowing, a soft smile on her face. I was glad to see it. I would tell her this story over and over again if it distracted her from the horde beyond our dwelling. If it distracted her from Lygath's rejection. If only for a brief reprieve. "You were meant for it, this life."

This story grew bittersweet, though it needed to be said. So she would finally have a deeper understanding.

"My mother became deeply ill in Sarroth when I was a child," I said. "The healers in Elysom called it the *arasykin shy'rissa*. The heartstone sleep. We don't know why it happens. Some think it's because Sarroth is the farthest away from the core of the Arsadia, the center of Karak. The Sarrothian claim that as a badge of pride almost, like outsiders can't survive here, only the toughest of Karag can. But I don't believe that."

She frowned.

"One healer my father consulted believed she'd been born with it. A defect in her blood. Some are just unlucky, even in Elysom. The sickness began to shut down her body. It started slowly, her movements and strength becoming weaker," I said, remembering finding her on the floor one day when my father had been out in the fields. "By the time I was ten, she couldn't walk anymore. She stopped going into the village. She was so tired all the time. Then, a year later, she couldn't move her arms. The year after that, it was her tongue."

Klara bit her lip as tears sprung to her eyes, despair written there. "Sarkin...I'm so sorry."

I breathed deep. "And then one day...Tyzar and my father left."

"Left?"

"He told me to watch over my mother, that he had to go meet with a healer in Elysom. He was gone for nearly a week. And when he returned..." I sharply exhaled, remembering the shock and disbelief of that night. "He had two Elthika eggs with him. Stolen from a nest he'd found along the western cliffs."

"But *why?*" she breathed.

"Because one healer believed that Elthika eggs, the hatchlings in which possess heartstone energy, the purest form of it, could help her. Not heal her completely, but at least give her a life back, a life worth living. Because at that time, she was only a shell."

Klara said nothing, only looked at me solemnly.

"My father stole the eggs, that is true, even knowing the consequences," I told her. "But it wasn't for nefarious purposes or to sell to our enemies, as Elysom tried to claim. The eggs didn't work, needless to say. We kept them warm and he returned them to the nest, but his theft had been discovered. The Elthika he'd taken the eggs from had been bonded, not wild. Her rider was a council member in Elysom. And so Elysom let the Sarrothian decide my father's fate. And our *Karath* sentenced him and Tyzar to death, but he gave them six months of time until their execution."

My lips twisted bitterly. "Because he was a farmer and they needed his next crop yield before he could die."

"That's awful," she whispered, her lips pressed together as her eyes gleamed in the low light. "And Tyzar? I thought the Karag would never needlessly kill an Elthika. Isn't that against your laws?"

"The Elthika have their own laws, and stealing hatchlings or eggs is among the highest of offenses. So yes, they were both sentenced to execution. And that's why he sent Tyzar away. That's why people say that Tyzar rejected their bond. Because he left, but not by his choice. So that he wouldn't be killed, my father commanded him to leave, to fly north as far as he could, though it nearly broke him."

Klara's hand pressed to her mouth as tears from her wide, beautiful, sad eyes dripped down her face.

"And with only six months left, my father decided on mercy for my mother. She'd long asked him to help end her life. Before she'd lost her ability to speak. The thought had been unfathomable to him. But then? He didn't want to go to his own death, knowing what she wanted, knowing he could give it to her. His last gift. The last sacrifice he would make for her," I said. "He asked me to start rider instruction that year. I was fourteen by that time, older than some of my peers already. I refused at first.

How could he ask that of me? To leave him? But what I didn't understand…what I couldn't understand then…"

"He loved you so much that he didn't want you to watch him die," she said softly. "Oh, Sarkin, you were just a child yourself."

"One who'd grown up too fast already," I said quietly. "He didn't want me to watch him fall apart. He didn't want me to be around for what he would do, so my conscious would be clean. I was so angry when I left because I knew I was saying goodbye to him, to my mother, and it was not *my* choice. But he asked me to watch for Tyzar, and I promised him I would. And those first few months of training, the Arsadia was so different. I felt guilty for enjoying it. I felt guilty for the relief I felt at being away from home."

She reached out to take my hand, leaning down to kiss my scarred, calloused palm. I felt her shuddered breath on my skin, the drip of her hot tears. There was a reason I never spoke of this. It made me feel raw. Like an old, festering wound.

"When I learned of both of their deaths…it was Kyavor who told me. He'd been my instructor then too. He'd received a message from the *Karath*, who was angry that my father had chosen death early and that he'd taken my mother with him. Two *mysar* commands were laid upon me by Elysom as penance, and they could be whatever they wanted. The commands are like debts that need to be paid. Whatever two tasks Elysom asked of me, I would have to obey without question."

"The Dakkari scouting missions…and…"

"Marriage," I said, my lips twisting. "That one in particular was my aunt's doing, and she gave it to me only recently. She knew how much that *mysar* command would *cut*…because I'd vowed to never take a wife. And that was common knowledge in Elysom and certainly to her."

"What?" she asked in astonishment. "You never wanted to marry?"

"After witnessing the tragedy of my parents' marriage? For

years?" I asked, shaking my head. Sad understanding reflected in Klara's eyes. "*Never.* But my aunt, Kethra...she thought my father murdered my mother, her beloved sister. She blamed him for her sickness, for her death, for taking her away. She wanted to make me remember that, so that every time I looked at *my* wife, I might remember the one my father took. The one he vowed to protect."

I gazed at Klara, seeing her process that information—that I'd never intended to marry. That *mysar* command had once felt like a cruel twist of a dagger in my belly. Only now...I saw it much differently. My aunt had instead given me a gift.

"It all makes sense now," she whispered. "Especially why you were so angry in the beginning."

I gritted my jaw. "I never meant to hurt you, Klara. But you have to understand, I—"

"I do understand," she said quietly, rising up onto her knees until she was right in front of me. Her arms wound around my neck, and I *saw her.* She wasn't withdrawn right now, she was *here.* With me. And she was shining so brightly as she looked at me. "But even when you didn't want me, I could see that you were *good.*"

"I want you now," I confessed to her. *More than I ever thought possible.* "And always."

She smiled, pressing her lips to mine in a soft kiss. "I know." She sniffled. "Thank you for telling me, Sarkin."

I pulled away so I could see her fully as I said, "I told you this because I want you to understand that I know something about shame and how it follows you. How it can feel unshakeable."

Her chin lifted as she absorbed the words.

"I'm not saying it's easy, *aralye*," I told her. "It took me a year after I bonded with Zaridan before the challenges to my title stopped. Because of my father's memory, because of events that people knew *nothing* about, sacrifices he made that they cannot fathom. But I earned my right as *Karath* in their eyes. You will need to do the same. Perhaps not through claiming an Elthika, but through other ways. You are kind. Giving. You are open to *everyone* because you know you can learn from *anyone*. Those are your strengths."

I brushed my hands over her cheeks, catching the last of her tears.

"And you can throw a mean dagger if all else fails."

The small chuckle that emerged from her felt like a win in itself, though it was short-lived.

"Maybe I *will* 'dagger' the Sarrothian," she said, pulling away to look up at me. "Not in a literal sense, obviously. I mean that… I learned how to throw daggers so well because people said I *couldn't*. You know I hated that most of all."

My lips quirked, and I ran my hand over her face, thinking her so lovely. I trailed my fingers through her hair, observing how the ends curled around my fingers. "I can so easily imagine you sneaking out at night to practice throwing daggers on the wildlands."

She guided me back until we were lying down, her head on my chest. It felt so natural with her. So easy. And I felt like a weight had been lifted from me, now that I'd told her about my father. It had been like a scar that had never healed properly, one that always pulled and itched.

"Do you feel shame for what your father did? You said you felt it follow you…but what your father did was out of love. There's nothing shameful about that."

"I wish he hadn't stolen the eggs," I confessed. "He should've known better, but I also know how much he hated watching her suffer. We both did. He was desperate. Desperate to help the person he loved."

She nodded against me, though I couldn't see her expression. "Whatever happened to Tyzar? Did you ever find him?"

I smiled as I dragged my fingers down her arm. "That is a happy story, at the very least. He fled north, as my father commanded him. After I claimed Zaridan, I made it my mission to find him. He lives close to Muron's Spine. A peninsula in the North, a sacred place. He has a mate. Two hatchlings that are growing strong by now. Soon we might see them at Tharken, and I hope one or both will choose a Sarrothian rider."

Maybe even our *child,* came the sudden thought. How fitting that would be.

I dragged in a deep breath, feeling how much the knowledge pleased Klara.

"I still visit on occasion, if I'm ever in the North to meet with the Kylothian," I informed her. "One day I will bring you to meet him too."

"I would like that," she whispered. "I would like that very much."

Silence stretched between us, and I heard the distant, dulled sounds of the celebrations of our horde. Klara sighed, reality flooding back in.

"Can I write your story?" she asked quietly. "Your father's story?"

Something tightened in my chest. Longing? Grief?

"I believe very strongly in recording stories. Putting them to parchment. They are our history, after all," she said. "How many stories would have been lost if not for scribes who took the time to record them…and I think it would be a shame if yours was lost too. People should remember your father, your mother, and Tyzar."

I clutched her to me tighter, my heart speeding in my chest. I'd done everything I could to build a careful, impenetrable wall around me after the losses of my life.

How had she wiggled between the cracks?

I repeated her words. "I would like that very much, *aralye.*"

CHAPTER 38
KLARA

The meadow was familiar.

I felt the wind brush across my face as I trailed my fingers through the grass at my ankles, seeing it light up beneath my touch.

I was in the starfall meadow, the one Sarkin had brought me to. I could still see the indent of our blanket, pressed into the grass. The night sky was quiet though, the stars hanging perfectly still.

I was dreaming, I knew. The sensation of it was familiar. But it also felt more *real* than other dreams had. As if I was really there, standing in the meadow, alone, on that dark night after the *illa'rosh* had come to an end.

There was a sound behind me, and I turned slowly.

Lygath.

He was sitting, watching me, halfway between where I was standing and the twinkling lake down below that trailed along the edge of the forest.

His silver scales were gleaming. His wings were lightly colored, a gray that seemed translucent, especially when he flared them wide. With the moonlight behind him, I could see the outline of his thick bones within them.

He was smaller than Zaridan, though not by much. But he had her eyes. Gold like the statues in Dothik. Gold like the pieces of metal—Kakkari's gifts, we called them—that we unearthed in the soil in the wildlands, using it for weapons and tradable goods.

"Lygath," I said. "What are you doing here?"

I knew he might not be able to understand me, though Sarkin had once told me that Elthika were more intelligent than we were. That they had their own language, but that they might understand ours.

The Elthika shifted when I began to approach. My heart was thundering in my chest, but I wasn't afraid. There was a dream-like quality to this reality, an extension of my gift, my magic that I had yet to fully realize. *I might never,* I thought.

I stopped on the small hill that overlooked where he was sitting. There was an edge to him, and I halted my approach, not wanting to scare him.

And so I sat, right on the grass. I was in the shift dress I'd gone to sleep in, and the grass tickled my bare legs. I waited until Lygath settled again, though he never took his gaze off me.

"I see you in my dreams all the time. I have since I was a child. I still remember the first time," I said, talking to him even though I didn't know if he could understand me. "I thought you were so fearsome...but so sad. You were calling out, this mournful cry, as you flew. I think you were in the Arsadia, from the landscape I can remember. I think, now, that maybe you were looking for Zaridan. Only...that hadn't come to pass yet. I saw your future without her."

His ears twitched at his sister's name. Those eyes were so piercing that if I looked into them long enough, I felt goose bumps pebble over my flesh.

"Sarkin says that you don't want a rider," I continued, dragging my knees up to my chest. "If you don't, that's all right. But I have this feeling inside me that you don't want to be alone anymore either."

A sound rose in his throat, a gruff chuff, that had the edges of my lips curling.

"And I know what it's like to be alone," I confessed. "I know how frightening it can be. Maybe you're not scared. You are a Vyrin, after all. One of the most revered and fearsome of your kind, from an ancient bloodline. But even though you're a Vyrin, it doesn't mean you're not lonely. Elthika like companionship, don't they?" I shrugged at him. "So, what are you afraid of? Are you afraid of your sister's rejection? Were you angry that she chose Sarkin? Did you feel that she left you behind? Abandoned you? Or do you feel shame, that you have hidden away for so long?"

His tail thumped on the earth, but I didn't flinch, even when the hill trembled with the force.

"She looks for you all the time," I told him. "Sarkin told me she's always looking for you."

Lygath went still. Then he huffed out a breath, and I thought I saw another tendril of *ethrall*, making me swallow.

Then he lowered himself to the ground. No longer sitting but lying down, the starlight grass illuminating and rippling beneath him. His head came to rest on his forelimbs, the wicked gleam of the talons reflecting in the moonlight. And when he turned his head, I saw the mark of Muron. On the lower right side of his neck, it looked like black ink was spread over his silver scales. Like wild, untamed roots of a tree, though I knew now it was the mark of heartstone lightning.

Still, it was a familiar shape that I could trace in my sleep because I'd studied it in the mirror—cursing it—for nearly my entire life.

"Zaridan chose her rider well," I told Lygath, feeling a smile stretch over my lips. "Sarkin is...he's..."

I didn't know if there was a single word that could describe him aptly.

"He was the best choice she could make," I said finally, thinking that I felt that way too about him. "He's a good leader to his people. Fair but honorable. And he has a kind heart, though he holds it close. Your sister chose well. She loves him. And so do I."

The quiet confession felt easy slipping from my lips, especially to Lygath.

I took a deep breath and stood. The Elthika's head raised to regard me, his eyes watchful as I approached, but he didn't stand. He stayed in his position as I drew nearer and nearer.

"You smell like home. Like the wildlands. One day, I hope I'll show them to you," I cooed to him softly when I was close enough. I smiled, raking my eyes over him, observing the way his silver scales tapered to points like teeth. "You're very beautiful."

He huffed.

"I mean very, very fearsome," I corrected, biting back a smile.

He huffed again, though it was shorter. Zaridan could be proud. Perhaps Lygath was as well.

I was within arm's reach of him. I walked until I looked into one of his eyes. Golden and slitted black. I could see my reflection in them, so clear, even in the darkness. His pupil contracted on me.

I felt the warmth of connection. Like I knew him. I *had* seen him the majority of my life. He was familiar.

"I know I'm meant to be yours and you're meant to be mine," I said quietly. "Can you not feel that, Lygath?"

A breeze shuffled between us, blowing the ends of my hair, the tendrils caressing the Elthika's scales. He watched me closely. I had the sense he could see *all* of me. Every facet of my being.

I heard the rustling. I held my breath because it was familiar. The *sy'asha*. The song of his scales.

But then he quieted it, as determination rose in me. He *did* feel it. He did know. My hand rose between us. His pupil flicked to it. A shudder racked through him, a low growl rising in his throat, but it didn't sound ominous. More like a purr, though perhaps that was my own delusion.

Slowly, with bated breath, I pressed my hand to his snout. His nostrils flared, the muscles pulling and flexing beneath my palm. He was cool to the touch, his scales like armored silk. I traced my fingers over his cheek until they were right below his eye. His pupil contracted before widening.

Dannik and Sora had always wanted me to fight more. Fight more for what I wanted.

There is always defeat in your eyes, sister, Dannik had told me once.

No longer. Their words, their belief in me gave me strength. Sarkin gave me strength, especially knowing what I did now.

"I will be at Tharken again," I said, the determined words pulled from me.

I knew what I had to do. To carve a place for myself within Sarkin's horde. To claw my way to his side, where I wanted to belong. I didn't have to prove it to Sarkin. But his people would never see me as their equal if I didn't do this.

"If you'd like, come find me there. I'll be waiting."

Then I sat down next to him, gazing out at the lake.

"But until then, let's just sit here together for a little while."

I woke next to Sarkin, though I felt as awake as I had next to Lygath in my dream.

Calm had settled in place of shame. I felt determination rise in me, a wave that washed over me and gave me strength.

I watched my husband breathe as he slept, pressing my hand to his bare, warm chest to feel the steady beat of his heart.

Deep affection burst in me until I felt like I couldn't breathe.

He was every bit the mate I'd always dreamed of…one I'd never allowed myself to believe I'd actually find.

And he was stronger than anyone I'd ever known.

His story, the tragedy and loss he'd endured, losing everyone he'd loved so quickly…I couldn't imagine his strength to withstand that. To come out on the other side as a *Karath*, taking the role of the male who'd sentenced his father to death.

I felt like I understood him better now. He told me he'd been reckless once, that Zaridan had taught him patience. I wondered if during rider training, with his newfound freedom far from home, far from his responsibilities, he'd taken his freedom too far, pushing limits he never could before. Maybe his anger had driven him, or perhaps the unfair fate he'd been given.

Only now, he seemed like the opposite of that young rider. His loss had made him strong but detached from the world. Never truly a part of it. I'd often felt that way in Dothik after losing my mother. We had more in common than I'd believed. We'd both lost those we loved dearly and felt the sting of their absence.

Compared to my woes of Lygath's rejection, his story had only reminded me that the limits of our will knew no bounds. What was one rejection in comparison to what Sarkin had experienced?

There was no excuse for it. I'd been feeling sorry for myself, pitying myself.

No more.

Sarkin deserved a great queen at his side, a queen who could pull herself out of the shadows, just as he'd done. His horde would learn that they could not dismiss me. I needed to prove to them that I was worthy of their king.

Because for the first time…*I* believed that.

As I felt the reverberation of Sarkin's heartbeat, my eyes trailed to his wrist. To the black cuff.

Slowly, I reached forward and unhooked the hidden metal

clasp. Sarkin had barely slept since we'd left the mountain village. I hoped he was tired enough to not notice I was gone because if he knew what I would do, he would try to stop me.

I took the cuff, clutching it tight in my hand, and held my breath as I rose from the bed. Years in the quiet archives had taught me stealth. The carpet dulled the sound of my footsteps as I hurriedly dressed, not bothering to change from my shift dress but simply pulling up riding trews and shoving my feet into my boots.

The tether that I'd used on Lygath—the one that had slipped from my grip and fallen below into the shadows of the cliff pass —was hanging slung over a stool. Sarkin had retrieved it when they'd recovered the acolyte's body. He'd said nothing, but I'd noticed its appearance that first night. Now I reached for it, winding it around my fist as I untied a few laces on the tent's entrance, just enough that I could wiggle through.

It wasn't yet dawn, but it would be here soon. The air was biting cold, and my nipples pebbled underneath the thinness of my dress I was using as a tunic. The encampment was deathly quiet. All the revelry from the celebration had died down, and I prayed to Kakkari that everyone was still sleeping.

No one roused as I snuck through the camp, keeping to the edges. I didn't want to risk Sarkin hearing Zaridan land, so I dipped into the trees that grew up the mountainside, knowing there was another flattened landing not far from camp.

When I reached it, the stars sparkled in the indigo sky, as the moon lowered. I clasped Sarkin's cuff onto my wrist to keep it secure. Though it was a tight fit on him, it drooped on me, and I hoped it wouldn't fall off. Taking a deep breath, I pressed the button on the side. I heard nothing, but I knew Zaridan would hear the signaling call, no matter where she was.

Sure enough, a few long minutes later, I heard the telltale beat of her wings. She landed before me, her head moving meaningfully to look for Sarkin, but I approached her instead. She lowered her head to regard me as I pressed my hand to her snout. Her cool scales beneath my palm felt so much like her brother's.

"Take me to Lygath," I said quietly. "Take me to Tharken. *Hanniva.*"

CHAPTER 39
KLARA

Lygath appeared at dawn.

His scales sparkled like morning dew as the first rays of the sun broke over the cliffs. He came gliding into the Tharken Pass, heading straight for me.

The sight felt so familiar, even in sunlight. But as my gaze darted around the opposite cliffside, I knew this wasn't like the *illa'rosh*. I didn't truly have any concept of how this would be regarded by the Karag. Technically the choosing was over, the last of the acolytes relented.

Though by their own laws, an Elthika could be claimed at the Tharken cliffs at any time of the year. And here Lygath was…

As I'd known he would be.

I'd crossed the distance to him in my dreams, calling him here. And this time, I knew he wanted to be claimed. He'd been given a choice. Mine had already been made.

And now he'd made his.

Across the cliffside, I could see the Sarrothian horde's encampment, dotted along the flattened mountain peak. Some horde members were beginning to rouse, and soon they would know that Lygath had returned to Tharken. Sarkin would wake any moment to find me gone, if he hadn't already.

Zaridan was below, patrolling the pass to watch for me, an exercise Sarkin had told me they'd done endlessly.

The tethers tightened in my grip.

Lygath drew closer and closer. I stepped up to the ledge to draw his attention. Those golden eyes flashed in the sunlight, and then his speed increased, a mighty gust of his wings preceding the burst, and a roar unleashed from him. It boomed along the cliffs, echoing deep and long. It raised the hairs on my arms, nearly making me shudder.

The call of a Vyrin.

Now everyone will know you're here, you proud thing, I thought, grinning.

I backed up as much as the ledge would allow. I gazed at the spot where I would meet Lygath, ignoring the rising sounds of alarm from the Sarrothian horde that echoed in the pass.

Closer…

Closer…

Closer.

"*Now.*"

I sprinted along the ledge, the tethers tight in my grip.

I swore I could see my reflection in Lygath's golden eye, flying as close as he did to the cliff.

I jumped.

CHAPTER 40
SARKIN

"Where is she?" I growled to Feranos, stalking toward the cliff's edge, the horde parting for me until I reached my wing commander.

"She's at the pass," he said quietly. "Sarkin…Lygath is there too."

Fear spread like ice in my veins. I'd known something was wrong the moment I'd woken to find Klara gone.

"And Zaridan?" I asked, wrapping my hand around my bare wrist. I didn't remember the last time I'd been without my cuff.

"She's down there," Feranos told me, pointing to the lower pass. We couldn't see her from this angle, but I knew that my Elthika would be watching Klara. "The *illa'rosh* is over. What is she *doing*?"

My teeth snapped together. "Claiming her Elthika."

Feranos's expression looked grim when he met my gaze.

"Call Vorna," I ordered him, watching his fingers immediately flash to his cuff. "I need him. I need to get to her and—"

"Lygath! He's there!" I heard the cry from a horde member. My head whipped to the Tharken cliffs, and I saw his shimmering scales in the morning sun. In the far distance, I watched him glide through the pass.

"Where is she exactly?" I asked Feranos when he stepped up beside me.

He pointed his finger toward the top of one of the cliffs, very close to where she'd been situated during the *illa'rosh*. "There."

Klara's form was just discernible from this distance.

And Lygath would reach her in mere moments.

"I'll never make it to her in time," I rasped, my heart thudding in my chest in realization. The only thing that wasn't making me lose my mind with fear and worry was that Zari was down in the pass. She would catch her if Klara fell. But what if something went wrong? What if Lygath attacked her this time instead of allowing her a death fall?

The only thing predictable about Lygath was his unpredictability.

"Fuck," I breathed, watching Lygath reach Klara's ledge. I felt helpless—as helpless as I'd felt watching Haden fall off the very Elthika that my wife was hell-bent to claim.

Kyavor appeared, coming up on the other side of me, clasping his hand onto my shoulder. "Breathe, Sarkin," he murmured quietly, though his eyes were rapt on his pupil along the cliffside. "She wouldn't do this recklessly."

She needs to do this, came the realization. A realization I hated. I hated everything about this. But I couldn't control her. I couldn't cage her to make sure she was safe. The purpose of my training her had always been to *prepare* her. That was how I could protect her best.

That was how I could love her best.

A collective rippling gasp among the horde made time seem to slow. The world quieted. Even the wind. Everyone was there. Every Sarrothian soul at Tharken had come to see their queen. Even Klara's peers. Vyaria. Kan. All watching with bated breath.

Lygath flew close to the cliffside.

I watched the small speck of her back up on the ledge, and then she sprinted. My nostrils flared wide, my heart beating at its bony cage so hard I thought it might burst free. I watched the heart that was outside of my own body, the heart of vulnerability that was flayed wide open, leap off the cliff, silhouetted against the gray stone of Tharken.

She landed on Lygath's back cleanly, just as she'd done a couple nights prior.

"Come on, *aralye*," I whispered, watching for the flash of the tether. *There.*

"She latched it—it's on!" Kyavor exclaimed, straightening as his gaze tracked her every movement. "Now to see if he'll…"

There was a rippling of energy going through my horde behind me. No longer was it trepidation. It had now turned to *hope*. Scarce, unbelievable hope.

"He's not fighting her," I said softly, with dawning realization, watching Lygath soar through the pass with Klara on his back. *He wasn't fighting her.*

Klara took the primary riding position—bent low over Lygath with a straightened back and locked thighs. She had a good grip on the tethers…and *Lygath wasn't fighting her.*

"She's claimed him," I said, throat tight.

"On Muron, she has!" Kyavor said, a broad grin—the biggest I'd ever seen on the aging male—appearing.

Raising his voice, Feranos cried out to the horde, "The *Sorrina* has claimed Lygath!"

The cheers erupted. So loudly that it nearly shook the entire mountain.

Another Vyrin for the horde. Another descendent of Muron. Zaridan's own blood. Sarroth would speak of this day for the rest of our history as we watched the *Sorrina* take her first flight with her bonded Elthika.

Klara Dirak'zar of Rath Serok and Rath Drokka. Rider of Lygath. Queen of the Sarrothian horde.

Pride burned so brightly it nearly stole my breath.

Yet it was mingled with hot anger, bubbling relief, with pricking love and sharp desire. My emotions were such an overwhelming mess that I didn't trust myself to move. I didn't trust myself to speak or react as I listened to the loud celebration that erupted around me. And so I stayed as still as a statue, though my eyes were only on Klara as Lygath ascended above the Tharken cliffs.

Something dark shot from the shadows beneath the pass. *Zaridan.*

The horde quieted, a hush of awe descending as Zaridan hurtled straight after Lygath, her wings close to her body. Lygath roared. Zaridan's response was a call of her own, beautiful and chortling. They spun around one another as they ascended together, and then the rising dawn blotted them from view.

The two Vyrin siblings, descendents of Muron, reunited once more.

Another Vyrin for the horde of Sarroth, claimed by a Dakkari princess, who everyone had underestimated. Even me.

Sarroth would never underestimate her again.

She'd ensured that, hadn't she?

Long moments later, they appeared again. And they were flying straight for the horde. The Sarrothian began to race for the landing field to the right of the encampment.

Feranos and I moved with them, and the horde parted for us as I walked to the front.

"*Sorrina, Sorrina, Sorrina,*" came the chanting cries, the closer she drew. I could see her now. Her cheeks flushed, hair windswept, eyes glassy with her success and relief.

The horde erupted into cheers when Lygath landed before us, gusting his wings. He kept as far away from the Sarrothian as he could without going over the cliff edge, Zaridan landing beside him. Still ever mistrustful.

And Klara straightened on his back, looking over the horde

that she had just won over. She might always feel the sting of their prior rejection. Sometimes I still remembered it. But she would have to accept it, just as I had.

Never before in our history had a rider tried to claim the same Elthika twice.

But Klara had.

A Vyrin nonetheless.

The noise, the chanting, the cheers were thunderous. Klara sought me out among the crowd, and I stepped forward. Lygath huffed out a sharp breath, and I looked at the Elthika, a torrent of emotions at the sight of him channeling through me. I didn't know how to feel. But now that he was my wife's bonded—and Zaridan's sibling—we would have to learn to get along. It would be hard. Especially since whenever I looked at him...I couldn't help but remember Haden.

I passed to his side, and his golden eyes kept me pinned. Klara was looking down at me, swinging her leg over, her grip on the tethers loosening. She unclasped them, keeping them in her fist as I held out my arms for her. Lygath still needed to be trained on basic commands. He wouldn't lower his wing for her yet.

She slid off the side, and I caught her in my arms. My heart still thundering, relief so potent spiraling through me that I went dizzy with it. But I was still trying to get a handle on my fear. My anger.

"I'm sorry," she breathed into my neck. It was miraculous I heard her over the noise. "I'm sorry."

I said nothing. Instead, I looked at Zaridan, my displeasure likely rolling off me in waves, and nodded at Lygath. "*Thryn'ar.*"

The flying command. Zaridan let out a sharp chortle in the back of her throat, which made Lygath's ear twitch. Then she took off, her brother following shortly after.

Then I left the landing space. The horde was still celebrating, though their exuberance died down as I left with Klara still in my arms, heading toward the forest at the back of the encampment. I needed to be alone with her, but I thought the walls of the tent would feel too suffocating.

Once we were far enough away from the horde, deep in the forest, when we could no longer hear them, I set her down on her feet.

She was biting her lip, looking sheepish and hesitant, when she met my eyes. "Sarkin…"

"I don't know whether to yell, celebrate, kiss you, punish you, or fuck you," I growled.

She sucked in a sharp inhale through her nostrils, those dull little teeth still buried into her full bottom pink lip.

"So you tell me, *aralye*, what you want me to do," I finished.

"A kiss would be a good start," she breathed. I saw something black dangling off her wrist. My rider's cuff. She saw where my gaze had dipped, and her fingers brushed over the metal. "Though I understand if you want to start with the yelling part."

I strode up to her, sliding my hand into her hair, *tight*, pulling her head back as she stared up at me in surprise.

My kiss was hard and angry. I poured my fear and frustration into her. My other hand came up to her cheek, and I *fucking* hated that it trembled as it did. A growl wound its way up my throat.

One thing had become apparent to me this morning—I was no longer an impenetrable force. She was my glaring vulnerability, the soft place that could so easily destroy me.

My aunt had succeeded in one thing.

She'd made me like my father. I knew I would do anything for my wife to protect her…and that made fear rise in me like nothing else had before.

I *loved* her. I loved my wife.

I broke the kiss with a rough gasp, feeling her pant against me as I leaned my forehead into hers. I glared at her.

"Next?" I asked.

I saw the desire bloom and heat. This moment felt like when I'd trained her at Tharken. That dizzying adrenaline was still pulsing in her blood, making her wild. She was still on a high of claiming Lygath.

I grinned, but it was sharp. "I know exactly what you want."

Her chin lifted. "Do you?"

She dropped the tether to the forest floor, winding like a twisting serpent. Her hands drifted to the laces of her riding trews.

"You stole from me," I rasped, watching her as my cock thickened, as blood pulsed and rushed and sharp, punishing desire rose with it. "Snuck away in the night like a common thief."

She swallowed, but her fingers never stopped gently untying the laces. My cock pulsed with excitement, my abdomen dipping like I was free-falling.

"I may be your husband, Klara Dirak'zar, but I am also your *Karath*. Your king. Or have you forgotten that?" I asked softly, watching her.

Her tongue darted out. Slowly, she toed off her boots and her riding trews dropped. She stepped out of the material, and then her hands went to the dress she'd worn to our bed the night before, pulling the delicate fabric over her head until she was naked before me.

Naked, save for the riding cuff she'd stolen. It stood out against her skin, and the sight of it only made me more crazed. My gaze snapped to hers. Her hands were shaking when she brought her fingers up to her lips to rub at the reddened flesh. Her nipples were pebbled tight, her shoulders raising and lowering, the curves of her hips and breasts tantalizing.

"And what would my king ask of me?"

I nearly groaned at the sultry words. My anger was steadily being replaced by lust, but I would *play*. I would play with her. I would play along. Because she'd still have to deal with my ire when we were done, but at least we could work out some frustration with each other beforehand.

"Get on your knees," I ordered her.

I heard her thick swallow, but she did as I asked, lowering herself to the soft forest floor. We'd never done this act before, but I had fantasized about it, imagining how her mouth would feel on me, the heated lash of her tongue.

She thought to distract me? To fuck away my ire?

It might work, I admitted as I stepped forward, tugging firmly at the waist of my trews. Klara pushed them down when I reached her, my cock springing forward.

I hissed when she wrapped her hand around me, bucking into her grip.

I saw her hesitation. She'd never done this before, but her enthusiasm and curiosity was evident. Her eyes flickered to the line of the forest, but then I saw the heated burn in her eyes. She *liked* this. The idea of getting caught aroused her, and my cock jumped with the realization, drawing her gaze.

She didn't wait for me to give her another order, however.

She licked, almost demurely, at the tip of my cock, which made me surge in her tight fist. I blew out a shuddering breath, thinking of the hell she'd just put me through…and the sweet, sweet hell she would put me through in the next few moments.

"Suck me, wife," I growled, my patience snapping, especially when she teased her thumb over what I knew she called my *dakke*, the sensitive bump above the root of my shaft. She pressed into it, and a rough groan spilled from me. My hand went to fist in her hair. "Enough teasing. I'm tempted to come on your tongue, to find my relief and not allow you yours. Maybe that will be how I punish you."

Her head lowered, and the heat of her mouth made my eyes nearly roll to the back of my head. My eyelids closed, neck craning.

"Oh, fuck, *aralye*," I breathed. I licked my bottom lip, and then I sucked in a sharp breath when I felt her cheeks hollow around me, the pulling sensation nearly making my knees tremble. Her mouth was stuffed full of me—so much so that I felt the searing brand of her tongue on the underside of my cock with nowhere to go. It moved and quivered under my length, and I gasped, my hand tightening in her hair as I shuffled closer.

I cursed again when she retreated, dragging her lips over the sensitive tip, the hot lap of her tongue finding the trickle of pre-come at the seam.

"Where did you learn this?" I asked, my nostrils flaring, chest heaving.

Her eyes flashed up to me knowingly. "Books, *Karath*," she teased.

Books.

I nearly groaned. Books could only take her so far. This was instinct, and on Muron, she was made for it. Made for *me*.

I grunted when she stole my breath again, taking me deep, seemingly trying to learn how far she could fit me between her lips. Her thumb pressed to my *dakke*—teasing and stroking, emulating the hot lash of her tongue.

I'd meant for this act to balance our power over the other. She'd taken from me, and I would take from her. Selfishly, I'd ached for her to pleasure me, to give while *I* received. I wanted to be the one in control of this moment.

Only…I had the maddening feeling that it might be just the opposite. Especially when I saw her other hand move between her thighs, when I heard the wet slick of her arousal and her soft, desperate moan rumble down the length of my cock.

And I didn't mind it one bit.

I'd thought the desire I'd felt for her in Lishara's temple would be the worst I'd ever felt. That clawing, desperate need had been unimaginable. I'd thought that the severity of it—the overwhelming, pressing need to claim her as my own, to sink my body into hers until I lost myself completely—had been heartstone-magic induced.

But I'd only felt it rise, even stronger than before. This desire was all our own. Lishara had no part in this. It was only us, deep in this mountain forest.

I felt my sac tighten, and I rumbled out a rough groan. Selfishly, I continued to pump between her lips, catching her surprised sound. Once, twice I thrust into her before I pulled out suddenly, hearing her ragged breaths.

I joined her down on the forest floor, pushing her back as she spread her legs for me. I needed her right now. I wanted to feel the tight sheath of her sex around me. Only then could I feel grounded again, fucking *sane* again.

Her cry filled the air when I surged into her. She was so wet, so hot, she fluttered and squeezed around my cock. I leaned down, biting and nibbling before sucking on one nipple hard. My hands found hers, taking them in my own, intertwining our fingers and bringing them over her head. She felt exposed and vulnerable this way—like I could do *whatever* I wanted to her—lighting my blood on fire.

"Sarkin," she gasped out. Raising my head, I met her eyes. Her cheeks were flushed pink, her eyes glassy with her pleasure and need. She was tightening on me.

"Mmm, getting even wetter for me, my *Sorrina*," I purred, surging my hips into her harder, going as deep as I could until she felt my *dakke* pressed to her clit. She cried out, her back arching, her fingers squeezing my own.

It had been too long since we'd last made love. We hadn't since we'd left the mountain village. Mere days of going without felt like *months* with her.

"Kiss me," she pleaded. "Make me come."

I lowered my head, giving her her kiss. She sighed contentedly into my mouth, which she knew drove me wild. Her taste was sublime, her tongue soft. The longer we kissed…the more gentle it became. The pace of my hips slowed, instead focusing on deep strokes that stole both of our breath, every retreat making me shiver.

Our fucking suddenly became less about power, about fear, about the high of adrenaline and the sharp vulnerability I'd felt watching her jump off that ledge without me close to be able to protect her. It became less about punishment and more about... reconnection.

These last few days, I'd *missed* her. I'd missed this. There was an unexpected eroticism in that connection, one that felt like a startling discovery.

When we both orgasmed, it was a breathless wave of steady pleasure—deeply, deeply satisfying. With it was a release of all the events that had happened during the *illa'rosh*. It allowed us to piece ourselves back together, reinforcing the rips and tears.

When it was over, I collapsed onto her, making sure to keep half my weight pressed to the ground. I buried my head into her neck, feeling her shudder and her sex pulse around my cock, drawing out the last of my orgasm. Our hearts were rapid with no sign of slowing. Her hands dislodged from my grip and came to the back of my head. Her fingers raked through my hair, and she cupped her palm over the back of my skull, holding me to her as if afraid I'd pull away.

It did work, I thought. All the anger had left my body with my release. I felt boneless, the panic of the morning making me tired.

My rider cuff, still on her wrist, brushed the back of my head. Against her neck, I murmured, "You've fucked the fight out of me, my love."

Her hand in my hair stilled.

"So," I murmured, groaning as I pulled away, propping my hands on either side of her head so I could look down at her, "I want you to tell me what you were *thinking*. I'm listening now."

CHAPTER 41
KLARA

I got dressed as Sarkin watched me, leaning against a nearby boulder next to a thick tree as big as a *thalara* trunk. He hadn't taken off a single stitch of clothing during our lovemaking, the erotic thrill of that surprising as I smoothed my nightdress in place and shoved my feet back into my boots.

My body was humming with life from the memory of his touch.

But he was upset with me and he was demanding his explanation. Our lovemaking had perhaps softened his ire, but it wasn't gone completely. I thought he might even be hurt by what I'd done. Which, yes, was understandable. I'd stolen his cuff and his dragon…all to claim an Elthika he'd asked me explicitly not to choose.

At my wrist, I unlatched the rider's cuff and approached my husband. I reached for his wrist, sliding it over and replacing it where it belonged. I fastened the latch tight and then intertwined our fingers.

I brought our hands up and brushed my lips back and forth over his knuckles, thinking how best to explain. He watched me all the while, a dark curling lock of hair dipping low over his multicolored eyes.

"I won't be a source of shame for you," I finally said.

His brows furrowed. "What?"

"What your father did…" I began, sighing, "even though his heart was in the right place, his actions haunted you and followed you for so many years. You were challenged relentlessly. Even before I knew about what happened with your father and Tyzar…I know how important it was for the horde to accept me as one of their own. I was already an outsider—a Dakkari from across the sea. But to be an outsider who couldn't claim an Elthika? To the Sarrothian, that was unacceptable."

"And I told you," Sarkin growled, "I didn't care what they thought. I gave you the choice to claim an Elthika or not. *Me.* Not them. If you didn't want to go through with the *illa'rosh*, I would've brought you back down myself that morning without a second thought."

"It was more than that though, Sarkin," I breathed, getting frustrated because he wasn't understanding what I was trying to say.

"Then tell me."

"I needed to prove to myself that I was worthy to claim an Elthika of my own!" I exclaimed, feeling my throat tighten. "I needed to prove it to myself *and* to you. That I was worthy to stand by your side in the eyes of your horde."

His jaw tightened, his eyes flashing. He looked like he wanted to argue, but I brushed my other hand across his lips to silence whatever it was he was about to say.

"Ever since my mother died, I've felt like an outsider. Long before I ever came to Karak. I know what it feels like to be dismissed. Overlooked. I know what it feels like to be whispered about, for others to judge your worth before you ever even speak to them," I said, thinking about all the years living in my father's palace. Dannik had tried to shield me, but he'd only been able to do so much. "Then I came here, and I was on trial all over again in the eyes of your people. I will *not* live my life here feeling as I always have. I will not be ignored. I will not be made to feel small. And so, I would have been back at the Tharken cliffs, year after year, if that was what it took to prove myself. *I* needed to believe that. I needed you to believe that too. Your horde is your everything, Sarkin. I couldn't disappoint you because it would've been a disappointment to myself."

"You're my everything now, you fool," he said simply, so nonchalantly that for a second I thought I hadn't heard him right. "Can't you see that?"

I blinked. "What?"

Sarkin scrubbed his hand over his face. He looked *tired*, I realized. The first time I'd ever really seen him this tired. *Worn.*

"I felt fear today that I haven't felt—*ever*," he confessed, those eyes burning into mine as the words dripped from his tongue. "Seeing you on that ledge, I was faced with the possibility that I couldn't save you if something went wrong."

"But I—"

"No, now it's my turn," he rasped. I bit my tongue. "You *scared* me today, Klara. Scared me to the point that I was confronted with a reality in which I could *lose* you. And that frightened me. More than anything ever has."

My heart went fluttery and heavy all at once. "Really?"

"I felt so fucking *helpless*," he said gruffly, raking his hand through his tousled hair. "This morning, I realized that you've somehow managed to steal this cold, shriveled thing I call my heart…just like you stole my Elthika, you little thief."

I thought it inappropriate to smile, but he sounded so damned grumpy about it that I couldn't help the small one that slipped.

"Really?" I whispered, my eyes going watery.

Sarkin closed his eyes, breathing in deeply. I watched them shift beneath his lids, going back and forth, and I reached forward to place my other hand on the center of his chest. To my surprise, his heart *was* rapid, a pounding drum beneath my palm.

"Zaridan would do whatever you asked of her," he finally said. His eyes flashed open to regard me. "And I would too."

A bloom of realization, soft and gentle, spread like warmth from a fire. Something I'd only ever dared to wish for.

"You love me," I declared.

He inclined his head. "On Muron, I do. I love you, *aralye*."

I grinned, feeling like sparks of joy were sizzling in every vein of my body. Sarkin might never be the type of male to express exactly what he felt. He *was* a Sarrothian, after all. A king. He could be brooding and detached, internalizing many of his emotions—out of necessity and stemming from his old wounds. But he could also be passionate and sensually bold. Cutting yet charming. They were all the facets that made him who he was, and I wouldn't change it for anything.

"I love you too," I breathed, smiling though my vision blurred, "in case it wasn't *completely* obvious."

I reached up to wind my arms around his neck. He was comforting and warm, a solid presence against me and an unyielding pillar of support. How could I not have fallen in love with him?

He breathed in deeply, embracing me back.

"I should've listened to you, Klara," he said softly. "When you told me about Lygath."

I pulled back so I could meet his eyes. "Please know this, Sarkin. I would have *never* risked my life, knowing how you would feel, if I believed Lygath would reject me again. I wouldn't do that to you. I was as certain about him as I am about you."

"How did you know?" he asked.

"I found Lygath in my dreams. Early this morning. He was in the meadow where we watched the starfall. I think he might've seen us there, that night. I think he called me to him, leading me there, like a beacon."

"You can dream walk," he said. There was a prick of awe in his tone.

I swallowed. "It's possible. My ancestor, Vienne…she could speak to others in her dreams, even if they were dead. She saw things. It's possible part of her gift is now mine, passed down through bloodlines."

"And what happened with Lygath?"

"I just talked to him," I said. "He was so…lonely. He's not vengeful or full of rage. He's *sad*. He felt the bond though. He started to give me his *sy'asha*. I knew what I had to do after you told me about your father. I was never going to rest until I could be seen as an equal in your horde's eyes. And Lygath gave me that gift of a bond. He'd already made his choice when he came to Tharken. So, you see, I was never in any danger."

He brought his forehead to mine. "Never sneak away like that again, Klara. *Please.* I should've listened to you, yes. You felt you couldn't tell me what you needed to do, and I will forever feel the guilt of that. But from now on, we never hide anything from each other. *Lysi?*"

I didn't like that he felt *guilty*, but I knew that he wouldn't hear otherwise. And so, I nodded against him. I pressed a kiss to his lips.

"*Lysi,*" I whispered in agreement. "That I can promise you."

His relief was palpable.

"Sarkin?" I murmured.

"Hmm?"

"*Lo rune tei'ri,*" I said, meeting his eyes, seeing all the strings of different colors in them. Greens and golds and browns. My heart was beating out of its chest as I grinned. "It means *I am yours* in Dakkari."

He started to chuckle, the sound like a reward in itself, but then an Elthika swooped low overhead, a loud roar shaking the forest, making us part.

Sarkin frowned up at the canopy.

"A rider?" I asked, turning to track the dragon. It was a glittering deep red in color, unlike any I'd ever seen even after the *illa'rosh*.

"A *Karath*. From Grym," Sarkin corrected. "That's Samryn, his Elthika."

"Another *Karath*?" I breathed.

"Likely here to congratulate you, my *Sorrina*. It's not every *illa'rosh* a Vyrin is claimed," he said. And it made everything in me *sing* to hear that small thread of quiet pride in his voice, despite his complicated history with Lygath. "Come. We should return to meet him. Oh, and Klara?"

"Yes?"

"*Lo rune tei'ri*," he repeated, brushing his lips against the sensitive shell of my ear as he whispered the words. A shiver raced down my spine. He sealed his words with a kiss at my temple.

I thought my face would crack apart with my smile as he took my hand. I made sure all my clothing was in place before we ventured from the forest. I was acutely aware that I still had Sarkin's release inside me and that we both looked a little worse for wear. But it couldn't be helped.

And I was too deliriously happy to care.

When we emerged from the forest long moments later, I saw the red Elthika—blood red, *human*-blood red—perched on the landing space. He was even bigger than Zaridan, and I couldn't help but notice that the Sarrothian kept their distance even though the *Karath* appeared to have come alone. I couldn't see him from this angle, for his Elthika's head was shielding him from view, but when Sarkin pulled me forward, I saw him sitting on dragonback, waiting.

I only got the impression that he was an imposing figure, spying a flash of silvery-gray hair before he was sliding off his Elthika, landing onto the stone in a crouch before rising.

Then he approached, and I felt the rake of his gaze over me, sizing me up. Perhaps he'd never seen a Dakkari before, unless he'd been one of the *Karaths* on patrol in our homeland.

My first impression had been correct—he *was* imposing. He appeared only slightly older than Sarkin, and he sported a silver scar that almost matched his hair, curving down his sharp jaw and onto his neck. Human hair silvered and grayed like that with age, but he wasn't physically old by any means—though the glint in his eyes belied a soul that struck me as *ancient.*

Eyes that were piercing blue, like the glow of a powerful heartstone.

He stopped in front of me, and I had to crane my neck to look up at him.

"*Sorrina*," he murmured in greeting. "I have come to pay the respects of the Gryms as we congratulate you on your claiming of Lygath." The edge of one lip curled, and he never took his eyes off me, despite Sarkin edging forward. "You must be a fearsome creature to claim such a Vyrin, Klara Dirak'zar."

I swallowed, my tongue heavy in my mouth. He was intimidating and slightly cutting, just as Sarkin had been. I couldn't get a read on him, and so I settled on what I had always done when meeting members of my father's court, who I knew were trying to get a read on *me.*

I smiled. Soft but detached.

"*Kakkira vor*," I said in Dakkari. *Thank you.* "You know my name."

"Of course," he said. "You have been the topic of much conversation for quite some time among all of the Karag." His eyes flickered to Sarkin. "Even in Elysom."

I was still on a high of claiming Lygath, of knowing that Sarkin loved me. Nothing would dull it, not even this male.

"Then I feel like I'm at a disadvantage because I don't know your name, *Karath*," I replied.

The edge of his lip curled, the side that held his scar.

"I am Alaryk Arn'dyne, rider of Samryn," he said, stepping

away so that I could meet his Elthika's vibrant red gaze, nearly stealing my breath, "and the *Karath* of Grym."

To the east, I knew. The territory that shared a border with the Hartans, if I was remembering correctly. Where the last war had taken place.

The Karag were onto something that the Dakkari didn't yet realize.

Names *should* be feared, not hidden. And this *Karath* had a fearsome one, just like my husband.

"Alaryk Arn'dyne, I'm pleased to meet you," I replied. My eyes went behind him, and I added, "And your Elthika, Samryn."

"Our horde is departing soon," he said, his gaze going to Sarkin. "But there is another matter I had wished to discuss with you. I met with a messenger from Elysom shortly before we departed for Tharken."

I thought I knew what that message pertained.

Sarkin jerked his head further toward the forest, highly aware of the eyes of his own horde, ever watchful. We went to a more private place, and when we were out of earshot and protected by Samryn should anyone venture too closely, Alaryk asked, "Is it true that there is a living *thalara* tree in Dakkar?"

Sarkin gestured to me. Alaryk's responding gaze was piercing.

"Yes, I saw it," I said quietly. Alaryk's brows lowered. "I have a gift of heartstone magic, through my bloodlines of Rath Drokka and Rath Serok. I saw a *thalara* tree deep in one of our forests. I believe I know where it is. It's near where we used to call the Dead Lands."

Alaryk's shoulders raised with his deep inhale. He looked back to Sarkin. "You are making plans to ride to Dakkar?"

We hadn't talked about it, but even I looked to Sarkin. I knew he'd been flying to Elysom prior to the *illa'rosh*, to discuss plans with the council on how best to approach the negotiations with my father. I knew that time was working against us, but I'd been so consumed with the *illa'rosh* that it nearly slipped my mind entirely these last few days.

"Yes," he replied, casting me a look when he reached down to take my palm. "We are both going. Along with a few Elysom council members and some of my trusted riders."

My breath hitched. Hope too. I would see my home again. My brother.

"I'll be joining you," Alaryk declared.

Sarkin's nostrils flared. "Given the delicate nature with our relations with the Dakkari, I think it would be best to keep the rider horde small."

"I'll get Elysom's approval," Alaryk said, easy arrogance—or perhaps confidence—pouring from the soft words. "I wanted to let you know my intentions in person."

Sarkin scoffed. But then he smirked. I couldn't tell if they were friends or not, if they liked one another or not, if there was a history here. But like most kings, they didn't like others to over-step into their territories. And that was exactly what this *Karath* was doing.

"The Hartans are getting restless again," Alaryk informed Sarkin. "I thought you should know because we're both aware of how secretive Elysom likes to be about these matters."

My husband stilled. "The council knows?"

"Yes," he said. "My spies inform me that the Hartans have heard rumblings of heartstones, rumors from across the sea. They know that Dakkar has them. My interests in going with you are to ensure that Grym is not overlooked in these negotiations, espe-cially since it is *my* territory and *my* riders who have defended the border since the war. At great cost to us."

"I know," Sarkin said. "My intention was never to cut you out. Especially you, Alaryk. You know that."

"You'll forgive me if I will still demand to be there," the *Karath* said. "You would do the same, if the situation was reversed."

Sarkin was quiet. Then said, "I would."

"When do you leave?"

Sarkin cast me a brief look. Then he said to Alaryk, "We will wait for you. We are still in the Arsadia. Meet us at Rysar in a few days. We'll make the flight to Dakkar together."

Alaryk stepped forward, extending his arm. I watched as Sarkin clasped his forearm, bringing them close. "I'll be there."

Then the *Karath* of Grym stepped back. He looked to me. His chin lowered. "*Sorrina.*"

"*Karath,*" I said back.

His lips lifted again, his eyes tracing over me.

He sees more than most, came the thought. Did he have heart-stone magic too? I couldn't decide.

Then he was walking back toward his Elthika, leaving nearly as quickly as he'd come.

Sarkin asked, "I should have told you. About Dakkar."

"I didn't ask," I said, looking at him. Even in front of his horde—because I could still feel their eyes—he cupped my face in between his palms, tipping my chin up so I could meet his eyes fully. "I'd been a little nervous about the *illa'rosh*," I admitted.

"I didn't want to distract you," he admitted. "But we decided at the last meeting in Elysom."

"And I can go?" I asked, wanting to be sure.

Sarkin's lips quirked. "Like you would have stayed behind, *aralye?*"

"Good point."

"You'll take Lygath. Your first flight. To show him your homeland."

My lips parted. "It doesn't… Lygath won't…"

"What is it?" he asked, brows furrowing.

"After Haden…" I said. Realization dawned over his expression, a frown dropping into place. "I didn't know how you felt about Lygath being among the horde now."

"Whatever came before…it happened. I cannot change it. And so we must start new. We have to. That is *also* a choice, and it is one that I have already decided I will make. For us. For you."

I love him, I thought quietly. The sacrifice he was willing to make for me pulled at my chest.

Then his expression changed. A flash of sadness.

"I just realized that Haden has been gone for more years than I ever even knew him. Isn't that strange?" Sarkin asked.

"People come into your life, and they change you forever," I said. "It doesn't matter how long you knew them—they'll always be there."

Just like Sarkin would always be with me.

For evermore.

CHAPTER 42
KLARA

One thing I'd learned riding on the back of Lygath for nearly four days on end?

New harnesses took ages to break in.

That and the fact that my husband was a hoverer—literally—especially when it came to me. He kept Zaridan firmly behind us so he could keep me in his view at all times. Feranos had taken lead at the very front, flanked by Samryn, Alaryk's bloodred Elthika.

Sarkin might've decided to accept Lygath's presence within the Sarrothian horde and as my bonded. That didn't mean he trusted him yet.

The relationship and bond with an Elthika was one established over years. Lygath and I were still getting used to one another. He didn't know the basic flying commands I'd learned in instruction, and there hadn't been enough time for any training before we'd left the Arsadia to make the long journey to Dakkar. Zaridan had communicated with her brother when necessary, allowing us to fly relatively smoothly. But the harness made him itchy, just as it rubbed against me in all the wrong places. He had some breaking in of his own to do.

But there were moments on our flight when Lygath seemed almost *happy*. When he caught sight of Zaridan, or when we happened to fly low over a place he'd never been before, his head swinging wildly to observe what he could. When we flew over Sarroth on our way farther south, he roared, as if he knew where his new home lay. Perhaps Zaridan had told him. The Elthikan language was impossible for us to replicate, and it was a great mystery still among the Karag. But they still communicated. Riding with Lygath, with his sister close by, they'd been *talking*.

And I'd been utterly fascinated to find that the other Elthika in our travel party seemed to eavesdrop every now and again, until Zaridan snapped her jaws and they floated farther away, chastised by the Vyrin.

There might always be mystery when it came to the Elthika. No matter how long the Karag had assimilated with them.

One other disadvantage for traveling for nearly four days without reprieve?

I missed Sarkin.

Though he was close, we couldn't speak to one another mid-flight like our bonded Elthika could. Every now and then, he would quicken Zari's pace so that we could fly side by side, as if he wanted to look at me, wanted to *admire* me. And every time, I grinned like a silly lovesick fool until he smirked and returned to his place behind Lygath.

When we camped at night, we cuddled close, separate from the others...but that was the only time we had before dawn would break.

Only a little while longer, I thought, my eyes on the peek of land that I could see in the distance.

All I'd seen was Drukkar's Sea for the last day, every glittering, twinkling wave below us, the sea breeze refreshing though it made my hair a wild mess. Once, when I'd been younger, my uncle's horde had stayed close to the coast in the South Lands. I'd woken to the briny air every morning and would walk along the cliffs with my mother, usually early if she'd had a dream.

The world had seemed too wide, so endless then when I'd looked across the sea.

Now I knew it was.

There was so much that I hadn't seen. Even of Dakkar. Even more of Karak. And what lay beyond those seas?

My heart began to race when we passed over the shores of Dakkar. My heart raced as we flew over typography that I could trace in my sleep. And it never slowed, even with the hills of the West Lands under us, which gave way to forests and endless plains of the wildlands.

And when I saw Dothik come into view in the distance, I felt a strange pricking of excitement, acceptance, and grief.

Sarkin had listened to my advice when I'd told him we should send a messenger ahead of us, informing my father and his council of our arrival. There was always a possibility that the message would give them time to coordinate an offensive attack…but given what they'd seen of Zaridan's *ethrall*, I didn't think they would try. Sarkin had been right to frighten us with it. It ensured obedience, a demonstration of how much more powerful the Karag were.

But I hoped we could come to a peaceful negotiation. Especially if Dannik was present, especially if I could speak with him.

I couldn't wait to see my brother. To let him know that I was safe. That I was happy. That he didn't have to fear for me anymore because I knew he did.

And maybe one day, if the Dakkari and the Karag could reach a peace, he could come to Sarroth. To the Arsadia. There was so much I wanted to show him, so much I wanted to share of the fantastical things I'd experienced during my time in Karak.

Dothik's sparkling turrets in the lowering sun shone like beacons. Just like when I'd left, I could see that the East Gate was open, that a group was gathered out on the wildlands, awaiting our arrival. There were about three dozen Dakkari waiting, the majority of them guards, though, thankfully, I saw no archers on the walls. Sarkin likely wouldn't have let me land near the city gates if there had been.

Lygath didn't land right away, like the others in the traveling party, which consisted of Sarkin's *kya'rassa*, Alaryk Arn'dyne and his chosen commander from Grym, and two Elysom council members, luckily neither being Sarkin's aunt, Kethra. He'd made that a stipulation in the agreement with Elysom.

I pounded my fist three times along Lygath's side. Though we were still learning to fly with one another, Lygath began to circle downward at my command, eventually landing next to Zaridan.

My eyes immediately went to the group of Dakkari, the sense of familiarity overwhelming.

Dannik.

All the Dakkari were staring right at me when I tapped on Lygath's wing. He extended it after a bit of fuss, and I descended, my legs feeling a little wobbly after my long flight.

"Klara," Sarkin called out in warning, but my heart was about to burst out of my chest.

I grinned when my watery eyes met my brother's, and the moment I reached the earth, I ran to him.

He was dressed so familiarly. A pressed black tunic, embroidered in golden thread in the swirling Dakkari style. Leather pants that had been well-worn from his long days at the training grounds. His long golden hair was pulled back from his face, the hilt of his sword peeking out from behind his back. The golden beads sung musically in his hair when we collided.

"Klara," he rasped, his arms immediately coming around me. "You have a damn dragon."

There was disbelief in his tone. I laughed. He smelled just as I remembered, like the soap that was sold in the marketplace. My fingers met the metal of his sword.

"I do," I said. "I missed you so much, Dannik."

I pressed a kiss to his cheek and pulled back to look at him. My brother's face held a serious expression, eyes running over me, inspecting and cataloguing me.

"You're all right?" he asked me, so quietly that I knew no one else would be able to hear us.

"More than all right," I answered, knowing that my answer would be especially important to him.

His brow furrowed. His eyes flashed to the horde of Elthika, situated on the wildlands. Lygath was prowling closer to me, making the Dakkari guards a little skittish. Despite our bond being new, my Elthika would be driven to protect me, to watch over me and ensure that there were no threats against me.

Sarkin too, I thought, seeing my husband appear out of the corner of my eye, his hand coming to my lower back.

"I'm happy, Dannik," I told him, my words laced with unspoken meaning as I looked deep into his golden eyes. I pressed my hand to Sarkin's side. "My husband, Sarkin."

"I remember," Dannik said, eyeing the Karag male next to me, the edge of a glare in his eye.

Sarkin held my brother's gaze. I nearly sighed at the posturing between the two males. "There is a lot we have to discuss."

"*Lysi,* there is," Dannik agreed.

My gaze went beyond my brother, who'd been the only one of the Dakkari to approach us, stepping past the safety of the guards to come to me. I looked at my father, my stepmother. Alanis was here but not Lakkis, and she was looking at my Elthika behind me, brow furrowed. She'd probably never been so close to one.

My father was ever watchful. When I met his eyes, it pained me that there was little emotion there. No relief, no happiness. Just an empty stare as if I were a stranger. It hadn't always been that way, but ever since my mother's death in the North Lands, he'd grown more and more detached.

I wondered if it hurt him to look at me, considering I looked so much like her. He had loved her, deeply, once.

I took my brother's hand, knowing that he was the future of Dakkar. He could turn my father's head if needed. Not even Alanis could do that. And that boded well for all of us. Dannik was reasonable. I could make him understand what was at stake and how our negotiations could only help the Dakkari people.

I sensed the *Karath* of Grym close by. Observing closely. Listening. I saw my brother glance his way before his eyes went to his red Elthika behind him.

"Shall we?" Dannik asked, gesturing toward the East Gate.

"With conditions," Sarkin said, keeping me in his hold. "My riders will make camp out here while we are in negotiations. No one goes near our Elthika. And if we see archers or guards approach, we will use *ethrall* to defend ourselves."

Dannik's lips pressed together. "I am not foolish enough to endanger the citizens of Dothik."

"I am only ensuring the safety of my own people and our Elthika. I'm sure you understand," Sarkin answered, ever patient. "And when it comes to my wife, I want a guard with her constantly while within the city."

"You think one of our own would try to hurt her? She's a princess of Dothik and my *sister*. I would kill any who try to hurt her."

"Then we have that in common," Sarkin replied.

I sighed. "I can watch out for myself in Dothik."

Sarkin looked at me. "No. Guard with you at all times. I will not risk your safety. It's not negotiable, Klara."

I met his eyes. He was serious and wouldn't relent. I saw that clearly, and it was not something I would argue with him about.

"Very well," I said, squeezing his wrist.

Dannik was watching the exchange closely. Whatever he saw, he seemed…*relieved?*

"You'll stay at the palace?" he asked Sarkin. "We have rooms prepared."

"I stay with my wife," Sarkin answered. He gestured his hand toward the two Elysom council members and at Alaryk and his commander. "They can decide where they wish to sleep."

Dannik inclined his head. "Then let's get started. We have much to discuss."

"That we can agree on, Dakkari," Sarkin said.

It was going to be a long couple of days.

CHAPTER 43
KLARA

"This is the last remaining heartstone?" Sarkin asked me, his voice hushed as he inspected what was nestled into the ancient sword.

We were below my father's palace, in the room I knew like it was a part of me.

It was the day after our arrival. Though we were tired from endless discussions, tired from *waiting* for my father to meet with his council to go over our terms, I'd still wanted to bring Sarkin down here. We were waiting for their decision, after they'd heard what we'd had to say about the *thalara* tree. Dannik was in with them, as were the council members from Elysom. Alaryk was, apparently, wandering around and observing Dothik up close, making quite a stir wherever he went, or so Sarkin had told me.

"Yes," I replied. "The very last one."

It was even dimmer than when I'd last seen it, the power of it dying. Heartstones were not ageless, and this one had been used before, to vanquish the fog in the Dead Lands. Not to mention it had once helped Bekkar, an ancient horde king, shape Dothik into the kingdom it now was.

"I used to sit here all the time," I murmured, walking to the stone bench that I was surprised wasn't permanently imprinted with my backside. "I always felt calm down here. More connected to my bloodlines than even when I was out in the city."

Sarkin took a seat beside me, threading my fingers with his and bringing the back of my hand up to his lips. His kiss was soothing. I hadn't expected how stressful negotiations like these would be. How mistrustful my father and his council would be, fighting us at every turn, even though every last person in that throne room knew that it was the Karag who held all the power.

"Did you expect it to be like this?" I wondered, thinking about the demands of the Dakkari.

"Yes," Sarkin replied. "It is always like this. It's a dance, nothing more. We just have to go through the motions."

I supposed he would know.

When we'd told them that we knew about the location of a heartstone tree within Dakkar's border, I had felt the palpable shift in the room. At first they'd wanted Elthika of their own as payment for the tree. They argued that they couldn't be equals— that they couldn't be allies—when the power balance was so skewed. If we gave them Elthika, then perhaps they would feel more secure.

Sarkin—and Alaryk—had laughed outright. Having two Karag kings at the negotiations had been…interesting. I didn't think my father and his advisors really stood a chance.

The representatives from Elysom—an older male I recognized from Sarroth, named Gevanth, and a shrewd-eyed female named Harnek—had been the ones to calmly explain that was not even *remotely* an option. The Elthika were a race of their own. They were not owned by the Karag. They were allies of them, and they were not for bartering and trading like property or goods.

The *Dothikkar*—and my stepmother, the queen—had harrumphed at that, as if they didn't believe it.

When they'd pressed, growing bold, it had been Sarkin to shoot up from his seat, glaring over at my father across the long table as Dannik observed with his arms crossed, leaning against one of the columns of the throne room.

My husband had said in a calm yet icy voice, *Let us make one thing clear, Dothikkar. We are here to negotiate for heartstones out of respect, not out of necessity. The Hartans were the last race that tried to take Elthika that were not ours to give. Do you know what happened to them? We went to war and nearly razed their cities to the ground. They now bend a knee to the Karag—and the Elthika— and we no longer ask what they want.* He'd glared. *We are here for one thing only.* Heartstones. *If you wish to share in those heartstones, that is what we offer you. We are offering you peace as* allies, *mostly in part because of my wife, because you are her father and these are her people. She is the queen of the Sarrothian now, and her title demands respect given to her kin. But I'm growing tired of these demands when every last person in here knows that, eventually, we will leave here with exactly what we want.*

That had brought the meeting to a swift end as my father and his council met.

I heard footsteps travel down the spiral staircase, heavy on stone. A moment later, Dannik appeared.

"Any news?" I asked, straightening.

"I said my piece. Now we wait. Our father is still *Dothikkar,* and what he decides goes," Dannik said. His eyes traveled to Sarkin "I'd like to speak with my sister. Alone."

Sarkin looked over at me. When I nodded, he inclined his head and stood. "I'll check on Zaridan and Lygath…and update my *kya'rassa.* I'll return in a little while."

When Sarkin passed Dannik at the staircase, he said, "Watch over her."

"I always have," my brother replied, raising a brow.

I bit back a smile. Despite their constant pissing matches, I thought they might've respected each other. In another life, they might've even been friends. Or killed each other. Either was possible, I supposed.

Sarkin left us, and Dannik came to sit with me.

"Last time we were down here together," I began, smiling, "was the night that *he* came. The night everything changed."

"And everything is changing again," Dannik replied. He sighed. "This is what you want? You're not just saying these things because the Karag are telling you to or—"

"Dannik," I said, my tone pleading. I faced him on the seat, and he peered at me carefully. "I know what you must've thought when I left. I know how scared you were for me."

"Klara, I couldn't sleep. For weeks. I kept imagining the worst thing. And remembering that I didn't fight for you as much as I should've. I can't ever forgive myself for that."

"And what were you going to do? You cannot stand against an *Elthika*. You saw what we all did that night. Your *only* choice was to let me make my own decision and go with them," I said. "I wish that I could have told you that I was okay. Sarkin…he's not what I expected. He's a good leader to his people. He cares about them, and he almost always puts them above his own wants and needs. Except when it comes to me," I amended. "He's not the villain you imagine him to be. Quite the opposite."

"You really love him, don't you?" Dannik asked, frowning as he studied me.

"Yes," I said easily. "He made it easy. Dannik…I know how this must seem. But believe me, these terms are what's best *for* the Dakkari. You have to make our father understand that. Do you really think that I would stand by and *not* try to help our people?"

"What you ask…it would bind the priestesses' power. They will not stand idly by and allow that to happen," Dannik said.

I'd brought up the terms to Sarkin, and he'd presented them. In exchange for the location of the *thalara* tree and half of the heartstones that were still rooted within the earth, my father would have to agree to strip the priestesses' power in the North Lands. He would have to return back to the old customs, where the only people allowed to step foot within the temple were priestesses who *chose* to dedicate their lives to Kakkari, our goddess.

No longer would they have free rein to take anyone who showed signs of having heartstone magic. No longer would they try to create heartstones with experimental practices, killing innocent people in the process. It was an abomination, what they'd been allowed to do. Too long my father had ignored their growing, hungry power. If it wasn't checked and bound now, I feared what would happen.

"It's for the best," I repeated. "Surely you know that."

"I do. But their power stretches far, Klara. They have their influence in every horde, every outpost, every district in Dothik. It will not be easy to extinguish their reach entirely," Dannik pointed out, sighing.

"This will be a start," I said. Lowering my voice, I said, "And once you take the throne, I know that you will be a strong king, one whose mind is not swayed by greed and power."

"And what if I don't want it?" Dannik asked quietly, a strange tone in his voice that had me straightening.

"What?" I whispered, quick and sharp.

He smiled, but it didn't quite meet his eyes. He stood while I frowned up at him, my heartbeat quickening in my chest.

I...I had never asked him if he even *wanted* the throne. I supposed I had always assumed because he was so well suited for it.

"Do you think that King Arik and Queen Kara intended the throne to always pass through bloodlines? Wasn't that the knotted mess that they'd been trying to unravel in the first place?" Dannik asked. "Maybe it's time for the people of Dothik to choose their king or queen. Maybe we should be more like the Karag in that regard. Or like the hordes of our wildlands that have withstood centuries of hardship and still have managed to flourish."

I stood, taking his hands in mine. "If that's what you want," I replied, sincerely. "Perhaps we can help you make that change, but I don't think it will be easy."

"*Nik*," he replied. *No.* "It won't. Don't listen to me. It feels like years have passed since you left. I'm merely…tired. And I don't have the luxury of being tired."

"Sarkin gets like that sometimes," I told him. "When so many rely on you, the weight of it gets heavy."

"How does he stand it?"

I laughed. "Maybe you need a wife. He says that I've helped him."

"Maybe I do," Dannik said, the corner of his lip quirking, though the rest of his expression remained serious. "Regardless, I do think the heartstones would help. Because when this one dies…" He gestured behind him. "I fear what will happen."

"Then sway Father," I said, squeezing his familiar palm. "That's the only way forward. That's the only way to a stronger Dakkar—one allied with the Karag. It would be a new age for us all."

His eyes were bright. "It would," he agreed.

I smiled. "And I, for one, would love to see that."

CHAPTER 44
SARKIN

One week later…

Deep in a forest called the Ancient Groves, I stood by Klara's side as we watched the Dakkari-steel chains fastened around the *thalara*'s wide trunk.

It was a beautiful tree—black with graceful, regal boughs and white, velvety leaves, highlighted with blue veins.

It was an old *thalara* tree. And it was different than all the ones I'd ever studied. This might've been the oldest I'd ever seen, and I could feel the raw power swirling from it, drawing in energy from its surrounding, feeding on it to grow the dying heartstones at its roots.

Across the clearing, the *Dothikkar* stood with Dannik. The old king and, potentially, the new one. There were a few of his council members. Gevanth and Harnek stood close by. Alaryk had remained as well, though he'd sent his commander back to Grym to relay to Elysom that what were now known as the Heartstone Accords had been struck with the Dakkari.

In these accords were our agreements.

Each nation would get half of the heartstone yield. Seventy

percent of each yield would be replanted into careful groves of *thalara* orchards, just like the forests that used to grow in the Arsadia. A handful of experts would come from Karak to assist the Dakkari in their growing and care, ensuring that the trees would be healthy to sustain heartstone yields for centuries.

The remaining heartstones could be used as we saw fit. But the *Dothikkar* had finally agreed to curb the priestesses' power in the North Lands, to stop trying to create heartstones, especially after we had told him such a thing was not possible. Did I believe it would happen?

I would like to. But I had seen greed for decades, even in Sarroth before I'd taken the throne from the previous king. I was more than a little jaded, especially when it came to the promises of strangers.

It was important to Klara, however, and for that reason alone, the Karag would be monitoring the Dakkari progress on that front, ensuring that the agreements were met.

And in exchange on the Karag's part, for the heartstones were growing in Dakkari soil, we would allow a small population— warriors, mostly, though Klara had also requested scholars—to live among the Karag. They could enter rider instruction if they so wished, choose to take part in the *illa'rosh* if they passed train- ing, and claim an Elthika of their own. We would let the Elthika decide on their riders, as it had always been.

The territories of Sarroth and Grym—on Alaryk's agreement —would be the first territories to accept new citizens from Dakkar. With time, however, it might extend into Elysom, Elarin, and Kyloth.

If the Dakkari wanted to bond with an Elthika…they would have to earn the right.

Today marked the first day of our accords, and it would begin with uprooting the heartstones.

Klara took a deep breath. She whispered to me, "What if they're not there?"

I almost chuckled. Was this what she worried about?

"What if I made a terrible mistake and we negotiated for nearly a week for nothing?"

My hand drifted to her hip. Truthfully, I couldn't wait to get her back home to Sarroth. I couldn't wait to have her in *our* bed, to show her the territory that was now hers, where we would spend over half the year when we weren't at the mountain village in the Arsadia.

I couldn't wait to have her all to myself, at least for a little while. I *dreamed* of mornings where we could spend lazy moments, taking our time to get out of our bed. Where we would just be with each other.

But duty came first. At least for now.

"They'll be there," I said, leaning down to murmur into her ear as we watched the chains being tightened by the guards.

In a small clearing close by, just large enough for her to land, Zaridan waited. The chains were attached to her harness, and she would be the one whose power and strength uprooted the tree.

"How do you *know*?" she asked.

I gazed into my wife's beautiful gray eyes, tipping up her chin. The color of them reminded of the fog that flowed over Sarroth on misty mornings, calming and peaceful. Slowly, I said, "Because you said they were. And I believe you. It's as simple as that."

She blew out a small breath and tried to hide her pleased smile and the flush that colored the tops of her cheekbones. She was so lovely sometimes, it hurt.

I pressed a small kiss to the scar that curved over the side of her face and then turned my attention back to the tree. She went quiet, but I could tell that her mind was racing.

"The past intertwines here," she whispered. A shiver traced gently down my back. "It's all around us. We just have to listen for it. *I hear it.*"

"You're thinking of your ancestor, Vienne?"

She nodded. "It saddens me to watch this, even though I know it's for the best. Because this tree once saved her life and the life of her husband, her horde king. It gifted her the heartstone that gave her the power to save her people. There is history here. And it wouldn't surprise me if the last people to lay eyes on this tree had been Vienne and Davik of Rath Drokka," she said. "There's something…awe inspiring about that. Magnificent and humbling. Like our past is closer than we ever imagined. Not separated by centuries, but rather like a bridge. A bridge to that past…and it's right here."

I was in love with the way her mind worked because she thought so differently from me. She saw beauty in places where I'd never even thought to look. She found art in the folds of this life, where I had only ever seen duty and necessity.

"Sometimes you have to destroy in order to create, *aralye*," I told her, squeezing her hip, pulling her closer to me. "Don't be saddened by this. Your ancestors gave us this gift. You knew where this place was, you knew the stories passed down your bloodlines of this specific tree. That was *not* an accident. That was fate. All of this information is just pieces of torn parchment. Pieced back together and rearranged so you can see the entire story. Because of your bloodlines, both of our people have another chance. This might be the last *thalara* tree in existence, and you knew exactly where to find it. That's magic *and* history. Perhaps they are the same thing."

Klara looked up at me with parted lips as she absorbed the words. "I love that thought," she said.

Just then, Feranos, next to one of the Dakkari guards, called out, "Attached. We're ready, *Karath*."

My eyes met Dannik's from across the way. He inclined his head.

"Zaridan," I called out.

I couldn't see her because the Ancient Groves was a thick,

overgrown forest, but I could sense her presence. I felt the ground shake when she stomped.

"*Thryn'ar!*" I commanded. The flying command.

A roar shook the trees as my Elthika jolted into flight. She knew to go slowly…but it only took her mere moments to uproot an ancient tree.

"*Faryn,*" I ordered. *Stop.*

The trees shook when she landed back to the ground, the black Dakkari-steel chain rattling.

Klara had gasped, her eyes on the *thalara* tree, lying on its side, black earth spilling from the underside of its roots like dripping ink.

The sudden blue glow of the heartstones was almost blinding as it filled the clearing.

"There," I said finally, wanting to see her reaction more. "You were right, Klara. They were here. All this time."

She turned her watery gaze onto mine. I knew her emotions were out of relief, of happiness…but also of grief. Her mother had been killed trying to create the very thing that had been under Dakkari earth for centuries. That would cut her, deeply, for a long time. It might never *stop*, and I wished desperately that I could shield her from that ache.

But…there was also hope in her gaze. Hope for a new future. One in which our people would work together, creating tighter bonds, pushing us toward greater things *together*. She'd told me that Dannik might be struggling with the call for his own destiny, the weight of it…but I knew that he was part of that future. That we wouldn't be able to succeed without him.

"Sarkin."

"Hmm?"

Klara turned into my arms as life burst in the clearing. There was excited chatter from the guards and my *kya'rassa*, the scholars here to write about this day—her friend Sora among them, the

Dothikkar even, Dannik, Gevanth and Harnek. It was a celebration. A day to remember.

"I know we still have work to do here," she said to me. "But after it's done…I want to go home."

I couldn't help the small smile that edged its way onto my features. "And where's home?"

She grinned. "Sarroth, though truthfully…it's wherever you are."

Briefly, I rubbed at my heart when it fluttered in my chest.

"*Lysi?*" I asked, my tone teasing, before winding my arms around her back.

"*Lysi.* I'm eager to get back home. To start a life with you, by your side. To train Lygath. To begin chronicling the first Dakkari hordes. To learn everything I can about being a *Sorrina* to the Sarrothian. That's what I want. So…"

Behind her, I saw Dannik crouch down at the roots of the *thalara* tree, his face glowing blue from the magic as he reached out his hand. My eyes returned to Klara.

"So?" I asked quietly, leaning down briefly to brush my lips with hers, unable to resist stealing a kiss.

"Will you take me home?" she asked.

"Yes, *aralye*," I replied.

Dannik's fist curled around the heartstone, the first of many, plucking it from the roots of the dying *thalara* tree.

A new age had begun.

"Let's go home," I said.

EPILOGUE
KLARA

Lygath was snapping his sharp teeth at a wild shearling that was getting too close.

The shearling was no larger than an Elthika egg and was covered in soft brown fur, its tufted paws peeking out from beneath it. It hopped closer and closer to Lygath, the small mammal seemingly not intimidated by the Vyrin, though its long ears straightened and twitched as it approached.

Lygath and I were in a forest clearing. Private, quiet, and peaceful. It had become our afternoon routine after I was done with my interviews in Lakir. I'd review my notes, and Lygath would snooze happily.

I tried to bite back my grin, watching the exchange with the shearling under my lashes. Every time Lygath raised his head to glare at me—as if telling me to deal with the small nuisance—I darted my gaze down to the notebook spread open in my lap, my quill scratching hurriedly across the parchment.

Lygath huffed. Then he growled, a guttural sound in the depths of his throat. And yet, though my bonded Elthika *was* considered a somewhat unpredictable danger—or at least, he used to be—I'd never seen him hurt even an insect. So I didn't fear for the shearling's life.

It was a dizzying yet harsh juxtaposition. That he'd let riders fall to their deaths—my husband's friend being one of them—yet he was infinitely careful with the creatures I'd seen him interact with.

What I was still learning was that we would never fully understand the Elthika. Scholars in Elysom could write endless books on them, hefty tomes that rivaled the length of the ones on Dakkar's entire history even. They could give their symposiums and lectures on one facet of their existence—their mating habits and customs, the circumstances of whether they chose a wild birth or whether they entrusted their eggs to a hatchery, their courtships, the dances of their flights—and still it was a widely accepted truth that they would always be a mystery.

They were not meant to be understood by us. Not fully. It was arrogant to believe that they could be. And I learned that every day with Lygath, especially during his ongoing training.

My Elthika narrowed his eyes at the small animal, who was now sniffing at his tail. I saw a puff of red smoke emerge from his snout—my stomach tightening at the sight—but it was only a sigh. Finally, he decided to ignore the shearling, turning his head away to admire the forest grove we'd tucked ourselves into.

I relaxed as the fog dissipated. I would never get used to the sight. Such power he had. Such destruction he could unleash. The responsibility of it was humbling.

As if to make a mockery of my thoughts, the shearling curled up next to Lygath's deadly claws, no concern for its own safety, staring up at my Elthika as if content to study him, as I often did.

I chuckled, and Lygath cut me a sharp, impertinent look.

"You've made a friend," I noted, grinning before looking down at my notebook, shaking my head in amusement.

The pages were filled with scribbled notes, unreadable to anyone except me. Sarkin had said so. He'd told me my penmanship was horrifying, though he'd said it with the telltale curl of his full lips, a sly but gentle look in his eyes as if charmed by the discovery.

Of course my writing was terrible when I was recording notes and stories from my interviews. I'd come up with a series of symbols and half-written words so I could take notes without interrupting my discussions with the villagers. Sarkin lamented over the messiness, though he could appreciate the efficiency.

We'd spent more than one evening in our bed of furs laughing over his ridiculous interpretations of what I'd written… which had ended with him using his tongue to trace my made-up symbols all over my body as I squirmed beneath him. He'd chuckled against my skin, asking me to guess what he'd drawn.

I cleared my throat, straightening against the tree I was perched against, trying to ignore the aching heat that had begun to burn in my belly at the memory.

Merciless male, I thought, biting back a smile. I was thoroughly addicted to my husband, and he would only smirk if I told him that out loud, as if it wasn't obvious every single day.

For the next two moon cycles, I'd be focusing on the southern village of Lakir for my research. Where Sammenth and Ryena had grown up. The first time I'd stepped foot in Lakir, I'd known it was the right starting point. Dakkari blood ran strong there, stronger than in the other southern villages I'd visited, the portion of the country that was rumored to be where the lost hordes had landed on Karak soil centuries ago.

I feared that I was, roughly, three hundred years too late to make definitive progress on my research. Even the records in Dothik, which I'd checked when we'd last been there, didn't have the names of the hordes that had disappeared during the third *Dothikkar's* reign. And yet there was unmistakable evidence that the hordes had come here. That they'd lived here, flourished here.

I was making it my duty and purpose to repair those frayed memories. As best as I was able to in conducting my interviews, asking mostly elderly villagers to recount stories of their childhood, their ancestors, tales passed down from generation to generations, recipes, clothing, heirlooms, *anything*.

In doing so, I hoped that I could help build a bridge between the Dakkari and the Karag. A bridge that was, truthfully, already forming after the Heartstone Accords, but one I wanted to reinforce and strengthen.

Lygath made a sound in the back of his throat, one I recognized.

"Zaridan?" I asked, shutting my notebook, though it bulged so much with loose notes and records that I had to tie it shut with a long leather cord.

He made another sound, guttural and short. An affirmative. My eyes went to the sky as Lygath stood, sending the brave shearling at his back limbs finally skittering away into the cool darkness of the forest surrounding us. We'd been here a couple hours already, the sun beginning to sink.

There in the sky, I saw the familiar shape of Lygath's sister. When she spotted us, she let out a call, high pitched and trilling. Sarkin had sent her, to bring us home to the citadel.

I bit back a smile. He worried. Lakir wasn't such a great distance from Sarroth, but even still, he still liked me back home by sundown. Especially tonight.

"We're called home, it seems," I said, approaching my Elthika, carefully tucking my notebook into my leather satchel.

Without my command, Lygath stretched out his wing, and I ascended.

The preparations for Akymor were well underway.

As Lygath flew us over Sarroth, I saw that lanterns had appeared since I'd departed this morning, lining all roads within the territory. With the lowering sun, they were being lit one by one. A beautiful warm glow illuminated the pathways, showcasing a great network of roads that led from the center of Sarroth, stretching out in all directions—across the farmlands, over the river, winding through the valleys, even ascending up into the mountains where I knew one small village was tucked away.

Akymor was a Karak-wide celebration that heralded the end of the mating season for the Elthika. Feasts and parties would be going well into the night. Sarkin had told me about it a few months prior, when he'd brought me gifts from Elysom. A dress had been one of those gifts, one I'd been saving to wear to the festivities tonight.

We were expected to make an appearance at all the villages throughout the course of the evening, as *Karath* and *Sorrina* of Sarroth. But the holiday would begin tonight at our citadel, where we were having dinner with Sarkin's *kya'rassa*, including Kyavor, who had flown from the Arsadia for the occasion.

When Lygath circled down onto the terrace of the citadel, Sarkin was waiting for me on the back steps. After I descended off the mount, I went to Lygath, pressing my fingertips just below his eyes.

"*Sen endrassa,*" I murmured to him. "Enjoy your night, my friend."

Lygath tipped his snout into my touch. When I turned, I felt the power of his launch behind me. I tilted my face back, watching the two siblings come together in the sky overhead.

Then my eyes were only for my husband, lounging against the stone wall.

"Welcome home, wife," he murmured, those multicolored eyes warming on me.

"Sorry I'm a little late," I said, my eager grin widening on my face. I rushed into his arms. They came around me, and I thought, *This is home.* It didn't matter where we were—in Sarroth, in the Arsadia, in Dothik.

Sarkin was home, and I breathed him in shamelessly, savoring his heat and the comforting press of his unyielding body. Though I'd just seen him this morning—pressing a kiss to his cheek as I'd rushed out of the citadel to meet Lygath, eager for a day of interviews—I felt like it'd been much too long.

His lips met mine as my hands stroked through his hair. My fingers clenched the dark strands as his bit into my hips, holding me close. Desperation was rising. I'd been thinking of him all day. A small madness we both shared. I often woke with him between my thighs, to sweet but wicked kisses along my breasts...yet I felt like we *always* wanted each other. That need would never be satisfied.

"Oh," I heard, and we broke apart when we realized someone had managed to sneak up on us. It was Droshin, the head of the household staff in the citadel.

Sarkin was a minimalist when it came to his own creature comforts. Before me, his residence in the citadel in Sarroth had been used for sleep and nothing more. Most of his time was spent in the Sarrothian villages, meeting with the councils there, or with Zaridan and his riders, traveling between the territories and patrolling his homeland.

But he'd expanded the staff when we'd returned from the Arsadia...and I knew it was for me alone. He'd hired more cleaners—for it was a large house, one with rooms that I'd yet to even explore—two cooks, and personal helpers for me, should I require their assistance.

"My apologies, *Karath, Sorrina*," Droshin said, though he was no stranger to finding us in compromising positions in the last few months.

"What is it?" Sarkin asked, recovering more quickly than I did, though his hands never left my hips. I knew he preferred to have as few people in his home as possible, even though the citadel was grand and we very rarely ran into a single soul, as discreet as they were. He was fonder of our home in Rysar, in the

Arsadia. Our quaint little dwelling up on the hill at the base of the mountain, where we had more privacy than we knew what to do with.

"Brear would like to know if you prefer the wine from Grym this evening or the brew from Elarin."

Decisions like *that* my husband hated most of all, I knew, and so I smiled at Droshin. Kyavor was partial to brew, not wine, and he was our honored guest tonight.

"The brew will be fine. Thank you, Droshin," I replied.

He inclined his head, seemingly eager to leave us be, and I chuckled after he left.

"Three more months," Sarkin sighed, pressing a more chaste kiss to my lips lest we get carried away again. "And then I won't have to worry about interruptions when we are back in the Arsadia."

Another riding season would begin soon.

"There will always be interruptions, *Karath*," I murmured, untangling myself from his arms before intertwining my hand with his, pulling him through the back door of the citadel. "But if it means having you, then I don't mind them."

"Then let's go lock ourselves in our wing until our guests arrive," he suggested. "Tonight will be long. I want to savor you while I can."

It always felt like I was free-falling off Lygath's back when he said things like that. The rush and flurry in my belly felt like a sweet, exciting thrill.

"All right," I whispered, anticipation surging, and he led us up to our private section of the citadel, where even Droshin wouldn't bother us unless it was absolutely necessary.

Our rooms in Sarroth had once been…sparse. The first time I'd seen them had been the night I'd dreamed of Lygath and taken a tumble off the cliffside. Sarkin had brought me here to bandage my wounds and tie me to him in sleep. Other than a table near the fireplace, a large cushioned chair that had been well-used, and the bed, it had been bare bones, befitting the Sarrothian king who always seemed to be on the move.

It hadn't worked for me, however, and Sarkin had given me free rein to change whatever I saw as necessary.

Over the last few months, I'd made various purchases throughout Sarroth. Smooth and soft rugs for the stone floors—which had already gone a long way toward adding color and life into the room—window dressings, paintings and glass mosaics that glittered in sunlight, decorative silver vases filled with blooms and greenery that reminded me of the Arsadia. A new foot stool here. An expertly woven blanket there.

Sarkin had often observed new furnishings within our wing with soft yet bemused amusement, his eyebrows quirking on me whenever he spied new decor on the gray walls or a trinket that I'd purchased from the marketplace, displayed proudly on the mantel.

My husband never made comments or gave his opinions about specific items I purchased…but I knew he enjoyed seeing them. He'd told me once that he liked me "nesting." Feathering our home with things I enjoyed. He liked seeing my mark on our dwelling, evidence I was burrowing into our life. I'd often caught him observing the little pieces I'd acquired, a peculiar yet pleased expression on his face.

My favorite addition to our wing, however, was the wall of books in our sitting room by the hearth. The citadel *did* have a dedicated library, much to my endless delight. It needed some love and care, a project that I planned to focus on after the bulk of my interviews were done in Lakir. Most of the books were in Karag, however, and while I did work with a tutor in the nearest village to help me with my husband's native tongue, I'd decided to lug all the books in the universal language up to our rooms for safekeeping.

Having shelves built into the walls had been one of my first projects upon arriving to Sarroth, as any good scholar worth her ink might do. Most of the books in the universal tongue had been trade ledgers from village to village, oddly enough, but I'd still read nearly every single one. Others, however, had been translated Elthika tales, mostly fables meant for children. But some were useful tomes on Elthika and Karag history, much like the book Sarkin had gifted me from Elysom. Those were the ones I repeatedly reached for whenever I needed a break from my research or if my husband was away from Sarroth.

"Thinking of your books again," Sarkin said, cutting through my thoughts. I averted my eyes from the shelves as he drew me into his arms, now that we had a brief but private moment together. "I always know when you do. Should I be jealous of them?"

"Of course not. How can you be jealous when you know how much I love *you*?" I teased, laughing.

"Mmm," he murmured, pressing a kiss to my lips. "How much?"

I thought about it, trying not to get distracted by his touch. The truth that came to me was humbling. "Enough that if I was forced to choose, I would choose you over ever touching another book again."

For someone like me, that reality was tortuous.

But that was how much I loved him.

Sarkin made a sound in the back of his throat, those eyes flickering between mine. He frowned, briefly, a slight pulling of his lips, and then he said quietly, "Then it's a good thing that you never have to. Because I wouldn't ever want that for you, my love."

I grinned, my gaze going to his lips. I reached up, pressing my index finger to their full softness. Such soft lips for such an intense, intimidating male, I couldn't help but ponder.

I went to my tiptoes, desperate for a taste of him. The kiss was hungry and raw. His fingers dug into me, and I pressed as close as I possibly could, like I was trying to climb inside him.

It was the same ache that had possessed us at Lishara's temple, all those moons ago. Only now it wasn't heartstone induced.

Lishara's blessing had been a *promise*, I realized, a glimpse of our future come early.

I gasped when Sarkin pressed me up against the wall, caging me in. Against my belly, I felt his cock thicken with a surge.

I had just popped open a clasp of his riding armor—which I was getting quite good at—when he groaned, "Wait, *aralye*. The *kana*."

I moaned. "You didn't get it?"

"No," he rasped, lowering his forehead to mine, even though his fingers began to dip into the waistband of my riding pants. He stroked my skin. Maddeningly. "Sina is still drying out the leaves. She said the next batch won't be ready for two more days."

Kana was a plant, I'd discovered, that grew in both Dakkar *and* Karak. A shared plant with a shared purpose. The deep green leaves of it were stripped and dried to be used in tea to prevent pregnancies. I'd used the last of it yesterday morning.

We both shared a desperate look.

"I can't wait," I pleaded. It was unlikely I would get pregnant at this part of my cycle. Not impossible, but not likely.

Sarkin's gaze burned, his fingers flexing on my hips. There was a primal part of him that *loved* risking it. That part of him that ached to see me heavy with his child. He'd spoken of his fantasies, his deeply buried wants, and it was a fantasy we often played out in our lovemaking.

My words set him on fire, just as I'd known they would, and before I knew it, he had my pants pushed down, his fingers finding me wet and aching. He huffed out a sharp breath and flipped me around, pressing me down until my arms were braced on the wall and my back was flat, ass exposed to him.

There was one breathless moment of delay as he ripped through the laces of his pants…but then I cried out when he slammed into me with a swift thrust.

Then he didn't stop. My teeth chattered together with every powerful pump of his hips. I rocked back into him, biting my forearm to keep from screaming.

His hand landed on my ass hard. "Let me hear you. Don't ever hide that from me, Klara."

I moaned but removed my teeth from my flesh. On his next sublime thrust, I let him hear just what he did to me, and I didn't care who heard, even though we were expecting guests any moment.

Our lovemaking was quick and desperate and exquisite. He knew the angle that made little pinpricks of light burst in my vision, and all too soon, I was tightening around him, crying out my pleasure as the orgasm ripped through me. My legs shook with it, but he kept me steady, always my anchor, keeping me rooted.

"So fucking perfect, my love," I heard him groan. "Oh, I can feel you. *Gods*, you're going to make me—"

His words cut off with a hitch of his breath. Then his thrusts became erratic, chasing his pleasure down, and I nearly whimpered in my triumph when I felt the hot lashes of his come spill inside me.

In the aftermath, once we'd cleaned up, my legs continued to shake. I heard Sarkin's low, deep chuckle. I felt it reverberate up my spine, and he tugged me to the plush chair by the unlit hearth, close to my books, pulling me into his lap, my legs dangling off the side.

My body was still tingling and I was still catching my breath. He pressed a sweet kiss to my cheekbone, stroking his fingers through my hair. I smiled, snuggling closer.

"How long do we have?" I asked, trying not to grow too sleepy in the aftermath of our lovemaking.

Sarkin grunted. "They can wait for us. Let me keep you here a while. We've both been so busy."

"I know," I said, placing my hand on his chest. I looked up at him, my eyes tracing the sharp lines and hard curves of his chest-twistingly handsome face. "While I'm looking forward to tonight's festivities, I'm looking forward even more to having you all to myself for a little while."

"I'll be all yours," Sarkin promised. "No more trips to Elysom or to Grym. I'm staying right here until we leave for the Arsadia."

I smiled, content with his answer.

"And maybe when we return from the Arsadia after this next rider season," he continued, brushing his thumb over my lips, "there won't be a need to take *kana* tea anymore."

A pool of warmth and affection spread like ink in my belly, filling all my empty places until it felt like I was bursting.

"That's what you want?" I asked. "Truly?"

Sarkin inclined his head. "That's *exactly* what I want, *aralye*."

My grin was so wide that it hurt my cheeks. "Then no more *kana* when we return to Sarroth."

The reaction my words wrung from him was unmistakable. His body went tight with it, and then he was growling, tugging me even further into him. I laughed as my arms wound around his neck, as his kiss consumed me.

We'd decided to wait for our first child—to get settled in Sarroth, with me as their new queen. Lygath still needed training, and dragon riding would be a near impossibility if I was pregnant. With our bond so new, we thought it best to wait. Not only that but with the Heartstone Accords now in place, Sarroth and Grym would be accepting their first new residents within the coming months. There was still much to be done.

So…we'd decided to wait as we settled into our new life. And if I happened to get pregnant before we were ready, so be it. We would see that through together.

But this was the first time we'd talked about a future date. A plan. It surprised me how much Sarkin wanted a child. But I knew, without a doubt, that he would be an incredible father.

"When we go to the Arsadia," I said, pulling away from his kiss, "can you take me north so that can I meet Tyzar?"

Sarkin's gaze warmed even though his brows furrowed. He stroked my face with the back of one finger. "What makes you think of that now?"

"With a child in the not-so-distant future," I began, smiling, "I was thinking of your own childhood. How much Tyzar meant to you and your own hopes for his return to Sarroth. If not him, if the memories are too painful for him, then perhaps his children. Perhaps our child will be a blood born, if they want that, and maybe your line and Tyzar's can be joined once again."

He pressed his forehead to mine. My husband was not one to show emotion readily, but I saw how much my words affected him. His shoulders were bunched, and he held himself very still, the want pouring out of him.

"You speak of a future that only seems like a dream to me," he whispered, closing his eyes. I cupped his cheek, holding him close. "The sweetest of dreams. And a future I will hope for. Ardently."

"Dreams have a way of becoming reality," I reminded him. "At least in my experience."

"Yes," he replied, opening his eyes. "And so it will, my queen."

I smiled.

"I love you," Sarkin murmured. "Every day I am surprised by how much more that love grows."

"Let it," I told him, "because my love for you is a wild thing, and I have stopped trying to tame it."

I pressed a kiss to his lips, purposefully chaste.

"Now, we really should prepare for our guests," I teased.

My husband chuckled. "If we must, *aralye*. But later, in the early hours of morning, you're all mine. *Lysi?*"

"*Lysi.*"

ACKNOWLEDGMENTS

I always wanted to know what lay beyond Drukkar's Sea…and that's why I wrote this book. After I finished *Throne of the Horde King* in 2022, there was a sense of sadness as I wrapped up that series. But there was also excitement because I knew that I still had many, many stories left to tell about the world of Dakkar. *The Horde King of Shadow* is only the beginning.

These days it takes a small village to publish a book. *The Horde King of Shadow* is my 25th novel and I've been blessed to have so many supportive people in my life that helped make it happen.

To Naomi, I don't know how I ever functioned without you. You are a superstar assistant and your continued enthusiasm for this book always kept me moving forward. "No pressure…but a little bit of pressure" definitely needs to be printed on a shirt! Thank you for being the best PA an author could ask for, not to mention a great friend.

A big thank you to Mandi Andrejka, my editor. Simply put, you make my books better. You spot the smallest of things with your eagle eyes and I always love your reaction GIFs sprinkled throughout a manuscript. You've been so kind, generous, and helpful over the years (!!) we've been working together.

Thank you to my producer, narrator, and friend, Marcio Catalano, not only for being a supportive force, but for also encouraging me to explore different paths of creativity and to step outside the norm, especially when it comes to audiobooks.

To two of my author friends, Emma Hamm and Juliette Cross—waking up to a plethora of voice messages from you both always made my morning. Thanks for sharing your guidance and opinions on all things publishing and being wonderful friends.

To my IRL family and friends—hi Hayley, Pierce, Katrina, and Beth—thanks for the emotional support cocktails, cat sitting, and putting up with my scattered brain when I'm on a deadline.

Last but not least, a big thank you to YOU, the reader. Whether I was honored to meet you at one of the signings or conventions this last year or whether you are someone who is just stumbling upon my books for the first time, thank you for your support! I wouldn't be able to do this thing that I love so much—telling stories—if it weren't for you.

CONNECT WITH ZOEY
Scan the QR code with your phone to access her links:

I'm mostly hanging out on
Instagram. Come say hi!

ABOUT THE AUTHOR

Zoey Draven has been writing stories for as long as she can remember. Her love affair with the romance genre started with her grandmother's old Harlequin paperbacks and has continued ever since. As an Amazon Top 50 bestselling author, now she gets to write the happily-ever-afters—with an otherworldly twist, of course! She is the author of Sci-Fi and Fantasy Romance books, such as the *Horde Kings of Dakkar* and the *Brides of the Kylorr* series.

When she's not writing, she's probably drinking one too many cups of coffee, hiking in the redwoods, or spending time with her family.

Website: www.ZoeyDraven.com
Facebook group: Zoey's Reader Zone